NIGHT RISE

FRANCES DE LA ROSA

Editors: Kim Halstead,
Jen Boles
Cover Artist: Cristiana
Leone

D1698776

Copyright © 2022 by Frances De La Rosa

All rights reserved. No part of this book may be reproduced in any manner whatsoever without written permission except in the case of brief quotations embodied in critical articles and reviews.

First Printing, 2022

Acknowledgements

I am overwhelmed by the love and support I've received from so many people over the course of this journey, so a huge thank you to everyone.

First, my editor Kim, who helped shape this story through multiple drafts, and who made this adventure seem possible.

To my proofreader Jen, who cleaned the last of my grammar, making a truly enjoyable reading experience.

Next, Cris, my beautiful cover artist, who made something beyond what I could have dreamed.

To all the readers, those who braved my rough first draft, and all others who forged through the rest with me, catching plotholes and asking questions.

Great big hug to all my family and friends, from those I bounced ideas off of, to those that ask me how it goes every time I see them, and anything in between.

To my grandpa, who taught me to make what I know.

And the biggest thanks to my husband, who believed in me so much, I finally believe in myself.

NIGHT RISE

Prologue

Dawn squealed when she arrived at breakfast and saw which fairy was sitting at the miniature table next to her plate.

"Dusk!"

"Morning to you too," he replied. His shaggy dark hair fell into his eyes, and he shook his head so he could watch her bounce around the human table to sit next to him. She wiggled in her seat for a few moments, then beamed at him in his tiny chair.

"Guess what! I'm meeting the prince today!"

"Yes, I'm aware," Dusk said as he sliced his raspberry, carefully separating the individual drupelets.

"I'm kind of nervous," she whispered loudly, her big blue eyes shining with childish worry. "What if he doesn't like me?"

"I don't know how he couldn't," Dusk replied, half smiling as he ate a drupelet.

Dawn kicked her feet while a servant filled her plate with jam-covered toast, then happily shoved some into her mouth.

"He's also meeting the Court, so you'll meet him too, right?" she asked as she swallowed, her cheeks now speckled with bread crumbs.

Dusk started to speak, then frowned and looked in his waistcoat pocket. Light leaked out and he sighed, closing the pocket again.

"Unfortunately, I need to return home immediately," he said, getting to his feet.

"Oh," she said and chomped her bread, thinking. "When will you be back? Will it be before he leaves?"

"It shouldn't be too long if everything goes well," he said, fluttering his wings and floating into the air. "Though it won't be before Geoff is gone."

Dawn wiped at the crumbs on her face with a napkin, mostly succeeding in spreading the sticky jam more. "Then I'll tell you about it when you come back."

He half-smiled as he turned away, and she focused her attention on her food. It was always boring when Dusk left suddenly, but at least this time she'd have something else to keep her busy. Maybe the prince would be even more fun than the fairy.

"So, how was it?" Dusk asked a few weeks later as they sat down at the table together.

"He was weird," Dawn said, bouncing while they waited for dinner to arrive. "He just wanted to watch the Court the whole time."

"That's not strange for someone used to being involved in politics," Dusk said. "Or for someone unused to fairies, for that matter."

"I guess it was that he's so much older," she mused. "He's older than Alex."

"Age isn't anything really, especially once you're old enough to marry him," Dusk said.

"I hope so," she replied. "Guess I have twelve years to figure it out."

Dusk smiled at her as servants carefully placed plates of food in front of them. "You know, I have my best friend beat by a good two or three millennia. I think you can manage half a decade."

Dawn stared at him for a moment, her eyebrows furrowed as she thought hard on what he said. "I don't think Alex liked him much, and they're a lot closer in age."

"He's your brother. He has a different job than you," Dusk said.

"I guess." Dawn sighed as she poked at her plate. "But I don't want this job. I'd much rather stay here and play with fairies."

"Don't want to be without us then?" he asked, half-smiling.

"Who would?" she replied, grinning at him. "You're too fun."

* * *

The late morning sun beamed through crisp middle-winter air, reflecting on the thickly piled snow that covered the world. Fluffy flakes were caked in every crease and crevice, smoothing the stone walls that encompassed the castle and painting the roofs of the buildings white. Footprints ran all over the grounds, approximating where paths were. Voices were heard calling out, conversing, and even laughing as people went about their day.

Childish squeals rang out from the main yard, making several heads turn as they walked past. Usually, the yard was full of shouting and metal clanging as knights and squires trained, but today it was occupied by Dawn and her friends playing in the snow.

The young princess was usually with one or both of her companions, when her favorite fairy wasn't around, of course. Robert, or Rah as Dawn referred to him, and Sarah were a prospecting squire and handmaid, respectively. Sarah had only moved to the castle with her father two years ago, while Rob had been born and raised within the walls.

Dawn was working on a snow sculpture while her friends threw snowballs at each other. Rob hit Sarah and she shrieked with glee and pranced past Dawn, bumping the snow pile.

"Oh, sorry!" she exclaimed as the pile fell over.

"It was almost done," Dawn pouted, then sighed and smiled. "But it could have been better. I'll just make it again."

Rob tossed some snow at them and Sarah chased him away, leaving Dawn to restart. She worked diligently on her new pile until it was a couple of feet tall and very lumpy, almost resembling something human-shaped.

"And what are you making?" someone asked, making her jump and turn around.

"Dusk!" Her smile was brighter than the snow around them. "Don't look. It's not ready yet."

"Ahh," he said, turning around. "Tell me when."

She piled and shaped until she was satisfied. "All right, you can look."

He turned and saw a very basic human-shaped lump, with four bumps on its "back".

"It's a snow-fairy!" she declared, beaming proudly.

"It's wonderful," Dusk said, floating closer to look it over.

"Not as good as a real one," she said. "But the wings won't go any longer."

"I could make them cooperate," Dusk said, eyes glinting impishly. "If you'd like to see."

"Oh! Yes, please!" She wiggled with excitement, rocking on her heels.

Dusk chuckled and gathered snow for his own sculpture. The snow moved and stuck to itself easily, guided by magic, and in no time he had a perfect scale likeness of a fairy.

"Well?"

It was a male fairy, with a birdlike physique and youthful yet mature features that seemed so otherworldly. His narrow wings were transparent and stretched as far as he was tall. The top edge of each was almost perfectly straight, and the bottom gently curved towards the rounded ends. Dusk had positioned them mid-flap, the upper pair sticking up almost vertically, and the lower pair out to either side. All four pivoted against each other for a thrust that would keep the fairy stationary.

"It's beautiful," Dawn said softly, unable to look away. "I've never seen him, though. Who is he?"

"This is Diya," Dusk answered. He was the only fairy Dusk knew well enough to make entirely from memory, and the only one Dusk would want to emulate.

"You should show it to him—I bet he'd like it!"

Dusk smiled wryly. "He's seen others like it I've made in the Realm."

"But he needs to come here and see this one," she said, stomping her foot and crossing her arms. "Then we can play together. You said he likes playing."

"You have your own friends to play with," Dusk replied as Sarah and Rob passed nearby, still chasing each other and throwing snow. "And I have work to get to."

"Oh, all right," Dawn said, drooping as Dusk flew up and away. Once he was out of view, she knelt by the Diya sculpture.

"Don't worry," she whispered. "We'll meet someday, and we'll have lots of fun."

* * *

Dawn sat with Geoff under the willows, listening to the river and watching the sunlight dancing on the grass. Once they'd been sent off to spend time alone together, he'd asked to leave the castle walls, and she'd brought him to her second favorite place.

The prince's last two visits had been dull for her, and she was glad he wanted to do something besides hang around her parents and the Fairy Court this time. In four years he would have to choose between her and the other princess, Isabella, and she needed to really impress him if she wanted to secure the marriage. The princess he chose would ultimately become queen of the rich Kirkjufell kingdom, and could thus ensure her own kingdom's prosperity.

Geoff was quiet while he worked on something, completely focused on his fingers as they wove grass and tied knots. Dawn liked this chance to study him. Until now, she hadn't been that interested in the prince when he'd visited, but this time she noticed his chocolate curls and deep brown eyes. She'd recently started to take an interest in boys, and it was strange to be around the one she was intending to marry one day—in a sweaty palms and nervous fidgeting kind of way.

"Here," he said and placed a finished goat on the grass in front of her.

She picked it up and carefully turned it in her hand. "It's adorable."

"Keeps me busy, anyway," he said, then touched the goat with his fingertip. "Watch this."

They were still for a moment as he channeled magic into it, then he pulled his hand away and the goat lowered its head and nudged Dawn's palm as though it were grazing.

"That's amazing," she said, smiling. "Do you do other animals?"

"I can," he replied, putting his hands behind his head and lying back on the grass.

"What about a bird? Could you make it fly?" she asked. Would it float above the ground and flutter into the tree branches? Less graceful than a fairy, but no less magical.

He stared up at the sky through the willow branches stirring in the light breeze, choosing for the moment to be quiet. Eventually, he took a deep breath and sighed. "I like this."

"The willows?"

"Just...being here," he said, shifting his eyes to look at her. The goat continued moving, lowering and raising its head at intervals. "I don't get to leave the palace much, except to go hunting. Nice to just *be*, you know?"

"I do," Dawn replied, keeping her eyes on the goat. "I only get to leave the castle when we visit Riverglade, and even then I have to have someone watch me."

"Fun life for us royals," he said, then closed his eyes. "Wake me up when it's time to eat, all right?"

That evening, they arrived late to dinner, and Dawn brightened even more when she noticed who was at the high table.

"Dusk is here," she told Geoff quietly as they crossed the room.

"That's the one I haven't met, isn't it?" Geoff asked. He spotted Dusk and studied him.

"He is," Dawn answered.

They reached their places next to the fairy, and dinner was presented once they were sitting. Geoff kept her attention as they ate, nudging her and whispering in her ear, and she almost missed Dusk as he finished and flicked his wings to go.

"Dusk," she called before he got far.

He paused and looked at her. "Dawn."

"You're leaving?" she asked sadly, and he shrugged.

"Well, I'm done."

Geoff watched them speak with interest, and smirked as Dusk turned to leave. "Bit of an odd name, isn't it? For a lux fairy," he remarked. "And shouldn't you be blond?"

"Excuse me," Dusk replied crisply and landed on the table in front of Geoff, glaring up at the prince. "That might be true, were I only a lux fairy, but I happen to be arcane."

"Arcane," Geoff repeated, rolling the word around. "So you have all the fairy abilities?"

"Exactly," Dusk said as he floated back into the air. "Good night, Dawn."

She watched him fly away before returning her attention to the prince.

"So what did you think of him?" Dawn asked at dinner a few days later, when Geoff had gone home.

"You seemed to like him," Dusk replied, not looking up from his plate.

"Meaning you didn't," Dawn said, setting her fork down to look at him. "Why not?"

"I didn't dislike him," Dusk argued, meeting her eyes. There was an odd glint to them Dawn had never seen before. "But it does no good for me to get on with him, does it?"

"I suppose not, since I'll leave and we won't see each other again," Dawn said, sighing as she picked her fork back up. The visit had gone well, and everyone was optimistic Geoff would choose her. "But at least I'll have a prince charming."

Dusk stared blankly at his plate. His fork was suspended above it while he thought. "We still might see each other for special occasions."

"If you happen to be here, when I come visit," Dawn speculated. "Father could always let you know when I do."

Dusk shook his head and smiled. "Then I'll make sure I'm here, whenever you come."

* * *

"Come on!" Rob whispered.

Dawn laughed as she followed him into the rain, and they ran through the night. "Shh! They'll find us!"

Behind them, lights bounced around the castle, and they could hear their names being called.

"They won't think to look out here," Rob replied. They reached the north gate and he quietly opened it.

A glowing fairy was floating on the other side, waiting for them. No raindrops touched him; instead, they changed direction as they fell around him.

"Dusk!" Dawn said, pleasantly surprised to be caught by him. "What are you doing here?"

Dusk sighed and rolled his eyes. "Finding you. What did you get up to this time?"

"Nothing," Rob answered, glancing nervously between Dawn and the fairy. "None of it was her idea. It was all me."

"I thought it was Sean's idea," Dawn said.

"Well, he thought of it, but I did it," Rob replied.

"Whoever is at fault, it doesn't explain why you felt it necessary to run away with Dawn to avoid a ruined dinner," Dusk said, his eyes sharp as he glared at Rob.

"I wanted to leave," Dawn replied. "I thought we might get away unnoticed with all the excitement."

"Well, now you're going back in to get dry," Dusk said, and Dawn drooped. "And tomorrow I'll bring you out for an hour or two to do whatever you feel like."

"Not without me," Rob said as Dusk led them back.

"If you are able, you may join us," Dusk replied without looking back. "Though I doubt you'll be free of punishment for this evening's antics." Rob grimaced and was silent.

"Can we leave the castle?" Dawn asked.

Dusk slowed slightly and glanced at her, his face alight. "If that's what you want, then it's what we'll do."

"So, where too?" Dusk asked when he met Dawn outside the keep the next afternoon.

"Well, I'd say the Fae Realm, if you didn't always tell me no," Dawn said, grinning while she adjusted the satchel strap on her shoulder. "So I guess the meadow will have to do."

"I've explained to you plenty of times why I won't take you there," Dusk replied, flying towards the west wall.

"I know," Dawn said, only rolling her eyes a little. "It isn't for you alone to decide. No humans have set foot there in over a century. It's just not done..."

Dusk paused by the wooden gate, letting Dawn pull the latch and swing it inward before flicking through to the other side.

"And I take it you plan on writing?" He nodded at the leather satchel as Dawn closed the gate behind them.

"After we wander a little," she replied, glancing over the meadow that stretched in front of them. The castle wall sat right on the edge of the fragrant, flower-filled expanse.

"Working on another fairy poem?" Dusk half-smiled at her as he followed her deep into the overgrown grass. "Or have you finally found something else to write about?"

"I was hoping I'd find some inspiration here," she answered, blushing with the exercise. There were rocks to trip over and thorny plants to catch her skirt if she wasn't watching.

After a few minutes of aimlessly wandering together, Dusk froze. "Dawn," he said softly, "I need you to stop here for a moment. I'll be right back."

"What are you doing?" she asked as he flicked away.

She followed his path with her eyes and found his destination a few paces away. A large sheep with heavy curled horns stood facing them, nostrils flared as it breathed heavily. It was also orange. Dawn made an "o" with her mouth and slowly, so as not to draw the sheep's attention, knelt in the grass to watch.

Dusk approached the sheep with his hands out, softly calling to it. The sheep bleated and jerked its head around, stepping back. Its bright orange wool darkened to red. Some movement behind the sheep caught Dawn's eye, and she focused on the dots that were floating around. One buzzed toward her, landing on a nearby flower, and she noted the yellow and black stripes.

"Dusk," she whispered.

He glanced at her, and she pointed at the bumblebee. Dusk grinned, then zipped around the sheep to the swarm. After a moment of nothing seeming to happen, the swarm moved, drifting away from the sheep. Dusk slowly moved back in front of the sheep, cooing softly to it. The wool went back to orange, and Dusk carefully placed his palm on the sheep's nose. Its wool turned yellow, then green. Once the sheep was blue, and no longer breathing heavily, it set to grazing and Dusk flew back to Dawn.

"Mood-sheep," he said, shaking his head. "Good catch on the bees, or I might not have calmed it down."

"You're welcome," Dawn replied, smiling as they returned to their wandering. "And it seems I found some inspiration."

"The sheep?" Dusk asked, cocking an eyebrow at her, and she shook her head.

"The bees," she said, watching the one she'd noticed float around lazily before finding the rest of its swarm.

* * *

"This way," Dawn said as she led Geoff through the rose gardens, her favorite place, and they stopped in front of a bush that was in full bloom. "This is my second favorite rose."

Geoff stared at the large white and yellow roses and shrugged. "Doesn't look any different than the bush you sent us."

A cut from the Morning Blossom had gone to Kirkjufell last year in order for Geoff to send messages to Dawn. Her father's mirror had been set up with the additional signature specifically so she could correspond with the prince.

"Well, I'd still like to send you one," Dawn said. She'd started sending him pressed roses about a year ago. Roses she liked or that he didn't have in Kirkjufell. Her favorite roses, though, she was saving until he saw them with her. That way they could be special to him, too, and tied to a memory they shared.

"Oh good," he replied flippantly. "Still reminds you of your friend, right? That squire boy."

"Rah," she answered, nodding. "Although he has been knighted since you were last here."

"Has he," Geoff said, still studying the roses. "And Sarah? She do any magic yet?"

"Oh, no," Dawn said, lowering her gaze briefly. "But she will someday, I'm sure."

His eyes flicked to her face for a moment, and he almost smiled. "You're lucky, you know, to have friends and family who care about you."

"My friends care," she said. "But I think all my parents care about is that I marry you."

"They have a kingdom to run. Of course they're interested in that," he replied. "But at least they're nice to you, treat you well."

"Isn't Henry a kind father?" she asked.

Geoff turned away from her to watch a fairy flit around down the path, tending roses. "They break, you know. The birds."

"The birds?" she repeated.

"When I try to make them fly," he said, turning back to her. "The effort is too much for grass and they break themselves. So I don't make birds."

"That's too bad," she said. She would have loved to see a little grass bird flying around the garden, playing with the fairies.

"What about the other rose, then?" Geoff asked. "The dusk thing."

"Oh, the Heart of Dusk," Dawn said, returning to the present. "It won't be blooming for a couple more weeks. After you've gone home." And after her sixteenth birthday, the reason he was visiting.

"Show me anyway," he said, and she nodded. He held her hand while she led him to the secluded clearing, and they stopped in the corner. She indicated a small, scraggly bush.

"Dinky little thing," he mused. "Not a very big flower, either. You sure you like it?"

"I sent you a drawing once, didn't I?" she asked. "The colors are beautiful, more than I could convey."

"Like a sunset," he said. "Or a sunrise."

"I suppose so," she said, hiding her blushing cheeks behind a curtain of strawberry blonde waves.

"But why's it dusk and not dawn?" he asked.

She pushed her hair out of her face and stared up at him. "What do you mean?"

"The rose," he answered, and she felt something in her chest move. "Why isn't it Heart of Dawn?"

"I'm not sure," she replied. "That's just what it's called."

"Didn't you tell me the fairies make a lot of the roses? Especially the magic ones."

"Yes," she said slowly, wondering what he was thinking. "Why?"

"Did that arcane one make this, you think? Named it after himself."

Her chest thumped again. "He could have."

"You really like him, don't you?" Geoff asked, catching something in her face that he didn't like. Something Dawn wouldn't have been able to explain if she knew it was there.

"He's my friend."

"Is he. Think you'll miss him?"

"I'll miss all the fairies."

"But you'll have me."

"I will, and that's enough," she said, though she wasn't sure who she was trying to convince. Geoff smirked and wrapped his arms around her.

"Do you like me?" he breathed in her ear.

"I do," she whispered back. She felt her heart thumping against him, but she heard his beating to a different rhythm where her ear was pressed against his chest.

"Good girl," he said, putting his mouth on hers, and she melted against him. When they finally stopped, she breathed deeply to slow her pounding heart and blinked until her vision returned.

"Next time I see you, you'll be coming to me and we'll do more," he rumbled in her ear.

"Oh," she remarked. Was he saying what she thought he was? "Does that mean you're choosing me?"

"I've always intended to choose you," he said. "I like you being around. How you're happy to just be with me. You get it."

Get what, exactly? Whatever it was must be good, if he was choosing her because of it.

"Oh," she repeated, and he laughed.

"First kiss, was it? That's good. Good, you saved it for me. Just make sure you don't forget to save anything else, all right?"

"I promise," she said with her lips almost touching his neck. It wasn't like there was anyone else she would do something with. Of her two male friends, one was like a brother to her, and the other was no larger than a hummingbird.

"Good girl," he said and squeezed her tightly. "Better give you more then. Make sure you really remember."

She gasped and pressed herself against him as his lips found hers again, and he laughed in his throat.

Three weeks later Dawn went to the rose garden alone and found Dusk tending a bush. She wandered over to him and watched him for a few minutes until he paused.

"Need something?" he asked as he looked at her.

"I was wondering about the Heart of Dusk," she said. "Is it yours?"

"Of course it's mine," he said and grinned. "Thank you for noticing."

She took a deep breath, not knowing why she was nervous. "Is it all right with you if I send it to Geoff?"

"Why wouldn't it be?" The smile left his face.

"Well, I remember you didn't like him, so I wanted to know how you felt about him having one," she answered, running her fingers through her hair.

"It's fine. You can send him one." The bright gleam of joy in his green eyes was gone, replaced with a shadow of sorrow.

"No, it isn't," she said and stopped playing with her hair. "You don't want him to have one. I won't send it."

"If he's expecting it, you should send it," Dusk argued. "Really, you don't have to worry about me."

"No," Dawn said. "You're my friend, and even if I'll only be here two more years, that's two years we have together, and I want to be the best friend I can. I won't send him one."

Dusk stared at her intensely for a moment, then flew away quickly

"Where are you going?" she called, but he was gone from her sight and didn't answer. A few minutes later, he returned with a rose in his hands.

"Send him this one," he said, holding out the Heart of Dusk.

Dawn looked at the perfect flower and the fairy offering it, and wondered why her chest was thumping again.

"If you're sure," she said as she carefully accepted the stem, heart desperately trying to escape its cage.

"Yes," Dusk said. "However I feel about him, you'll have this to look forward to when you go to Kirkjufell. It'll remind you of me."

"Then I'd better get in to press it," she said, wondering how he couldn't hear her heart still beating like crazy. He smiled a sad smile as she left him, and she glanced down at the rose. A bittersweet gift it was—something to remind her of her favorite person. Something that would always carry the memory of his mysterious sorrow.

"Did he like it?" Dusk asked at dinner.

Dawn stared at him in confusion, her mouth open to take a bite of food. "Did who like what?"

He half-smiled. "Did Geoff like the rose? It should have reached him by now."

"Oh, well, I didn't send it," she replied sheepishly, lowering her fork. It was currently sitting in her room, on her desk where she'd enjoyed seeing it every day for the last few months.

"Did it not turn out nicely?" Dusk remarked. "You do so beautifully usually, but perhaps this particular rose doesn't press well."

"No, it's perfect," Dawn said, shaking her head. And it was hers— her rose, her memory. "That's why I didn't send it because I wanted to keep it myself."

"Do you need another bloom?"

"No, I only ever want to press that one," Dawn said. "Geoff will just have to see it when I bring it with me."

"If that's what you want," Dusk replied, and smiled a happy smile.

"It is," she said, smiling back at him. And with that, the lingering sadness she felt whenever she saw the rose was turned into joy.

* * *

Dawn was in the library trying not to doze when Sarah poked her head around the shelves.

"Message for you, Dawn," her friend said. "From Geoff."

Dawn looked to her mother, who nodded her consent, then smiled as she followed Sarah. She was just reaching the point in her economics lesson where her mind would start to wander, and it wouldn't be long before her mother lost her patience. A quick break from studying would do them both well.

The Mantrisa keep was built almost exclusively of stone, with cobbled walls, stairs, and floors, held together with mortar and magic. Brilliantly colored tapestries lined the walls, separated by windows and nooks for flowers.

Sarah led Dawn to her parents' rooms—past tapestries of flying dragons and wildflower arrangements—and she let herself into her father's study where Geoff's message was waiting on the mirror. They had been writing to each other more regularly since her sixteenth birthday when he'd told her he meant to pick her, and only more so after Isabella had gone to see him. Dawn had sent him the Heart of Dusk she'd pressed right when Isabella arrived with the intention of ensuring he'd think of her while the other princess was there. He wrote back that day to tell her he got the rose and was all the more set on her because of it.

Just after Isabella finished her visit though, he'd gotten sick. No one knew what was wrong, and it was a tense couple of weeks until Henry wrote that Geoff had been seen by a skilled physician and was healing. Dawn continued sending him messages while he was sick, and once he was recovering, he wrote back. It was a relief when she started getting his messages again, but sometimes they were odd and unlike him. A few were nearly illegible, as if he'd forgotten how to write, and others would ramble about things that made no sense. But, always, he would remind her that he wanted her.

Today's message was no exception. She settled at the desk and glanced over the mirror while she readied her quill to copy it. There was rose petal dust on the glassy surface from two roses, the Scarlet Rain to send the message to her father's mirror, and the Morning Blossom to show it was for her. She blew the dust off to reveal the message, then sighed with relief when she saw the words were clear and concise, as Geoff's hand should be.

Dawn,

I showed the girls some of the roses you've sent me, so they can be used to your scent before you arrive. They weren't very fond of Isabella, but I think you'll get on well with them if their response to the roses is any indication. I didn't show them the last one though, the Heart of Dusk. That one is only for me. I worried when it didn't come, that you'd forgotten, but then it did and I knew you waited for the perfect moment, smart girl. One more month and you'll be here, and I'll have all my girls together finally. The anticipation is thrilling, like the moment before you catch your prey and end its life. I like it. You be a good girl, don't forget.

Geoff

"More sweet nothings?" Sarah asked when Dawn returned from the study with her message copied, and they headed down the hallway to the northeast tower. The floor runners were a rich amber color with scrolling green vines, and were so thick the girls left faint footprints.

"Yes," Dawn said, skimming the message. "Though it's still a bit strange for him." The most recent messages were no longer troubling, as they had been when he was sick, but the tone had never quite returned from something darker. Thankfully, her parents never read the messages, or she'd have some explaining to do.

"They *are* still better, aren't they?" Sarah reasoned as they started up the stairs. She was the only person Dawn had confided in, and she would take the secret to her grave. "He's just not fully over the sickness, that's all."

"Yes, that's all it is, I'm sure," Dawn agreed. She reread his older messages constantly, trying to remind herself who he had been when she'd seen him last and how well they'd gotten along. Maybe her care and presence would help? Could she brighten his mood?

"He mentioned the rose again," she said. They reached her room at the top of the tower and entered.

"That's good," Sarah said. "It means he's thinking of you."

"If it were ever any other rose, I'd agree," Dawn replied. She opened a box on her desk and placed the message inside, nestling it carefully among the others. "But it's only the Heart of Dusk."

"So, what, you're worried he's thinking about the fairy?" Sarah teased, making Dawn laugh.

"I guess not," she said. "I must just be overthinking. That was where we had our first kiss, after all." Surely that was the only reason he was so interested in the rose, never mind that he was the one to point out Dusk had made it.

Of course, while Dawn had kept the rose, it had only reminded her of her friend. Her friend, who was right that she would look forward to seeing his rose when she left. Her friend whose smile she thought about daily, even without the rose to remind her. Her friend who she wouldn't see again before she was gone for good.

I

Dawn broke slowly over the Tail Spike Mountains and danced along the Claw River. The light dazzled the fishing and trade boats ambling along. Some were going up toward the lake, and some down to the ocean. A light breeze stirred the water and shifted the willow branches that dangled above it before finding its way to the Mantrisa Castle.

The breeze and sunlight gently reached the northeast tower of the castle keep and caressed the bedroom window, hoping to gain entrance as Dawn Mantrisa awoke and rolled over in bed. She pulled her silk sheets around her and settled into her feather pillows, studying the gold embroidery in the deep red canopy above her while she waited.

As if on cue, there was a soft knock on the door. Sarah entered the room, with a hydro fairy flitting in after.

"Morning, Dawn!" she chirped as she walked to the window and threw open the drapes, bathing the room in the golden glow of sunrise. Her soft brown hair was tied together with a ribbon, though a few strands not quite long enough to be held back with the rest hung in her face. The edges of her cerulean tunic were covered in a wild mixture of embroidery in every shape and color imaginable, with a few patterns finding their way down her beige skirt and all the way to her hem.

"Morning," Dawn replied. She yawned and took her time leaving the bed and pulling off her gauzy nightgown.

In one corner of the room was a clawfoot washtub with a small table full of soaps, oils, and plush cloths. Naia, the hydro fairy, flew over to prepare the bath, pulling water along special pipes from the river and through a fairy-powered heater until the tub was filled close to the top. Dawn went to her washtub and stepped in, gently lowering herself into the warm, lightly scented bath.

"Perfect as always, Naia, thank you," she said, and the fairy fluttered her wings happily.

Sarah got the door, and the pair of them exited while Dawn washed. Half an hour later Dawn finished her bath, and Sarah returned with a wispy aer fairy. She gently dried Dawn's strawberry blonde hair with magic while Sarah laced her dress—gold silk with three-quarter sleeves, princess waist, and A-line skirt.

Once Dawn was dressed, the girls hurried down the stairs. They passed quietly through the carpeted hallways to the lesser dining hall, pausing momentarily to watch a flora fairy repairing a tapestry. A basket brimming with colorful threads sat under her, and she pulled out a single pink strand. The strand wiggled in her hand, and as if on its own, wove its way into the tapestry, making knots and changing direction as needed until the entire string was gone.

Sarah tugged on Dawn's arm as the fairy reached for another thread, and they went through the doors of the dining hall. Tall, narrow windows lined the north side, letting in the sunrise that made the room sparkle as it bounced off gold flecks in the stone walls. Four round tables comfortably filled with nobles were neatly arranged in a diamond, and on a raised platform against the far wall was a long table for the royals and the highest-ranking officials.

King Leopold sat front and center at the high table, smartly dressed but with no crown on his head, just his own golden blond hair shining like a halo. Queen Eleanor was on his right, her fiery red hair blazing in the morning light. On the king's left were Sir James, the head knight, and Cedric, the only wizard of the Mantrisa house—and Sarah's father.

The Mantrisa's magical needs were more than met by fairies, but at least one wizard was beneficial when dealing with other kingdoms who didn't think much of the minuscule creatures they'd never seen. A kingdom's power and influence directly correlated with the number of mages under the king's employ. A fact that made the newly reclaimed Mantrisa kingdom all the more desirous to unite with the Kirkjufells. The oldest kingdom in the known world, the Kirkjufells had an envious thirteen wizards, more than double the average five or six of any other kingdom.

Sarah took her seat next to her father, and Dawn went to her place on her mother's right, glancing at the final seat. The Fairy Court was invited by the king to have a representative at every meal as a tribute to their friendship. It was a purely symbolic act for the fae, who didn't require food to live. Today's occupant was a welcome surprise.

"Dusk!" Dawn exclaimed softly as she walked behind him, peering at him curiously.

Most fairies opted for backless clothing to allow for wing movement, but Dusk preferred the more elaborate system of flaps and ties that wove between the individual wings, giving him a more noble, less fanciful appearance. His silk mulberry shirt was one of Dawn's favorites, especially when paired with his onyx waistcoat like it was today.

His hair was in his face, and he made no move to allow her to see his eyes as she sat. He adjusted his transparent wings, which were hanging on either side of his chair, folding them in neatly behind himself like a gossamer cape as he leaned back.

While being quiet was perfectly ordinary for him, something in his current mood was different. It was distant and fuzzy like he wasn't used to whatever it was, but it still had a familiarity about it that Dawn had never identified.

"Nice to see you today," she said as food was presented and she picked up her fork. Really, he wasn't supposed to be here, and she wanted to know why he was.

He nodded but didn't say anything, just picked up his fork and poked at a strawberry slice on his plate.

"I thought it was Harpullia's turn next?" she tried again, moving her eggs around without eating anything.

"He had business elsewhere," Dusk said, perfectly formal. He took a bite and chewed slowly, moving his mouth up and down more than necessary.

Dawn grinned, knowing an angle that would at least get a reaction. "Oh, really? Is it something in the Realm?"

Dusk shook his head to move his hair out of the way and scowled at her. "Where Harpullia Pendula is needed isn't my business to share," he said, then turned his scowl back to his food and continued eating.

Dawn giggled softly, unable to help herself. "Come now, that isn't very friendly of you."

"Dawn," her mother chided wearily before Dusk could respond. "Please, just let him eat."

Dawn turned to Dusk to apologize, only to find him leering at her.

"Yes, let the poor fairy eat," he said before returning his attention to his plate.

Dawn shook her head, laughing silently, and focused on her own plate. She shot an occasional simper at Dusk, who smirked at her in return.

The castle was peaceful as Dawn and Sarah walked through the halls of the keep, leaving their footprints behind as they padded along. Morning had flown by and turned into early afternoon with a dress-fitting, history lessons, and vocal practice. In spite of Dawn's short remaining time in Mantrisa, her schedule was kept full with her usual activities—and included several new ones in preparation for her upcoming birthday celebrations.

"How is the song coming?" Sarah asked, startling Dawn out of her pondering. "Think it'll be ready in time?"

"Hmm? Oh, yes, it'll be wonderful."

"Everything all right?" Sarah asked gently. "Julia seemed a bit exasperated when I came to get you."

"Did she?" Dawn said innocently, then sighed when she saw Sarah's expression. "No, I wasn't focused on singing, so she wasn't very pleased."

"Going to tell me what it was, or do I have to keep pestering you?" Sarah teased.

Dawn shook her head slowly, smiling to herself. She couldn't hide anything from Sarah. "Fibrill just got me thinking about Kirkjufell, and how I'm leaving here."

"Is that all?" Sarah replied, knowing there was more to it.

"Well, it made me realize what I won't have anymore," Dawn said.

"Besides Bert, you mean?" Sarah asked. "At least you won't be without me."

"Him, yes," Dawn agreed, smiling for a moment about Rob. "And all the fairies. I've never lived without them, so it'll be strange."

"That won't be so bad," Sarah said. "I'm used to life without them to do things like dry my hair. I can help you."

"Thank you," Dawn replied. Of course, there was more to it than that, but she didn't know how to explain it was really one fairy in particular whose friendship she would miss. One fairy that she hadn't expected to see again, and whose mood only served to puzzle her more. "But speaking of Kirkjufell, how are you feeling about returning?"

"I barely remember it," Sarah answered as they made it outside and blinked in the brightness. "It was a very long time ago we moved here."

"And Cedric rarely talks about it. It must be difficult for him," Dawn considered.

"Actually, I've been worried about him lately," Sarah said. "He's been acting strangely."

"Oh?" Dawn remarked. "How so?"

"He's been talking to someone," Sarah said quietly. A pair of servants were walking toward them, and they moved to the side of the gravel path to make room. "I've noticed his mirror glowing at odd hours, but when I ask him about it, he denies there's anything going on."

"But who could he be talking to that he wouldn't want you to know about?" Dawn asked as they angled back onto the walkway. Mirrors were difficult to set up, and they were regulated so only the highest powers owned them—namely, kings and mages. The fact that Cedric arrived in Mantrisa with a mirror had been his biggest selling point. "Have you checked the signature?"

"That's the thing, he's always keeping it cleared so I can't," Sarah replied. With very few mirrors in existence, and all owners knowing each other's signatures, finding out what signature he was using would be a dead giveaway. "He usually only talks to Edmond but that's infrequent, and he's never minded telling me."

"You don't think he's met someone, do you?" Dawn asked, not really believing the idea. "Since you're leaving soon, maybe he doesn't want to say anything."

"No," Sarah said, shaking her head. "I mean, it's not the sort of thing he would hide from me, if it were that. But I guess I don't know what else could be going on."

They reached the northwest corner of the grounds where a pair of buildings sat together. One was a wooden cottage with a thatched roof where Sarah lived with Cedric. It was built to the preferences of the wizard who felt uncomfortable living in the keep. Squatting to the left of the cottage was a grey stone-brick chunk of a building that wasn't any larger than Dawn's bedroom—the magic lab where Cedric spent most of his time.

The windowless cube was lit inside with four lamps, one in each corner. They were maintained by lux fairies who came out once a week to replenish the spells. On the back wall was a rough oak table with a pair of matching chairs. Next to the table was a short bookshelf with worn leather books neatly organized on the two shelves. Another set of shelves was against the right wall filled with glass beakers in metal stands, writing and drawing materials, and a variety of tools like tongs, measuring cups, and hammers.

Cedric was sitting at the table, poring over a spell book when the girls entered through the single door. Though still in the prime of his life, the wizard held himself as someone twice his age, tending to lean and sit to rest weary limbs whenever possible. His skin had an odd assortment of wrinkles that seemed out of place on the otherwise springy, healthy-looking flesh.

"Ahh, here you are," Cedric said as he looked up. Dawn paused by the equipment shelves while Sarah grabbed a book and sat next to her father. "Why don't you bring over some beakers and we can try that light spell again."

Dawn selected a corked beaker and stand from the shelves and brought them to the table. "Will this do?"

"Perfectly," Cedric replied, nodding at the seemingly empty beaker. "Do you remember the spell?"

"I think so," Dawn said. She uncorked the beaker and tipped it into her palm, almost shivering as magic touched her skin, making it tingle. Once she felt it was enough, she placed the beaker back on the stand and went to the middle of the room. She closed her eyes and thought of the spell, then whispered the words to herself. The magic tingled again, and she opened her eyes. In her palm was the slightest glowing ball, only bright enough to light her hands as she cupped them together.

"Very good," Cedric said, coming over to look. "Now see if you can make it brighter."

Dawn nodded and closed her eyes again. The thing she needed to do, and that she'd failed at every attempt so far, was connect her own magic to the raw magic in order to fuel the spell herself. The problem was that without knowing her alignment, it was difficult— at best—to manipulate her magic.

In centuries past, one mage had found a way to read alignments, and magic was easy to come by for many. He'd never shared his knowledge, and since his passing alignments had become a guessing game based on whatever spells a person could manage. While mages of all varieties were common in the past, now they were few and far between, limited almost entirely to wizardry.

Every living thing had an alignment, and humans, in particular, could be aligned to anything imaginable, excluding alignments already claimed by other third-degree creatures. Aside from healing, which was for unicorns, and rebirth, which always aligned with phoenixes, humans claimed a wide variety of alignments from musical ideas like beat and rhythm, to learning and scholarly things like language and details. Many others, like color and collecting, couldn't be neatly categorized.

The light in Dawn's hands dimmed as she thought about the spell, trying to think of a connection to it she hadn't tried yet. Light, of course, would have been an obvious choice, if it wasn't already one of the seven fairy alignments. Not an option she, a human, had available. Maybe something to do with energy? Perhaps sight, or even guiding. The more things she tried, the farther she reached from the basic idea until the raw magic ran out, and the light faded completely.

Sarah cleared her throat, standing to reshelve her book. "We should be heading in now. They've likely already started the meeting."

"Thank you," Dawn replied, nodding once to indicate she'd gotten Sarah's meaning. "Your help is just invaluable. Don't you think so, Cedric?"

"Sarah's?" Cedric mused as he put away Dawn's equipment. "I do find her to be quite helpful, yes."

"But you'll have to care for yourself soon, won't you?" Dawn said. "That'll be a big change."

"Perhaps," Cedric replied, eying Dawn sideways. "If I were to be alone."

"Who will you have?" Sarah asked.

"Well, I will still be here, will I not?" Cedric gestured sharply around himself. "One is never truly alone in a castle."

"And when you're not in the keep?" Sarah raised an eyebrow and tilted her head at the northern wall of the lab. "Our cottage is a separate building."

"What are you two getting at?" Cedric asked, sighing as he returned to the table and his spell book. He'd long since passed the point of being irritated by the girls' antics, and knew the best thing to do was go along with it. "Please, make your point."

Dawn raised an eyebrow at Sarah, who pursed her lips for a moment before speaking. "Are you seeing someone?"

"What?" Cedric stared at the girls, face colored by shock and something else Dawn couldn't put her finger on. "You think I am courting someone?"

"Well, are you?" Sarah asked gently.

"You know I couldn't be with anyone, even if I wanted to. Your mother is the only woman I'll ever love." Cedric dropped his gaze to the floor like he thought it would crumble away if he moved.

2

The sun hovered above the west castle wall, a few hours from dipping behind it, as Dawn and Sarah ran across the castle yard. They reached a small servant entrance to the keep and ducked inside. The hallways here had fewer tapestries, no flowers, and the rugs, though still plush, lacked the vibrant patterns of those in the public areas.

Once they were out of the service passages they slowed, jogging through the last few hallways until they arrived at the minor dance hall. They quietly opened the door and snuck across the room to the far back corner.

The hall was busy with servants and fairies alike bustling about. Glowing lux fairies played with dancing lights that made their window-pane wings look like stained glass. Petal-clothed floras wove silk for table coverings and napkins. Willowy aer fairies zipped around with their faster speeds, delivering materials and communicating progress of each task to the queen.

With Dawn's birthday just over a week away, many decorations were being staged here before moving to the grand hall within a few days for the real event. The preparations, while always extravagant, were especially so this year, doubling as a grand farewell to Dawn before she left for Kirkjufell—and Geoff.

"...is perfectly manageable, of course, but the exact design hasn't

NIGHT RISE ~ 31

been decided yet. I think we need to talk to the sculptor more before he starts," Eleanor was saying as Dawn and Sarah reached the table and took their seats among the handful of humans and fairies on the project.

"Begging your pardon, but the ice has already been procured, and it would be easier for my team to maintain it if he were to begin now," replied the thermal fairy Eirwen, flicking her wings impatiently from where she stood on the table in front of the queen. She was in charge of the kitchen fairies, who worked on a variety of temperature-related tasks. Her porcelain skin marked her as specializing in cold spells, though her team included several dark-skinned, hot-based thermals.

Eleanor nodded understandingly. "Well, since Dawn has finally joined us, I suggest we decide on the design now, and Alfonso can get started this afternoon."

"A splendid idea," Eirwen said, wings relaxing before she floated into the air. "I'll go let him know we're ready for him."

The Antwerpian artist Alfonso was in the opposite corner of the room surveying his ice block—a chunk so massive he craned his neck and still couldn't see the top, even with his towering height. It had taken some doing from Leopold to convince the Antwerps to allow an extended stay in Mantrisa for their exclusive artist.

"I hope you don't mind we started without you," Eleanor said once Eirwen was out of earshot. "I've other important matters to attend to."

"It's no trouble," Dawn assured her.

"Doesn't look like you got much done without us," Sarah added, earning her a hard look from the warrior queen. Before she could respond, Eirwen returned with the sculptor.

"Your majesties," Alfonso said, smiling and bowing dramatically. "May I say what an honor it is to be working with you for the princess's birthday. I've prepared a few ideas to best commemorate such an occasion, for your most esteemed consideration."

He set several drawings on the table, and they looked them over and deliberated. Alfonso went through a nice variety of options: birds and other animals, Dawn standing tall with a ball and scepter, and even an overly embellished number eighteen. After much discussion, they unanimously voted for a crowned sun rising above an intricate landscape.

An hour later the committee was going over food selections when the door was flung open and Rob jogged over to their corner. He was out of breath and stopped next to them, leaning on his knees. Once his breathing was under control he straightened and ran a hand through his dirty blond hair, pushing sweat from his forehead into the short soldier cut.

"Robert," Eleanor addressed him, one eyebrow raised as she looked him over. "Have you brought your father's list of ingredients he wants for the festivities?"

"Ahh," Rob said, wincing. "I apologize. I didn't think to stop by the kitchen on my way here."

"Then why have you come?" Eleanor's other eyebrow joined the first as she waited.

Rob's eyes flickered with mischief as he glanced at Dawn, then he fixed a serious look on his face and turned to the queen. "I've been sent for the princess."

"Have I gotten a message?" Dawn asked, grinning at Rob as she guessed his real intention.

"I've only been instructed to retrieve you," Rob said, shrugging.

Dawn winked at him and turned to her mother. "I really ought to check. It seems important."

"Very well," Eleanor said, offering her daughter the slightest of smiles. She knew what was going on but didn't mind playing along. "Just don't be too long—we've plenty of work to finish here."

"I'll be quick," Dawn said, already leaving her seat and hooking her arm through Rob's. They raced out of the hall, and she grinned at him as he closed the door. "So where are we really going?"

"Well, I was thinking the rose garden would be good," he replied, grinning back at her. "Figure we're safer staying in the castle, but you still need some free time."

"The garden sounds perfect," Dawn said, never unhappy to visit her favorite spot. "Remember that one time we were playing hide-and-seek in there, and it took you three hours to find me?"

"How could I forget?" Rob said with a chuckle. They found a nearby exit and walked casually towards the gardens. "I suppose you'll want to go see that rose while we're there."

"Which one?"

"You know which one," he said, nudging her gently. "You wouldn't even like it if I didn't get stuck in it."

"And whose fault is it that you chose there to hide?" She laughed.

In minutes the smell of roses subtly filled the air as they entered the garden. A few bushes were covered in buds almost ready to open, and several early-spring blooms were fully opened. Most were middle-spring bloomers, and by late-spring it would turn into a kaleidoscope of roses in every color imaginable.

Scattered throughout the garden were statues of many kinds of magical creatures. Dragons danced, pegasi pranced, and the regal phoenix rested. Notably missing were any likenesses of fairies. Instead, dragonfly-like wings sparkled in the light as flora fairies tended the plants with magic, bringing out a level of beauty only they could achieve. All fairies were drawn to such places of natural tranquility, so there were others relaxing, playing, and enjoying the atmosphere.

"I hope they have roses there," Dawn said, looking around the garden as if she'd never see it again and wanted to memorize every detail. "Although they won't be as pretty if they do."

"No, they wouldn't be," Rob said, watching his friend's rapture. "But maybe they'll have something else that you'll like just as much. Are you ready to go see our bush?"

"Yes, I'm ready," Dawn said as she took one last glance around.

It was a short walk from the entrance without any twists or turns to get lost. They were in front of the bush in moments.

The roses were white with yellow edges and skillfully gradated so even the most discerning eye couldn't tell where one color ended and the other began. It was the same Morning Blossom bush that Dawn had shown Geoff, and every visit to the garden since then had felt different, colored by his lingering presence in her mind.

Being here with Rob helped it feel more grounded and comforting. "It's nice we get to enjoy this before we leave," Dawn said and gave Rob's arm a little squeeze. "I'm really glad you get to come. It'll be much more fun with you there."

"Yeah," Rob replied. He looked at the roses for a while, deep in thought, then looked at Dawn, a glimmer of mischief in his deep blue eyes. "Of course, we don't have to wait to have fun. How about a game of hide-and-seek while we're here? For old time's sake."

He nudged her playfully and she laughed. "Sure, that'll be nice. You hide first though, so we aren't here forever."

"Would that be so bad?" Rob said as he went off to hide. Dawn just laughed again and closed her eyes to count.

"...eight...nine...ten! I hope you're ready!" she called out and started wandering around the garden. "Now let me see, he likes to hide...here. No, well maybe over... No, not here either. He's found some new places... I should check... Wait." Dawn retraced her steps to where she'd seen the fairy. "Dusk?"

Dusk was working on a rose bush that had yellowing, droopy

leaves and dark splotches on the half-open flower buds. He finished clearing one bud, then glanced back at her.

"Oh, hello Dawn," he said and returned to his work.

"Is this one of yours?" she asked as she walked closer to look. While Rob was comfortable to have around in familiar, expected places, Dusk always seemed to belong wherever she met him. And he extended that sense to her.

The fairy paused working and turned to her, half-smiling. "It is."

"It's lovely," she said. The roses were medium size, with deep red and violet petals. They would bloom in a few days, somehow bright despite the disease.

"They were a prototype of sorts for the Heart of Dusk," he replied as he set about working again.

"That would explain it," Dawn said sadly. The rose was one that she had sent to Geoff, and knowing it was also one of Dusk's made her stomach uneasy. "It's too bad I'll be gone before they bloom."

"They'll be ready before your birthday," Dusk said, giving her a quizzical look. "I'll have them healed in plenty of time to be picked for the celebration."

Dawn giggled softly. "I meant the Heart of Dusk, though that is nice to know about this one."

"At least you have the one you pressed," he said, and she winced.

"Right," she said while her cheeks grew warm. It hadn't come up before that she'd sent that rose, and somehow the idea of Dusk knowing about it terrified her. "But, I'd still like to see them blooming if I could."

"Then why don't we go check on them?" Dusk asked as he finished working and cut his magic. "I was going to stop by a couple of other bushes first, but no reason I can't skip ahead for you."

"Dawn?" Rob's voice interrupted her answer. "I thought you wanted to seek so this didn't take all day? Not that I'm complaining, or anything... Oh, there you are. What are you doing?"

"Rah! You're just in time," Dawn said as he walked up the narrow path to them. "Dusk and I are going to check on my favorite rose. You should come."

"Dusk?" Rob remarked, grimacing as he stopped next to Dawn and noticed the fairy. They stared at each other, and Dusk shrugged, unbothered by Rob's appearance. Rob glanced at Dawn uncertainly and shifted his weight from one foot to the other. "Well, actually, I was thinking I ought to go soon. Sean was wanting to get a few of the guys together for some sparring, and I did tell him I'd try to be there."

"If you're sure," Dawn said, disappointed to lose him but not unhappy for some alone time with Dusk.

"Whatever you'd rather do," Dusk muttered, smirking.

"Right," Rob said, throwing a scowl at the fairy. "Well, I'll see you later, then."

He tramped off towards the entrance, turning down a path a few strides away. Dusk took a moment to look over the diseased rose bush before flicking into the air and leading Dawn in the opposite direction.

The path they took had some twists and passages in hedges, covered in ivy that blended into the shrubbery. Eventually, they emerged through an arch into a secluded clearing with a fountain in the center and a two-person swing in the far right corner.

Dusk grinned as he led her to the small, nondescript bush off to the left side. It was covered in tiny, firmly shut buds, offering not even the slightest hint at the nature of the roses.

"It'll be about a week or so before they start to open," Dusk said as he looked over the buds and rubbed a leaf between his fingers. "Not early enough for you, unfortunately."

"They never are ready for my birthday," Dawn said. "Although that reminds me, you weren't going to be here either."

"No," Dusk replied, shrugging like it was nothing. "Like I

mentioned at breakfast, Harpullia couldn't come, so I volunteered. It is meant to be my turn after his, so this is the most logical option."

"And here I was hoping that you did it for me," she teased, though it bit at her that he wasn't there for her. "But really, I am glad you're here. The last of my time before I leave will be much better with you."

He smiled at her, making her wonder if he really wasn't there for her after all. "I certainly hope so."

3

Dawn awoke the next morning to someone pounding on her door. She cracked one eye open and wondered what was going on. There wasn't any light slipping in through the drapes, so she assumed it must be the middle of the night.

"Come back when it's light out," she sleepily called and rolled over in bed.

The pounding stopped and the door flung open. Sarah rushed in, agitation etched on her face in the light from her lamp. She went to the window and threw open the drapes.

"Dawn, look!"

Dawn sighed and got up slowly, feeling oddly well rested for it being so late. She went to the window and looked out at the mountains in the distance. It was dawn, and the sky should have been filled with morning, but strangely she was able to look directly at the sun as it crept above the mountain peaks. There was no light coming from it, and the sky was black as night.

"What's going on?" Dawn whispered.

"I don't know. I came straight here when I saw," Sarah explained, her face pale in the flickering shadows of lamplight.

Dawn slowly digested the scene. Her nerves tingled, and she struggled not to shake. "Then we'd best find out."

The king and queen's rooms were full of anxious attendants and fluttering fairies when Dawn and Sarah arrived. They shoved their way through all the moving bodies to the king's study, where they found Leopold in deep conversation with Cedric and the Fairy Court. The fairies had started for the castle practically before dawn failed to break, arriving in record time with aer fairies speeding them.

"It's certainly not natural," Harpullia said. He was pacing on Leopold's desk and his wings were flicking as he spoke. Though he was speaking loudly for a fairy, the activity around them nearly buried his words. "In thousands of years, we've never seen anything like this. Something that only affects one kingdom."

"But there is no human in my kingdom with the ability to cause such a thing," Leopold replied. "Nor any who would wish to, to my knowledge."

"And we are certain the fae are not behind it," Cedric mused, almost matching the fauna fairy's lower volume.

"We've no need for such accusations," Harpullia sniffed, the sharpness of the words cutting through the noise. "If you have no more to add than the continual reminder of our technical ability, you may leave."

"Please, may we stay focused?" Leopold said. "We've only been here an hour and we'll make no progress like this." Dawn caught her father's eye and waved to him.

"Can we be of any help?" she asked.

"Why don't you check on your mother," he suggested.

James rushed into the room, almost knocking Dawn over. "Sire! Word from Antwerp. They'd like to speak immediately."

"Of course they would," the king grumbled, putting his head in his hand tiredly. "Did you tell them their trade agreements will have to wait until the current crisis has passed?"

"That's why they want to hear from you," James said, pulling out a pocket mirror and showing the king. "They believe they've reason to adjust the terms in their favor."

"Nova's fangs," Leopold muttered, glancing over the message. "Thank you, James."

Harpullia flitted into the air as Leopold pulled his full-sized mirror out of the desk drawer and placed it on the surface.

"Shall we leave you to work?" Cedric asked. "A short recess might do us all well."

"Yes, why don't you," Leopold replied as he prepared his quill. "Dawn, your mother?"

"Right!" She jumped and darted toward her parent's bedchamber. As she reached it, Eleanor burst out in full plate mail with her helmet tucked under her arm.

"Is my horse ready?" she shouted to no one in particular.

"Dearest, we're not ready for you to leave yet," Leopold called from the study. "Someone needs to see the Court to the high council room."

"The Court can see themselves there. I need to go out to the people," Eleanor asserted. "They'll be restless if no one attends them. Do you want riots?"

"Darling," Leopold sighed. "We've already sent out a company, and James is preparing his to go as well. Your effort would be better spent here."

"Dragon droppings! You know I work best with the people," Eleanor argued.

"Mother," Dawn said softly, putting her hand on Eleanor's elbow. "Perhaps it wouldn't be safe for you to go alone? Maybe I could come with you and help."

"Dearest, if it isn't safe for me to go on my own, it wouldn't be safe for you," Eleanor replied gently. "You wouldn't want Geoff to worry about his future queen, would you?"

"Listen to your mother, please," Leopold called before Dawn could reply. "I can't have you going out with everyone panicking. Eleanor may go, as she can take care of herself."

"I suppose," Dawn said, looking at her feet. It was hard to take such advice from the same Eleanor who had led an army at sixteen, but Dawn was in no position to say so. "But you should still travel with someone."

"All right, we'll compromise," Eleanor said gently. Dawn glanced up to see the queen smiling at her. "I shall travel with James."

"Fine. Now will someone get the fairies to the high council room?" the king grumbled as his mirror glowed. "I'll be there just as soon as I deal with the Antwerps."

Dawn happily helped the Fairy Court, feeling much better having something to do, even if it was small. She led them down the hall and upstairs to the high council room, a spacious room with a large table in the center and maps on every bit of wall space.

The back wall was lined with windows that reached to the ceiling and usually flooded the room with light. If the day were ending rather than starting, the darkness on the other side of them would be perfectly ordinary. As it was, the windows were subtly chilling when noticed from the corner of an eye, and downright terrifying if looked at directly.

As soon as they arrived, the fairies broke up into small groups and spoke quietly to each other. Harpullia stood in the center of the table, and the groups took turns checking with him as they made plans. He directed a few to gather resources from the library, a pair of floras to find plants to bring in for studying, and luxs to spell windows throughout the castle to give "natural" light.

"Excuse me," Dawn said when Harpullia was between groups. "Is there anything I can do?"

Harpullia Pendula put his upper wings straight in the air and stepped across the table to her, delicately placing his leaf moccasins on the grainy surface. "All of our needs are being met currently, but thank you for the intention."

"Are you sure?" Dawn asked. "I mean, I know that you're perfectly capable, of course, but I would like to do something. Perhaps I could help bring books from the library?"

"The references we are after are all fairy materials," Harpullia said, smiling patiently. "So it would be better if you left it to us."

"Maybe I could bring something else? What about the plants you sent for?"

The flora fairies returned with a plant each, set the miniature pots on the table, and then flew away to bring more.

Harpullia's pointed nose twitched. "As I said, we are meeting our own needs."

"Right," Dawn said, feeling perfectly useless as she glanced around the room. "Then I'll just stay out of the way."

She sat at the end of the table and watched the fairies fly around until Sarah and Cedric arrived, having gone to the kitchens to arrange breakfast. Sarah grinned as she took a seat next to Dawn.

"What are you so happy about?" Dawn asked glumly.

Sarah leaned in close to whisper as she wiggled excitedly. "I know how you can help. You should ask if the fairies would let you use the lantern."

"What lantern?" Dawn whispered back.

"Ask," Sarah said quietly as the king entered the room. Dawn nudged her, but she drew her fingers across her closed lips and tilted her head at the king. If Dawn wanted to know more, she'd have to do as Sarah suggested.

"All right, let's have some ideas," Leopold said as he took a seat across from his daughter. The fairies stopped fluttering everywhere, settling on the table, and everyone stared at each other silently. "Well, don't all start at once."

Harpullia cleared his throat and stepped forward toward the king. "We have already sent the majority of lux fairies around the kingdom to provide aid where they can."

"Good," Leopold said. "Are the floras out as well?"

"Yes, Sire. Except for those of us here and in the Realm, all able fairies are out," Harpullia replied.

"And you're sure there isn't anything else you can do?" Sarah asked, prodding Dawn with her elbow. "There's really no other light sources you know of?"

"And what else might there be?" Leopold inquired. Cedric raised an eyebrow at his daughter, who shrugged and prodded Dawn again.

Several pairs of fairy eyes shifted to the princess, and she gave in.

"Maybe a lantern?" she asked quietly. The fairies gasped, and Leopold gaped at her. Clearly, Sarah was onto something. "Well, there is one, isn't there? One that we could use."

Several fairies buzzed their wings and others bolted to the ceiling, where they darted around like flies trying to escape.

"Everyone, calm down," Leopold soothed, watching the agitated fairies uneasily. "It has only been mentioned. There's no reason for distress. We will only consider it as a last resort should nothing else work, and even then I leave it to your discretion."

It took a few minutes for all the fairies to relax enough to return to the table, and when they did most remained anxious and twitchy, running their hands together and shooting Dawn wild glances.

"It is well that Dusk is not here to have heard such things," Harpullia said, giving Dawn a harsh look.

"Why? Does it have something to do with him?" Dawn asked. If Dusk was aware of it, perhaps there was a way to act on the idea after all.

"He is the only one that could access it alone," Harpullia answered after a moment's consideration. "Though I doubt if he were to be so willing."

"But maybe someone could convince him," Dawn whispered to herself as breakfast arrived.

Once she was done eating, Dawn excused herself and dragged Sarah with her out of the high council room.

"What is this lantern?" she asked as they jogged through dark, empty hallways. Occasional candles in nooks marked turns and rooms.

"Apparently it's magic, and it could make light," Sarah said between breaths. "But the fairies have to get it for us, and they don't want to. Where are we going?"

"To the library," Dawn replied. "I'm hoping one fairy, in particular, will be more inclined to your idea."

They found the stairs to go down and went through the last few hallways to the library. Dangerous creatures seemed to lurk around every corner, but it was just shadows on the tapestries turning a flock of sheep into a leviathan, or a mountain into a gaping, toothy mouth. Sarah waited in the library entrance while Dawn felt her way to the far back corner, where a small structure sat on a table.

The structure resembled a dollhouse, with three walls and a floor and roof. Instead of couches and beds, it had tables and shelves full of tools and equipment that looked like miniature versions of shelves in Cedric's lab. This was the fairy lab, and Dusk was busy inside heating beakers filled with magic, combining spells, and writing down notes in a journal.

He pulled something out of his pocket and frowned at it, noticing Dawn approach as he put it back.

"Morning, Dawn," he said. His voice was on a level with humans, with his aer abilities increasing the volume. "Rather unfortunate about your namesake, or else it would have been a good morning. Do you need something?"

Dawn licked her lips and took a deep breath. She didn't know enough for this to be a good idea, but similarly, it wasn't a bad one either. "Actually, yes. You see, I suggested an idea to the Court—well, Sarah told me to suggest it and I did—but they weren't too thrilled by it. And Harpullia said you would be able to help, but you might not want to."

"And what might this idea have been?" he asked with a smirk.

"I thought we could use the lantern," she said and his smirk disappeared.

"*No*," he whispered, and Dawn felt the word slam into her, trying to push her away. "I'm sorry, but that isn't an option."

"Why not?" she asked as she knelt by the lab and rested her arms on the table.

"Because—" Dusk started, then sighed and looked down at his hands as he clenched them. "I'd rather not explain why not."

"And there's nothing I can do to change your mind?" she asked, her eyes shining.

Dusk unclenched his fists and looked at her, a strange depth in his stare she'd only ever seen in fairies, and only in moments of intense feeling. "There's nothing you could offer."

"No?" She sighed and dropped her eyes, unable to hold his gaze.

Dusk stared at her face for a long minute, then reached out to place his hand on her thumb. "Maybe there is one thing. In order to do it, I'd need to talk to Diya. Would you want to come to the Realm?"

"You know I would," Dawn answered, focusing on her thumb. She'd only spent her entire life wanting to see the fairies' home and meet the mythical Diya. Whatever the reason for going, she wasn't going to miss it.

Dusk squeezed her thumb lightly, then pulled his hand back. "Then you get ready while I finish up here, and we'll meet by the east gate in an hour."

"Rah! I'm so glad I caught you."

Rob looked at Dawn panting in his doorway and smiled. "Me too. My company's helping with animals that are stampeding around. I don't know how long we'll be gone. Just want to say goodbye before I go?"

"Actually, I need a favor," Dawn said as she walked into his room. "I'm going to the Fae Realm and I wanted to borrow some trousers."

"What? Why are you going there?" Rob exclaimed.

"Dusk is taking me so we can get a lantern that will give us light," she explained. Saying it aloud didn't make it less crazy. "I'm meeting him soon to leave, so if I could get those clothes, please."

"Right," Rob said and went to his dresser. He found trousers and a tunic he'd grown out of years ago and threw them on the bed. "These should do. You change here, and I'll be right back."

"What are you doing?"

"I'm letting James know I won't be able to go with the company," he said. "Since I'll be coming with you instead."

"You can't tell him I'm going!" Dawn looked at him with wide, fearful eyes. "Father can't find out until it's done—he told the Court we wouldn't use the lantern."

"Then why are you going?" Rob asked.

"Because Dusk agreed to do it," she mumbled. "And he wants to take me." Even to her, it was flimsy at best, but she'd already made up her mind. Whatever else happened, at least she would see the Fae Realm and meet Diya.

"Are you saying he only wants to go if you do?" Rob asked.

She blushed and looked down at the worn clothes on the bed.

Rob groaned and rubbed his forehead. "This is the dumbest thing I've ever done. Fine, I won't tell James what I'm doing. Just that it's for you."

"Thank you," Dawn said. The door closed and she was left alone.

Rob returned a few minutes later wearing a leather gherkin and carrying a short sword at his side. "Ready?"

Dawn finished tying the rope belt at her waist and let the drab tunic fall over her hips. Rob's old shirt hung on her frame, concealing her petite figure in folds of fabric. The tan pants reached past her feet, so she folded them up at her ankles and tucked them into her boots.

"When am I not?" she asked. She hadn't adventured in forever, or really at all, and the excitement was getting to her. The discovery of the new, the fun time with her friends, and even the idea of danger around them wasn't something she wanted to miss.

"Right," Rob said, grabbing his pack and throwing it over his shoulder. "The guards are keeping an extra eye out, but I bumped into Sean, and he'll look the other way while we sneak out."

"You didn't mention what we're doing, did you?" Dawn asked as she followed him out of the barracks and they slowly crossed the yard to the east wall.

Rob's reply was quiet, "He knows it's better not to ask questions."

A light bounced in front of them, and he pulled them behind a shed. They peeked around the corner to watch, and after a moment Dawn grinned and led them back into the open.

"I didn't realize you'd be bringing Robert," Dusk said as he met them.

"Why wouldn't she?" Rob replied, glaring at the fairy.

"It'll be much safer with him," Dawn said. "Sarah's meeting us as well, then we'll be ready."

Dusk frowned, and Dawn thought he might decide to call the adventure off, but the frown left as he exhaled. "If you feel you need them. Of course, that will mean we'll travel slower."

"Speed isn't as important as safety," Rob said, and Dawn smiled at him.

Dusk opened his mouth to argue, then looked down at his hands as he curled and uncurled his fingers. After several moments he sighed and his eyes flicked to Dawn before he regarded Rob. "No, time is the most important thing. And with that in mind, we'd best meet Sarah and get going."

4

⚉

By late afternoon Dawn and her friends were deep in the forest that sprawled across the east side of the kingdom. There were several towns and farms bordering the forest, with a few houses scattered just inside the tree lines. They were all marked by candles sparkling in windows and lanterns left on top of fence posts to help travelers, even though Dawn and her companions were the only people out.

Dusk led them along a rough, overgrown trail that avoided all signs of civilization once they were inside the tree line. He explained this was the route he and other fairies used to get between the Fae Realm and the castle, but it was almost never traveled by humans. Rob followed directly behind Dusk, shoving branches and foliage out of the way for the girls to pass unhindered.

"Do you really think we can fix this?" Rob asked, glancing uneasily at the sky through the tree branches.

"The lantern isn't meant to fix it," Dusk replied without slowing or looking back. "It's only to provide some light until we can find the cause."

"Oh," Sarah remarked. She walked carefully behind Dawn, carrying a small lamp. "That's much less exciting than I thought. You sure we can't do more?"

"It depends what the problem is," Dusk answered. He went

through a dense, scratchy bush and waited while the others shoved around it. "And from what I can tell so far, I doubt it. I know it wasn't fairy magic that did this, so the possibility of removing the issue with the lantern is slim at best."

"But maybe we could use it to help find where the problem came from," Sarah mused.

"How it's to be used is up to the Court," Dawn said. "All we mean to accomplish is ensuring that they have the option."

"No, it's up to Diya," Dusk said, his tone sharp. "No matter who wants it, or for what reason, it's only for him to decide."

Dawn bit her lip as the words cut her, wondering what was so important about Diya that Dusk would act like this. She knew the fairies were close, but wasn't she also close to Dusk? Then again, how could she, a human, hope to make a similar impression?

"Any idea how much longer?" Sarah whined before Dusk started moving again. "I'm getting tired."

"We should stop for the night soon," Rob said, decidedly not moving any farther. "There's a clearing nearby we could use."

Dusk glanced around the area, checking the sun's position in the sky while he considered the idea. "Can you lead the girls there?" he asked Rob. "If you're ready to make camp, I'd like to go ahead to the Realm on my own, stay there for the night."

"I can lead," Rob said, looking at the fairy apprehensively. "But is that a good idea?"

"Assuming you can take care of things, why wouldn't it be?" Dusk answered.

"Who cares, as long as we get to eat?" Sarah asked. "Go on, Bert, show us this clearing."

Rob took a moment to check his direction, then turned off the path they were on and foraged towards the clearing. Dawn watched Sarah go after him, then turned to Dusk.

"You'll be able to find us, won't you?" she asked.

"Of course," he answered. "Now go on, before you lose them."

"Take care, then," she replied. She hurried to catch up to Sarah's quickly fading lamplight, but turned back to see Dusk's glow staying exactly where it was as he watched her.

"Welcome to our home for the evening," Rob said as he and the girls emerged from the undergrowth into the clearing.

The clearing was cozy, with soft moss under their feet and a creek gurgling along one side, and just spacious enough for the three of them to camp. Dawn looked around and frowned, noticing the remains of a campfire in the light of Sarah's lamp.

"Rah, how recent is that?" she asked softly. Rob knelt next to her and poked at the ashes.

"Very," he answered. "Possibly from this morning."

"Does that mean we'll have company?" Sarah asked. She was a few feet behind her friends and glanced back, half-expecting something to jump out from where they'd entered.

A high-pitched whine hit their ears, and they turned towards the far end of the clearing next to the creek. A brown fox emerged, head down, tail drooping. She cradled her back left paw, limping along on her other three legs until she collapsed at the far edge of the clearing, bright eyes imploring them to help. Dawn stepped closer, but Rob held up a hand to stop her.

"Don't," he said quietly as he stood, eying the fox warily.

"But she's hurt," Dawn replied.

"Then I'll check." Rob slowly walked over to the fox, hands out in front of himself like he was afraid she would jump at him suddenly. She whimpered and winced away from his touch as he knelt next to her and laid his hands on her back. As he lightly ran his fingers over her leg, she yelped and bit at his face, making him lurch back.

"Careful," Dawn called, and Rob shook his head and turned towards her.

"Doesn't seem like anything's wrong," he said, eyebrows furrowed. The fox was still whining and licked her foot like it was bothering her. "Maybe it's—oof!"

A young boy dropped from the tree branches onto Rob, wrestling him to the ground. His nut brown skin and dark clothes hid him in the shadows like a wraith. Rob fought against him, but the youth was springy and evaded all attempts at throwing him off. He pulled weighted cords from around his waist and got them wrapped around Rob's limbs before the knight could throw him off.

As soon as the boy appeared, the fox got to her feet and leapt towards Dawn, snarling and baring her teeth. Sarah tried to run over to help, but was grabbed around her waist by a man in a trench coat who seemed to materialize behind her. The lamp fell from her hand and rolled away, the flame spluttering but remaining lit.

"You got him, Paul?" the man asked, calmly holding Sarah off the ground as she squirmed and fought his grip. His ginger hair was neatly combed, and every piece of clothing was perfectly crisp as though just pressed. Reddish stubble speckled his chin.

"Got it!" the boy cried happily as he trotted over to the man with Rob's sword. The knight was busy untangling himself from the cords and glowered after the youth.

"Only because you fight dirty," he grumbled, struggling with the cords on his wrists.

"You've a lot to learn, boy, if you don't expect opponents to take every advantage they can," the man replied, shrugging. "Good work, Paul. Now tell me which one of em's worth the most."

Paul smiled and looked closely at Sarah, still fighting, and then glanced over to Dawn. "That one."

"And why's that?"

"She's got the noble posture," Paul answered. "And her hands are smooth, so she doesn't work."

"No, you're wrong," Rob said, finally free of his ties. He placed

NIGHT RISE ~ 53

himself between the fox and Dawn, knife in his right hand. "It's the one you've got who's rich. Ask her."

"It's true!" Sarah cried, looking back at the man. "It's me, so let them go."

The fox made a sound like a laugh and bounced around Rob, sniffing at Dawn.

"You won't fool any of us with this little act," the man said, nodding at the fox. "'Specially not when Mina's got the scent. Now, you just give us whatever money an' goods you have on you, and we'll consider letting you all leave."

"We don't have anything," Dawn said before her friends could argue more. It was touching, what they were willing to do without her asking, but she couldn't lose them. "Please, just let us continue on our way and we'll forget we ever saw you."

"And where might you be going?" the man asked. "Odd to find such prestigious travelers in the forest at night, 'specially during a crisis."

"That's none of your business," Rob said, glaring at the man.

Mina snarled at him, and he waved his knife at her, reminding her he was armed. She backed up slightly, haunches raised. The man clicked his tongue and the fox sprang at Rob, knocking the knife away. He stumbled back a step, then threw her away from his body. Paul was already nearby, holding the knife.

"Anymore?" the boy asked with a grin. Rob's face burned with rage, but he remained silent, staying between the boy and Dawn.

"He's out," the man said, smirking, then clicked his tongue again. Mina yipped, then jumped around Rob and knocked into Dawn, sending them both to the ground.

Before he could interfere, Rob was attacked by Paul, who giddily brandished the knife, cutting the knight's cheek. He had more cords, and Rob was again immobilized. Mina made the laughing sound and snapped at Dawn's face, who winced away from the animal's teeth.

Sarah shrieked as she watched her friends struggling, and a maroon glow shimmered around her. Magic surged through her and into the man, making him drop her in surprise.

"The hell?" the man grumbled, only thrown for a moment as he grabbed Sarah's wrist.

"Zan!" Paul cried, looking over with concern.

"I'm all right," the man said, wrestling with Sarah as he tied her with his own cords. "Not bad, girlie. Maybe you *are* worth something. Help Mina with Blondie, will you? Even if this one's a mage, that one's got the money."

Paul collected the cords he'd used on Rob before and brought them to Dawn. She watched him approach and noticed a tiny flicker of light just outside of the clearing, that seemed to be growing.

"Dusk?" she whispered.

"Yeah, that's what time it is," Zan replied. He finished tying up Sarah and stepped over to help Paul. "'Course it hardly matters with the Night Rise."

"Night Rise?" Dawn glanced up at the sky, where the stars glimmered as if it were the middle of the night, as they had been the entire day. Shadows played in the clearing, eerily bouncing from unsteady lamplight instead of stretching in the last drops of sunlight as they should be.

"Well, the sun rose, didn't it?" Zan said, reaching Dawn and tugging on the ties Paul had bound her with. "But instead of light, it brought more...night."

"I suggest you release myself and my companions," Dawn said. Help was here; she just had to keep their attention. "I am Princess Dawn Mantrisa, and if you do not, you will face dire consequences."

Paul's eyes grew wide and he looked at Zan, but the man smirked. "Nice try, Blondie, but let me give you some advice. No one's going to believe a story like that if you don't have a—"

"Fairy!" Paul grabbed Zan's arm and pointed at the undergrowth behind them.

Dusk burst out of the foliage, glowing hot from the flames engulfing him, and shot across the clearing. Mina yelped and sprinted into the undergrowth as a fireball raced at her, Paul close on her heels. Zan dodged the bolt of magic Dusk shot at him, rolling expertly out of the way, then with a smirk, he bowed dramatically to Dawn.

"Another time, Princess," he said, then flicked his coattails and was gone.

"Are you all right?" Dusk asked Dawn as he hovered around her, checking for any injury. He was no longer on fire, but still shone brightly as he undid the cords holding her.

"I'm fine," she said, rubbing her wrists before standing. "How did you know we needed you?"

"I heard Sarah scream," he answered.

"Are we that close to the Realm?" Sarah asked as she wormed her way out of her own ties. She'd gotten her hands in front of her and used her teeth to loosen the cords. "I thought it was still a couple more hours of hiking."

"Can someone untie me?" Rob complained, having trouble with Paul's second job on him. Sarah finished releasing herself and skipped over to help.

"Did you not make it there?" Dawn asked quietly, and Dusk shrugged, not looking at her. "Well, thank you for saving us."

"Dusk, can you heal this?" Sarah called over, and pointed to Rob's cheek as they stood.

Rob grumbled, "I don't want it healed. It's fine."

"Well, at least let me clean it," Sarah said and pulled a handkerchief out of her tunic pocket to wipe up the blood. Rob glowered but bent down to allow Sarah to tend the wound.

"Can I go now?" he asked when Sarah finished. "I want to scout around, make sure they're really gone."

"You're not going anywhere," Dusk said, scowling at the knight. "I can tell they've gone, and someone needs to make camp."

"Are you staying?" Dawn asked.

"Someone has to take care of you."

"I can take care of things," Rob argued. "Really, it's not my fault they were here."

"But if you'd paid better attention, you would have known before you arrived," Dusk countered. "I only left because I thought Dawn would be safe with you. Now I see that isn't the case, so I'll be remaining here tonight."

"That's ridiculous," Rob exclaimed. "Not even James could have taken them alone. You don't need to stay—I can watch things tonight."

"Rah, he said he wants to stay, so he's staying," Dawn said. She, at least, felt much more secure with him around. "Now why don't we get a fire going? Then we can have some dinner."

5

The forest was eerily quiet the next morning as Dawn emerged from her tent and looked up at the still dark sky. The sun was just visible through the trees, dressed like a new moon and in no hurry to bathe the world in light as it marched along its path.

"Morning, Dawn!" Sarah called. Dawn smelled potatoes frying as she walked over to sit by the warm fire.

"Morning," she yawned. "Where are the boys?"

"Bert went out to make sure we were still alone, and Dusk is over that way somewhere," Sarah replied.

Dawn followed Sarah's pointing hand and saw a fairy glow high in a tree. The glow bounced and floated over to them.

"Did you sleep alright?" Dusk asked as he landed on the mossy ground next to Dawn.

"It wasn't terrible," she answered. Of course, knowing Dusk was around had put her at ease, and even Rob couldn't argue with someone who didn't need sleep keeping watch. "And what about your night? Anything happen?"

"Thankfully, no," he said. "I was able to spend the night star-gazing."

"Great for you," Sarah muttered, scowling. "I know I didn't have such a nice time, and Bert didn't look like he slept any better."

"While I am sorry you had an unpleasant evening, it was in no way my fault you encountered the mercenary," Dusk said.

"Because it's my fault, right?" Rob asked as he entered the clearing. He glowered as he stomped to the fire and sat on Dawn's other side.

"Well, if I had been properly informed of your capabilities, it wouldn't have happened," Dusk argued.

"Bert was just fine," Sarah said, poking at the potatoes roughly. "He did fight before they tied him up, you know."

"And you used magic," Dawn said quickly. The moment it happened was surprising, and the reminder was a suitable distraction from the current mood.

"Magic?" Dusk asked, curious in spite of himself. A new mage's first magic was something indeed. "Sorcery? Or was it intentional?"

"Not really," Sarah said, looking down at the potatoes and scraping them around the pan. "It just happened by itself. But it didn't do anything."

"It surprised us," Rob said. "And them, which didn't *not* help."

"You did more," she said, cheeks turning pink.

"You both did well," Dawn said. Seeing them willing to sacrifice themselves for her wasn't something she would readily forget, nor be able to repay. They were better friends than she deserved.

"I suppose you did well enough," Dusk said, shrugging. "Dawn wasn't harmed, and that's all that matters."

"Because we're so unimportant?" Sarah exclaimed.

"Of course not," Dawn said before Dusk could react. The one thing her friends had in common was how much they cared about her, even if they did so differently. If she could only help them see it. For now, though, they had a task to finish. "Are the potatoes ready? We don't want to waste any time getting to the Realm."

Everyone was quiet as Sarah prepared plates and handed one to Dawn and Rob before sitting down with her own.

"I should mention," Dusk said once the others were eating. "The Realm is protected to prevent humans from entering, and I only intend to bring Dawn through."

"You're going to leave us out here alone?" Rob remarked.

"You're only here to help Dawn travel. There's no reason for you to come into the Realm with us," Dusk explained very calmly, considering. "It won't be dangerous, as the defense spells will warn of any nearby threats."

"Don't worry, Bert. I still trust you," Sarah said, throwing Dusk a withering glance that he ignored. "I know you can take care of the two of us."

"Are you sure this is the way?" Sarah complained as they continued through the forest. "Doesn't look like we're going anywhere."

"This area is spelled to confuse you," Dusk explained. They had gone quietly the last hour and a half, and everyone's moods had settled closer to where they had been the day before. "The only way to reach the Realm is to follow this trail, and only fairies are able to stay on it."

Dawn looked at the trees and noticed the leaves beginning to lose their color where Dusk's light fell on them, making the forest feel like middle-autumn instead of early-spring. It occurred to her that it didn't feel like the path led nowhere, but instead felt like she had traveled it many times, and was returning to a place of safety and comfort. A place like home.

Dusk stopped them as they reached a small ledge, and they could hear the stream rushing by a couple of meters below them. "Here is where we'll part," he said. "I don't know how long we'll be in the Realm, so go ahead and make yourselves comfortable. Just be sure you stay put. When you're ready, Dawn."

Dusk brightened himself so Dawn could see as she climbed carefully down the ledge. She went slowly, testing each stone or branch that she placed a foot on. It was good she had thought to borrow pants—this would have been impossible in a dress.

Directly across the stream was a dense patch of forest, shrouded in a depth of darkness beyond what even the Night Rise could achieve. It fit neatly in Dawn's view if she stared right at the center, with the edges cutting off cleanly where the regular forest met the magical section. The Fae Realm, with its spells to keep out everything. Everything except fairies, and whatever guests they chose.

Once Dawn was on the edge of the stream, Dusk held his hand out to her.

"Are we flying?" she teased and held her hand up to meet his.

"No, you're walking," he answered. She felt a tingle run through her body as Dusk channeled magic into her. "Go ahead."

Dawn looked at the rushing water and bit her lip. The stream wasn't any wider than she was tall with her hands stretched above her head, but it *was* equally deep. "You're sure?"

"Do you trust me?" Dusk replied, and she nodded shakily. "Then walk."

Dawn took one long, deep breath, then closed her eyes and stepped forward. Her foot touched the water and it was still and solid. She took another step, and another until the tingle of magic stopped and she finally opened her eyes. She was on the other side, on a narrow strip of rocky ground between the stream and the dark foliage wall.

"Good job," Dusk said as he removed his hand from hers. "The Realm is just past the wall."

He touched a bush, and the prickly foliage lifted and pulled away, revealing a tunnel just large enough for Dawn to pass through. The far side was bright, blindingly so, and Dawn squinted until she made it through and the light was no longer harsh.

The foliage wall was a perfect circle on the inside, covered in jewel-toned berries. Dawn saw a bluebird on her right poke at a red berry, and as it ate, its feathers shifted to scarlet. It chirped, then gobbled a green berry and shifted to jade before flying farther into the Realm.

A meadow stretched across the ground, a springy carpet of flowers and ferns, soft enough to sleep on like the fawn Dawn spotted on her left. It spread seemingly forever, easily three times what she would have guessed from the outside.

She took a deep breath and scrunched her nose, trying to decide what she was smelling. One moment it was the flowers—roses, lavender, chamomile—the next, deep evergreen forest after rain. There was even a salty scent she'd only ever smelled on visiting Antwerpian dignitaries, that she was told was the ocean.

In the center of the Fae Realm, only a few short paces from the wall, was another perfect circle of a dozen trees surrounding a crystal clear pool. The giant trees, decorated in a rainbow of flowers and fruits, alternated gold and silver leaves that sparkled when a fairy went by. The trunks were speckled up and down with windows, doorways, and even balconies higher up.

Around the base of each tree was a ring of bright red mushrooms with white spots, their caps covered in dewdrops that looked like sugar crystals. In and around the trees, a handful of lux and flora fairies were working to keep their home from deteriorating like the forest around them.

Dusk paused just inside the clearing and pulled a small piece of quartz out of his pocket. It didn't always glow when Dawn saw it, but every time it did Dusk returned home. It was glowing now, and Dusk put it away.

"Diya's by the pool," he said, then led her inside the tree ring.

The pool was a perfect circle with smooth pebbles along its circumference. It filled the space inside the trees, surrounded by a carpet of plush grass for animals to lounge around the sides. Tiny stone benches sat right at the water's edge, allowing fairies to rest and dip their feet in the cool water. Colorful fish swam in and out of a coral garden, and on the surface lily pads floated delicately along, ferrying frogs and fairies from one end to another.

"I'll go find him and bring him to you," Dusk said, seeing where Dawn's attention was. "He'll feel better if I talk to him first anyway."

"Oh, right. That sounds good," Dawn answered. She knelt by the pool while he floated away and imagined herself riding the lily ferries, fingers trailing through the water as she conversed with frogs.

"Dusk!" Diya exclaimed as he was wrapped in a hug from behind. They were on the far end of the pool across from Dawn, and could only make out her general shape in the shadowy lighting. She was no more than another fawn seeking refuge in the Realm. "What're you doing here?"

"Why didn't you let me know how you were?" Dusk replied. A pair of fairies floated close by, whispering quietly to each other. Dusk eyed them, and they went silent and sped away.

Diya settled into Dusk and rested his head on his shoulder. "You know why. You're supposed to be enjoying your last second, not worrying about me."

"That was before this," Dusk said and looked up at the dark sun above them. "It isn't something that any lux fairy is fine with. Of course I've been worried."

"Well, you shouldn't. I'd survive on my own. And even if I didn't, it isn't worth what you gave up just to check on me," Diya replied, glancing down at the water and splashing with his foot.

"Well, perhaps if I had truly given it up," Dusk muttered as water droplets bounced around them.

Diya studied his face for a second, then glanced across the pool and smirked. "You bastard, using this as some sort of cover to bring her here? What, you just stopped caring what other people would think all of a sudden?"

"Not exactly," Dusk said. He tensed slightly and Diya frowned. "We didn't come without purpose. She wants to ask about the lantern."

"She's here because she wants that thing?" Diya's frown sharpened and he squirmed uncomfortably. "You brought her so she could ask about it? And you're supposed to be the smart one."

"That's why she wanted to come, but I only intended to let you two meet," Dusk explained. "At the very least, she feels like she's doing something to help, and I get to be with both of you, even just for a fraction of a second."

"Guess I can't argue with that," Diya said, shrugging, and Dusk relaxed again.

"Not when you're the one who told me to go," he replied, chuckling. "Now will you come meet her?"

Dawn looked up as Dusk returned to her end of the pool, leading a faintly glowing lux fairy by the hand. Diya was exactly how she imagined at a glance, with sharp features and lithe frame that all fairies shared, and white blond hair that was common for lux in particular. But while other fairies had the liveliness of a roaring fire, he seemed to be flickering embers, undecided if they were relighting, or going out.

His bark fiber shirt wrapped around his neck—leaving his shoulders exposed—and barely reached where his navel would be. Similarly, his low-waisted trousers only went to midcalf and draped ragged above his bare feet.

"Dawn, this is Diya," Dusk said as the fairies came to a stop next to her, their hands separating.

Dawn stood and held out her index finger to the lux fairy. "Pleased to meet you."

"So I hear you want the thing," Diya remarked, making no move to accept her hand. His voice was harsh, not anything like the playfulness she'd expected.

Dawn pulled her hand back and grasped her wrist in her other hand. "Yes, I was hoping we could borrow it."

"*Borrow?*" Diya snorted. "Dusk, what'd you tell her?"

"Only that we could ask you what you thought," Dusk answered.

"So you're giving me the choice," Diya muttered. "Well, I'm not gonna decide. You do it. You're the one who likes helping them."

"Diya," Dusk groaned.

"Excuse me," Dawn said, eyes darting between the fairies. Of all the things she had imagined for this meeting, the fairies fighting wasn't one of them. "Is there some problem? We really only want to help with the Night Rise. I have no intention with the lantern beyond that."

"Yeah? But what happens to it when you're done?" Diya asked. His voice was measured and calm, but his body was tense, like a harp string waiting to be plucked.

"Well, we'd give it back to you, I suppose," she answered after a moment's consideration. "Since it's yours."

"Mine?" Diya spat. "You think I want the thing?" His wings twitched and he darted off.

"Diya! Wait!" Dusk called, but the lux fairy didn't stop.

"What happened?" Dawn looked at Dusk, her vision almost blurring. She wanted to be friends, for Diya to be happy to meet her. His behavior was shocking, and Dusk wasn't mediating as he should.

Dusk sighed and rubbed his forehead. "I'm sorry, I should have warned you this might happen. Come on, we have to find him."

He flew off the way Diya had gone and Dawn followed. Their effort had failed as far as she was concerned, but Dusk was determined to try again. If he thought the mission could be salvaged, maybe there was hope for Dawn to befriend Diya as well.

Outside of the main tree circle grew a sturdy ash tree with fairy doors and windows scattered throughout the upper branches. The single fairy home on the edge of the Realm. Dusk disappeared into one of the lower openings as Dawn reached the tree. She stood on her toes, but even the lowest hole was too high for her, so she put her ear on the trunk, hoping she could hear at least some of the conversation inside. To her surprise, Dusk and Diya's voices were perfectly clear, as if she were in the tree with them.

"I'm sorry," Dusk's voice was gentle. "You know I didn't mean for it to go like this."

"Should of known better than to try it," Diya replied. "But I get why you did. I'm not mad, really."

"I know," Dusk said softly. "But I wish it hadn't bothered you."

Dawn's stomach rolled at their words. Whatever Dusk tried, it had to do with her, right? If it did, that meant Diya was bothered by her. But why would he be? He should be happy that Dusk had another friend, shouldn't he?

Diya snorted. "Yeah, 'cause it's that simple. You're an idiot, you know, letting your feelings get you into this kind of crap. Lucky you're my idiot, or who knows what you'd do on your own."

Dusk chuckled. "I wouldn't get into any kind of trouble. That was always your job."

"Yeah," Diya replied, a smile in his voice. "If you want me to, I'll give it another try. You deserve that much."

At least there was something they agreed on. All Dawn had to do then, was show Diya that she cared about Dusk as much as he did. That shouldn't be difficult—there wasn't anyone she cared more about than him.

The fairies were quiet for so long Dawn thought they might have snuck out without her noticing, and she almost missed Dusk's whispered "Thank you."

She jumped away from the tree and watched Dusk lead Diya out, their hands tightly clasped. Dusk caught her eye and winked as they descended. Once they stopped at eye level, Diya pulled his hand away from Dusk and stared anywhere but at Dawn.

"So," Dusk began. "We don't know what we'll do after the Night Rise, but I think it would be reasonable to at least consider finding the lantern."

"Wait, it isn't here?" Dawn asked, and Diya laughed.

"You thought I had it?" he mocked. "Guess you really don't know anything."

"Diya, please," Dusk groaned, and his friend shrugged.

"Sorry. I'm trying."

Dusk raised an eyebrow at him, and Diya glared back. Eventually, Dusk sighed and turned to Dawn. "And are you prepared to help us retrieve it? It could be dangerous, but I do need a human to help."

She wasn't prepared for anything that had happened yesterday, today, or really anything she was heading towards after this adventure was done. The only thing that had gotten her this far was Dusk, and she saw no reason to change that now.

"Well, I suppose whatever you think is best," she replied, and Diya finally looked at her. His eyes darted around her face like he'd never seen a human before and was trying to find the similarities to his own kind.

"Yeah, all right," he said, icy eyes burning into Dawn. "Whatever *Dusk* thinks is best."

6

Late morning turned to afternoon, though without sunlight filtering into the forest—or anywhere in the kingdom for that matter—the sun's position in the sky was the only tell, and it was difficult to read through the dense tree canopy.

There was just enough room at the top of the ledge for Rob and Sarah to comfortably sit while they waited for Dawn and Dusk to return from the Fae Realm. At first, they huddled together, feeling exposed and jumping at every sound, but after several minutes of nothing happening, they relaxed away from each other.

"I can't believe you brought these," Rob said as he shuffled a deck of cards and dealt them out.

"Well, we're using them aren't we?" Sarah said. She picked up her hand and looked at her cards.

"I guess. Hey! You aren't supposed to look," Rob remarked.

"Aren't we? I thought we were changing games," she replied, allowing him to grab the cards. It was quiet while he shuffled again, and she nervously watched the shadows flickering at the edges of the lamplight. "They sure are taking their time. Think we should go after them soon?"

"We were told to stay here," Rob grumbled. "Unless you want the fairy to yell at us more."

"What I want is to actually do something," Sarah said, putting her chin in her hand. "I thought this was going to be fun, but so far it's been nothing but bad."

"I thought you using magic was something," Rob replied. "You hadn't managed anything before, no matter how hard you tried."

"Glad you were impressed," she remarked, rolling her eyes. "I'd love to know how I did it."

"Rah?" They heard Dawn call from down the ledge, and both hurried over. She was standing at the bottom, with Dusk and Diya floating next to her.

"I could use some help getting back up."

"Can't he do it?" Rob muttered as he knelt down and grasped her forearm.

"I could, but she asked for you," Dusk replied. He and Diya floated up the ledge once Dawn was steady at the top.

"Well, weren't you supposed to be getting a lantern or something?" Rob grumbled. "Where is it?"

"The lantern is in the Ruins," Dusk said. "So we'll be going to the Mansion."

"Let me guess, Sarah and I are staying there while you get it?"

"Both of you, stop," Dawn said. It had to be the Night Rise putting everyone on edge, right? They were so close to a hot meal and comfy beds if they could just hold it together a little longer. "Rah, you came to help me, and this is not helpful."

"Like he's done nothing wrong?" Rob argued. Diya snorted at him, and he glared at the lux fairy. "And what's your problem?"

"Enough," Dusk said, simmering. "This venture may have been Dawn's idea, but I am in charge when it comes to the lantern. You'll follow my plans, or you can go home on your own. Your choice."

"Fine," Rob relented. "Lead the way."

On the north edge of the forest was the quaint city of Riverglade.

The area had been a swampland until mages drained it, and many of the buildings stood high on stilts to stay above the water during flooding season. Between the oldest buildings stretched bridges that swayed gently in the breeze from the Claw River that flanked one side.

Lamps were scattered along the bridges and hung under buildings, lighting the town as if for a festival. The few people around hurried with their heads down, hardly looking up as they went home for the evening.

On the other side of town from the river, sitting high on a bluff, was the Ruins. A century ago it was the Academy, a prestigious college for all mages to practice and hone their craft. People had traveled from all over Arrtelagon to study there until the Great Shaking, a disaster that destroyed the school, and most of the knowledge it contained was lost. A single dormitory survived the catastrophe, and the few remaining mages transformed it into the Mantrisa Mansion.

The mansion foyer had five crystal chandeliers that were only lit for special occasions, and when they were, the building glowed like a beacon, guiding boats and travelers to Riverglade. The chandeliers were bright tonight as Dawn knocked on the mansion door.

"I'm coming! I'm coming!" They heard some movement inside and the door was opened by the butler.

"I assure you the Duke and Duchess are doing everything they can to find—" he paused, realizing who was there. "Why, if it isn't Dawn! What are you doing here?"

"Hello, Charles. Would you get Alexander for me, please?" Dawn asked.

"Of course, come in, come in! I apologize. I wasn't informed you were coming," Charles said and ushered the five of them into the foyer.

"That's all right, Charles. It wasn't planned," Dawn assured him.

He gestured at a couch, mustache quivering as he spoke. "Please wait here, I'll return momentarily."

Dawn and Sarah sat together while Rob remained standing and the fairies perched on the back of the couch. The instant everyone was settled they heard an excited screech, and a head of curly blonde hair streaked across the room, crashing into Dawn.

"Daw'!" June squealed as she attacked her aunt with hugs.

"Hello to you too," Dawn said, hugging the excited toddler back. "Where's your Papa?"

"Papa! Papa!" June jumped up and down and pointed at the swooping twin stairs that led to the upper rooms.

Alex stood at the top, leaning on the banister. He was easily a head taller than his sister and took after his father in terms of looks with golden hair and boyish charms.

"I didn't think we'd be seeing you for another week," he said as he descended the right stairway. "And weren't we going to the castle? Charles will have a heart attack if we move the party here last minute."

"Carles! In the kit'en!" June cried and ran off to find the butler, disappearing through a door on the far wall. Alex smiled after her as he made it to the bottom of the stairs and crossed the foyer to them.

"So, why are you here?" he asked and cocked an eyebrow at the group.

"We came to check on you. Mother is running around with a company, and Father is busy so I volunteered," Dawn explained. They had come up with the excuse on the way, and she hoped it sounded better to her brother than it did to her. She didn't think he would entirely believe it, but neither would he comment to the contrary, assuming he also didn't guess their real reason for being there.

"Busy? Must be why they didn't send a message about it," Alex reasoned. "But why did you come on foot?" His eyebrow crept higher like it was trying to leave his face.

"All the horses are being sent around the kingdom with supplies, so there weren't any available for us," Rob said. Dawn marveled at his ingenuity, and he gave her a sly wink. It was true all the horses were busy; if he'd gone with his company he'd have ridden.

"And what about you?" Alex asked, shifting his piercing gaze to Dusk. "Shouldn't you be helping the rest of the Court?"

"Yes, that's why they sent me along. I'm meant to talk with the fae here," Dusk said, so fluidly Dawn almost believed him.

"But your friend isn't with the Court," Alex replied, squinting at Diya while he tried to remember if he'd ever seen the lux fairy.

Dawn bit her lip and tried not to give them away by fidgeting, then jerked as they were interrupted by June.

"It's dinnah time!" the toddler beckoned them from a doorway on the left.

"That's our cue," Alex said and led them over to the dining room. "We just finished eating, but the food is still warm."

Charles proudly presented the table that was set for three people and two fairies, with the remnants of a roast pig and vegetable dinner.

Behind the head of the table a fire crackled in an enormous fireplace, and above it hung an ornate mantle covered in creeping ivy. The wall opposite could fold and tuck into a slot on one side, allowing the dining room to expand to fit a crowd or be smaller for a family. It was currently closed, creating a cozy and companionable atmosphere.

Alex sat at the head of the table and signaled his guests to sit. Dawn took the right side with the fairy seats, and Rob and Sarah sat opposite her. Dusk made himself comfortable next to Dawn, but Diya flew over to the mantle and settled in among the leaves, tucking his wings down with him out of view.

"Enjoy," Charles said, then nodded to the bouncing toddler. "I'll send Catherine down to collect her."

"Thank you, Charles," Alex said as the butler disappeared. "So, how was the journey? Run into any trouble?"

"We did run into a mercenary," Dawn said as she prodded her carrots. "Thankfully no one got hurt."

"What about me?" Rob asked around a mouthful of meat. The cut on his cheek was deep red and struggling to scab over.

"That's deeper than I realized," Dusk said, and Rob made a face at him. "I could heal it for you if you'd like."

"Already said it was fine," Rob mumbled and returned his attention to his plate.

Alex winked at Rob. "A boy wants to keep a wound like that—it impresses the ladies. If you're lucky, it'll scar."

"What's this about scars?" Catherine asked as she entered the room.

"Mama!" June cried. She jumped over to her and grabbed onto her leg, giggling uncontrollably.

"Hello, darling," Alex said. "Rob was showing off his. Apparently, they fought with a mercenary on the way here."

"Yes, hello, June," Catherine said as June squirmed around, then looked at Rob. "We've heard someone was running around making trouble. Could you describe them?"

Rob nodded and swallowed. "There was a man in a trench coat, a boy who looked about ten, and they had a fox."

"That fits reports we've had," Alex replied, rubbing his chin thoughtfully. "We should discuss it more thoroughly tomorrow."

"Fine by me," Rob said and returned to eating. Catherine hobbled over to Alex and gave him a peck on the cheek.

"We'll be upstairs," she said, then scooped June into her arms and headed out.

Alex watched her go, then turned to his sister. "You can tell our parents we're doing fine here. Being close to the Fae Realm makes it easy for them to help us out. The townspeople have been worried about the situation, so I've got my forces wandering around to offer any aid they can. You've heard what they're calling it?"

"Night Rise," Dawn said, nodding. "It's quite dramatic."

"It's a dramatic event," Alex replied, shrugging. "Had a few kids running around pointing at the sky and shouting 'Night Rise!' all yesterday morning. I mentioned it to Father when I sent him a message. He said he'd let us know what's going on once he knew more."

Dawn fidgeted as her brother stared her down, unable to think of a good response.

"It's something magical," Dusk said, and Dawn relaxed. "We know it isn't us, and it doesn't look like dragons."

"You think it's human magic?" Alex asked soberly.

"I've tested it myself. There's nothing else it could be," Dusk said. The leaves on the mantle rustled as Diya shifted around.

"Well, that's something else we'll need to discuss tomorrow," Alex said as he stood. "Now, if you'll excuse me, I've got a toddler to get in bed. Speaking of which, Charles will have some rooms ready for you once you're done here."

"Thank you, Alex. We're quite ready for sleep," Dawn said. Of course, it would still be awhile before she could get to bed, as she had plans for the night.

Charles returned shortly after to take them to their rooms. They almost forgot Diya in the ivy, but Dusk coaxed him out. The butler led them to a small, single room on the first floor for Rob, then brought the girls and fairies upstairs.

He let them into a small common room with two bedrooms branching out from either side, a plush couch in the middle, and a bathtub tucked behind a screen in one corner. Night clothes were laid out on the beds, and the tub was filled with warm water for them to enjoy before turning in. Dusk and Diya hovered around the glass doors that led to the balcony as Charles left.

"You take the first bath," Dawn said as she crossed the room to the fairies. "I should wait until after I go crawling around in rubble."

Sarah agreed but glanced between Dawn and the fairies uneasily. "Are you sure you don't want to take Bert with you? It'll be easier with him."

"We don't need his help," Dusk said, looking at Sarah's reflection in the window.

"But what if something happens? There could be crazed animals in there, or what if you need to dig or climb or something else he's good at?"

"I am more than capable of handling anything we might run into," Dusk said as he turned to face her, his expression hard.

"Really, you don't need to worry," Dawn said. They had made it here all right; they could get through one more night. Just one more night with Dusk before they went home and back to relatively normal. If only it could be longer. "But you can keep an eye on us from your window if you like."

"Well, all right then," Sarah conceded. She obviously didn't like it, but seemed as tired of fighting as Dawn was at this point. "Just signal me if you get trapped or anything, and I'll send him after you."

As she spoke, Diya inhaled sharply like he'd been struck. His wings stilled and he went limp, dropping out of the air.

"Diya!" Dusk cried and dove to catch him before he hit the floor, barely grabbing his arm and slowing his descent until they both landed in a tiny pile.

"Leave us!" Dusk glared at Sarah icily, and she paled and dashed into her bedroom, pulling the door closed behind her.

"Is he all right?" Dawn whispered fearfully, but Dusk ignored her.

"Diya, breathe. I'm here, don't worry. It's all right, you're all right now. Stay with me." Diya shuddered and breathed heavily, slowly calming as Dusk spoke until he was still.

"I'm okay now," he said quietly and Dusk held him tightly.

"You can stop. We'll take you home. We don't have to retrieve it."

"No. You said you wanted to get it. We're getting it," Diya said and took a long, shuddering breath. "I'm ready."

"Will you get the door?" Dusk asked quietly.

Dawn took a shaky breath as she reached for the handle. Something was going on. Something that might explain why Diya never came to the castle. Why his attitude was odd and sporadic. Why Dusk seemed so protective of his friend. She'd have to ask him about it, but for now, they had a lantern to find.

They all relaxed as the door opened and cool night air caressed their cheeks. Dusk held Diya's hand as they got to their feet and flew outside, and Dawn crept after them.

The southern wall of the mansion was covered with magically-attached clematis as old as the building, giving Dawn a ladder to climb down with. She hopped over the railing and grabbed a vine, giving it a tug to see if it would hold her. Once she was satisfied she wouldn't fall to her death, she worked her way down until she was near the ground and dropped the last half floor. She landed softly, then looked back up towards the balcony.

Sarah was in her window watching, and when she saw Dawn safely on the ground, she waved. Dawn smiled and waved back, then turned towards the fairies and the Ruins.

7

From a distance the Ruins appeared decent enough, with only some crumbling on the outer walls—nothing more than normal weathering would do. The doors of the main entrance had fallen off their hinges, and past the rotting wood, the truth was revealed. Inside were broken stairs, collapsed hallways, and piles of rubble too dense for even a fairy to squeeze past.

Dawn breathed in the stale, musty air and shivered with dread at the idea of going farther in. The light Dusk cast on the deteriorated floor quivered with his flicking wings, making sinister shadows that threatened to creep out of their void and steal whatever light they could.

"All right," Dusk said, surveying the destruction. "I'm going to have to clear a way for Dawn. It'll be slow, but she can't get through some of this. Strange how familiar it feels, even after all this time."

"It'll never be long enough," Diya muttered, taking in the destruction like he'd eaten a fresh cranberry. Bitter, yet a sweetness underneath. "Can you go on your own for a while? If it's going to take her some time, I'd rather not be in there while I don't have to be."

"I'll signal when we need you," Dusk agreed.

Diya flicked across the short yard back to the mansion as Dawn followed Dusk inside. He waited while she climbed over the doors, then slowly floated forward, lighting the way for her.

The silence got to her more than the gloomy setting as they went farther in, and she decided to fix that. She had plenty she wanted to know, and now might be her best chance to ask, anyway.

"Is there something wrong with the lantern?" she began softly.

"What do you mean?" Dusk replied, pausing for her to climb over some broken stone.

"I mean that the Court was very agitated when I brought it up, and you and Diya are being rather mysterious about it," she answered, sliding down the other side of the stone.

"It isn't something any of us are comfortable with," Dusk said. He waited while Dawn straightened and found her balance, then continued leading. "It was a painful time for us; something we wish we could forget."

"Then why did you agree to help me find it?" she whispered, and Dusk was silent. She watched him floating in front of her, and almost tripped as her foot caught on the uneven floor. She'd better watch her feet for now. "What about Diya? Why did we need to ask him about doing it?"

"He has a certain authority when it comes to the lantern," Dusk answered.

"But he gave it to you," Dawn remembered. "Why did he have it to begin with? Does he know more about it?"

"In a sense," Dusk said carefully, measured, clearly not pleased with her line of questions.

"Well, maybe I ought to ask *him*?" she said, and Dusk winced.

"I'd rather you not bring it up with him," he said.

"No, of course not," she said irritably. When had he ever shared anything about Diya? Beyond the occasional mention that implied a happier fairy, Dusk wasn't keen on telling her anything about Diya, as if he didn't want her to know about something so important to him.

"I'm sorry, but this isn't anything to do with you," Dusk explained, sighing heavily as he stopped and stared at his hands. He slowly squeezed them into fists before relaxing them again. "Diya is very important to me, and however much I want to help you, I have to look after him first."

Dawn was quiet as they moved again, focusing on where her feet went. She still had questions, but some progress had been made. Clearly, something was going on with Diya, and while Dusk wasn't sharing yet, neither had he indicated she wasn't allowed to ask again later.

Dusk stopped in front of a doorway that was blocked by a fallen wall and frowned. "We need to get past this. I'm going to see if there's another way around, you wait here."

"Alright," Dawn said. She watched his glow grow smaller until it was gone, then fumbled around for somewhere to sit. As soon as she settled herself on a fallen pillar, she heard shuffling nearby.

"Dusk?" she whispered, and squinted at the spot the noise had come from. Of course, it wouldn't be him—Dusk didn't shuffle, he glided—but no one else should be in there.

A lumpy shape she had assumed was just more rubble let out a low growl and shifted. Dawn jumped up and held her breath. The shape turned around, and a pair of glowing yellow eyes stared menacingly at her, narrowed slits of a hunting animal. Lips parted, and Dawn saw sharp white teeth glisten as it howled.

Dawn stepped back slowly until she bumped into the blocked doorway. The beast crept towards her until she felt its hot breath on her hands clenched in fear in front of her. She closed her eyes as it smelled her, bracing herself for the inevitable attack.

Instead, the beast let out a whimper, and she opened her eyes.

Dusk was returning, and in the glimmer of light she could make out a medium-sized dog. Under a layer of dust and other filth, she could barely make out a short, dark coat. It had big, floppy paws, and ears that stuck up partially then folded at the tips. Around its neck, it wore a loose rope that was as grimy as the dog. She smiled and held her hand out for it to sniff.

"There are other ways around, but they'll take longer than if I just clear—" Dusk cut off when he saw the dog sniffing Dawn nervously.

"Dawn!" Dusk lunged at the dog, and it jumped around at the noise, growling.

"No, stop. I've got this," Dawn said, keeping her eyes on the dog. Surely it just needed a gentle approach, to know it was safe with her. If Dusk could manage an orange mood-sheep, she should be able to do this. She crept forward slowly with her hand out and made soothing noises.

"Shh, shh. That's right, you're okay, shh, good boy…" The dog sniffed her again and settled down enough for her to run her hand along his back. "There, that's better."

Dusk hovered by Dawn and looked over the dog. His glow revealed a mottled grey coat that was shiny and soft under its layer of grime from the Ruins. "He looks healthy and well-kept until a day or so ago. I'd guess he's owned by someone from town. Probably got spooked by something and ended up lost in here."

"We can return him tomorrow," Dawn said.

"If you want to," Dusk said, shrugging. "At least he can keep you company while I clear this for you." He went up to the doorway and put his hands on the rubble. There was a rumble, and the pile started falling away.

The dog fidgeted nervously and Dawn coaxed him away a few feet to sit with him and watch Dusk work. She found it quite extraordinary to see something so small moving something so big, like watching a sorcerer bring down a mountain. Bit by bit the dirt and stone pile crumbled away until only a mound she could climb over remained.

"There," Dusk said when he finished. "Let's hope I won't have to do much more of that."

Dawn went up to the newly opened space and inspected it. "That was impressive."

"You've never seen a terra fairy at work, have you?" Dusk asked, half-smiling. "That was nothing, comparatively."

"And I suppose next you'll try to tell me your roses are plain," Dawn said as she climbed carefully through. Very little terra work was needed around the castle, and the most she'd seen of it was moving building materials for repair work. She straightened herself on the other side of the doorway and waved to the dog. "Come on, Fred."

"Fred?" Dusk asked with amusement.

"He looks like a Fred, doesn't he?" Dawn asked and waited while the dog jumped over the mound. "Good boy, Fred. Let's go fetch that lantern."

"Whatever you say," Dusk said as he flew deeper into the building. "Just don't expect me to clean up if 'Fred' leaves any messes."

"He wouldn't do that, would you boy?" Dawn teased, and Fred woofed happily.

Dawn was glad to have the dog, who gave her something positive to focus on. She forgot for a while about the sun and the weirdness with Diya. She forgot her upcoming trip to marry Geoff, and how she was losing her life as she knew it. And she especially didn't remember that this was the last she'd see of her friend—the one friend she'd miss the most and would almost never see again.

The going was harder the higher they went, with broken furniture, stairs that could give way, and gaping holes that grew wider and deeper. They picked their way carefully through the building,

Dusk occasionally stopping to move another blockage or add support where Dawn was too heavy to walk.

Eventually, they reached a room on the third floor that looked to be intact if the door in front of them was any indication. Dawn tried the handle, and it creaked inward on rusty hinges. Inside the walls were in decent shape, filthy and crumbly like everything else, but still standing. The floor was a different story; it was completely gone. They looked over the precipice of the hole and saw the contents of the room several floors below them in yet another rubble pile.

"Time to get Diya," Dusk said as he pulled out his quartz. It flickered crankily and he frowned at it, then sighed and tucked it away. "Looks like I'll have to physically bring him. Wait here with Fred for now." He flew away, taking his light with him.

It was eerie sitting in the dark, and Fred huddled next to Dawn comfortingly in the hallway just outside the doorway. Something about this particular room was foreboding, and Dawn felt like she wasn't supposed to be there. She focused on Fred breathing in and out against her, then recalled seeing a lamp hanging just inside the door when Dusk had flown past. Perhaps it still had some oil.

She stood and felt around the doorframe. Her hand bumped into the lamp and she lifted it off its hook. It was a small glass bowl with a twine handle, and there was still a wick in the metal teeth at the bottom. But of course, it was empty of oil. It hardly mattered anyway—how would she have lit it, if it wasn't?

Dawn rubbed her thumb along the side and a flame sputtered to life. She jumped, almost dropping the lamp, then steadied herself and sat back down with Fred, who was much more relaxed now that he could see. Soon, Dawn noticed two fairy glows approaching.

"Where did you find that?" Dusk asked, looking quizzically at the lamp as he and Diya fluttered to a stop.

"It was by the door," Dawn said, pointing at the hook.

"Lemme see it," Diya said, oddly insistent. He reached out to touch it and shivered as his fingers met the glass. "Like I thought. Dusk, look at this."

Dawn glanced between them curiously as Dusk touched the lamp and gasped.

"Do you know what this is?" he asked—wildly for him like he was excited but nervous—and Dawn shook her head. "The magic it's spelled with, the way you light it, it's fairy magic."

"Fairy magic?" Dawn repeated. Was this something to do with alignments, then? But fairy magic, when she was a human? "So I shouldn't have been able to light it."

"Correct," Dusk answered, eyes glinting as he shook his hair out of them. "It will only light for a fairy alignment."

"What?" Dawn exclaimed. She couldn't have one, she knew. One of the seven alignments that were only fairies, that no human should have. But there was only one possibility here, no matter how impossible it was. "Does, does that mean I have—"

"A fairy alignment," Diya finished.

He stared at Dawn with a strange intensity she couldn't return, and she looked at Fred instead. Of all the things that had happened today, this was possibly the least expected, impossible to explain. But somehow, it felt true, truer than anything else she knew about herself, that she would be so related to fairies.

"Dawn?" Dusk asked gently after a minute. "I don't mean to press you, but we do have a task to finish."

"Right." Dawn shook her head to clear it and took a deep breath. She'd have time to process things when they were done in the Ruins. "So, what are we doing?"

"Diya and I will locate the lantern, then I'll use the rubble to make a way down for you," Dusk explained. "It could take some time, as we can assume there's raw magic, and broken spells I'll have to untangle."

"Then, I'll just wait here with Fred," she said and patted the dog.

Diya flicked over to Fred and rubbed his chin before following Dusk into the hole. "Good dog. You found him in here?"

"Dawn found him," Dusk replied. "I left her alone for a moment and came back to her befriending him."

"Really," Diya remarked with a touch of admiration as the fairies took their light down the hole.

They were mostly silent as they searched, and when they did speak it was too soft for Dawn to hear, so she closed her eyes and rested her head on Fred. She felt the cool glass of the lamp in her hand and wondered why it would be here. Why would a school for humans use lamps that required fairy magic? All the lights in the castle were spelled by fairies, but they were carefully designed so humans could use them. Anyway, as far as she knew, the fairies had nothing to do with the Academy.

Eventually, the fairy glows made their way up from the hole as Dusk and Diya returned.

"We're ready for you," Dusk said.

"My turn, Fred," Dawn whispered as she set the lamp down and followed Dusk.

Diya landed on Fred's shoulders, and Dawn thought she heard him whispering as she descended the rough stairway Dusk had crafted for her.

"We've exposed the lantern, but it's still stuck," Dusk explained when she reached the bottom. "It's been wedged in a support point, so you'll have to take it out slowly while I fill in behind it. If we don't, the weight of the rubble could cause an avalanche and we'll fall through the remaining floors."

"Could you dig it out any further?" Dawn asked.

"Any more and I'd risk touching it accidentally," he said.

"And that's a bad thing?" she remarked, and Dusk nodded silently.

He led her through the pile and hovered by the top of the lantern, his light revealing a copper ring. She knelt next to him and grasped the handle.

"Tell me when," she said.

Dusk landed on the rubble next to her and carefully placed his hands near the lantern. "Now we'll just ease it out. Take your time; I'll follow your pace."

They worked together, slowly pulling it out, and after a few tense minutes, Dawn was holding the lantern. It was a plain rectangle with no decorations. The glass was miraculously undamaged in spite of everything it had been through, and the wrought iron frame was rust free. Dusk studied Dawn's face while she looked over it, and after a minute his tense muscles relaxed.

"Let's get out of this hole," he said.

They climbed up the stairs and found Diya lounging on Fred's back, humming softly. Dusk coughed and Diya shot into the air.

"You got it," he said when he saw Dawn, a sharpness in his eyes. Dusk flew over to him and hugged him.

"I need to help Dawn get out, but if you want to go now, there's no need for you to stay," he said.

Fred whined, and Diya shook his head. "Actually, I promised Fred I'd stick with him until he gets home."

Fred woofed, and Diya settled onto his shoulders. Dusk smiled and led them out of the Ruins. Everyone was relieved to be leaving, and Dawn's steps felt lighter as they got closer to the exit. When they made it through the broken entrance back to the yard, Fred barked happily and pranced around with Diya holding on for dear life.

"Fred, settle down, boy," Dawn whispered loudly. He slowed enough for Diya to hop off safely before continuing to prance around excitedly.

"So, what are you planning to do with the dog?" Dusk asked.

Before Dawn could answer, the kitchen door of the mansion opened, and Alex sauntered out to meet them.

"Out for a little night stroll?" he asked, looking between Dawn, the dog, and the lantern in her hand.

"Shouldn't you be asleep? It's been hours since you put June to bed," Dawn replied.

Alex smiled wearily. "You'll understand someday when you have children of your own. Let's get inside and you can tell me what's going on."

"We'll be inside," Dusk called over to Diya, who had started playing chase with Fred. Diya waved to acknowledge he'd heard.

Charles was waiting for them just inside the kitchen. "The tea is ready. Shall I find a bowl for the pooch?"

"Yes, and set up a place for him to sleep. The Fairweathers will be glad to have him back," Alex said as he sat down at the kitchen island.

"So he *is* lost," Dawn said, sitting across from her brother. She set the lantern carefully in her lap and grabbed a biscuit from the tray in front of her.

"Apparently he ran off yesterday morning," Alex said, watching Dusk as the fairy landed next to the teapot. "The family has been by a couple of times to see if we've had any luck finding him." He poured a pair of cups and slid one over to Dawn, then took a deep drink of tea and sighed, relaxing. After a moment, he looked at his sister.

"Well, let's have it," he said, and Dawn stared at him blankly. "You know what I mean. The lantern."

Dawn glanced at Dusk, who nodded, then she carefully set the lantern on the marble counter. Alex pulled it closer and turned it slowly.

"Never thought I'd actually see it," he mused. "I almost thought it wasn't real. I'm surprised you agreed to this." He eyed Dusk, who half-smiled.

"Believe me, so am I," he replied.

"Just here to check on me, was it?" Alex said and glanced at his sister. "Does Father even know you're here?"

Dawn put her nose in her teacup and sipped. "No, he doesn't."

Alex laughed. "Now that you have what you came for, what are you going to do with it?"

"We're going to make light. Just for a while until the problem is fixed," Dawn said.

"I see," Alex said and poured himself more tea. "What about after?"

"We haven't decided that yet," Dusk said.

"It's Diya that's out there, isn't it?" Alex asked, jerking his head at the door. How was he able to guess? What did he know about the lantern, and how it was connected to the fairies? "I'm greatly impressed you managed this, little sister. He wouldn't do this for just anyone."

The warmth from the tea turned Dawn's cheeks red. "Actually, it was Dusk who convinced him."

Alex looked between Dusk and Dawn a few times, then drained his cup. "Well, I bet you're ready to get to bed. I certainly am."

Dawn drank the rest of her tea and hopped off her stool. "Let me just check on Fred first."

"Fred?" Alex asked as she left. Dusk looked up at the ceiling and sighed.

"Don't worry about it," he said and followed after her.

8

The gentle light of a fairy glow eased Dawn awake the next morning. It bounced off the lantern in the corner and made the bedroom sparkle as Dusk turned away from the window to look at her.

"Morning," Dawn said as she blinked. Gradually, she got out of bed.

"Did you sleep well?" he asked. The sparkles shifted and vanished as he floated with her out to the common room.

"Better than yesterday," she said, glancing around. The other bedroom door was open, the room vacant. "I take it Sarah's up."

"She left an hour ago," Diya's voice came from the couch and his head popped up from the blanket he was buried in. His hair was messy, and his eyes were drooping with sleep like he'd also just woken up, a strange appearance for a fairy.

"You look like you rested well," Dawn said, grinning at him as he rubbed his eyes and stretched.

"Wasn't a bad night, considering," he replied, yawning. He flapped his wings slowly like he was testing they still worked, then flew over to Dusk.

"We'd best leave you to get ready. Shall I get a light for you?" Dusk asked.

"No," Dawn said, raising her cupped hand. "Let me try something."

If she really did have a fairy alignment, then she had a guess which one it would be. She closed her eyes and thought of the spell she knew while picturing Dusk and his glow. Her palm tingled, and she opened her eyes to see light radiating from her uplifted palm.

"Lux," Dusk said, half-smiling. Diya grinned and whispered in his ear, making him laugh and push the lux fairy away. "Enough. Dawn, if you don't mind?"

Dawn got the door for them and giggled at Diya, who pouted as he followed Dusk out. She watched the fairies drift down the long hall, and after a moment their hands reached for each other and their fingers entwined.

An hour later Dawn headed down to the foyer, damp hair braided and over her shoulder. Charles was seating a family of four on the couch as she descended the stairs. The son was fourteen or fifteen, with short brown hair, and the daughter looked around twelve, her yellow hair in twin braids.

"I'll just be a moment," the butler said as they settled. He turned, noticed Dawn, and smiled. "Ahh, Miss Dawn, your timing is impeccable. These are the Fairweathers, the owners of the pooch. I'm just off to fetch him if you wouldn't mind entertaining our guests."

"Of course, thank you, Charles," she said. He bowed and disappeared into the kitchen.

"Excuse me, but are you the princess?" the girl asked. Her eyes were wide and she held her breath.

"Suzie!" her mother said, face coloring with shock. "That is no way to address her highness. Please forgive my daughter. She normally has better manners."

"Oh, no, it's perfectly all right," Dawn said, unable to help smiling. She offered them a small curtsey. "I am indeed the princess, and it is a pleasure to make your acquaintance."

Suzie grinned and nudged her brother. He narrowed his eyes at her and shifted over, trying to put space between them.

"John, look!" Suzie pointed, and Dawn turned to see Charles returning with the dog. Behind them was the source of Suzie's excitement, a pair of glowing fairies.

Dusk and Diya hovered a few feet away as the dog woofed and jumped on his family, who were overjoyed to see him. Dawn crept over to the fairies and waited with them until the Fairweathers were ready.

"We can't thank you enough for finding him," Mister Fairweather said to Charles, who shook his head.

"It was Miss Dawn who found him. Along with the fairies present."

John was on the floor rubbing the dog's belly and looked up at Dawn like he was just seeing her.

"It was nothing," Dawn said. "We merely happened on him last evening while we were out. He's quite the gentleman." The dog got to his feet and stepped over to Dawn, who held out her hand for him to lick.

"No one's better behaved than our Colonel Woofbottom," Missus Fairweather said, smiling. "I'm not surprised he took a liking to you."

"I'd love to see him again before I leave," Dawn said, an idea popping into her head. "Perhaps Suzie and John might come visit the castle? They could come with Alex for my birthday."

"Oh! Can I?" Suzie bounced on her heels and gave her parents her best puppy eyes.

Missus Fairweather raised her brows and looked to her husband. A ghost of a smile passed his lips, and he nodded. "I see no reason why not," he said. "But that will mean you'll need to get ahead on your chores."

"I can do that!" Suzie said and raced to the door. "I can start right now!"

Colonel Woofbottom barked and leaped over to her. The Fair-weathers took their time following Suzie, and eventually, they made it out. Charles headed to the kitchen to resume his duties, leaving Dawn alone with Dusk and Diya.

"Well, I'd better go see if there's any breakfast left for me," Dawn said, watching the lingering fairies. "Would you like to join me?"

"Nah," Diya said. His face was relaxed, but his hands were clenched by his sides. "Don't really like eating. I'm just gonna wander a little."

"We'll find you when it's time to leave," Dusk said, offering Dawn a half-smile. He started to drift away, but Diya grabbed his arm and stopped him.

"No, I want to be alone. You keep the girl company, alright?" Diya flew quickly away, darting out of a window before Dusk could respond.

"Guess that's decided," Dusk muttered. He sighed, then looked at Dawn and smiled fully. "Shall we?"

When Dawn finished eating, Dusk went off to find the rest of their group while she went to her bedroom to collect the lantern.

She grabbed it from the corner, and as she reentered the common room, she noticed a faint light bobbing out on the balcony. She went over to the glass door and saw Diya pacing along the railing. He didn't seem agitated, but neither was he settled enough to stand still.

Dawn tried to back away quietly, not wanting to disturb him. Before she got far, he turned in his pacing and noticed her. He stared at the lantern in her hand, then slowly lifted his eyes to meet hers, his face expressionless.

Maybe he'd give her some of the answers she wanted, now while she had a chance to ask him alone. He was already disrupted anyway. She held his gaze as she set down the lantern and went out on the balcony. They stood silently together for several moments, reading each other.

Finally, Dawn spoke. "Please, will you tell me what's going on with the lantern?"

Diya continued staring at her face. He was quiet for so long that it seemed he wasn't going to answer.

"I can't," he said just as Dawn started to step back. "Don't like remembering. But I'll tell Dusk he can explain it to you."

Dawn was glad to be making progress. "Thank you. It means a lot that you trust me."

"Dusk trusts you," Diya said sharply, shattering her illusion as he moved his gaze out to the Ruins. But there was more to him, that she'd heard in his voice when he spoke to Dusk in the Realm, that she'd glimpsed earlier. She had to keep trying.

"You two are very close."

"Closer than you could possibly fathom," he said, the edge gone from his voice. That was something.

"He mentioned you've been friends for centuries," she said, trying to keep the focus on Dusk, hoping that wouldn't strike a nerve.

"Yeah, if you wanna think of six thousand years as a few centuries," Diya said, snorting. He turned his head to look at her, sighed, and turned back. "He saved my life, you know."

"He did?" she whispered, too intrigued to stop herself.

"He kept me from falling," Diya said, his hands tensing into fists. When she didn't reply he glanced at her and saw her bewildered expression. "Doesn't he tell you anything?"

No, that's why she was here, talking to Diya instead. She'd heard about fairy falling once or twice in her life, but each time the whispering fairies went silent as soon as they realized she was there. Whatever it was couldn't be good, and it was little wonder Dusk had never mentioned this part of his and Diya's past.

"We're getting ready to leave. I should get back to everyone," she said.

Diya made no move to follow her, only gesturing at the lantern. "I'll catch up when it's time. Don't forget to take that thing."

Dawn hurried through the mansion and found everyone in Alex and Catherine's living room. They had a similar setup to Dawn and Sarah with a couple of bedrooms on either side of a common room. There were a pair of couches with a low table between them. Scattered all over the floor were cloth dolls, wooden blocks, and leather balls spelled to sparkle or make sounds when played with. Sarah was playing with June in the corner while Rob and Dusk went over reports with Alex and Catherine.

"Ahh, there you are. About time you joined us," Alex joked as Dawn came in.

"Someone had to entertain the Fairweathers," she said. She sat next to Rob and placed the lantern on the table, as far from where Dusk was sitting as possible.

"They've had that dog longer than we've had June," Catherine said, looking up from some papers in her lap. "I remember the ceremony they had for him when they gave him his title. I'm glad you reunited them."

Alex started gathering the scattered reports into a pile. "We're just finishing up here. Rob's account of the mercenary matches what we've been seeing. Now we've got a much clearer idea of who we're dealing with."

"I hope you catch them soon," Rob said.

"It'll certainly be easier now that we know one of their hiding places," Alex replied. "You kept good track of all the pertinent details. Commendable work."

"What about me?" Sarah called from the corner. "I reminded Bert of most of it."

"You certainly helped," Alex said with a smile.

There was a small clatter of blocks falling, and June started fussing. "No, not tha' way!"

Catherine was up and by her daughter in an instant. "I think someone needs some air. Would you like to go outside, June?"

June stopped pouting and reached up to her mother. "Mama! Yis yis!"

Catherine picked her up and walked out of the room. "We'll be in the garden if you need us."

Alex smiled after his wife then turned to Dawn and was serious. "Charles is getting some horses ready for you—the sooner you get home, the better. I only wish I could see Father's reaction when you arrive with it."

"You would," Dawn teased. "But I was wondering, how did you know about it?"

"The lantern?" Alex asked, glancing at Dusk. The fairy was watching Dawn with a raised eyebrow. "Father told me what he knew years ago."

"So why didn't he tell me?" she said, dropping her gaze to her hands clasped in her lap.

"Because we didn't want anyone outside the Mantrisa family to know," Dusk said. "And you are meant to be leaving soon."

Dawn winced inwardly at the reminder. Just because she was leaving didn't mean she wasn't part of this family. But, even she didn't want someone like Geoff to know the lantern existed if it could be helped. Practical to never mention it to her, even if it still hurt.

Sarah finished tidying June's toys and slumped onto the couch next to Alex. "That's it?" she asked, nodding at the lantern. "Doesn't look like much."

"And why would it?" Dusk asked.

"I just thought something so powerful would be a little nicer, I guess. Less ordinary," Sarah said, shrugging.

"This is actually far more sensible," Alex said. "It helps protect it from falling into the wrong hands."

Sarah sighed. "All right, that's reasonable. But still boring."

"Well, when you make your own magic capacitor, you can make it as fancy as you want," Dusk said.

There was a knock at the door and Charles entered. "The horses are ready for your departure."

"Wonderful," Alex said, stretching and standing. "That means I can get back to work."

"And since when do you work?" Dawn asked, following her brother to the door.

"Since I was put in charge of a city," he replied, rolling his eyes at his sister. "When you get married, you'll talk to me about all sorts of exciting things like trade, taxes, regulations on boats in the river..."

"Or when you'll be coming to visit so I can see my niece," Dawn said, passing into the hallway.

"Yes," Alex said, rubbing his chin. "And I'll leave all of my work for Charles." He winked at the butler, whose mustache twitched in amusement.

"A simple enough task," he said, leading them to the stairs. "Without the lively young lady, or her impish father making more work."

Dusk went to collect Diya while the humans went out to the stable, and then it was only a few minutes until they were out of town and trotting along the main road that ran along the river to the castle. The fairies sat on Dawn's horse, watching Rob and Sarah in front of them. Sarah's horse had a lighted lantern attached to the saddle that made bouncing shadows across the paved road as they passed.

Eventually Dusk broke the silence. "Sarah, Robert, why don't you ride ahead for now? I need to have a word with Dawn."

"Sure, I guess we could," Sarah said, glancing at Dawn with concern.

"We'll be fine," Dawn said, smiling. "Just don't go too far."

"Come on, Sarah," Rob said. "I'll teach you some riding songs. Don't worry, they're easy, even for someone as tone-deaf as you."

"Look who's talking! You can't carry a tune in a bucket," Sarah teased back. They moved their horses into a canter and were quickly out of view. Dawn could still hear their voices as Rob started a jovial marching tune and Sarah joined in.

"I think I'll fly for a while," Diya said. "Want to stretch my wings." He rose into the air and drifted along behind. Very faintly, Dawn could see his light if she turned around.

Dusk fixed his attention on the road, away from Dawn. "So, you talked to Diya."

"I did," she replied, staring down at the shadows bouncing on her hands as Dusk's glow moved with the horse.

"You asked him to tell you about the lantern after I specifically told you not to."

"You two don't exactly make it easy to pretend I'm not curious."

"Curious enough you'd risk breaking my trust to find out."

Dawn's chest felt tight, and her heart skipped. "I'm sorry, but it isn't fair of you to bring me on this adventure, and continue to tell me nothing. I deserve to know what's going on, even if you don't trust me anymore."

Dusk turned around to face her, his expression gentle. "On the contrary, I fully expected you to go to Diya."

Dawn's eyes tingled and she wiped at them. "You did?"

"You're right that you deserve to know some things," he said. "And I know I don't act it, but I would like to share the story with you. Actually, I hoped Diya would be willing to tell you himself, but I understand why he can't."

"He doesn't trust me," she said bitterly. Risking the trust of one fairy to talk to the fairy whose trust she had yet to earn—what had she been thinking?

"Not exactly," Dusk said. "He trusts you as much as he can trust any human. What do you know about how fairy and human magic interact?"

The question surprised her, and she thought a minute before answering. "I know that they can't be combined, or affect each other directly."

"And have you considered which type of magic is in the lantern?" Dusk asked.

"Oh, I hadn't really," Dawn said, glancing at the lantern bumping against her knee as the horse walked along. In a way, neither type made sense. The lantern was in the Ruins, implying human magic, but the fairies were in charge of it, implying theirs. "Well, since it has something to do with Diya, I would think fairy magic makes more sense."

"Correct," Dusk said, half-smiling. "The reason it is related to Diya is because it's *his* magic."

"Diya's magic," she repeated, some of the pieces falling into place, while yet more questions were raised. Her friends' song changed to a slow ballad, and Dawn heard only occasional, sorrowful harmonies.

"Yes," Dusk said softly, the half-smile falling away. "And the reason it was in the Ruins is that the human who made it was Coma."

Coma. Everyone in Mantrisa knew who he was. It was Coma who had drained the swampland Riverglade was on, vastly improving the city's quality of living. It was Coma who built and ran the Academy, teaching magic and all but ruling the area until his death. And it was Coma who learned to read alignments, knowledge he had taken with him to his grave.

"At the time of the Academy, we fairies kept to ourselves," Dusk continued. "We stayed all but exclusively in the Realm. This was due almost entirely to Coma and his decision to make the lantern. He wanted power; no matter how much he had, it was never enough."

"And what better source than a fairy?" Dawn said quietly. The creatures were superior to humans in this regard, being entirely made of magic that was self-sustaining. A fairy never stopped generating energy, and as long as they didn't overexert themselves, they would continue to do so for eternity.

"Indeed," Dusk said, nodding slowly. "The problem he faced was that no fairy would be willing to share their energy to the extreme he desired it, and so he designed the lantern to contain a fairy against their will. He ultimately captured Diya and kept him in the lantern for centuries. Because of the spells he'd sealed it with, the lantern absorbed anything Diya put into it, making it impossible to escape and giving Coma all the fairy magic he wanted."

The horse walked on, each step thudding with Dawn's beating heart as Dusk continued.

"Diya lost part of himself while he was in there. He tried nonstop to get out for the longest time, but eventually, even he had to admit it was hopeless. It was your ancestor, Aaron, who eventually let him out."

"It's only been a hundred years?" Dawn asked softly. Aaron was the first Mantrisa king, and one of the last to study at the Academy before it fell. It was a long time for a human, but not for a fairy. "So Diya's still learning how to live again, isn't he?"

"There are times he wishes Aaron had never come because living with the memories can be worse than when he was in the lantern," Dusk said, closing his eyes while he breathed deeply. "It's been difficult for both of us, but I've only ever been grateful that he was returned to me."

Dawn silently digested his story, eyes drifting between the fairy nearly sitting on her hands and the lantern bumping her knee in time with the horse's hoofbeats. Everything Dusk had ever told her —and not told her—about Diya made perfect sense now. And what she'd experienced herself, with Diya's strange and suddenly shifting moods, must have been because of what he'd endured.

Now she was only more determined to befriend the lux fairy. Maybe she could help him, take some of the weight off Dusk. It must be so hard on him, to be there for Diya constantly, with no one to help him in turn. She could change that—she could do something for both of them.

"I can't imagine how this adventure has been for either of you," she said, glancing back at Diya, who was maintaining his distance behind them. "I'm sorry. If I had known I wouldn't have asked about this...thing."

"No," Dusk said, putting his hand on her thumb and giving it a light squeeze. "It had to happen eventually, and I couldn't have asked for a more suitable person to do it."

Dawn breathed out slowly, trying to steady her nerves. "Then I'm glad I could help. Why don't you go let Diya know we're done?"

Dusk flicked into the air. Seconds later he returned with Diya, and they resumed their place on the horse's shoulders.

Dawn watched Diya as he wiggled around getting comfortable, then when he was settled she hesitantly held her index finger out to him. He stared at it for a long moment, then just as hesitantly touched her fingertip with his palm. He coughed and pulled his hand back, shifting closer to the horse's neck. Dusk watched the exchange closely, then relaxed and smiled to himself when they finished.

Rob and Sarah were on yet another song, and they screeched ear-splittingly as they tried for a note neither of them could reach.

"Let's get back to your friends," Dusk said, grimacing. "Before we hear more of that."

Dawn giggled and kicked the horse into a gallop.

9

The sun was settling on the horizon, bringing a sense of normalcy with the true night that followed, as Dawn and her friends reached the castle. Rob caught Sean's attention as he marched along the wall on his patrol, and the guard hurried down to open a gate for them. Dusk dimmed his glow as they snuck across the yard and into the castle keep, then hurried through the long, dark hallways to the high council room.

Dawn raised her hand to turn the door handle, but her fingers curled away as her stomach rolled. Even if her father would be happy they'd gotten the lantern, she'd still get into some amount of trouble for running off like she had.

"Perhaps I should go in first," Dusk offered.

"Would you?" Dawn asked, her stomach settling. If he explained things first, it might go better for her.

"The Court should hear it from me before you bring it in," Dusk said with a nod to the lantern. "Come on, Diya."

Dawn scooted to the side as Dusk landed on the handle to push it down. He magically eased the door open a crack, and the two fairies flicked into the room. After a moment Dawn leaned on the door frame, trying to hear the conversation.

"...Dawn is fine, I've been with her," Dusk said. "And I believe you've guessed where."

"And where is my daughter now?" Leopold replied, a mixture of tired and cross. "I must speak with her immediately."

"Sire, I took her, it wasn't her doing," Dusk said. "There's no need for punishment as the decision to acquire it was made by me."

"That is not the issue," Leopold said, his voice getting louder as though he were moving closer. "Now tell me where she is."

There was a brief pause, and then very softly Dusk answered, "In the hallway."

Dawn jumped back from the door as her father opened it fully.

"Thank Nova," he muttered. "Rob, Richard is in the guardhouse. Go see him for an assignment, as James isn't back yet. Sarah, Dawn, come." He turned and walked briskly down the hall and the girls trotted to keep up.

"Father?" Dawn asked after a few paces. "What's going on?"

"Geoff has been writing to you," Leopold explained without slowing. "He sent you a message yesterday, and when you didn't reply, he continued sending them. Cedric volunteered to watch the mirror for us, but I think he's ready to be relieved."

Dawn paled as she considered what Cedric might have read. What Geoff might have written. Why hadn't she thought of him, of what he might think of her running off?

"I'm sorry," she whispered.

"Tell him you're sorry. I don't know what we'll do if you've jeopardized your chance at marrying him."

They reached Leopold's study where Cedric was sitting at the desk, mirror in front of him while he read a book. "Sire! You've finally found them."

"Apparently they've been adventuring," Leopold grumbled and yanked the lantern away from Dawn, pushing her into the room as he did. "Sarah, come with us. Dawn, you've some reading to do."

Cedric followed Leopold out of the room, and Dawn tentatively touched his arm, stopping him.

"Father didn't see anything, did he?" she whispered.

"No, I am the only one who read the messages," Cedric said softly.

"And you won't tell him about them?"

"It is not my place to inform him how the prince behaves," he replied. "Particularly if you have never mentioned it to him."

He closed the door as he left, and Dawn was alone in the study. She took a deep breath before sitting at the desk to look at the letters from Geoff.

Dawn,

We just heard about your light. You aren't taking it poorly, are you? I bet you're fine. You're always a good girl.

Where are you? Not too busy for me are you? Better not be, or I'll think you aren't being a good girl. But that can't be, you promised you would be.

Why aren't you answering? I'm getting angry. Don't want to be angry with you, though, so write me.

Spent some time with the girls, feeling better now. But I won't be completely until you respond. Why aren't you? Not forgetting about me, are you?

Damn it, Dawn. This isn't funny. Doesn't matter what's going on over there, you make time for me, now.

Where the fuck are you? This shit better not happen when you're here, or you'll be sorry. Damn it, I said I didn't want to be angry with you. Not my fault, though, if you're the one who breaks your promise.

Dawn's breathing got fast and shallow as she read until she felt lightheaded and breathed into her hands. Of everything he'd sent since his sickness, this was the most dramatic. Of course, it was also the first time she wasn't immediately available when he'd tried to reach her. Once she had herself under control she grabbed her father's quill and held it shakily over the mirror.

Geoff,

I'm here. I'm sorry.

She pulled a bottle of goat hair out of the desk drawer and sprinkled a few strands on the mirror. The words faded with the hair and she dropped her head on the desk to wait. In seconds, the mirror glowed and petal dust covered the surface. She swept the dust off with her hand, and Geoff's response appeared.

Don't do that to me again.

I won't, I promise.

Good.

* * *

The fairies of the Court were everywhere in the high council room, doing studies and experiments. A flora fairy tended a plant that was covered to keep it in shadows, a thermal fairy tested his flame under a variety of materials to see how much light got through, and a hydro and terra fairy worked together to build a small-scale terrain model with mountains and rivers.

"What are we doing with this?" Leopold said as he entered the room and placed the lantern on the table. He returned to his dinner, and Cedric and Sarah sat across from him. Many of the fairies left their tasks and gathered on the table, keeping a distance from the lantern.

"There is nothing to do," Harpullia said. "We deliberated amongst ourselves and have determined there is no one able to use it that we would find acceptable."

"I may not have skill equal to your kind, but I am capable enough for this," Cedric said, gesturing sharply at the lantern.

"No," Diya said from a window. He was sitting between Dusk and the pane, and leaned around his friend so he could see. "The wizard's not doing it."

"Then this endeavor was useless," Leopold said. "We've gotten no closer to an effective solution, and now we have a tool we won't be using but must ensure doesn't pose any threat."

"I didn't say no one could use it. Just not the wizard," Diya said as he got to his feet. "I'll allow its use by Dusk."

"But he cannot use it!" Cedric exclaimed. "It requires a human, and I've the only ability with spells."

"Yeah, but there's a way around that," Diya said as he cleaned his fingernails. "See, Dawn's got a fairy alignment."

"My daughter," Leopold said, his eyes focused on the lantern. "If you are truly suggesting what I think you are, you'd better have a damn good reason it's required. Have you fully considered what will happen? What you would be sacrificing?"

"He hasn't," Dusk said with a glare at Diya. "And neither have I, so while I acknowledge the possibility, it isn't a real option currently."

Diya shrugged and sat down again, stretching out his legs as he laid his head against the stone wall. "That's the only way I'll allow the thing to be used. Dusk can link with Dawn, or it can rot somewhere for eternity."

"Excuse me," Dawn said from the doorway as she entered, catching the end of the conversation. Surely she hadn't just heard what she thought she did. "Dusk may do what with me?"

"You know, connect your magic with his, like fairies do," Diya explained. "Then he could work the thing through you."

Link. Like fairies did. The thing fairies did that enabled them to share their magical abilities, as well as have children if they chose to do so. The idea was ludicrous, of course, but that didn't stop Dawn from wondering what if. What if Dusk said no? What if he did want to, but her father said no? What then? What if she spoke up and said she wanted to?

Dusk swiftly got to his feet and opened the window he was sitting next to. "Diya, let's go. I need to have a word with you."

Diya shrugged and followed Dusk outside. The window latched behind them, and their glows faded. Dawn stared at the window until her father cleared his throat and she jumped.

"Dawn, perhaps you should sit and we can talk," he said.

"Of course," she said. It took her a few tries to pull a chair out, and she bounced her heel once she was sitting.

"Did you take care of things?" Leopold asked, and she nodded. "So you're ready to explain to the Court why you went to get the lantern after I told them we would not?"

"I'm sorry," she said, her eyes focused on her hands in her lap. "I shouldn't have gone to Dusk on my own."

"We've little qualm with your decision to speak with him yourself," Harpullia said, his wings flicking like tiny knives waiting to strike. "As it was his own choice to uncover the lantern, our concern is for why you determined to suggest it in the first place."

"It was my idea!" Sarah said before Dawn could reply. "I told Dawn to do it so she could help, but I didn't think we'd end up going alone like we did."

"And how did you learn of it?" Leopold asked, giving her a withering stare.

Sarah bit her lip and glanced at her father. He watched her carefully, his eyes screaming for her to stay quiet.

"I don't know," she mumbled at the table. Dawn glanced at the king to see if he caught the lie. If he did he didn't show it.

"Sire, if I may take my daughter to our cottage, I will speak with her privately," Cedric said.

"Fine," Leopold said with a sigh. "You come see me first thing tomorrow if you learn anything."

"Of course," Cedric replied. He walked stiffly to the door and Sarah dragged her feet after him, looking at the floor like she hoped it would suddenly open under her.

Harpullia watched the door close, then stuck his nose in the air, wings still twitching. "It seems apparent to me where she learned of it."

"You guess that Cedric told her?" Leopold asked. "That is my presumption also. I'll get what I can out of him tomorrow."

Dusk led Diya around the castle grounds, wordlessly floating around the yard in a random pattern, turning and changing altitude without thought.

"So, are we talking or not?" Diya asked after many minutes had passed in silence.

Dusk froze and stared at the dark ground so far below them that their light didn't reach it. "Diya," he said after a pause. "What the hell were you thinking? Saying such a thing as if it weren't the most insane thing anyone has ever done."

"Already told you about it," Diya replied with a snort. "You know what I'm doing, and don't act like you don't want to. I know you. If I don't help, it won't happen, then you'll be a sorrier mess than I am."

"You can't do this to me!" Dusk turned on him, his face dark in spite of the light coming from him. "Please, Diya, not now. I can't think about it. Stop making me think."

"That's exactly why I have to, right there," Diya said. "Just like when we met. You won't give anything to yourself even though you deserve it, so I have to make it happen for you. Only this is something I can't give you. You have to do it—you're the only one who can."

"It's not only me that needs to be considered," Dusk retorted, his voice sharp. The glow coming from him flashed crimson. "You're messing with someone else now. Someone who has a life and job to do beyond just me. You can't involve her for your own selfish ends."

"But they aren't selfish," Diya muttered. He turned away from Dusk and his wings twitched like they wanted to dart away. "If anyone stands to lose from this, it's me. But I have to. I have to give you whatever I can, whatever you want. If you're not happy, I can't be, and you know how little I've had since then."

He shrugged nonchalantly, but his eyes sparkled with unshed memories as he turned his head back to his friend. Dusk instantly closed the space between them and was holding Diya tightly.

"Fine, make me think," Dusk said softly. "I can't trust myself, but I know I can trust you. I'll think, and maybe I'll try, but you have to leave her alone as much as possible, all right? Let me handle it with her."

"Sure," Diya said as he clung to Dusk. "Just don't take forever, you know? I'm not very patient, and Nova knows you don't have that much time anyway."

Sarah followed her father through the empty halls of the castle, his countenance matching the grey stone walls around them. Once they were outside, she breathed in the cool night air, trying to calm her quivering nerves.

"Thank you for not exposing me," Cedric said, so softly Sarah almost didn't hear him.

"It was nothing," she mumbled, watching her feet.

"Still, it is a relief to know you will side with me when I need you to."

The darkness prevented her from reading anything in his expression. "But, why do you need me to? I mean, now that the lantern is found, why does it matter who came up with finding it?"

"Child, I warned you the fairies would not be pleased if it came from anyone but the royal family," Cedric said. "And if they know that I specifically suggested it, they may wonder why I did, and start to imagine I want it for myself."

"Do you?"

Cedric stopped as they reached their cottage and looked at his daughter, the darkness now concealing her intention. "For what reason might I want such a device?"

"I don't know," she answered as they entered their common room. "But why would you worry about them thinking you do if there's really nothing?"

"Because their assessment of my character is a heavy influence on the king's opinion of me," Cedric said. "I cannot afford to lose favor with him because the fairies believe less of me than is true."

"I guess," Sarah said. The entire business was silly to her. They needed light, and the lantern could give it to them. What more was there to know? She yawned and slowly felt her way to her bedroom. "Good night, Father."

"Good night, child," he replied as she closed her door.

She lit her lamp and got ready for bed, then as she put it out she remembered the fight in the forest. Her father would be thrilled to learn she was a mage, wouldn't he? She cracked open her door and peered out, checking if he was already in his room. His bedroom was directly across from hers, and the door was closed. A faint light came from the bottom of his door and she tiptoed over. As she paused to knock, the light grew brighter momentarily, indicating a message being received by his mirror. She waited and heard faint writing sounds as he dipped a quill and responded, then retreated back to her room without a sound.

10

Dawn stirred awake the next morning, having slept better than the last two nights but still not perfectly. If the eerie darkness of the Night Rise lasted a hundred years, she didn't think she'd ever grow used to it. There was a gentle knock on her door, and Sarah entered with Dusk.

"Morning, Dawn," Sarah said, attempting her normal brightness as she opened the drapes. Her movements were stiffer than usual, betraying her unease.

"Morning. I see we have some new help today," Dawn said, watching Dusk fill her tub. She didn't wonder that Sarah would be nervous after last night, but what Dusk wanted certainly intrigued.

"I found him waiting outside your room," Sarah said, shrugging. "I think he was there all night."

Dusk rolled his eyes as he finished the bath and flew over. "If you two are finished gossiping, I do have a reason for being here. Dawn, we need to discuss what Diya said last night."

"You really don't have to. It's all right," Dawn said, pulling her hair over her shoulder and playing with it. It didn't seem like he was here to say he wanted to link, and she didn't need it confirmed if he wasn't.

"No, it isn't," Dusk said, wings buzzing. "Beyond the comment being wildly inappropriate, it puts a decision on you I don't want you to have."

"Then I won't consider it," Dawn said. It was clear where he stood on the matter, and though it hurt, the decision wasn't for either of them alone. "But would it really be possible?"

Dusk raised a brow at the question. "The only factor that determines its possibility is alignment. You are lux, and thus would be able to. But Diya didn't consider that the process may be more...dramatic for you."

"How so?" Dawn asked. If Dusk didn't want to do it, he could at least let her know what she was missing out on.

"Your size would require a higher quantity of magic," Dusk explained. "And paired with fairies having a denser concentration means that you receiving the needed amount for the linking would be physically difficult. Possibly even painful."

"That doesn't sound appealing," Dawn begrudged. Dusk's wing flaps softened as he relaxed, and Dawn tried to ignore her heart aching. "But since you're here, I think Sarah has something to tell both of us."

"I do?" she asked, her brow furrowed.

"Did Cedric tell you about the lantern?" Dawn asked.

"Oh, well, yes," Sarah answered. "But he doesn't want Leopold to know he told me."

"That's how this idea came about?" Dusk asked, and his wings buzzed again. "Why doesn't he want the king to know about his involvement?"

"I think he'll be explaining that himself," Dawn said. "Father asked to see him this morning, so perhaps you'd like to be part of their conversation?"

"I would," Dusk said and flicked to the door, pausing for a moment while Sarah opened it, then dashed away.

Leopold was at his desk in his study when Cedric came to see him. Papers were scattered all over the room in piles on the desk, the bookshelves, and even on the chairs not occupied by the king. A few kept landing on the floor as he tried to keep up his regular duties.

"Sire," Cedric announced himself, bowing.

"Ahh, Cedric. Thank you for seeing me," Leopold said, carefully adding more papers to the biggest pile on his desk.

Cedric coughed and stepped into the room, wringing his hands. "I would like to apologize. I was unable to get any further explanation from my daughter."

"Really?" Dusk remarked as he flew into the study. He landed on the desk, gingerly placing himself on the most stable stack of papers, and faced Cedric, a steely expression on his face. "Then why did she say you told her about it?"

Cedric gulped. "I do not think you have any reason to be here. This is between myself and His Majesty."

"No, this has everything to do with him," Leopold said, and Dusk nodded gratefully. "Is what he says true? Did you tell her about the lantern?"

"Perhaps I mentioned the idea to Sarah of the lantern being found and used, but I certainly did not intend for her to take your daughter to find it. She came to that idea herself."

"Indeed. And why did you say anything to begin with?" Leopold asked.

"I don't recall what I was thinking at the time. It must have slipped out accidentally," Cedric answered nervously. "You have had me very busy these last few days."

Dusk frowned. The only person who should fully know about the lantern was Leopold, and come to think of it, hadn't Dawn said the idea was from Sarah when she first came to him? He ought to have noticed right then, but other things were distracting him. He shook his head to settle it. Time to focus on the present. "But how did *you* know about it?"

"Well, I believe I read about it somewhere. There are records of it here," Cedric said, gesturing around the room halfheartedly.

This wasn't exactly wrong, but rather far-fetched that he should happen to stumble on the only scroll that mentioned it—which was kept with Leopold's collection in the secret room, no less.

"I see," Leopold said with finality. "We'll consider this matter cleared up, though I expect more discretion from you in the future."

"Yes, of course, Sire," Cedric mumbled and left quickly.

"Did you believe any of that?" Leopold asked Dusk once they were alone.

Dusk snorted. "No."

"I got the sense he wasn't telling us everything," Leopold said. An oversimplification, though politically correct. "But perhaps Sarah could help us with finding out more if she'd be willing to share with you again."

"She's certainly willing to help Dawn," Dusk replied. "I can speak to her."

"Just take care what you say," Leopold said. "She may not be aware of Cedric's motive, but she is his daughter. It'll be difficult for her to choose sides if she feels forced to."

"I'm certain she has no idea what Cedric is up to, but I agree. My opinions of him aside, I wouldn't want to come between a man and his child," Dusk remarked.

"See to it you don't," Leopold said as he straightened his desk slightly and stood. "Now let's get to breakfast."

Dawn and Sarah arrived at the dining hall last as always. Leopold and Cedric were sitting a bit tensely at the high table without James between them, and Dusk was by himself, two human seats away on the other side. The girls took their seats, and Dawn smiled mischievously at the fairy as food was presented.

"So, what should we talk about without Mother to interrupt us?" she asked.

"Haven't I answered enough questions over the last few days?" Dusk said with a sigh. He put half a blueberry in his mouth and chewed slowly.

"You know it'll never be enough," Dawn said, slicing her melon into small pieces. "There hasn't been any time for the fun stuff."

"Wasn't the Realm enjoyable?" he asked, carefully cutting the other half of his berry into smaller bites.

"It was," she said, daydreaming for an instant about the pool. What she would give to be a fairy for a day and explore everything the Realm had to offer. But as fun as the Realm had been for her, the Ruins would have had a very different effect on the fairies. "But were you all right? It can't have been easy for you."

"It wasn't all bad," he said, offering her a side smile before taking his last bite of berry. As he chewed, he pulled his quartz out of his pocket and it glowed. He stared in shock for a moment, then drank his water and stood. "I need to check on Diya. Could you let Sarah know I'd like to speak with her?"

Dawn coughed as she swallowed too fast. "Oh, yes. I can do that."

"Thank you. I'll be in the high council room," Dusk said and flew off, waving to Leopold as he went.

Dusk found Diya lounging on a windowsill in the high council room and landed at his feet. Diya cracked an eye open, saw Dusk, and closed it again. "So what'd she say?"

"Diya, do you have any idea where your communicator is?"

"Course, it's right here," he said as he put his hand in his pant pocket. He frowned and checked his other pocket, then stood up and patted himself. "All right, where is it?"

"In the Ruins," Dusk said, pulling out his quartz and handing it to Diya. "I've told you that you needed to hold onto it better, and now you've lost it somewhere we can't get it back."

"No," Diya said, staring unhappily at the glowing crystal. His face scrunched up like he was in pain and he threw his arms around Dusk's waist. "What're we gonna do, then?"

"There's nothing we can do," Dusk said as he held Diya. "At least you're here with me."

A few minutes later, Dawn and Sarah found them still holding each other. When Diya noticed the girls, he twitched and separated himself from Dusk.

"You wanted to talk to me?" Sarah asked, watching Diya carefully.

"Yes, if we can go out in the hallway for a moment," Dusk replied, floating into the air. "Dawn, would you stay here and keep Diya company for me?"

Dawn watched Sarah pull the door closed behind them. It was strange enough that Dusk wanted to speak with Sarah, but for him to do so alone was entirely unlike him. He *had* been curious about Sarah's magic—was it perhaps something to do with that? But why so pointedly leave Dawn out, if it were? Unless she was the subject... Dawn shook her head to stop that line of thinking and focused on the room around her.

The window magic had been maintained since Dawn was gone, and the high council room was lit with sun-like light that glittered on the wings of the Fairy Court, who were still hard at work on their experiments.

A pair of flora fairies fluttered around a line of houseplants on the table—all in varying intensities of magicked light from lux fairies— pausing to adjust spells or add new ones, and observing the effects on the plant's health. On the end farthest from Dawn, a hydro fairy started water flowing in a mini-terrain, and a terra watched how well the soil held together under withering, sun-deprived flora.

Dawn and Diya avoided looking at each other, both pointedly watching the other fairies in the room. After a few moments of silence, Dawn found herself comparing Diya to the lux fairies. His glow was significantly dimmer, and he stood still while they danced around, aiding their fellow fae. She realized Diya was looking at her and blushed, lowering her gaze to the floor.

"Don't worry about it," he said casually. "It's not like I don't know."

"I wish I could make it better," Dawn replied, lifting her eyes to meet his. Getting the lantern must have been hard for him, and she wondered if he was really as all right as he tried to convince her.

"There's nothing you can do—the damage is done," he said, shrugging. His gaze shifted to the lantern sitting on the table, and he closed his eyes. After a moment he opened them again. "I need to get some air. Do you mind?"

He flicked to the door, and Dawn crossed the room to open it for him. Dusk and Sarah went quiet as they entered the hallway. The fairy was glowering at the floor, and Sarah was smiling sheepishly like she'd been caught misbehaving.

"I'm going out," Diya said, wings beating impatiently.

"We'll follow this up later," Dusk said to Sarah, then flicked after Diya.

"Come on, let's get you to Fibrill," Sarah said, pulling Dawn away as the fairies disappeared through a window. "I bet she's anxious to see you."

"What did he want?" Dawn asked.

"He asked about my father," Sarah explained as they walked quickly through the still dark hallways. "Apparently he told the king that mentioning the lantern was an accident. I said that wasn't really what happened."

"And why was Dusk angry?" Dawn asked.

"He asked me exactly what Father told me, which wasn't much. It seemed to bother him when I said Father had a friend who knew about the lantern."

"He doesn't like people knowing about it," Dawn said. If the fairies only wanted the immediate Mantrisa family to know, it was reasonable that someone else entirely would be an issue.

"Well," Sarah said, coughing. "What really seemed to do it was what he said about the friend."

Dawn raised an eyebrow, and Sarah took a steadying breath before continuing.

"He said it was an old colleague who knew the maker of the lantern," she said softly. "I didn't think it was important, but you saw how Dusk took it."

"Knew *of* him? Or *knew him*, knew him?" Dawn exclaimed.

"Knew him, knew him," Sarah answered skeptically. "Why? Is that bad?"

"Very," Dawn said, slowing as they approached Fibrill's room. It was no secret that Coma had lived well beyond the expected life-span of any human, and all the more so one who practiced magic as heavily as he had. The general presumption was that his alignment, something he never revealed, enabled him to live beyond what would otherwise be possible. But if someone was still around today who had known him personally, they would have to be well over a hundred years old, at least. The implications alone were enough to make her skin crawl.

"I can't share what Dusk has told me, but the maker of the lantern has been dead for a century now. There shouldn't be anyone alive who knew him," she said softly.

"Then I guess someone's just mistaken," Sarah said, shrugging as they stopped next to Fibrill's room. "I'll be back in an hour or so."

Before Dawn could respond, Fibrill's door was thrown open and the seamstress stood there, looking harried.

"Dawn! Finally! I've been wringing my hands with nothing to do since you've been gone, and now we've lost three days. Three days! It'll be a miracle if the dress is ready in time now..." She pulled Dawn inside and shoved her behind a changing screen, ending any further questioning.

Within minutes Dawn was changed and standing on Fibrill's platform. All that was left to do was hem the skirt, but Dawn would be back every day until the birthday celebration to ensure it was perfectly level. Fibrill took pride in her work. She spent no less than two days on the hem alone, and as much as a week checking and rechecking every seam. Today she worked quietly, wanting to focus entirely on her pinning.

Dawn didn't mind the chance to think. A lot had happened in a few days, and they weren't any closer to ending the Night Rise than before. Then there was everything with Diya, who seemed resigned to his fate. And what were they going to do with the lantern? Whether or not they used it, something would have to be done with it to keep it safe. Cedric was proving to be an issue as well, which only made Dusk more irritable. Nothing was going at all how she'd hoped.

"Everything alright?" Fibrill asked, still busy pinning.

"No," Dawn said, staring at herself in Fibrill's mirror. Her brow was furrowed, and she relaxed her face to neutral. "It's all a huge mess. I tried to help and just made everyone I care about unhappy."

Fibrill snorted. "That can't be true. Your family and friends care about you. I'd guess they're just sad about you leaving soon, and they're doing about as well as you pretending they aren't."

Dawn blinked at her in the mirror. No wonder everything was

so awful. Sarah had likely wanted to enjoy the adventure with her, and Rob was probably hurt that she'd tried to leave without him. Then she'd spent the entire time with Dusk, leaving them out of all the exciting parts and withholding what she knew about Diya and the lantern. They couldn't like being kept in the dark about what was going on.

"Fibrill, you're a genius. I think I'll have a nice chat with everyone," she said.

The seamstress smiled and kept working. "Glad I could be of service. Now if only this hem would roll for me..."

The instant Dawn was safely in Fibrill's care, Sarah raced through the keep, searching for Cedric. She'd neglected to tell Dawn the real reason Dusk had wanted to talk to her. It wasn't like she minded helping, but the way the fairy had asked—and what he'd specifically asked her to do—*that* she could live without. The conversation repeated itself in her mind and she shook her head as if doing so would make it stop.

She poked her head into the library, and when she didn't find her father, she headed outside to go to the lab. As soon as she exited the keep she bumped into Rob, knocking them both off balance.

"Sarah," Rob said as he steadied himself then put a hand out to help her. "Are you all right?"

"I'm fine," she answered as she accepted his hand to keep from falling over. "Just going to see Father. What are you up to?"

"Oh, it's nothing," he said, looking at the ground. "Just that Richard didn't really have any task for me, so I'm stuck running messages." Running was a low-level task usually given to squires, something Rob was more likely to assign than be assigned to in his current position. While it wasn't technically a punishment, everyone knew he was in trouble for abandoning his company.

"That's better than what I'm doing," Sarah muttered.

Rob furrowed his brow. "You'd rather run than see Cedric?"

Sarah sighed. "I'm spying on him, for Dusk."

"You're what?"

"I guess Father has been a bit inconsistent with his story, so Dusk wants me to watch him," Sarah explained. "The real issue is he doesn't want Dawn to know I'm doing it."

Rob rubbed his forehead. "And you agreed to it? Why don't you just tell Dawn?"

"Because," Sarah began and took a deep breath. "She's taken Dusk's side with everything, even when he was in the wrong. I'm not sure what's going on with Father, but I don't want the fairy of all people to be involved. If Dawn knew I was trying to keep him from learning anything, though, she'd be mad at me. So I don't want her to know until after I've figured out for sure what Father is doing."

Rob chuckled. "You little fox. I won't mention anything."

"Thanks," she replied, and they continued on their separate ways.

11

Fairy and lantern lights bounced around the castle as people hurried about their day, wishing it didn't feel like night. People with outside tasks were usually happy with their work, but in the current circumstances, many were finding any excuse to stay indoors. Launderers hung washing on indoor racks to dry as if it were raining, knights and squires kept their training in the barracks, and those with free time hid away in the library to play table games or read quietly.

Dusk's mind was racing as he trailed along behind Diya, who was wandering aimlessly around the grounds. His conversation with Sarah had been troubling, and he looked up at the sky every so often to try to clear his head, though it almost made it worse with the dark sun.

Diya eventually found his way to the rose garden and waited for Dusk to catch up before entering. "So, what's up?"

Dusk sighed heavily. "I think the wizard is working for someone."

"What sort of someone?" Diya asked, reading his friend's face and frowning.

"Someone we both know," Dusk said slowly, avoiding Diya's eyes. "Sarah said her father mentioned a friend who knew Coma."

Diya inhaled with difficulty and slowly descended to the ground, where he curled up and shivered. Dusk held him until the shivering stopped.

"You think it's Berniece," Diya said between his teeth.

"It's possible," Dusk replied quietly. "We never did confirm what became of her after the Shaking."

Diya looked up at the sky and got to his feet. "I don't want to think about it right now."

"All right," Dusk said, getting airborne. "I know the perfect place to avoid thinking."

He led Diya through the rose garden to the secluded clearing, going straight to the Heart of Dusk bush to check how it was holding up in the Night Rise. The buds were just starting to open, revealing an inky black color underneath.

Diya relaxed and drifted around the clearing, taking in the pleasant setting. Some of the roses were fully blooming, and he paused to sniff them. A dragon statue caught his eye, and he laughingly slid down its back, soliciting a chuckle from Dusk before moving on. He hovered by the fountain in the center.

"Fancy a swim?" he asked breezily.

Dusk finished looking over his roses, satisfied that the plant was doing as well as could be hoped. "I *could* use the distraction."

"What, that girl isn't enough of one already?" Diya asked. He pulled off his clothes and tossed them on the ground, then dove into the water. A moment later he surfaced. "You still haven't told me what she said."

Dusk scowled as he took off his own clothes and set them down neatly near Diya's before flicking up to the basin. He lowered himself into the water slowly, not making any splash.

"She agreed to forget about your idea," he said with a glance at his friend. "But that doesn't excuse you making the suggestion in the first place."

"No?" Diya snorted. "So you're still avoiding it. Too bad she knows, though. Won't just forget it because you told her to."

"I didn't tell her to—she chose to on her own."

"Yeah, 'cause it's what you want. Can't stop herself from thinking about it though—" Diya leapt sideways to dodge the arrow of water that zipped past his face. "Hey! No fair using magic."

Dusk shrugged, lowering his hands. "All right, no more magic, but I don't want any more ridiculous comments from you. To either of us."

Diya rolled his eyes and put his face in the water to blow some bubbles. "You want to have a race?" he asked after a minute.

Dusk smiled. "No, but thanks for trying."

"Suit yourself," Diya said. He turned and paddled off, leaving Dusk alone.

Dusk took a deep breath and folded himself, sinking down to the bottom of the fountain. He stayed there for what felt like forever, ignoring everything but the cool water around him.

Dawn and Sarah sauntered around the minor dance hall, giving opinions and instructions for the various decorations and amusements that populated the space for Dawn's birthday. With both Dawn and Eleanor gone, the effort had stalled; as no one had been available to make decisions necessary to continue. Now they worked double-time to catch up, still handicapped by Eleanor's ongoing absence.

The flora fairies had finished making textiles and were now focusing on flower arrangements. A pair of hydros were setting up small fountains, with water that flowed upwards, in corkscrews, and other impossible shapes. Hummingbirds and butterflies were practicing aerial feats by the ceiling, led by a trio of fauna fairies.

Dawn had tried to talk to Sarah after the dress fitting, then again after vocal practice, but she'd been quiet and distant, easily resisting

Dawn's probing. Once in the dance hall, there was no opportunity for talk, so Dawn accepted she'd have to try later and focused on the planning. In spite of the crisis, or perhaps because of it, everyone was happy to work on the celebration, trying their best to make it as magnificent as possible.

Alfonso was hard at work on the ice sculpture when they reached his corner, with Eirwen directing a pair of thermal fairies to keep the block solid as he worked. The basic shape of the sculpture had been carved out, and Alfonso was on a ladder chiseling away at the top. He stopped and climbed down when he noticed the girls.

"Princess! It's good to see you've returned safely from your journey," he said. By now word had gotten around that she'd gone to check on Alex, an excuse that worked better here than it had with her brother.

"Thank you. This is coming along nicely," Dawn said, appraising the block.

Alfonso smiled proudly. "It's been quite the learning curve working with limited lighting, but I do relish a challenge!"

Dawn noted the lamps that were hanging all over and around the sculpture, some close enough that the heat was melting the ice. "These certainly are unique circumstances, though it seems you've found a way to make it work."

"Yes, I've developed the lamps into a new method of sculpting," Alfonso explained, beaming as he gestured around the sculpture. "You notice how they're positioned randomly to give the landscape a more natural feel? I move them around every so often to enhance the idea." He picked up a lamp that was sitting on a lower shelf of the block and moved it to a higher place.

"Now, you see here how the ice has melted in an unusual shape, which gives a rough, hilly feel? I simply have it refrozen"—he nodded to Eirwen, who flitted over and solidified the water—"and voila! The definition of realism!"

Dawn inspected the spot closely, pleased with the concept. The surface was lumpy where ice hadn't melted fully and dipped where it had been water. It shifted from clear in some places to foggy in others. The overall effect was a perfect testament to nature's way of being anything but orderly. It was a level of freedom Dawn wished she could have for herself.

"It's a whole new form of art," she said.

"I'm very glad you like it. There is truly no better way to honor your grace than with this," Alfonso said.

"What if you melt too much?" Sarah asked.

Alfonso blinked at her. "Beg your pardon?"

"What if you leave the lamp too long and you melt more than you wanted to?" Sarah explained, pointing out an obvious flaw in the new "method".

"Ahh, easily remedied," Alfonso remarked and waved over one of his other helper fairies, who carried a small bowl. "We simply add a bit more water, and my lovely assistants can build up new ice into yet further compelling shapes."

The fairy poured water out one drop at a time, freezing it as she liked so there were now swirls and twists, giving the sculpture motion.

"And so what others would view as a mistake," Alfonso continued, tilting his head at Sarah as he spoke, "we embrace as an opportunity for improvement."

"It's marvelous," Dawn said, smiling at the sculptor. The addition of movement brought the sculpture to a new level of quality she was impressed by. "I can't wait to see it completed."

Alfonso bowed and went back up the ladder to continue working. It was hopeful that a man from outside of Mantrisa could work so happily with the fairies, and that they could be so welcoming and inclusive of him.

Dawn watched for a while, entranced by the thermal fairies

indulging their own creative impulses. She followed the fairy with the bowl as she ran out of water, then collected a small chunk of ice made by Alfonso's chiseling to refill it. In this way, all the ice used in the sculpture would be from the original block.

Sarah coughed pointedly and tilted her head at the violinist that was waving at them. "I think the musicians want to go over their selections."

Dawn startled out of her thoughts. "Can you take care of it? I need to talk to Dusk."

"I could, but do you really need to go now?" Sarah asked, not wanting to be left alone again.

"I'm sorry, but this can't wait," Dawn replied, already walking away. "Thank you, Sarah. You're the best!"

Sarah sighed and went to talk to the musicians. Even at the best of times, Dawn was prone to running off with Dusk. But even so, the princess never fully abandoned plans with her. She missed the days when they had afternoon picnics in the meadow, or spent evenings playing games by the river. But once they went to Kirkjufell, she'd swap roles with the fairy and be with Dawn while he was left behind.

The rose garden was usually breathtaking at night. Lanterns spot-lit the larger statues, and starlight glinted on fairy wings as they played. No lanterns were lit now, during the dark day, and the few fairies around were busy working as Dawn hurried through the maze of bushes and decorations to the secluded clearing.

She went through the arch and saw a lux fairy glow bobbing around in the fountain. It was too faint to be Dusk, which meant there was only one fairy it could be. She stepped closer and recognized Diya swimming laps around the fountain. He noticed her approaching and changed directions to meet her at the edge.

"Hey, Dawn, what're you doing here?" he chirped.

Dawn wondered at him. He was a completely different fairy out here in the garden. In this moment she saw his original self, the self before the lantern, the version Dusk had become friends with all those millennia ago, and she understood why Dusk was so protective of the now-troubled lux fairy.

"I'm looking for Dusk. I thought he might be here," she said.

"Oh, he's here," Diya replied and pointed at the other end of the fountain. "Just sitting at the bottom over there."

"At the bottom?" Dawn gasped. "Is he all right? Did something happen?"

"Yeah, he's fine. Could stay under all day if he wanted," Diya answered. "But I was thinking it'd been long enough for now anyway. Give me a minute." He dove and disappeared under the water. Moments later he resurfaced with Dusk.

"Someone's come to see you," Diya said and nodded at Dawn.

Dusk looked at her with mild surprise. "Did you need something?"

"Do you remember when Diya asked me what I wanted to do with the lantern?" Dawn replied.

"Yes," Dusk said slowly and raised an eyebrow at her. "What of it?"

"Well, I know what I want to do now," Dawn answered and paused to consider how to continue.

"Could we maybe get out of the fountain for this?" Diya asked.

"Oh, I'm sorry! I'll just wait over here," Dawn said, blushing as she realized they were naked and walked quickly back through the arch.

She heard Dusk chuckle as she left, then some splashing as he and Diya got out. Shortly after Diya came out of the clearing, damp but dressed.

"He's ready. I'll be around," he said, shaking his head and sending tiny water droplets flying everywhere.

Dawn blinked as droplets hit her face. "You're not going to stay?"

"Dusk can fill me in later," he answered and flew away.

Dawn took a deep breath and went back into the clearing. Dusk was sitting on the swing, watching the water in the fountain churn as it hit the basin. She carefully settled next to him, not wanting to shift the swing and disturb him. There was a large gap between them, almost enough space for another person. A distance Dawn wanted to cross but didn't feel she should.

"So I was wondering," she started, watching the fountain with him, "would it be possible to pull Diya's energy out of the lantern and give it back to him?"

Dusk blinked slowly and turned to look at her. "While that is an admirable idea, it isn't possible. He wouldn't be able to hold it."

Dawn sighed, frustrated to be so quickly foiled. "I just thought, since it was his to begin with, he would be able to use it."

"That's not the issue," Dusk said, shaking his head. "Diya's ability to store and use magic was compromised by the lantern. It works in such a way that anything he made beyond the bare minimum for existing was absorbed as long as he touched it, but even without being absorbed now, the magic cannot remain as it should. It's like a bucket with a hole in the side. No matter how much water you put in the bucket, it will never fill beyond the hole."

"You mean it broke him," Dawn said quietly. Her heart dropped. If it was something physical, something not even a fairy could heal, what hope did she have of helping?

"Yes," Dusk said, nodding slowly. "That's why we can't just give him back his magic. Although, perhaps the idea has some merit..." He trailed off and stood to think, watching his hands as he made small gestures and paced.

Dawn waited silently, glancing around the clearing to distract herself. Her eyes were drawn to her favorite bush, and she remembered the rose Dusk had given her, that she'd given to Geoff. Her stomach rolled and she tore her attention away, forcing herself to focus on the sound of the fountain instead.

"All right," Dusk said finally, nodding to himself. "I think it would be possible to draw the energy out and put it into something else. Something like a bracelet or a necklace that Diya could wear in order to have access to it. That would allow him to use magic again. It would *also* leave the lantern without any power, so it couldn't cause any more trouble."

"That's brilliant," Dawn said and smiled at him.

"The only problem is how," Dusk said. "Cedric alone has the ability to pull the magic out, but even if Diya hadn't vetoed him as an option, I doubt he'd be willing to help."

"So the only way to do anything would be..." She looked down at her hands, white from clenching them tightly together.

"You really want to help him?" Dusk asked.

"He's important to you," Dawn said, still staring at her lap. "If Sarah or Rah were in trouble, I know you'd be willing to do whatever you could for them because they matter to me. That's what friends do, don't they? Help each other, and each other's loved ones."

"And you realize the link is permanent?" Dusk said, his green eyes so intense that Dawn could feel them on her. "We can't break it once it's made, and I can only have one."

"All the more reason it's up to you," Dawn said. "Diya's your friend, and if you're willing to do this for him, I won't prevent you."

Dusk shook his head to get his hair out of his eyes, then climbed into her lap and knelt on her hands, forcing her to look at him.

"It's just as important that *you* want to do this," he said. "Linking will mean we'll stay together, always. Is that something you would want?"

Yes, a million times yes. Dawn closed her eyes to escape his stare but became more aware of his weight and warmth on her hands. She wondered what his heart sounded like, what it felt like. If it would match hers, or have its own rhythm like Geoff's did.

"Dawn?" he asked, and she looked at him, his eyes full of worry. "Are you all right? If it's too much, we don't have to do anything."

"No," she said, then shook her head. "I mean, it's not too much. I want to if you want to."

Dusk smiled and stood up, balancing delicately on her thumbs as he reached up and placed his palm on her cheek. "I wouldn't have offered if I didn't."

12

Dawn sat at her father's desk and kicked her feet while she dipped the quill to write on the mirror. Once she'd explained to her father that she and Dusk intended to go forward with Diya's plan, he'd informed her that she needed to check with Geoff before she did. If the prince didn't like it, Leopold had advised against the option, not wanting to risk the engagement.

With a deep breath, she placed the quill on the mirror and started writing. Hopefully, Geoff would be busy and wouldn't answer. Then she could tell her father she tried, and it wouldn't be her fault if the prince never found out.

Geoff,

We've found a solution to the Night Rise, and I'm helping to fix it.

Dawn

She sprinkled goat hair on the message, Geoff's signature that activated the sending spells, and the hair and message disappeared. When nothing happened for several minutes, she smiled and stood to leave. The mirror glowed as she left the chair, and her smile faded.

Rose dust appeared, and she slowly blew off the Scarlet Rain and Morning Blossom mixture, revealing Geoff's reply.

That's my girl, wanting to help. You're not doing anything dangerous, right? Not hiding from me again?

No, I'm not going anywhere. But I'm doing something with Dusk you should know about.

The fairy? The hell are you doing with him?

We're linking.
Geoff? Are you still there?

Like hell you are. That's that magic thing they do, right? I don't want you doing that shit, getting connected to him. You're mine. If you can't do something with me, you're not fucking doing it with him.
Promise you won't do it.
Dawn, don't you disappear on me again. Promise.
Promise, damn it! You aren't allowed to do shit without my permission. You know that.

I promised him I would. I'm sorry, I have to do it.

You do it, and I swear I'll make you regret it.

He needs my help. No one else can.

Like I care? You do it, you won't be a good girl. Have to break your promise to one of us. Be smart which one.

Back in the rose garden, Dusk went searching for Diya, who was easy enough to find, lounging on the back of a unicorn and humming little ditties to himself. Dusk chuckled when he saw him.

"Should I come back later?" he asked.

"Done already?" Diya said as he sat up and patted the statue under him. "Come ride with me and tell me about it."

Dusk flew over and sat behind Diya on the statue, holding the blond fairy around the waist. "Where are we going?"

"Wherever we want," Diya answered, smiling. "Now tell me what she wanted."

"She had an idea to give you back all the magic in the lantern."

"Yeah?" Diya stopped smiling. "That's nice of her, I guess. Did you tell her she can't?"

"I explained what the situation is," Dusk said. "But it gave me another idea. We could channel the energy into a new capacitor that you could use."

"Yeah? You're actually doing it, then?" Diya asked, turning around to look at his friend. "So this is really it."

Dusk sighed and pressed his forehead to Diya's. "It won't change us."

"No," Diya replied, putting his hand on Dusk's cheek. "Only you, but for the better."

Leopold was looking over paperwork in the sitting room when Dawn left the study. He glanced at her and set the papers on the low table in front of the couch. "Did you talk to him?"

"Yes," Dawn answered, gripping her wrist behind her back.

"And how did he take it?"

"He understands what's going on," she said, digging her nails into her palm. It wasn't exactly a lie.

Leopold read her face and raised a brow at her. She held her breath as she met his eyes, and he sighed. "Then let's go end the Night Rise."

He led her down the stairs to the throne room where a small crowd of nobles and fairies had gathered. They walked up the long aisle, footsteps silent on the deep red carpet that ran to the dais at the far end of the room. Tall, glassless windows lined both long sides, carefully spelled to allow air and light in but keep rain and other unfavorable weather out. Today they emitted a soft glow that lit the room as at dusk, creating just enough light to see the overall space, with long shadows hiding the finer details.

Dawn smiled and waved at her friends as she passed them, then focused her attention on the queen's throne. Her mother was still wandering the kingdom, leaving the seat available for new occupants. Dusk and Diya were sitting on either arm of the throne, and on the seat, looking particularly out of place, was the lantern.

Leopold stood in front of his throne and faced the room, taking a moment to look over the crowd before speaking.

"Ladies, gentlemen, and fae, we've asked you here to bear witness to a special event. As you are aware, our kingdom is under most unusual circumstances. We have been working tirelessly, day and night, to find a solution to the Night Rise. We profess that today, my daughter, along with a member of the Fairy Court, have offered one. And so we present the fairy Dusk, and the princess Dawn, who by way of great personal sacrifice will provide our kingdom with light once again." The crowd murmured with curiosity and concern as Dusk rose and hovered in front of Dawn.

"What do I do now?" she whispered.

"Put your hands like this," he said, cupping his hands and holding them out. She copied him and he landed on her fingers. "Just stay like this. I'll do all the work."

Dawn allowed her breath to loosen her tense muscles. "Will you warn me when it might hurt?"

"I'll do my best to prevent harming you," Dusk answered. He

placed his palms against hers and closed his eyes. Dawn felt a tingle where he touched her and jerked, almost throwing him.

"Sorry!" she whispered.

"Don't worry about it," Dusk replied, stifling a laugh. "Are you ready now?"

"Yes, sorry."

Dusk started again, keeping his eyes on Dawn this time. She managed to stay still when the tingle came back, though it was difficult. It was like trying not to sneeze when you really had to, and the more you tried, the harder it got. The tingle spread slowly through her entire body until she was practically vibrating with energy, then it increased, and she bit her tongue to keep from crying out. Every nerve in her body felt like it was on fire. She shivered and locked her muscles, bracing against the instinctual convulsions. Her vision went white and her head pounded.

"Almost there," she heard Dusk's voice.

Then everything stopped.

She became aware of a new sensation, of something flowing in her and out of her. Magic, hers and Dusk's, now shared between them. She felt a presence on the other end of the link, and recognized it as Dusk. He took his hands away from hers, but she continued feeling him. She blinked slowly as her vision returned to normal and saw Dusk looking at her with concern that melted into relief as she focused.

"How do you feel?" he asked.

Strange, new, better. It was completely indescribable.

"I feel right," she replied.

Dusk smiled and turned to face the king. "We're ready for the lantern."

Leopold picked up the lantern and handed it to Dawn. She accepted it with her left hand while Dusk remained seated in her right. Dusk placed his palm against hers again and the tingle returned.

Now it was more of a tickle, soft and comforting. It worked its way through her, leaving her warm and content.

The tingle reached her left hand and continued through her to the lantern, finally giving her a sense of how much power they were dealing with. She gasped as she felt the depths of energy, amazed that in spite of the seemingly endless ocean of magic, the lantern cried out for more.

Dusk expertly directed her energy and tapped into the ocean. It flowed into her and she shivered. The new magic went through her and out, forming into a ball of light above her head. She watched it grow until it was too bright to look at directly, and she looked at Dusk instead. He appeared relaxed, casually watching the ball of light, but she knew he was concentrating on the magic he was controlling.

The crowd around them watched with quiet awe as a tiny star formed in front of them. When it seemed the baby sun was taking up as much space as the room allowed, Dusk cut off the tap and pulled Dawn's magic back, disconnecting it from the lantern.

"We're done," he said.

The king signaled to Harpullia, who nodded and led the Fairy Court up to the baby sun. They surrounded it and absorbed the magic, glowing brighter and brighter as the ball shrank away into nothing.

"Thank you," Leopold said to Dusk, then addressed the room. "We are pleased to say this has been a successful step forward. Everyone, you may now return to your business as usual."

The luminescent fairies scattered, most of them heading straight outside and into the sky where they remade the baby sun. It shone down on the castle, not as magnificent as the real sun but still a welcome relief after days of darkness.

13

With fairies already heading across the kingdom with light and a message of more to come, the throne room slowly emptied. Cedric attempted to slip away with the crowd, almost reaching the door when he was noticed.

"Are you heading anywhere in particular, Cedric?" Leopold called, stopping the wizard. "I need everyone to come to the high council room for planning."

"Sire," he stammered as he turned to face the king. "I've business of my own to attend to is all. I've fallen behind in certain tasks from all this excitement."

Leopold raised an eyebrow. "Very well, then."

Cedric nodded timidly and dashed away while he had the chance.

"If you wouldn't mind going with him, Sarah," Dusk said from his seat in Dawn's hand. Sarah and Rob were standing nearby, waiting for the room to empty completely before moving as well. "He may try to contact his friend to inform her what's happened. If he does I need to know immediately."

Her? So Dusk knew who was behind the Night Rise? Or at least had a guess. Dawn glanced around, but if anyone else had caught it, they didn't show.

"Oh, do you," Sarah muttered, crossing her arms and glaring at

Dusk. She might have mixed feelings about her father currently, but it wasn't for just anyone to judge.

Leopold cleared his throat and they looked at him. "If you would go, Sarah, it's on my order," he said. She gasped and nodded, dashing out of the room. "Now, the rest of you with me."

Diya fluttered over from the queen's throne and Dusk joined him in the air. Rob offered Dawn his arm as she went by, and they followed Leopold and the fairies into the hallway.

"Are you okay?" Rob whispered. It had been difficult for him to stand by and watch her come very close to fainting—or worse. "That looked pretty intense."

"I'm fine," Dawn whispered back, giving his arm a small squeeze. It was much more than intense, but she didn't think Rob would understand that she would never be the same as before the linking. She felt a magical tug from Dusk and knew he'd been listening. For a moment she tried to poke him back but couldn't quite figure out how. She gave up the effort as they reached the high council room and settled around the table. The surface was covered in a map of the kingdom and a couple of fairies were flitting around it, placing figurines and counters.

The king's plan was simple. Every morning, Dawn and Dusk would pull energy out of the lantern, and a team of fairies would deliver it all around the kingdom, aiming to give a full day's worth of light to as large an area as possible.

"We'll need the fastest aer fairies to deliver energy to the farthest places," Leopold began once everyone was seated. "Others who can hold more energy like terras should stay closer and visit more area. These towns here are a high priority." He pointed out a few larger townships on the west side of the kingdom that produced the majority of goods.

Rob looked over the map and noted some smaller villages in the southern outskirts of the kingdom. "The farms out here will need extra help. We all depend on them for our food, after all."

"We've got all the lux fairies possible out there already," Leopold said. "I'd rather keep a heavier focus where the population is higher. If I don't keep people happy, they'll be grumbling long after this is over, even if they suffer no long-term issues."

"I disagree," Dusk said. "You need to focus your efforts on the ecosystem. If we don't take care of the trees here," he pointed at a patch of forest near the river, "we could end up with a landslide that would cripple the river."

"Even if it did, couldn't we clean it up?" Rob asked. "We really should be concentrating on the poorer people who can't care for themselves as easily."

Dusk shook his head. "Depending on the severity, recovery from a major disaster could take years. It's much more important to prevent any from happening in the first place."

"I can't risk losing our biggest trade route," Leopold cut off Rob's retort. "Not to mention the Antwerps would find a way to use it against us... We'll check the trees there regularly. I'll arrange a few fairies to rotate through the smaller communities and ensure they all receive something."

Dawn listened to them plan, not having much to add. Politics were interesting at times, but large-scale planning like this was tedious. She absentmindedly picked up a horse figurine and played with it, running it along the edge of the map. The horse galloped across the land, visiting the Fae Realm and the Mansion before continuing up the Tail Spike mountains to Kirkjufell. Suddenly, it found its way blocked by a mighty soldier.

Dawn looked up and found Diya had joined her game. He smirked at her and built a small wall with counters, daring her to challenge the swordsman he placed behind it. Dawn grinned and charged with the horse, crashing into the wall and scattering the small pieces everywhere.

"Oh, sorry," she said sheepishly as some of the pieces knocked into the rest of the map, disturbing the carefully marked areas.

"It's no problem," Rob assured her, glancing nervously at the king as he hurried to straighten the pieces.

"Perhaps you'd like to go to the kitchen and have them bring dinner now," Leopold suggested sternly, replacing the soldier that had landed in his lap.

"All right," Dawn said quietly and stood to leave.

Dusk's mouth twitched in amusement as he watched her. "Take Diya with you."

"Why do I have to go?" Diya complained, but flew up off the table and followed Dawn to the door. "It wasn't my fault."

Leopold was wrapping up the planning as they returned. "That just about covers everything. I'll have to meet with Harpullia and confirm a few points with him, and there are a couple of places that I need to look into more carefully, but we've got the bulk of it worked out. Thank you, boys."

Dawn quietly resumed her seat, while Diya flew to the windows and landed in one, stretching out and resting with his hands behind his head. Dusk watched his friend for a moment, then turned to Leopold.

"There is one more thing to discuss," he said quietly. "Sarah has brought to my attention the possibility that Cedric is working for someone."

"Oh?" Leopold sighed and leaned back in his chair. "And you have an idea who it might be?"

"Unfortunately, yes," Dusk said. "We believe it's Berniece."

It was a familiar name if spoken of rarely, belonging to the witch who had helped build and manage the Academy. Though she was regarded as a skilled healer, conversations including her name were always heavy, dark. There was a general sense that she wasn't remembered fondly, especially by the fairies who had known her.

Dawn glanced at Diya in the window. How did he feel about her? He was looking outside, and his reflection was calm like he wasn't entirely listening, but his hands were in fists and his body was tense.

Leopold closed his eyes and exhaled tiredly. "Fine time to decide she isn't dead. Do you have any proof it's her?"

"Not currently," Dusk replied. "But I'll be looking into obtaining some."

"You realize the implications of this theory," Leopold said, sitting up and gripping the table. "Allowing the underling of a public enemy to work not only in the castle but as one of my chief advisors is a major security breach, particularly if it is connected to the current crisis. Kings have been overthrown for less."

"Whatever happens, you know we won't allow the Night Rise to lead to any further issues," Dusk said. "No one wants anything like what happened to your parents."

Somehow it hadn't occurred to Dawn before that Dusk knew her grandparents and had been there for her father during his childhood. Had Dusk been one of the fairies that watched over the infant prince? Kept him safe until he was grown? Helped him retake the throne from those who'd killed his parents and sent him into hiding?

They were interrupted by dinner arriving. The room was tense as plates and silverware were set in front of them, and meat pies with steamed vegetables were served. Their glasses were filled with lemon water, and the pitcher was left on the table. Everyone worked on their food slowly, except for Rob, who happily shoveled bite after bite into his mouth.

Dawn poked at her food, more stirring her vegetables than eating. She tried to think of something else, anything less dower. Well, there was always the Kirkjufells, marrying Geoff. He wouldn't be happy about what she did today, but surely she could find a way to make it work. Actually, since linking with Dusk meant being able to use his magic, maybe she'd be able to help Geoff all the more. Fauna fairies were skilled with healing, after all. If he did have lingering effects from the sickness, she might be able to alleviate them.

She jumped as she felt a stab of magic from Dusk, which immediately softened and withdrew.

Leopold eyed her with concern. "Something wrong?"

"Sorry, it's nothing," Dawn said quickly, glancing at Dusk for half a second.

Rob watched the exchange with worry, then glowered and stabbed his food as Dawn looked at Dusk.

"You kids should finish up and get to bed," Leopold said. "It'll be an early start for all of us."

Dawn rubbed her eyes, realizing how tired she was. Yesterday had gone late, and today had involved a lot of running around, not to mention linking with Dusk—which was enough of a task on its own.

"I can walk you to your room," Rob said, shoving the last of his food in his mouth.

"No need," Dusk said as he set his silverware down carefully on his empty plate. "I'm going with her."

Dawn shook her head at them as Rob started to protest. "You can both come, or neither of you. Just no arguing."

Rob glowered but went quiet. Dusk shrugged and didn't say anything.

Dawn glanced at the window Diya had been resting in and saw it was open and empty. The fairy was gone. She gave her father a quick hug as she grabbed the lantern, then linked her arm through Rob's. Together they followed Dusk down the hall.

Rob tried to think of something to say, but he was too distracted by Dawn leaning against him to come up with anything worthwhile. And anyway, he didn't want to talk while the fairy was still around.

They reached the tower and climbed the stairs to Dawn's room, and she went in alone to change into her nightclothes. Rob stared stonily at Dusk, waiting for him to leave first. After a minute of neither of them moving, he coughed.

"Do you need something?" Dusk asked, cocking an eyebrow at him.

"Are you planning on going somewhere else, or are you going to sit here all night?" Rob asked.

Dusk sighed and looked at the ceiling. "I'm waiting for her to be ready, as I'm staying in her room tonight."

"Surely there's no reason for you to continue doing that," he said crossly. It hadn't sat well with him when he learned Dusk had spent the night in Dawn's room at the Mansion, and he was determined to stop it from happening again.

"What did I say about arguing?" Dawn said as she opened her door and glared at Rob. "He's staying because we have to pull energy out of the lantern first thing in the morning."

"Oh," Rob said sheepishly and looked at his feet. Clearly, he wasn't winning himself any favors trying to interfere. "Well, goodnight, Dawn."

Dawn smiled at him. "Goodnight, Rah."

Rob nodded and shuffled down the stairs. Dusk watched him go for a moment then fluttered into the room, going to the window to settle for the night.

"Sorry about him," Dawn said as she climbed into bed.

"You don't need to apologize for your friend," Dusk replied, turning to look at her. "He's just trying to look out for you."

She pulled her sheets around her, tucking the edges in to cocoon herself. "I just wish I knew what got him upset in the first place. I think it was right after you... What was that anyway?" There had been several sensations from Dusk in the short time since they'd linked. The last one had been particularly intense, and certainly not something she would have expected, seeming unrelated to anything else going on.

"Ahh," Dusk remarked, slightly embarrassed. "That would be me failing to keep my emotions in check. It has been a few centuries since I had to learn something new magically, and linking is a bit of a curve for anyone. It won't happen again."

"Your emotions?" Dawn got comfortable on her pillows and felt her eyes drooping. "I don't mind them, really. I only jumped because you surprised me."

Dusk smiled at her as she fell asleep, then turned back to the window. The sun they had made was fading, trickling away like sand in an hourglass. Under the shrinking ball of light, long, noon-like shadows grew grey and fuzzy around the edges until they disappeared completely, leaving them in total darkness for the night.

14

"Dawn, time to get up..."

Dawn awoke to Dusk prodding her just before the sun would break on the horizon. She rolled over sleepily, eyes refusing to open.

"Five more minutes," she mumbled.

"No, the first group of fairies is already here," Dusk said and nodded at the window, where fairy glows could be seen through her drapes.

Dawn sighed and got out of bed, then opened her window for the fairies, and went to sit at her desk where the lantern was waiting. Dusk landed on the desk and put his hand on one of hers. Once he was ready, she placed her other hand on the lantern. She felt the tingle from yesterday travel through her and tap into the lantern as Dusk pulled out power. Today the fairies treated the process indifferently, with each fairy taking their allotment quickly and quietly from Dusk one at a time.

Dawn caught herself dozing after the first handful of fairies and shook her head to stay awake.

"You can rest your eyes," Dusk said, smiling at her inability to wake up. "This will take a while."

"Thanks," she replied, already leaning her head back. "I almost wish I was a fairy so I didn't need to sleep."

Dusk chuckled. "Yes, clearly the best thing about being a fairy is not sleeping."

"That and the flying," Dawn said. "And it must be interesting to be so small."

"How so?" Dusk asked as he finished giving one fairy energy and the next in line approached.

Dawn cracked her eyes open and squinted at him.

"Well, the world must look so different from your perspective," she said, then closed her eyes again.

"That's one thing I don't mind never learning," Dusk said soberly.

"Only illustrating my point," Dawn replied. Personally, she enjoyed daydreaming about life as a fairy, though maybe it wasn't a common hobby among fairies, to think about being human.

"It is a fate no fairy desires," whispered Enara, who was receiving energy. The fauna fairy was usually soft-spoken, but her current demeanor was particularly nervous, even anxious. Her chestnut hair flowed freely behind her, and she pulled it over her shoulder, partially covering her face. "Although the fate you have given yourself is equally troubling, if not more so, considering who will be most affected."

Dawn squinted at her curiously. While being human was, quite reasonably, undesirable for an immortal fairy, the second fate eluded her. Before she could ask about it, there was a knock and Sarah came in.

"Morning! Oh, you're up," she said.

"Morning, Sarah," Dawn replied, watching as Enara left, disappearing out the window. There were only a couple of fairies remaining now. "We're almost done."

Sarah nodded and started the bath going while she prepared a dress. Soon all the fairies were gone except Dusk.

"I'll leave you to get ready," he said, breaking the connection to the lantern and flying to the door.

"We'll see you at breakfast," Dawn said.

"Actually, I'm skipping breakfast today," Dusk said. "But if you need me later, I'll be where you can find me."

"What are you doing instead?" Dawn asked curiously.

Dusk shrugged nonchalantly. "There's some business I need to address."

"You mean it's a secret," Sarah said crisply as she opened the door.

"He means it doesn't pertain to us, so it's none of our business to know," Dawn replied sternly.

"Exactly," Dusk said, half-smiling as he disappeared.

Sarah glowered after him, arms crossed. "I don't understand how you can put up with him."

"He's my friend," Dawn said. Finally, she had her chance to talk, and she wasn't going to miss it. "Just like you. I'm sorry I've been so distant these last few days. I should be making some time for you, but I've been so caught up in everything. It certainly hasn't been my intention to ignore you in favor of Dusk."

"It's not your fault," Sarah said, softening. "I shouldn't be so jealous of you having other friends who want your attention. Besides, it's not like we have limited time. I'll be your maid wherever you end up."

"No," Dawn said firmly. She stepped over to Sarah and embraced her. "You'll be my friend wherever I end up. That's what I need, not a servant."

"Thanks," Sarah said quietly. She gave Dawn a final squeeze before leaving her alone to have her bath.

Dusk flew around the castle grounds, pulsing his light so he flashed off and on in a seemingly random pattern as he searched. When he reached the south wall he saw a faint light return his signal, so he made a beeline for the blackberry bush it came from.

Diya was inside, watching a caterpillar spin a cocoon. He came out as Dusk approached. "What are you doing out here? Aren't you supposed to be eating or something?"

"Morning to you, too," Dusk replied. "I'm skipping it today. There's a task that needs doing, and I can only do it now."

Diya offered a half-smile. "Oh really? It's not dangerous, is it?"

"Very. So I assumed you'd be interested in helping."

The half-smile turned into a grin. "You assume correctly. It's almost like you know me or something."

"Come on, we don't have very long," Dusk said as he turned and headed to the northwest corner of the castle grounds.

Diya followed happily until he saw the small cottage they seemed to be aiming for, and he stopped smiling and slowed. "Isn't that the wizard's place?"

"It is," Dusk answered. "That's why we have to do this now, while he's gone for a set amount of time. I want to find some evidence that he's connected to Berniece."

"Guess I'm the most qualified for this job," Diya said softly.

Dusk nodded. "Exactly why I want you to come."

Diya shuddered. "Let's get this over with."

They flew past the lab to the cottage Cedric and Sarah lived in. No locks on the door, thankfully. Dusk put his hands on the heavy wood and slowly eased it open, manipulating it with magic until there was just enough space for a fairy to squeeze through. The cottage consisted of a small common room and two bedrooms—much like the rooms Dawn and Sarah had used at the Mansion, but cozier.

A quick glance at the left room revealed it belonged to a teenage girl. Garments haphazardly littered the floor and furniture, and needlework blanketed the desk. Dusk nodded to himself and went over to the door of the right bedroom. Sarah's door was cracked open, but this one was latched closed and had a metal lock.

"This complicates things. Keep a lookout for me while I get this unlocked," Dusk called over to Diya.

"Sure thing," Diya said absentmindedly, already sitting by a window.

Dusk focused on the lock, thinking how best to get it open. Breaking it would be fastest—but would also alert Cedric at a glance that something was wrong. He studied the shape of the lock for several minutes, then flew over to the tub in the corner to find some material. There was a small leak in the wooden tub, and water was pooling on the stone floor, eroding it slightly. Dusk smiled as he dug around the puddle and collected loose pieces of gravel. He brought them over to the door and took his time shaping them together into a rough key. Once it was made he tried it in the lock, slowly turning it until it clicked.

"We're in," he said as he eased the door open.

Diya left the window and joined Dusk in Cedric's room. It was simply furnished with only a bed, desk, and small trunk. In lieu of decorations, Cedric had an odd assortment of jars, plants, and small trinkets on the shelves that lined the walls.

"Looks more like a witch's room than a wizard's," Dusk said, unimpressed by the lack of magical equipment and reading materials. Obviously, there was the lab for those things, but it was unusual for a studious mage to have none of them in his bedroom.

"Do you see that?" Diya asked with worry.

He was looking at a very well-kept plant in the corner next to the bed. It spilled out of its massive pot, trying to encroach on every bit of room around it. Dusk regarded the leafy plant with apprehension.

"A begonia. It doesn't necessarily mean her," he said quietly. For all he knew the wizard might be an amateur botanist. Although if Dusk had to guess, he would have thought Cedric would keep some sort of lily.

"But why have it, if not for her?" Diya said, voicing Dusk's concern. He looked over the contents of the desk and inhaled noisily. "He's got a mirror system, an old one."

The original form of the communication system would display messages in reverse, so writing was done on paper, then applied to the mirror so it would be backward. Modern mirrors, like the king's, were double-sided so the messages could be written directly on the reflective surface.

Dusk looked over the system with Diya. Blank papers scratched with quill marks were scattered around, and a roller was half-hidden under them. In the corner of the desk was an open jar with dried begonia petals.

"That's her signature," Diya whispered, indicating the jar of flowers.

Dusk pursed his lips and placed his hands on the mirror carefully. The jar alone was very telling, but he wanted to make absolutely certain it was what it looked like. He skimmed through the active spells to check the last few messages, and sure enough, the begonia petals were on the sending and receiving end of several.

"That's enough evidence for me," he said as he closed the magic. "Let's get out of here."

"Don't need to tell me twice," Diya muttered.

They exited the room and Dusk closed the door and relocked it. He brought the key back to the puddle and broke it up into gravel again. With any sign of their trespassing gone, they vacated the house readily.

The castle grounds were lively again, with everyone happily returning to their usual routines in the sunlight. Though the light was notably less bright than usual—an intensity closer to middle- or late-winter than early-spring—people were relieved to be closer to ordinary, and at least able to see.

Rob stood on the east wall, watching the road. Messengers had been coming and going all morning with news of the fairies' effort to deliver sunlight around the kingdom, and he'd been assigned to watch for them. He glanced up at the baby sun hanging above the castle, grateful for the light but less-than-thrilled with how it had been obtained.

If only that fairy would go away and leave his best friend alone. If only he could go back and stop her from getting the lantern in the first place, then none of this would be happening. If only she weren't destined to go away and leave him behind.

"It isn't fair," he grumbled aloud.

"What isn't?" Sean asked, bumping into Rob as he patrolled the wall.

"Nothing," Rob said quickly, focusing his gaze on the road again.

Sean raised an eyebrow at him. "You look pretty bummed. What's up?"

"I said it's nothing," Rob replied more harshly than he meant to.

"Oh, I get it," Sean said, unaffected by Rob's outburst. "Heard there was some kind of fight while you were gone, that you couldn't beat a kid."

"Only because I didn't want to hurt him," Rob said, scowling. "And he cheated."

"Sure," Sean replied, not sounding convinced. "And how'd you get cut? Should tell people it was the big guy if you want any respect."

Rob touched his cheek, feeling the scab. It itched, and he scratched it without thinking. He could have beaten the boy, he knew, if he'd been willing to hurt him. But, then what? The boy would be the one with a scar, or worse, and it would be his fault. He pulled his hand away from his face and looked at the fresh blood on his fingertips.

"Hey, looks like we've got a returning company," Sean said,

drawing Rob's attention to the horse racing towards the castle. The rider carried a green-and-red striped banner.

"That's my company," Rob said, straightening. "And looks like he's got the queen's emblem too." He noted the waving gold flag with a red sun, then jogged to the stairs to open the gate.

15

The major dance hall bustled with servants, fairies, and animals readying the space for the birthday celebrations only two days away. Stout terra fairies scoured the floor, fixing any wear in the stone and smoothing it for an optimal dance floor. Flowers had been moved in, and sweet-smelling floras tended them, ensuring every arrangement was fresh and full. Supple hydro fairies tended their fountains, encouraging the water to move higher, flow faster, and make tighter turns in their gravity-defying flows. Birds and butterflies were going through their rehearsed routines, still watched over by gentle faunas.

Crystal-clear musical notes rang through the hall as Dawn sang, practicing for the celebration. The melody floated through the room above the commotion, guided by aer fairies to ensure the best acoustics. Occasionally, a tenuous aer would adjust the volume of Dawn's voice, or the accompanying musicians, for the perfect balance between the two.

"Yes, lovely," said Julia, smiling her most serene as Dawn finished the piece. Her short salt-and-pepper hair was combed back so it fell behind her ears, showing off dangling amethyst earrings. The vocal instructor was considered by many to be the epitome of elegance—an opinion Dawn shared. "Remember to be careful on that alliteration, especially the "W." Practice biting an apple in the mirror later to get your soft palate up." She pantomimed eating a big bite, and Dawn mimicked her. "Yes, just like that. And most importantly, have fun. If you enjoy singing, your audience will enjoy listening."

Dawn saw Sarah waving at her from across the hall and went over, weaving through the chaos and dodging attempts from servants to stop her for assistance.

Sarah smiled and bounced on her heels when Dawn reached her. "Your mother is back!"

"Oh, good. I'd better go say hello," Dawn said and practically sprinted out of the hall.

"Thank Nova," Sarah said beside her. "If I have to look at any more floral centerpieces, I'll die from boredom."

Dawn giggled and slowed down to a fast walk. "It'll be over soon, then we'll get so used to rocks we'll wish we had floral centerpieces back."

"Kirkjufell isn't that bad," Sarah said, brow furrowed while she tried to remember anything about it. "At least, I don't think it was."

"Stone castle, palace in a mountain, I guess they aren't that different," Dawn said.

They made it outside and crossed the grounds to the south wall. The giant double gates were thrown open and a company of mounted soldiers was coming in, led by Sir James and Queen Eleanor. A handful of people had gathered on either side to greet them, and Dawn and Sarah went to stand with the king.

"Leopold!" Eleanor cried as she dismounted and all but jumped on her husband. "The tour was marvelously successful, though I think it's more due to your effort here than our own attempt."

"Our effort was made possible by your daughter," Leopold replied. "Though most of her actions were contrary to what was desired."

"Claws, dear, it's hardly an issue for her to take things into her own hands if she sees the opportunity," Eleanor said, turning to Dawn to hug her. "I do hope you didn't put yourself in danger."

"Only a little," Dawn replied, face buried in her mother's red mane.

"Well, do try to make sure it doesn't happen again," Eleanor said, straightening to look at her daughter. "I doubt Geoff would be pleased if you arrived in less-than-perfect condition."

"No, he wouldn't," Dawn said, grimacing. As things were, he wasn't going to be happy anyway.

"And you'll keep on yourself to be ready for him, I trust," Eleanor replied. "Now, if you'll excuse me, I need to discuss things with Leopold and James."

"Actually," Leopold said, coughing, "you need to see to the preparations for Dawn's birthday. They're currently setting everything up in the major hall."

Eleanor blinked at him for a minute, face blank. "Are you telling me they aren't finished yet?"

"They couldn't, with both of us gone," Dawn said.

"Dragon droppings!" Eleanor threw her hands in the air like she was throwing someone. "They've had everything decided for months! I'm going to go and tell them to get a move on..." She stormed off towards the keep, hair blazing behind her on her fiery path.

"Should I go with her?" Dawn asked Leopold nervously.

"Better to let her handle things on her own for now," the king said, chuckling as his wife shoved past an unfortunate servant who got in her way. "Go enjoy some time to yourself."

"Absolutely," Sarah said, grabbing Dawn's wrist and starting to pull her away. "We'll keep ourselves busy, and won't make any trouble."

Dawn waved to Leopold as she was dragged away, then turned to Sarah. "So what plans do you have for us?"

"I've been thinking," Sarah said, pausing to check if they were alone. "This friend of my father's, that Dusk thinks is Berniece. I've had an idea about how that might be possible, for her to still be alive, and I want to ask Dusk about it."

"All right," Dawn replied, more than a little curious what Sarah thought. "I'm sure Dusk won't mind, if we can find him…"

She trailed off as she felt a strange shimmer of magic that was compelling her to follow it.

"And I think he's this way," she said, heading towards the rose garden. As they moved, the shimmer grew stronger and felt brighter, guiding them through the maze of bushes until they found him sitting in front of a statue of Nova. The rainbow dragon gazed down at the fairy with a serenity only a second-degree dragon could manage.

"You made it," Dusk said, glancing at Dawn and Sarah as they crept up behind him.

"You're not surprised?" Dawn asked with disappointment.

"I could feel you coming," Dusk explained, half-smiling. "Good to see you're experimenting with the link."

Dawn felt a warm tingle and smirked at Dusk. "I thought you said you weren't going to do that anymore."

"I said it wouldn't happen by accident," Dusk said. "This one is intentional."

"If you two are done, I wanted to ask something," Sarah said, crossing her arms at them.

"Of course," Dusk replied and flicked his wings, flying up to them. "What would you like to know?"

"It's about Berniece," Sarah said, and Dusk winced.

"I see," he said softly. "You've realized the issue with her." Sarah cocked an eyebrow and nodded. "In that case, we'd best sit down somewhere private. It isn't something to discuss in the open."

He turned and flew away deeper into the garden, and the girls hurried to keep up. After a few turns and ducking under a couple of archways, Dusk stopped them in front of a massive marble statue of three dragons.

Matur stood on his heavy claws, batlike wings half folded, Majik's long whiskers flowed along his equally lengthy body, and Metre spiraled around them both, his feathery wings stretched above them. Dawn and Sarah bowed their heads to the Great Dragons, the creators of everything, then sat together on the bench tucked under the statue.

"So," Dusk said, hovering in front of them, "you want to know how Berniece has lived so long."

"It's something to do with magic, isn't it?" Sarah asked.

"Not something about," Dusk said, eyes glinting. "That's what it amounts to, is magic. You've heard the saying, 'Magic is life'?"

"Everyone knows that," Sarah said, rolling her eyes. "As in life itself is so great, it might as well be magic. What does that have to do with Berniece?"

"That's not what it means," Dusk said, and Dawn felt a cold tingle run through her. "Every living thing has magic, and in most cases, the energy is used up over time. When it's gone, you die. The saying is meant literally, as the magic you are born with is your lifespan."

Sarah paled. "So the way to live longer would be..."

"To take magic from another source," Dusk finished. "You eat to essentially replenish some of what is used by daily living, but to extend your life you'd need magic from a larger source, and the most prevalent source that's large enough to matter happens to be humans."

Dawn pursed her lips as he paused, not liking where this was going in the slightest. "Are you saying Berniece kills people to steal their magic?"

"Indeed," Dusk said, hanging his head for a moment. "Beyond her skills as an alchemist, she always worked as a physician, midwife, all manner of jobs that deal with life. Unfortunately, that also means she is intimately familiar with death, and it's hardly any task to contain raw magic for one's self if the owner is unable to resist."

"*That's* who you think my father is working for?" Sarah asked, face red as she clenched her hands into fists. It was one thing to use magic to live a little longer, but her father working for a murderer? This was low, even for Dusk. "Why would he do that? And how would he have found her if you can't?"

"I don't think he is, I know it," Dusk said calmly. "I found proof this morning that he's communicating with her. I wish I hadn't, and that she had died like we thought. How your father got involved with her I'd also like to know."

"He's not a bad person," Sarah said, shaking her head as her eyes grew blurry. "He may not be good at magic, but he isn't a killer."

Dawn put her arm around Sarah's shoulders. The man loved his daughter, and did everything he could for her, only working as a wizard to give her a good home. Sarah was understandably upset, but it was important that she not forget how much she also cared for him.

"No one thinks that," Dawn said gently. "And it's possible he doesn't know what kind of person she is. Whatever happens, I'll give him the benefit of the doubt."

Sarah leaned into Dawn's embrace, tears flowing down her cheeks. "Sorry. I'm just so frustrated since we got back."

"You should talk to him, as his daughter," Dusk said. "Deep down he loves you, even if he seems to have forgotten that recently."

Sarah sniffled, calming. "He does, doesn't he? I haven't even told him I used magic yet. I bet he'll be so excited."

"Of course he will," Dawn said as she wiped at Sarah's nose with her sleeve hem. "He's probably a bit down right now and misses you too."

Sarah finished crying and took a deep, steadying breath. "Okay, I'll go find him. Thanks for the answer, I guess." She gave Dawn one more hug before heading off.

"I should go too," Dawn said slowly, in no hurry to actually move. "I ought to see if Mother succeeded in getting things finished. I'll see you at dinner? Unless you're sneaking off again."

"No, I'll be there," Dusk said, half-smiling.

"Good. Breakfast was boring without you," Dawn said, then took her time stretching before leaving Dusk alone in the garden once more.

16

Sarah entered the lab and sighed with relief as she glanced around. It was empty. She knew she needed to talk to Cedric, but all she wanted was alone time to think, and her father deserved better than to have her spying on him anyway. A couple of hours here would do her well.

She grabbed a spell book from the shelf and sat at the table to look it over. Maybe now that she'd proven she could use magic, she'd finally manage a spell. She flipped through the pages to an easy one, the light spell Dawn used. Although, it may have only seemed easy for Dawn because she was lux aligned. Considering the situation her magic appeared in, maybe something that went with defense would be better? Sarah certainly hadn't tried anything along those lines before.

As she searched through the book for a suitable spell, her father entered the lab.

"Is it only you today?" he asked, frowning as he crossed the room to his daughter.

Sarah jerked and looked up at him. "Oh, sorry. Dawn's helping Eleanor get things finished."

"So she no longer finds it necessary to learn from me," he

grumbled, lowering himself into the chair next to Sarah. "I suppose she has someone else to help her in that regard."

"He does know more about fairy magic," Sarah said, avoiding mentioning how she had also gone to the fairy. "But since I'm here, we may as well work."

"Did you want to learn magecraft?" Cedric asked, looking at her with surprise.

"Why wouldn't I?" she replied, crossing her arms and raising an eyebrow.

"I always assumed you only intended to be a suitable partner for Dawn should she need one," Cedric said. "I would honestly prefer my own child leave magecraft for others."

"But you're a wizard," Sarah said, more taken aback than angry.

"Yes, and as such I know how dangerous magic is for the user," he said.

"Only if she doesn't know how," Sarah said, closing the book roughly. "It's fine if you know what you're doing, which is what I'm trying to learn."

"My dear," Cedric said calmly, reaching across the table to take the book. "If you have been truly endeavoring to perform magic all these years and seen nothing yet, then perhaps you've not the magical gift."

"Have the magical gift!" Sarah stood quickly, knocking her chair back. "Like you? When have you ever done anything magical? But you at least know things, and you don't want me to learn, to try."

She stomped to the door, then turned back to glare at him. "I do have it. I used magic to protect myself in a fight."

"Sarah!" Cedric called after her, but she left, slamming the door shut behind her.

Dawn walked through the keep with her mother, having successfully gotten the preparations not only back on track, but ahead of where they needed to be. All it had taken was one look from the angry warrior queen to set the servants and artists into a frenzy that pushed them to finish their tasks.

"It's good you made it back today, or I don't think they'd ever get ready," Dawn said.

Eleanor chuckled. "They just need to be reminded that they already know what to do. They want someone else to be in charge, but really they can make decisions on their own."

"I wish I could be more like you," Dawn said, letting her hair fall in her face. "I don't know how I'll do as well in Kirkjufell."

"If you keep to your strengths you'll be fine," Eleanor replied, putting her arm over her daughter's shoulders. "Geoff is already a natural leader. He just needs a strong woman supporting him. Though you will need to be careful with Henry."

Dawn glanced up at her mother's face and caught a flash of repulsion. She knew her mother avoided dealing with Henry—ever since her birth when her parents had reached out to engage her with Geoff.

"Does he...dislike us?" Dawn asked softly. Did the powerful king think little of them and their small, one-wizard kingdom?

"Darling, if he did, why would he want for you to marry his son?" Eleanor asked, cocking her eyebrow at her daughter. "My problem with him is the lack of manners he often shows. But Geoff likes you, and as long as he's happy, you'll be fine."

Dawn forced a smile for her mother. While she wanted to be there for Geoff, it would be much more of a task than the queen knew. The years of hiding Geoff's poor behaviors from her parents were starting to wear on her, and she didn't relish the idea of continuing them with Henry.

They entered the dining hall, and she noticed two changes to the usual seating. On the left end, Sarah was missing, and on the right, Rob was sitting next to Dusk.

"Look at you, sitting at the high table," Dawn said as she sat on the other side of Dusk and smiled at the knight. "I take it James is happy with you?"

Rob blushed and nodded. "Yeah, he knew I was helping you and cleared that up with everyone."

"So you got promoted to the high table?" Dawn asked.

"I guess so," Rob said casually as food was presented. "How are things coming with the celebration? Did Eleanor get everything going?"

He bit into a chicken leg, and Dawn giggled and poked at her corn, glancing at her mother next to her. Eleanor was too busy talking with Leopold and James to notice her daughter.

"They're basically done now. She was just standing there and they ran around tripping over themselves," Dawn said quietly.

Dusk snorted and almost choked on his carrot.

"Sorry," he said, still chuckling.

Rob looked between Dawn and the fairy, and frowned. He ate slowly, focusing on Dusk in the corner of his vision while he did. There wouldn't be a repeat of yesterday as long as he could help it.

"Oh, Rah," Dawn said.

He jumped, startled out of his self-imposed watch duty. "Yeah?"

"I have a favor to ask," Dawn said.

Rob swallowed and cleared his throat. Good, something she needed his help with. "Sure, anything."

"Tomorrow, when Alex comes, do you think you could let John tag along with you when you train?" Dawn asked. "I wouldn't mind him spending the day with me, but I think he'll have more fun practicing with knights than watching me watch other people work."

"Oh, yeah, I'll do that," he said sulkily. At least she had asked him, and not the fairy. He just had to ignore the fact that the fairy wouldn't actually be interesting to a boy like John.

Dusk finished eating while they spoke and stood to leave. "I'm going to go see Diya before coming to your room for the night. Maybe Robert would like to walk you again?"

Rob gaped at him, then closed his mouth and nodded. "Uhm, yeah, yeah. I'll walk you if you want."

"All right," Dawn agreed dubiously. "I'll leave the window open for you." Dusk nodded and flicked away.

Rob ate the rest of his chicken quickly, then watched Dawn as she took her time eating her food. Eventually, she set down her fork, and he offered his arm.

"You've been really great recently," she said as they left the dining hall. "I'm sorry I haven't been available much to just talk or anything."

Rob smiled bashfully. "I haven't done much. I've only looked after you while you do all the hard stuff."

"That is the hard job," Dawn teased, squeezing his arm. "But really, thank you. For everything."

"I'm just doing my duty," he mumbled, watching his feet as they started up the stairs of her tower.

"You mean you're just being a good friend," Dawn said. They reached the top and stopped in front of her door. "I haven't been very present this past week, and I want you to know I intend to change that. I want to enjoy the last of my time with you."

"We still have a while," Rob said. "You'll be staying here until the Night Rise is over, and then I'm coming with you to Kirkjufell."

"Where you'll stay until I'm married," she said, hugging him. It wouldn't be more than a handful of days, but she knew he would do everything he could to make it count. "Thank you."

She smiled at him and he blushed and smiled back, then turned and descended the stairs. Once he was out of sight she entered her room and got dressed for bed, then opened the window for Dusk.

"Oh," she exclaimed as she pulled back the curtain and found him sitting on the outside, looking at the stars. She carefully eased the window open a crack without disturbing the fairy. "Have you been waiting here the whole time?"

"No. I did go see Diya," Dusk said as he fluttered into the room.

Dawn sat at her desk and assembled her journal and quill in front of her. She hadn't touched her writing in days and was itching to get something on paper. "Is that the only reason you left early?"

"I may have had another motive," he said, landing next to her inkwell and sitting.

"I hope it wasn't to get away from Rah," she said offhandedly as she dipped her quill. "The two of you have been having issues."

"On the contrary. You both wanted a chance to talk alone, so I enabled you to."

Dawn opened her journal to a blank page. "That's kind of you. We haven't been able to spend any time together lately and I know I miss him."

Dusk shrugged like it was nothing and watched her hand move across the page. "I'd be happy to give you more space, if you let me know when you want to be with your friends."

"I'd rather you get along with them," Dawn replied. "I understand Sarah being a bit rough, but I'm surprised Rah is having trouble. I thought, between them, he'd be easier."

"I guess it's a guy thing," he said simply, and she narrowed her eyes at him. He knew more than he was letting on, but he wasn't budging on telling her.

"Must be," she said and returned to her writing. After a few minutes of silence, she looked at him again. "I've been meaning to ask you something."

"When aren't you?" Dusk muttered, looking at the ceiling. "What is it this time?"

"Do you remember what Enara said this morning, about you choosing a fate no other fairy would want?" she asked.

Dusk winced like she'd slapped him. "I was hoping you were too tired to catch that."

"So it is something," Dawn said. She blew on her writing to dry it, then closed her journal. "I thought it must be when everyone was so quick to oppose the idea at first, and then Father said we were making a sacrifice. He's good at saying what the people want to hear, but this wasn't just for show, was it?"

"No, it was true," Dusk said and gave her a weak smile. "I should have known you'd notice."

Dawn stared hard at him. "So what did we do?"

"You did nothing," he said quickly, putting his hand on hers. "I'm the one who sacrificed myself. Now that we're linked, more than our magic is tied together. Since magic is, technically speaking, the same as your lifespan, I'll die when you do."

Dawn gaped at him, hoping she'd heard wrong. "You'll what? Die?! How could you do this without telling me what would happen? I can't believe you!"

"It's my only chance to help Diya. If I didn't try, I wouldn't be able to live with myself," he said, pulling his hand back and clenching it. "And he wouldn't have suggested it if it weren't what he wanted."

"But why would he?" Dawn asked. There was more going on, but what? And why wasn't he telling her? Why did he never tell her anything? "Would he really want to help so much he'd give you up?"

"Of course not," Dusk said, smiling. He unclenched his hand and dropped it as he looked up at her. "But we can worry about that later. You should sleep now, so you can be up early again tomorrow."

Dawn studied him, trying to read anything in his face, but he was much better at concealing his feelings than she was at discerning them, and he made good on his promise not to accidentally send them magically again.

"All right," she said, yawning. No point arguing while she got more tired, not to mention unfair since he wouldn't. She stood up and turned away from him as she crossed to her bed. "Good night."

"Good night," Dusk said as she got under her covers, then he darkened his glow and flew to the window for the night.

17

Dawn awoke to the first rays of morning creeping in through the window. She rolled over to get comfortable, thinking Sarah would be in momentarily to wake her up like any other day. It occurred to her that there was something odd about the sunrise and she wondered what it could be while her brain slowly turned on.

Wasn't there something going on? Her birthday wasn't until to-morrow, but Alex was supposed to arrive today. Wait, she'd seen him already, because of the... She sat up abruptly as she realized what was strange. The Night Rise, by all appearances, was over as suddenly as it had started.

Muffled voices could be heard from the other side of her drapes as she got up to open them, and she found Dusk speaking to Harpullia outside of her window.

"...the only place we haven't looked is farther south," Harpullia said.

"She knows better than to try the farmlands," Dusk replied. "Send one fairy to make sure, but it would be more practical to double-check the east side of the kingdom."

"Think she'd try to hide right under us?" Harpullia asked. Dusk cocked an eyebrow and Harpullia sighed. "I'll send out everyone I can, with extra effort between Riverglade and the Spikes."

"What's going on?" Dawn asked as Harpullia flew off.

"Morning, Dawn," Dusk said as if nothing were out of the ordinary. "They're looking for Berniece."

There was a knock and Sarah entered. She was less chirpy than usual, slower, and her eyes were dark like she hadn't slept. "Morning."

"Sarah? What happened to you last night?" Dawn turned to her, concerned by her friend's less than cheerful entrance. Even without the positive nature of the sun returning to contrast it, Sarah's mood was the lowest she'd ever seen.

"Nothing!" Sarah said as she crossed to the tub to fill it, avoiding meeting Dawn's eyes.

"Then why weren't you at dinner?"

She offered Dawn a sheepish smile, too tired to make any better effort. "I was in the lab trying to get a spell to work. Didn't notice how late it was until it was time for bed."

"Did you not speak with your father?" Dusk asked carefully, not wanting to upset her more, but trying to keep a focus on the important things. Surely their using the lantern hadn't gone unnoticed by Berniece.

"Nope," Sarah said, grimacing at her own lie. Dawn gave her a look, and she sighed. "Fine, I saw him. He wasn't happy to hear I did magic."

Dawn walked over to her and hugged her. This news, especially on top of Cedric's connection to the Night Rise, would strain even the healthiest of relationships. "I'm sorry."

"For what?" Sarah replied, hugging back. "Whatever he thinks of me being a mage, I know you support me."

"Not to interrupt, but he didn't attempt to contact Berniece again, did he?" Dusk asked, less patiently now.

"No, he didn't," Sarah said as she and Dawn separated. She still wasn't chirpy, but her mood was greatly improved. "What proof do you have it's her, anyway?"

Dusk sighed wearily and stared at the floor, wings slowing. "Unfortunately, it's too irrefutable to be anything else. Diya and I discovered that he's been sending messages to her mirror."

"And how do you know that?" Sarah asked, crossing her arms as her mood shifted down again. The only way he could know that was if... "Did you break into our cottage?"

"The only thing that matters right now is that Cedric used her signature," Dusk said, glaring at Sarah. His wings regained speed and sliced through the air. "Even if by some miracle it wasn't Berniece, there's still someone out there using her mirror. Someone Cedric doesn't want any of us to know about."

Sarah pursed her lips and stared at the wall behind the fairy while her eyes filled with angry tears. Her father wasn't perfect, but who was Dusk to stick his nose in the middle of it? His intentions didn't excuse his actions. She took a deep breath and left, calmly closing the door behind her.

At midday the south gates were open, and Rob jogged along the gravel path to reach them as the Mantrisa carriage rolled through. It came just far enough in that the gates could be closed, and the horses were reined to a stop. A few servants were waiting nearby to unload the luggage, and Rob watched from a few feet away.

Alex exited the cabin first, then helped his wife down, who was carrying a sleeping June.

"Come along, children," Catherine called back into the carriage, and John and Suzie Fairweather hopped out after her, followed by Colonel Woofbottom.

"This is amazing!" Suzie said as she looked around. Her brother seemed equally struck, but was too mature to comment.

Catherine directed them to the servants to get their luggage straightened out, and Rob stepped over to Alex. "How was the journey?"

"Afternoon, Rob," Alex said, taking a moment to stretch his long limbs. "Rather pleasant, actually. Did Dawn send you for the kids?"

"For John," Rob said, nodding, and Alex chuckled. "But speaking of kids, any sign of that mercenary?"

Alex sighed and ran a hand through his golden hair. "They've disappeared. I sent some men to the clearing to watch it, but they haven't returned or left any sign of where they've gone."

Rob scowled, dissatisfied. He'd wanted to hear that the man was in chains and the boy was with some caretakers getting a second chance at his childhood. "And what are you going to do?"

"Nothing," Alex replied, shrugging. As far as he was concerned, everything that could be done had been.

Rob rubbed at the cut on his cheek, still not fully healed. He'd likely never know now what would become of the boy that gave it to him, a fact he couldn't accept.

Suzie and John bounded over, preventing further conversation. Dawn had only asked Rob to watch John, so they waited a few minutes before he gave up and led them both across the grass to the training area next to the barracks, the dog trailing along after. Just when he was wondering if he shouldn't go looking for Dawn himself, she and Sarah approached from across the grounds.

"You brought the Colonel," Dawn said happily. The dog stopped circling and woofed at her, jumping up to lick her face.

"Dawn! You made it," Rob said as he put away the sword he was holding. Sarah made a face at him, and he grimaced back at her. "I was starting to worry I'd be in charge of both of them."

Suzie's hair was in a single braid pulled over her shoulder, and it bounced as she jumped excitedly. "Thank you so much for letting us come! I've been thinking about all the things I want to do! I can't wait to get started!"

"That's wonderful!" Dawn said, smiling at the girl's excitement. "The first thing I have set up for you is to visit Fibrill. She's going to fit a dress for you to wear tomorrow."

Suzie's eyes grew huge and, somehow, she stopped jumping. "I get a new dress?"

"Technically it's an old dress," Sarah said. "It was one of Dawn's favorites a few years ago. Should about fit you."

Suzie felt like she was going to faint. "I get to wear a *princess's dress*?!"

"Yes! Now let's get going so Fibrill has time to work on it," Dawn said. "We'll see you at dinner, Rah."

She waved goodbye and walked off with Sarah and Suzie, leaving Rob with John and Colonel Woofbottom. The dog yawned and made himself comfortable nearby, circling a spot of grass and laying down.

"Would you like to try a weapon?" Rob asked.

"Oh, sure," John said distractedly, turning away from the girls as they grew smaller. He inspected the rack full of practice weapons and chose a wooden great sword, hefting it with both hands. "Do they watch you practice a lot?"

"You mean the girls?" Rob replied as he pulled a long sword from the rack and tested its weight. "Sometimes. They're usually busy with their own things, but Dawn likes to come when she can."

John tried swinging the sword and stumbled forward several steps before regaining his balance. "Do you have a lot of girlfriends? You must get tons, being a knight and all."

"And why would I?" Rob said. He took a moment to set his feet and practiced blocking. "That isn't really the point of the job."

"Well, wouldn't they like you? If you saved them or something,"

John said, squaring off. Rob smirked and prepared for John's attack. Knights were peacekeepers and rule-enforcers, not some fanciful heroes like so many people thought.

"It's not about saving them so they'll like you," he said as he sidestepped to avoid John's charge and turned to jab his sword hilt gently between the boy's shoulders. "It's about protecting anyone who needs it."

John dropped his sword and fell, catching himself with his hands before he hit the grass.

"Ow," he complained, picking himself up and grabbing the sword. "That sounds boring. Maybe I'll be a musician instead. Then I can get all the girls and have fun."

"That's your problem right there," Rob said. He stepped towards John, ready to swing. "Nothing in life is about just getting a girl. There's real purpose in hard work alone, commitment to a worthwhile cause. And any girl that would want a guy who's in it for the wrong reasons isn't worth the time."

"I guess I see what you mean. I don't want Suzie's dumb friends," John said, grimacing at the idea. "But someone like the princess would be cool. Or her friend, she was pretty too."

Rob slowly charged, giving John plenty of time to dodge if he knew how. "Sarah? She's annoying," he said. "But you're right, she's not half bad to look at, as long as she keeps her mouth shut," he added under his breath as he swung above John's head.

John ducked as the longsword came at him and countered with a stab at Rob's waist. "Oh, I don't want a girl that talks too much. Suzie's bad enough."

"Then you don't want Dawn either," Rob said, nimbly changing direction to avoid being struck. "She's got more to say than anyone."

John shrugged and put away the great sword. "Maybe I should take my father's advice and not worry about it yet."

"That's a good idea," Rob said and set his sword on the rack. "Come on, let's find the guys and play some games or something."

John agreed happily and followed Rob to the barracks. Colonel Woofbottom barked as they left and trotted along after them.

Childish squeals of joy rang through the castle halls as Dawn, Sarah, and Suzie exited Fibrill's room. The seamstress had been more than happy to help, and Suzie got through the entire fitting calmly. Once released, though, she went right back to her contagious happy energy.

"That was so much fun! Do you really do that all the time?"

"It's not as exciting as it seems," Dawn said, smiling patiently at the girl. "After the first few dresses, it gets old. What were you hoping to do next?"

Suzie bounced on her heels. "I want to talk to a fairy!"

That was exactly what Dawn would want if she were in Suzie's shoes. "Sarah can check on your room and things while we do that, then it'll be time for dinner."

"I'll make sure everything's perfect," Sarah said. "Would you like an evening bath, or do you prefer morning?"

"Will it be a fairy bath?" Suzie asked, looking up at Sarah with her big doe eyes like she didn't believe her luck.

Sarah smiled sweetly. "That's the only kind we have around here. I'll have it ready for you after dinner, then, and you can have it remade in the morning if you decide to wait."

"Now to find you a fairy," Dawn said as Sarah went off down the hallway, leaving slight impressions on the golden brown rugs. "If you'll give me a moment..."

She closed her eyes and thought about Dusk. This is how it worked before, right? In seconds she felt a shimmer that seemed to pull her—and she opened her eyes and grinned. "This way."

They followed the shimmer through the keep and outside to the north gate. It felt stronger as they left the castle walls and headed to the willows at the river's edge.

"This one." Dawn indicated the oldest tree, whose wide roots reached into the river at a gentle incline, creating a platform for lounging over the water. Dusk was sitting in the middle of a root, weaving a willow frond into a circle.

"And what can I do for you this time?" he asked without looking up.

"I brought Suzie to talk to you, if you don't mind," Dawn said as she and Suzie climbed the roots and settled next to him. "She's got lots of questions."

"All right," Dusk said, assessing the frond. "Just let me finish this. Diya! Time to try it on!"

Dawn looked up and saw Diya swinging in the branches above them. He stopped and flew down, landing in front of Dusk.

"It's looking nice," he said.

Dusk placed the circlet on Diya's head, jiggling it slightly to check it was on firmly. It fit snugly against his forehead. "That should do. Keep it on and let me know if it stays well."

"Are you a fairy prince?" Suzie asked, completely smitten by the lux fairy.

"You could say that, yeah," Diya said. He shook his head quickly, trying to dislodge the circlet. "Feels pretty good, doesn't move much. I'll run around a bit and see how it goes."

"Oh!" Suzie exclaimed, realizing something. "You were the fairies who found Colonel Woofbottom."

"Yeah, that's right," Diya said, grinning. "How is the dog?"

"He's great! We brought him with us if you want to see him," Suzie said.

"I would, actually. Sounds like the perfect way to make sure this thing stays on," Diya replied. He fluttered in the air, giving Suzie a dramatic bow before flying back towards the castle to find his dog friend.

Suzie watched him vanish over the castle wall, then turned to Dusk, ready with questions. "If he's a prince, does that make you the fairy king?"

"Don't take him too seriously," Dusk said, laughing. "We don't have royalty or anything like that."

"Then why does he have a crown?" Suzie asked.

"Because he's special," Dusk said flatly.

"That's really what he chose? A circlet?" Dawn asked, giggling. She wouldn't have expected him to choose such a gaudy thing to keep magic in, and yet it made perfect sense that he did.

Dusk sighed and rubbed his face. "I couldn't convince him to pick something a little plainer. It's a good thing we're going to Kirkjufell because he also wants a pearl for it."

"Well, if you don't have a king, who's in charge?" Suzie asked.

"The Court is in charge, sort of," Dusk explained. "We don't have a strict ruler of any kind. Just a handful of fairies who are older and want to help with decisions that affect all of us."

Suzie considered his answer for a moment. "Are the older ones more powerful?"

Dusk furrowed his brow, not entirely sure how to answer. "Yes and no. In a sense, older fairies have more practice with magic, but we all have relatively the same amount of energy as each other. Linked fairies are arguably stronger because they can share power with each other, regardless of age."

"But I heard that you linked with Dawn," Suzie said, thinking she was onto something. "Does that make you stronger, or weaker than other linked fairies?"

"Neither," Dusk answered as he shook his head no. "The main

thing linking does for fairies is giving them access to magic they didn't have. I'm arcane so in a sense, I already had more power than any linked pair."

"What's arcane?" Suzie asked, scrunching her face a bit as she said the new word.

"It just means I have all seven fairy alignments," Dusk replied, shrugging like it made no difference to him that of the fairies, he alone was arcane. "I was a test of sorts for Nova to learn what he could do with fairies."

Suzie looked confused. "Nova? But he made people."

"Yes, he made people and fairies," Dawn said. "That's why we look so much alike."

"So he just made a bunch of fairies? All at once?" Suzie asked.

"He made two fairies, myself and one other, then later a few more, then a few more again until he worked on humans," Dusk said.

"Wait, so you know Nova?"

"I do," Dusk said, chuckling. "We fairies lived in the Sky Forest with all the second-degree dragons for millennia."

Suzie stared at him in wonder. "So you also know the three Great Dragons?"

"No," Dusk replied. "The first-degrees do not reside on Arrtelagon, being beyond our plane of existence."

Suzie furrowed her brow and turned to Dawn, who smiled.

"He means they aren't made of worldly materials," she explained. "So they cannot exist here. Like how ice can't exist in heat."

"Oh," Suzie said, nodding slowly. It still didn't quite make sense, but at least Dawn's attempt was something she could picture.

"We should get back for dinner soon," Dawn said. "There's time for one more question before we go."

Suzie nodded and considered what her last question should be. "What's the most impressive magic you've ever seen?"

Dusk grinned, ready with an answer to that one. "Aaron Mantrisa raising this castle. He moved a small mountain from the Spikes to here, then shaped it into the wall and buildings, entirely by himself."

"Wow," Suzie said, climbing carefully down from the willow roots. "That is pretty cool. I'll have to tell John."

She bounced ahead while Dawn ambled after with Dusk.

18

Dawn awoke as delicate pre-dawn light filtered into her room. In spite of everything, she was excited for today. She got out of bed readily and went to her window to watch the sunrise.

"Morning, Dusk," she said as she opened the drapes and found him watching the horizon.

"Good morning," Dusk replied.

They watched the sun rise up above the mountains and bathe the world in its golden light. A beautiful sight on any day, but extra special on this very important birthday.

"Thanks for staying the night, just in case," Dawn said, once the sun was too big and bright to look at.

Dusk turned to her, glowing with his usual light and a new affection. "It was no trouble. Rather peaceful, actually, since you were practically asleep before you got in bed."

"Sorry," Dawn replied, grimacing. "I didn't realize chasing a thirteen-year-old for an afternoon would be so tiring."

"You think that's bad, try dragging three almost-eighteen-year-olds through a forest, then one of them through ruins looking for a lantern," Dusk said, chuckling. He stopped smiling after a moment and was quiet. "I'm sorry I didn't tell you what would happen before we linked. It was wrong of me."

It was more than wrong—it was possibly the worst thing Dawn could imagine. But, were the circumstances reversed, could she have given her own life to help Sarah or Rob? Would she have gone to Dusk and trusted him to help, whatever that entailed?

"You need to let me know what's going on before I agree to things. No more surprises, all right?" Dawn said, holding her finger out to him.

"Promise," Dusk agreed and grasped her finger. The touch was comforting, and she sensed a depth behind it that hinted at possibilities she couldn't fathom.

They separated as Sarah knocked and entered.

"Happy birthday!" She jumped on Dawn, hugging her. "Oh, I wanted to be the first to say that," she said with disappointment as she let go and noticed Dusk.

"Good morning to you too," Dusk said, rolling his eyes at her.

Dawn shook her head, laughing. "Don't worry Sarah. He didn't say anything about my birthday yet. You were first."

"Then I also get to give you your first present," she said and pulled a small ivory cloth out of her pocket. "I almost didn't finish it, since we've been so busy the last week."

Dawn accepted the present and looked it over. It was a lacey handkerchief with a pink rose embroidered in the corner.

"It's beautiful. I think it's the best one you've ever done," she said, then showed it to Dusk.

"It's quite skilled," he said, reaching out to feel the cloth. As soon as he touched the rose Sarah had stitched, he raised his brows in surprise. "That's interesting."

"What is?" Dawn asked curiously.

Dusk glanced at Sarah. "Did you know there's magic in this?"

"Magic?" Sarah asked and pointed at herself. "*My* magic?"

Dusk let go of the handkerchief and nodded. "It must have come from you while you made it. It doesn't seem to have any purpose, just raw magic sitting in the threads."

Sarah shook her head. "How did I do it, though? And why?"

"It must relate to your alignment," Dusk said, shrugging. "You'll find magic has a tendency to appear on its own until you learn to manage it."

Dawn ran her thumb over the rose. "It won't do anything, will it?"

"No, it's harmless," Dusk said. "Nothing more than a small capacitor. I did say you could make it as fancy as you wanted when you made your own."

"Well, it matches the dress," Sarah mumbled and went to Dawn's wardrobe. She pulled out Fibrill's latest creation, a pink-and-cream gown with double sleeves, a front-laced corset, and a short train.

"Indeed," Dusk said, glancing between Dawn and the dress.

"I'd better go check on the Fairweathers," Sarah said. "Suzie had a bath last night, but I have a feeling she'll be taking another one this morning."

"She will if I come prepare it for her," Dusk said, smirking. He filled Dawn's tub speedily and met Sarah at the door.

Dawn giggled. "Good luck. She'll keep you for more than that if you let her."

Dusk snorted. "She can't be worse than you."

"Come on, we need to get moving," Sarah said and opened the door. "I'll be back in a bit to help you dress. Oh, and here, it's from Geoff." She reached into her pocket, pulled out a lumpy letter tied with string, and handed it to Dawn.

Dawn waited until the door closed to untie the string and found a bead bracelet nestled inside the letter. The beads were smooth and white, almost pearlescent, but unlike any she'd ever seen before. She fastened it on her wrist—a perfect fit—and read the message.

Dawn,

Finally, time for you to come to me. I made your present, special just for you. I'm sure you're wondering about the beads. You're so smart, you'll notice they're unique. They're bones, bones of things I hunted, things I killed for you. You wear it for me. Wear it when you come, don't forget. Be my good girl.

Geoff

Dawn's stomach turned as she looked at the bracelet, then finished the rest of the letter. The words were jagged and thick, added on after he'd finished and wrapped the bracelet, just before it was sent to her.

Heard you decided to break your promise to me, chose the fairy. I'll give you another chance, but you have to be perfect, can't do anything I don't want again. Don't forget who you belong to.

The letter fell from her limp hand, her eyes glued on her wrist, and the bracelet encircling it. She barely noticed her stomach fully rolling as she knelt to collect the paper. Numbly, she walked to her desk and settled it into the box with all her other letters from Geoff.

By late afternoon, the birthday celebrations were well underway. There were games and contests in the yard, small performances scattered everywhere, and delicious treats for all to enjoy. Dawn was following Suzie around the major dance hall, as the girl was taking in the excitement for the first time.

"Are there really going to be sky fires tonight?" she asked.

"It wouldn't be my birthday without them," Dawn replied.

Suzie almost squealed but remembered who her company was

and stopped herself. "John tells me how good the fairy made ones are all the time since I've never seen them but he has. We tried to use some from Antwerp once, but it didn't go so well."

"No?" Dawn asked, smiling. She'd only ever seen fairy sky fires, but she wasn't surprised anything else would be lower in quality.

"They went off too fast," Suzie replied. "Had too much...black salt or something. I almost didn't get away in time, but Woofbottom was there and he dragged me away before they exploded. That's how he earned his title, you know."

"That was you?" Dawn asked. The story was well known, usually told as a cautionary tale to younger children. Somehow, it wasn't surprising Suzie was the origin.

"So you heard about it?" Suzie deflated slightly.

"What I heard," Dawn said, putting her hand on Suzie's shoulder, "was that you were a very brave girl. I'm glad someone was there to help you."

Suzie grinned and returned to bouncing around the room. They came to the ice sculpture and she stopped for more than five seconds to stare in wonder at the monolith.

"It's so big," she said, craning her neck to see the top. "How did anyone get all the way up there?"

"With a ladder," Dawn said. "Of course, he did have some fairy help."

Suzie gasped. "I wish I'd gotten to see them."

Dawn glanced around the room and spotted Alfonso and Eirwen talking nearby.

"That's the artist right there, and one of the fairies who helped him," she said, pointing them out to Suzie. "We can go talk to them if you like."

"Oh, yes please!" Suzie said and bounced over to the pair.

Alfonso saw them approaching and smiled. "Princess Dawn! Are you enjoying your birthday? The decorations are particularly grand this year if I do say so myself."

"Hello Alfonso, Eirwen. They are indeed," Dawn said. "Suzie was just admiring your work."

"Ahh, and what does the young lady think?" Alfonso asked, turning to give Suzie his full attention.

"It's huge!" Suzie said with wide eyes. "What part did the fairies do?"

"I can show you what we did," Eirwen said and flicked to the sculpture to point out the specific places that were done with fairy magic.

"It's really incredible," Dawn said before Alfonso could protest. "Truly a work of genius."

"As long as you appreciate it, I've succeeded," Alfonso replied, smiling again.

"You couldn't have done better," Dawn said. Some movement caught her eye and she saw the musicians gathering by the stage. "It seems I'll be needed soon if you'll excuse me."

She made her way through the hall and Rob intercepted her just before she reached the stage. He was carrying a little wooden box with a ribbon on top.

"Happy birthday," he said, smiling.

Dawn stopped and smiled back. "Thanks, Rah. You were marvelous today. How many of the contests did you win?"

"Only six," he said. "Would have been seven, but I promised Sean I'd let him win archery."

"Ha! You've never been good at archery," Dawn said, giggling. His form was perfect, but his aim, less so; the arrow would fly straight and true, right past his target. Once, he'd nicked a noble's ear and couldn't go near a bow for months.

"Well, no," Rob said, shifting his weight around. "That's why I let

Sean have that one. Uhm, I've got your present. Raspberry cream truffles, your favorite."

Dawn accepted the box and opened it, sticking her nose inside. "Smells fantastic. Your father's really outdone himself."

"I actually made them this year with his instruction," Rob said. "I thought it would be more special."

"How sweet of you," Dawn replied. She tucked the box away in her pocket and hugged Rob tightly. "Thank you."

"You're welcome," he said softly as he squeezed her back.

"Dawn!" Julia called her from the stage, earrings dancing as she waved. "Time to warm up."

"Be right there!" she called back and let go of Rob. "I'll have to try them after the song. You should wait with Sarah."

"No problem," Rob mumbled, watching her walk away.

The major dance hall sparkled in the fading light as dusk approached, signaling the start of the musical portion of the festivities. A hush went through the room as Julia appeared from behind the curtains. Her piercing blue eyes swept across the audience, engaging each individual as though for intimate conversation. Once everyone was settled to her satisfaction she nodded slowly to the musicians, all but bowing to them, then walked backstage. The curtains slowly opened, and Dawn stepped forward. The lights dimmed as the musicians began to play, their soft melody rising gently from their pit and swirling around and up to the rafters above. Dawn took a breath and started to sing.

"The wind whispers through the willows,
The stream sighingly sings,
As the bumblebee buzzes, and busies
himself,
Gathering his bounty of spring.

Each flower he visits has a flavor,
Each meadow a life of its own;
Such beauty in being, no other can
know,
As intimately as this humble drone.

Fly on, then, little bumblebee,
Fly and live your sweet happy life,
Enjoy the serene and gentle existence
Of a creature without burden or strife."

Once the song ended, Dawn returned to the major dance hall and was immediately accosted by a swarm of people wanting to praise her. She smiled politely and did her best to acknowledge everyone one by one. Dusk reached her quickly, and she sighed with relief.

"Did you like it?" she asked.

"When have I ever not?" he replied, smiling. "Though it has been a while since the last one of yours I heard arranged. Your prose has improved since then."

"I am quite happy with it," she said, blushing. She remembered the day she'd first thought of the poem, how happy she'd been simply enjoying time with Dusk. "Of course, Julia was just as responsible, getting the music perfect to match."

Rob appeared through the crowd, shoving past everyone until he was next to her. "Um, Dawn, would you like to dance?"

"Yes, that sounds nice," Dawn said. "You don't mind if I do?"

"Not at all, go enjoy yourself," Dusk said. "You'll know if I need you."

Rob glowered after him as he flew away, then turned to Dawn and held out his hand, smiling. "Ready?"

Dawn shook her head to settle her thoughts and smiled back. "Yes."

The crowd around them parted as Rob led Dawn to the open floor. He hesitantly put his hand on her waist and she leaned into him. He relaxed as they started waltzing to the music, confidently leading.

"I'll miss this," Dawn said quietly after a few measures.

Rob looked at her skeptically. "I'm pretty sure you'll be able to dance in Kirkjufell."

"Not like this," Dawn explained, looking around them as they turned. "Surrounded by loved ones, spending time with you. We won't get to play anymore."

"You'll come visit, though," Rob said. "And if you don't, I'll come to you."

Dawn sighed and rested her head on his shoulder. "That would be wonderful. We'll both get sick of boats from going back and forth constantly."

"Exactly," Rob agreed. "There won't be any time to miss each other."

Dawn picked her head up as something caught her eye and giggled. "Looks like Sarah found a dance partner."

Rob followed her gaze to where Sarah was swaying with John, both of them holding the other a bit stiffly.

"Good for him," he said, chuckling.

"That's—oh!" Dawn jumped as she felt a shimmer. "Dusk wants me. Once this song is done, I'd better get to him."

Rob frowned. "That doesn't hurt, does it? If he's hurting you, I'll have to do something about it."

"No! No, it's fine," Dawn said. "I'm just not used to it yet. Please, I don't want you to start anything. You fight enough already."

"I'm not the one who does troublesome things," Rob muttered, scowling. "If he behaved better, I wouldn't have to fight."

"You don't have to fight because *I'm fine*," Dawn said, giving him a hard look. "Even if there was something, I can take care of myself." The music paused, and she stepped away from him. "The dance was lovely, thank you."

Rob sighed heavily. "I didn't mean it like that. You know I just want what's best for you."

"Oh, Rah," Dawn said gently. "Of course I know that. Don't worry, he could never replace you. Wherever I end up, I'll need my best friend."

"Good," Rob replied, relaxing. "As long as you don't expect me to like him, I can manage."

"That's fair, though I wish you could be friends. Save another dance for me, all right?" she asked and started walking away.

"Promise," Rob called after her.

The sun was just settling behind the castle walls as Dawn made it outside. She smiled to herself and continued following the shimmer, knowing where she was headed even without Dusk's trail.

In minutes she entered the secluded clearing in the rose garden and saw Dusk waiting for her on the swing.

"You didn't give me very long," she accused him lightheartedly as she crossed to him.

"Sorry, I didn't want you to miss the lighting," he said. "It's perfect right now."

The sky was deepening to navy and the first stars were visible, twinkling brighter by the minute. Over the west wall, the last rays of the sun were vanishing, leaving a sliver of orange in the sky.

Dawn smirked at him. "You mean at dusk?"

"You said it, not me," he said, winking at her conspiratorially.

Dawn laughed. "So why am I here?"

"The roses are blooming," he said.

Dawn followed him to the Heart of Dusk and looked at the

blooms with pure joy. The petals were inky black on the underside, seeming to be nothing but dark from a distance. A closer inspection revealed that the inside of the petals was a deep navy blue that slowly transitioned into brilliant reds, oranges, and pinks. Every rose glittered as if it were covered in tiny stars, as they did at dawn and dusk.

"I may have encouraged them to bloom a bit early for you," Dusk said.

"Thank you," she replied, unable to look away from the roses.

"There's one more thing," Dusk said. He floated above the bush, where she couldn't avoid seeing him. "Pick one."

"Pick one?" Dawn repeated uncertainly. "What for?"

"For your present. Or did you think I wouldn't get you anything?"

Dawn giggled. "I thought showing me the roses was my present."

"It's only part of it," Dusk said, rolling his eyes. "Do you want the rest or not?"

"Yes, sorry," Dawn said and looked over the roses. After several minutes she pointed out a smaller bloom that had particularly vibrant colors and glimmered pleasantly. "That one."

Dusk nodded and put his hands under the bloom to separate it from the stem, then landed on the ground and knelt.

"You can sit. This will be a while," he said. She nodded and sat on the swing to watch him work.

He set the rose down delicately and placed his hands on either side of it. Instantly, sand particles flowed and swirled around the bloom until it was covered by a sphere of grains. The sand turned faster and faster and started glowing red with heat, brighter and brighter.

Dusk watched closely until it glowed white-hot and there were no longer individual pieces of sand. He carefully picked up the still-roiling ball and carried it to the fountain to submerge it. The water hissed and a cloud of steam rose up as the newly formed glass cooled.

Dusk pulled the ball out of the water just before it was completely solid and shaped a small ring in the glass. He dunked it in the fountain again and left it until it set. Once it was ready, he checked it for any flaws and nodded, satisfied it was free of defects. He unwrapped a leather cord from around his waist and strung the pendant.

"Done," he said, flicking over to present Dawn with her necklace. She stared in amazement, silently studying the glass-encased rose for what felt like an eternity to him.

It was perfect. The rose, the fairy, this moment... She wished it would never end.

The last drops of sunlight slowly dripped away, and the pair of them were content to enjoy the warmth washing between them. It flowed back and forth across the link, multiplying their joy to the point of elation.

Eventually, Dawn raised her hands to her hair and pulled it up. Dusk smiled and flew behind her to fasten the cord around her neck. He tied the ends around each other, adjusting the length so the rose rested on her heart, then flew back in front of her. Dawn grasped the pendant with one hand and closed her eyes.

"Thank you," she whispered.

Dusk smiled and looked up at the stars twinkling above them. Almost an hour had passed, and the sun had long since sunk fully below the horizon. "You should get back inside before they send a search party."

"You don't think they already have?" Dawn stood, giggling. "Rah certainly thinks there's something untoward going on."

"Does he?" Dusk said, chuckling softly, and followed Dawn out of the clearing. "I might have to inquire what exactly he thinks is happening."

"He's concerned the link is painful," Dawn explained seriously. "It's getting frustrating that he won't believe me when I tell him nothing is wrong."

"I'll talk to him about it. I don't want him to continue giving you a hard time when it's me he has issues with."

"As long as you keep your temper with him," Dawn said, glancing at him.

"No guarantees," Dusk replied, shrugging. "But I'll try."

Dawn played with her necklace absentmindedly, and the beads on her bracelet clinked as her hand moved, reminding her of its existence.

"That's more than he'll give you, anyway," she said.

"He can be as unhappy with me as he needs," Dusk replied, eying the bracelet as she shook her wrist. "Tomorrow. For now, there's more celebrating to be done."

Once they entered the major dance hall, Dusk left Dawn to find Diya, who was playing with Suzie by the ice sculpture. He hovered nearby, happy to watch his friend have fun.

"Dusk," Alex called, and he turned to see a rather perturbed duke approaching. "I'd like to speak with you privately. It'll only take a moment."

"All right," Dusk said, turning to Diya briefly. "Don't move from here, I'll be right back."

"Sure," Diya said and continued dancing and flipping for Suzie.

Dusk rolled his eyes and followed Alex to a quiet corner of the room. They stopped next to an empty table, tucked behind a fairy fountain. "What is it?"

Alex looked at him hard. "What the hell are you doing with my sister?"

"Nothing at the moment," Dusk answered slowly, not unsurprised by the question, but certainly not in the mood.

"You convinced Diya to help find the lantern for her,"—Alex ticked off the faults on his fingers one by one—"then linked with her, somehow neglecting to mention that doing so will kill you, and now she's sneaking out of her own celebration to be alone with you. I thought I must have been wrong back at the Mansion, but here you are, proving that my hunch was right. You're toying with her, which I can't stand by and let happen."

"I'm not toying with her, and I'm rather offended that you of all people would think I was," Dusk replied crisply.

Alex scowled back at him. "I may have gotten into trouble with girls in my youth, but I never made anyone fall in love with me that I could never be with. She's not some commoner with nothing to lose. We need the protection of the Kirkjufells to ensure our own rule. You can't interfere with her life like this."

"You think I don't realize that?" Dusk asked angrily. Just when he'd reached a decision and was ready to act, here came the older brother to tell him no. "If I could go back and stop myself, I would. I wouldn't have gotten the lantern, wouldn't have agreed to link, wouldn't have fallen in love with her." He sighed and hung his head.

Alex studied him closely, almost sorry for the fairy. "Do you really believe that?"

"No." Dusk raised his eyes to meet Alex's, half-smiling. "I couldn't stop myself if I tried. I'd just fall in love again."

"What are you going to do when she marries Geoff?" Alex asked, shaking his head sadly. "I've got to go rescue my wife, whom I've left alone with the child all evening. I suggest you don't go any deeper than you already are and save both of you from more grief."

Dusk watched him go, then noticed Diya hovering on the other side of the fountain, smirking.

"So he's on to you too," he said.

"I thought I told you to stay where you were," Dusk muttered, flicking past him back into the open room.

"You know I'm terrible at doing what I'm told," he replied as he followed. "I'm kind of surprised he's the first one to figure you out, aside from me, obviously. I'd have bet on her knight."

Dusk snorted. "Robert is too busy trying to prove something against me to notice why he wants to. Besides, I've known Alex his entire life, and he's always been very perceptive."

"Are you going to take his advice?" Diya asked seriously.

"I don't know yet," Dusk said. "I was considering telling her tonight, but he did make some good points."

"So tell her, and let her decide," Diya said. "Just make sure you do it before she leaves, you know? You don't have to be scared. She'll make the right choice."

Dusk spotted Dawn sitting with her friends and laughing, the picture of happiness.

"The right choice for me, maybe," he said to himself. "But is it the right choice for her?"

19

Dawn was woken up well over an hour past sunrise by Sarah shaking her less-than-gently.

"Come on, Dawn. Time to get up now."

"All right, I'm awake," Dawn said and slowly got out of bed.

"I let you sleep through breakfast, but you'll miss Alex going home if you don't hurry," Sarah said, already pulling a dress out of the wardrobe. "The bath is ready. Dusk came in with me earlier to fill it."

Dawn put her hand in the tub to check the temperature and was unsurprised to find it had grown cold. She started to wish it were warmer and felt a tingle run through her arm and out of her fingers. In moments the bath was the perfect steamy warmth.

Sarah noticed the steam as she put a dress on Dawn's bed and squinted. "Did you just heat your bath?"

"I did," Dawn said, pleasantly surprised. "Must be the thermal. Dusk did mention some of the abilities will act on their own when I want them."

"That's convenient. Sure takes out the guesswork of magic," Sarah said. Her arms were crossed, but her voice was teasing. "Maybe I should find a fairy to link with so I can randomly do new things too."

"No," Dawn said, throwing Sarah a stern look. "Don't joke about that. It's not a good thing."

"Then why did you do it?" Sarah asked gently, really not understanding the issue, but picking up on Dawn's distress.

"Because I didn't know it was a bad thing to do," Dawn said, words catching in her throat. "And now I'm responsible for the death of a fairy."

"You're what?" Sarah stared at her wide-eyed.

Dawn rubbed her lips together and pulled her hair over her shoulder, gripping it tightly. It was a hard thing to imagine, and only harder to say out loud. "Apparently Dusk is now tied to my life, which means my death will also be his," she whispered.

"That is pretty awful," Sarah said, relaxing her crossed arms. "But it doesn't sound like it's your fault, especially if you had no idea what would happen when you did it. Dusk or Diya should have mentioned it when they suggested linking in the first place."

Dawn sighed and closed her eyes for a moment. She liked being linked to Dusk—loved it, even—but the cost wasn't something she felt she could live with. Regardless, what was done couldn't be undone, and it wasn't sensible to be angry with herself about it. "I suppose you're right. I shouldn't blame myself."

"Good, now get your bath before it cools again," Sarah said as she headed out of the room. "Don't want to miss saying goodbye."

Once she was bathed and dressed, Dawn made her way to the kitchen and had a pleasant meal with the cooking staff. Everyone smiled and humored her when she asked to heat the leftover porridge herself, and seemed impressed by her use of magic to do so. She ate her porridge quickly, then grabbed some pear slices and hurried to the main entrance of the keep.

After a few paces, Dusk turned into the hallway, and she stopped.

"Dusk! What are you doing here?" she asked, not trying to hide her pleasure at seeing him.

"You wanted to see me," he said, half-smiling as he floated in front of her. "Anything in particular, or did you just miss me?"

Dawn bit a slice of pear and chewed slowly before answering. "A little of both. It was lonely last night without you."

Dusk chuckled. "In that case, Diya wouldn't mind if I kept you company instead. Speaking of him, we should start draining the lantern today."

She nodded, swallowing her pear, and started walking again. "Right after I say goodbye to Alex."

In moments, they made it outside and headed towards the south gates where the carriage was preparing to leave. Many servants were bustling about loading luggage, with Catherine holding a squirming June and overseeing the process. Alex was speaking with the king by the horses as Dawn and Dusk reached them.

"...with no signs of her anywhere else, the Court feels it's the most likely area," Leopold was saying. "And I'm inclined to agree."

"We'll be sure to have as many men as possible searching," Alex said. He noticed his sister and smirked at her. "Now it looks like I've another farewell."

"It was marvelous to see you," Dawn said as she gave her brother a hug.

"Indeed," he replied. "And it won't be long before I see you again. If everything goes smoothly in Kirkjufell, I'll be up for the wedding." He cocked an eyebrow at Dusk, who held his gaze.

They all winced as June shrieked. Alex looked over at his wife struggling to contain the writhing toddler and sighed.

"I'd better assist my wife. Until next time, little sister," he said as he wandered over.

"That'll be you soon," Leopold said, smiling at his daughter.

"Will it?" Dawn replied, watching Alex take June from a strained Catherine and swing her around. As much as she loved her niece, she hadn't really considered having her own children at all. Seeing Catherine's fatigue and Alex's unending effort certainly made it seem a lot of work. Work she wasn't sure she was ready for, or even really wanted.

"That is the goal, is it not?" Leopold asked.

Dawn saw Sarah and Suzie heading towards the carriage and sighed with relief. "I should go say goodbye to Suzie as well," she said, trotting off to meet them. They caught each other a few paces up the path from the carriage.

"Thank you so much for having us!" Suzie said, throwing her arms around Dawn. "It was the most fun ever!"

"I'm glad," Dawn replied, hugging her back. "Hopefully you'll be able to visit again sometime."

"Oh, I plan to," Suzie said, grinning. "John does too. He was saying he might come train as a squire, even."

"That's wonderful," Dawn said. It seemed Rob's time with the boy had gone well, something she'd have to mention to him.

"Dusk!" Suzie squealed as the fairy floated over to them, and he half-smiled.

"It's been a pleasure, Suzie," he said, offering her a bow.

Suzie beamed, then glanced around and frowned. "Is the Fairy Prince not coming?"

"Oh," Dusk said, chuckling. "Give me a moment, and I'll find him. We'll need him for the lantern, anyway."

As Dusk drifted off, Catherine waved Suzie to the carriage and she bounced over. Once the luggage was situated, everyone leaving made one last round of hugs and farewells. Dusk arrived with Diya just in time to see Suzie before she climbed into the carriage. Once she was inside, the horses started on their way.

"So what was that about the lantern?" Sarah asked Dawn as they watched the south gates close behind the carriage. There were still several people milling about, including the king and queen, Rob and a few other knights, and a handful of servants.

"Oh, we're draining it," Dawn said, not sure how much Dusk would mind her sharing.

"Draining it? Sarah asked, surprised. "What are you doing with the magic? You can't just take it out and do nothing with it, can you?"

"No," Dawn said, then sighed with relief as Dusk and Diya floated over to them. "But you'll have to ask Dusk about it."

"Ask me what?" Dusk said, glancing between Dawn and Sarah with concern.

"Sarah is curious about the lantern," Dawn said. "She wants to know where we're putting the magic."

Dusk grimaced and looked at Diya, who shrugged.

"It's going in my circlet," he said casually.

Sarah nodded, satisfied. "One other thing. Why can Dawn use it?"

"What do you mean?" Dawn replied, brow furrowed.

"Because it's spelled by a human to contain fairy magic, shouldn't it absorb your magic? Since you have a fairy alignment?" Sarah asked.

"Did Cedric tell you that?" Dusk asked, scowling, and Sarah nodded. "Of course he did. Well, in most cases you'd be correct, as magical devices generally work based on alignment. The lantern was designed to circumvent the alignment and instead differentiates between fairies and humans by how the magic behaves—that is, whether or not it is self-sustaining."

Sarah squinted at him like she wasn't sure she believed him. "Isn't that harder? Why would anyone do it that way?"

"Sarah!" Rob called as he made his way over to them. "Do you have some time? I could use a hand packing for tomorrow."

"You aren't done yet?" she asked, rolling her eyes as she followed him. "Guess I'd better, then, so you actually get to come."

Dusk watched her leave, sighing as she disappeared from view. He turned to Dawn and offered a half-smile. "Shall we?"

Dawn eyed him as they headed towards the keep, going at a faster pace than he usually set. She glanced behind them and watched Diya floating behind a few meters, clearly in no hurry to work on the lantern.

A minute of silence passed, and they reached the main entrance to the keep. "Why didn't you want to answer Sarah's question?" Dawn asked.

Dusk looked sideways at her as they entered the foyer. "It's nothing she needs to worry about."

"Is it something I should worry about?" Dawn asked. She held the door for Diya, who lazily caught up. "It does sound like it's pertinent to me."

Dusk looked at Diya, who shrugged, and he sighed. "You're no help."

"Am I supposed to be?"

Dusk scowled at him and turned back to the foyer, continuing his faster pace inside. "We can talk once we're working on the lantern."

"Can I ask about other things?" Dawn replied. With Diya around to give his permission, she wondered how many topics she'd be able to broach.

"Like what?" Dusk asked warily.

"I want to know what fairy falling is, and why it was going to happen to Diya," she said.

Dusk froze as they reached Dawn's tower and faced Diya, glaring. "When did you tell her that? And why didn't you mention it to me?"

"Don't know," Diya said, shrugging. "Must have forgotten."

"You're impossible," Dusk muttered, shaking his head.

Dawn looked between them, wondering again what secrets they still had. How much more was Dusk going to keep from her? "Does this mean you aren't going to tell me about it?"

"No, it's fine," Dusk replied and started up the stairs. "I suppose since we have time, and you want to know, we may as well tell you about it."

They arrived at Dawn's room and she opened the door for them.

"Make yourself comfortable," she said as Diya floated around and inspected her things, checking the boxes of letters, the sheets of music, and the journals that were scattered everywhere as she packed.

"Nice place you have," Diya said, choosing to bounce a few times on her bed. "Shame you're leaving it soon."

"You're coming too, remember?" Dusk asked as he settled himself on the desk.

Diya jumped on one of the feather pillows and stretched out, barely filling the center.

"Yeah, I know. I have to watch that thing," he said and made a face at the lantern. "Here." He took off the circlet and held it out, shaking it around until Dawn took it.

In a few moments, Dawn was sitting at her desk, one hand on the lantern while Dusk channeled magic into the circlet. She felt the energy tingle, a little at first, then more and more as Dusk adjusted the amount. It decreased and increased a few times until it settled at a comfortable spot.

"There," Dusk said and relaxed into the flow he'd be maintaining for the afternoon. "Now we can talk. The story starts with the other fairy Nova made along with me, Cosmos."

Diya inhaled sharply and shifted around on the pillow. "Been a long time since I heard that name. Really takes me back."

"Are you going to be all right?" Dusk asked, concerned. "You don't have to stay and listen."

"I'm fine," Diya said. "Go on, I'll make sure you don't get anything wrong."

Dusk rolled his eyes. "All right. Cosmos was a talented arcane fairy with lofty ambitions. He was more skilled with magic than I am, and very persuasive when he wanted to be. I'm not sure what did it, but after centuries of living contentedly, Cosmos decided that he wanted to be as powerful as a second-degree dragon—and he was willing to do anything to achieve it. He started experimenting with magic, trying to get it to work in ways it couldn't, and he spent years among humans, watching and learning about their magic."

"Those were good years for us, without him bossing others around and making you miserable," Diya said.

"But then he came back," Dusk continued. "And he had new ideas for manipulating magic that he was eager to test out. The worst thing he tried was also the last. Do you know about third-degree dragons?"

"Only that they're powerful," Dawn said. "Of the third-degree creatures, they're the strongest in terms of raw magical potential."

"Very good," Dusk said, half-smiling. "A creature aligned to power would certainly intrigue anyone wanting more for themselves, so it's unsurprising that Cosmos quickly set his sights on them."

"He didn't try to experiment on them, did he?" Dawn asked with worry.

Diya snorted. "If only that were all he tried."

"Indeed," Dusk agreed morosely. "What he wanted to do was link with one. That much power, combined with an alignment to make it efficient to channel, would have put him close to second-degree —if he didn't match them outright. Unfortunately, no dragon was interested in linking with him."

"Because they're all too good for that," Diya said, squirming around uncomfortably. "And smart, besides."

"Diya misses them," Dusk said quietly.

Dawn looked sadly at the fairy wriggling on her pillow. "Can't you go visit them?"

Diya lifted his head to shake it. "We can't go to the Sky Forest, and none of them will come to the Realm."

"Which will also be explained," Dusk said before Dawn could ask why. "So Cosmos made a plan to link with a dragon against its will. He convinced Eachann, a fauna fairy, to help him. They selected a younger dragon who tended to spend a lot of time with fairies."

"Safaa," Diya said. "She was the sweetest dragon. Other than Dusk, she was my closest friend."

Dusk looked at Diya and sighed. "Thankfully, she was unharmed. Cosmos's plan was to sneak into her cave at night while she slept and link. Eachann was there to ensure she didn't wake up until it was done. Dragons sleep in groups, so they had to be quiet, and Cosmos couldn't glow or the light might disturb them. Eachann had just set up his spells on Safaa when Diya found them."

"I didn't find them—I followed them," Diya said. He rolled onto his stomach and rested his chin on his crossed arms, sticking his wings in the air and moving them back and forth as he spoke.

"I noticed them heading towards the caves and wanted to know what they were up to. As soon as I got there, Cosmos tried to wave me out, but my light had already bothered some of the dragons, and they woke up. Everyone was furious. The dragons couldn't tell that I wasn't with the other two, and they nearly destroyed the three of us on the spot. It was lucky there were a few older dragons in the cave who were more reasonable. They got the Court and the second-degrees together to decide on a punishment, which ended up being to turn us into humans, and for the rest of the fairies to leave the Sky Forest."

The magic flowing through Dawn sputtered for a moment as Dusk took a deep breath, briefly reliving the past.

"And I convinced them that Diya wasn't involved, despite what

Cosmos claimed," he said. "So only Cosmos and Eachann fell. Eachann was bitter for a while, but eventually, he accepted his new life and moved on to get married and have a family. Your family, in fact, which is why you have a fairy alignment."

Dawn furrowed her brow, not sure how to feel about her fae ancestry. Such a simple reason for her to have the alignment she did, stemming from a complicated history that was so close to Dusk and Diya. Almost as if she were meant to be around them.

"And Cosmos?" she asked after several minutes. "What happened to him?"

Diya sat up and moved off the pillow to the davenport, where he pulled the bed coverings around himself into a little nest.

"I'm good," he said once he was wrapped in the blankets. Dusk watched him for a minute, then faced Dawn.

"Cosmos became Coma when he fell"—he spoke deliberately—"which I believe is sufficient to answer your questions about the lantern."

Dawn felt the color drain from her face as she realized the implications. "So it wasn't by chance that he captured Diya, was it?"

"No," Dusk replied. "Coma blamed Diya, so he chose him. The lantern itself was used because it was Diya's light that was his downfall. Coma was always one for dramatics."

Diya's muffled reply came from the bed. "He was always one for being an ass." Only the rounded tips of his upper wings could be seen, so completely had he buried himself.

Dusk choked back a laugh. "Are you all right?"

The wings vibrated and the mound swirled around until Diya's head appeared. "I'm fine."

Dawn frowned as she thought of something else. "And are we sure he's dead? Not that I don't trust you, but if Berniece is around still, then he may be as well."

"Aaron made sure of it," Dusk said. "He caused the Shaking that destroyed the Academy entirely for that purpose. I personally checked for any sign of him to no avail. If Coma had escaped, he's not the type to lay low for this long."

Dawn felt relief. "I'd rather only worry about Berniece anyway."

"Indeed," Dusk said, half-smiling. "Well, now you know everything."

"You forgot something," Diya said and wiggled around in his cocoon.

"No, I didn't," Dusk replied, lifting his wings and holding them stiffly.

Diya smirked. "You forgot to mention Rose."

"Ah, yes," Dusk said, lowering his wings again. "I did forget her. Rose was a flora fairy who was linked to Eachann. That's how we know what happens when a fairy is linked with a human."

"It's also why you make roses," Diya said, still smirking.

"Speaking of which," Dusk said as he glanced around Dawn's room. "I was wondering where you were keeping the other one of mine that you pressed. Have you already packed it?"

"Oh," Dawn exclaimed, looking away from him. "Well, I don't have it anymore."

"You sent it to Geoff?" Dusk asked, and Dawn nodded. "When?"

"A few months ago," she mumbled, staring at the stone floor under her feet. "When Isabella was visiting him."

"I see," Dusk said, and Dawn felt him draw away from her, into himself.

Hours later Dusk cut off the magic channel just as Sarah knocked and stuck her head in the room.

"Time for dinner," she said as she stepped inside.

"We're ready," Dusk replied and held out the circlet for Diya, who fluttered over and put it on. "Go ahead and try it out, but don't overdo it. It's got a few years' worth of energy, which is plenty to get into trouble with if you aren't careful."

Diya shook his head and the circlet stayed in place. "Still feels the same. Don't worry, I won't do anything crazy."

"All right," Dusk said, looking at him dubiously. "Are you going outside while we eat?"

"Actually, I thought I'd stay here," Diya said and looked at Dawn. "If that's fine with you."

"Oh, well, I suppose so," she said. "Do you need anything before we go?"

"Could you just open the window for me?" Diya flew over to land on the sill. He left his wings up, poised to flick away in an instant.

"I'll just be a second. You two start going," Dawn said.

Sarah bobbed her head once and returned to the stairwell, but Dusk glanced between Dawn and Diya, refusing to budge.

"Go on, I won't do anything," Diya said, daring Dusk to question him.

Dusk narrowed his eyes at Diya, then slowly floated out after Sarah.

Dawn shrugged and went to open the window. Whatever was going on here must not have to do with her. "Anything else?"

"Yeah," Diya said. He flew over to the doorway and stuck his head out for a moment, then returned to Dawn, hovering just above eye level. "Why did you link with him?"

Dawn stared up at him, a mixture of surprised and confused. What sort of question was that? Hadn't he been the one to suggest it? "We wanted to help you, and you had said you wanted us to do it."

"Would you have done it if you knew it'll kill him?" Diya asked. His carefree attitude was gone, replaced by a cold and calculating opponent.

Dawn took her time answering. She would never do anything to harm Dusk, at least, not intentionally. But he wanted to do it, he'd said so, and she was just as incapable of denying him what he wanted.

"It would have been a much harder choice, but I trust him to know what he's doing," she said. "It's no different now than when we were in the Realm. I'll do whatever Dusk thinks is best."

Diya stared stonily at her. "So you did it for him, not me."

"I guess so," she said, glancing down at her necklace. Her strawberry blonde locks fell in front of her face, hiding her warming cheeks. "Should I not have?"

Diya softened, the sharpness in his icy eyes gone. "So we're at an impasse, you and I. We both want him to be happy, but we disagree on how to do it."

"What do you mean?" Dawn asked, furrowing her brow as she raised her eyes to him again.

"Simple," Diya replied. "You give him anything he wants without question, but I work to give him what he needs, even if he resists the idea. Especially if he resists."

Dawn frowned at him, not following his logic. "Are you saying he'd be happier if we hadn't linked?"

Diya stared out the window. "I'm saying he's happiest when I'm happy, and him dying doesn't make me happy." His eyes shifted to her, glinting like they had in the Ruins. "And what about your desires? Is this the outcome you want?"

"Of course not," Dawn said, and her heart thumped heavily.

"Exactly," Diya said, nodding. "You see? He says he wanted to link to give me this"—he pointed at his circlet—"but I don't give a damn about the magic. I only want my friend. He linked for himself, whether or not he knew it then. He knows now."

Dawn sighed with frustration as her heart somersaulted. Was

this about her after all? "Is there a point to this trial? Or are you just teasing me to bother Dusk?"

Diya smiled slowly and laughed. "Fine, I'm done. Just one last question, if you'll humor me."

Dawn raised an eyebrow at him and waited.

"If you didn't link to help me, why did you do it for him?"

Dawn gaped at him, not sure what to say or think of such a question. What did it mean, that she'd done it for Dusk? Because he was her friend and she wanted to help him. But Diya was also his friend, and they had very different views of what that entailed. So what else was there, what other motive for *her* to do it? Nothing came to mind, or at least, nothing she was able to admit to herself.

Diya floated to the window and watched the shadows stretching slowly along the world as the sun set. "You don't have to tell me; I just want you to think about it," he said. "Now, go eat dinner before Dusk realizes how long I've kept you."

20

Dusk woke Dawn up sometime before sunrise. She looked at him through bleary eyes, then blinked and rolled over.

"Not today, Dawn," he said, dragging the blankets away as far as he could without magic and brightening his glow.

Dawn groaned and covered her face with her hands. "I don't want to. Just another minute."

"No," Dusk said. "You asked me to make sure you made it to breakfast on time, so you have to get out of bed now. I've already gotten your bath ready, and it'll grow cold if you take much longer."

"I'll just warm it like I did yesterday," she said, reaching blindly for her sheets.

Dusk blinked at her and pulled the covers farther away. "Good for you, but you still need to get ready now. We're going to Kirkjufell today, remember?"

"I don't want to." Dawn groaned again and buried her face in her pillows.

"Honestly, neither do I," he said, sighing. "But you have a duty to your family to go, and we have the lantern to look after until it's empty. The longer you stall, the harder it'll be."

Dawn sat up slowly and looked at the window. "All right, I'm up. How early is it, anyway?"

"Half an hour or so until dawn," Dusk said. "Plenty of time to bathe before Sarah arrives, then you can be on time for once." He paused and looked her over closely. "Speaking of which, you were quite a bit later to dinner than I would have expected."

"I just took my time getting there, I suppose," she said, yawning.

"Indeed." Dusk raised a brow at her answer. "You're certain it wasn't Diya keeping you?"

"No, he didn't make any trouble," she said, wincing inwardly. He'd have to feel that and know she was lying.

Dusk considered her answer, wanting to give her a chance to be honest. "You seemed preoccupied like something was bothering you."

"I was just processing everything you told me," Dawn tried. That wasn't untrue, at least.

Dusk narrowed his eyes, not buying it. "Whatever he said to you, you shouldn't let him tell you what to think. He's very opinionated but doesn't always understand everything he preaches about."

"You two need to work out your problems on your own and leave me out of the middle of it," she replied testily and got out of bed. She'd finally had enough of everyone else fighting and bringing it to her. Didn't they know she had her own problems? "Now if you'll please excuse yourself so I can have my bath."

Dusk opened and closed his mouth a few times, trying to decide how to respond. Eventually, he stopped and hung his head. "Sorry. The whole situation is hard enough for everyone without us antagonizing each other." He flew over to the door and waited for Dawn to open it for him. "I'll have a word with him. We won't upset you again."

Dawn sighed as she cracked open the door. "No, I'm sorry. He did agitate me, and I didn't want to let you know. But you always know, don't you?"

Dusk smirked. "Now you're learning."

As soon as he heard the door close, Dusk found the nearest window and bolted outside. He raced to the garden and the clearing, where he stopped and glared around the space.

"Diya!"

A rose bush rustled, and Diya poked his head out. "What'd you do that for? I was almost done counting thorns. Now I'll have to start over."

"Would you care to explain what you did to irritate Dawn last night?" Dusk asked calmly. "She attempted to cover for you this morning, which I certainly don't appreciate."

"Did she?" Diya said as he clambered out of the bush. "It's not my fault if she can't handle hearing certain truths about you. And since when did you get mad at me?"

"Since when did you harass innocent humans?" Dusk countered. "Don't think you can get out of trouble with me by shifting the blame. If you're so well-intentioned, you shouldn't have spoken to her in secret. What did you tell her?"

Diya snorted. "She stopped being innocent the instant you decided to help her get the lantern. It's on you that she's involved in our lives, and you're the one refusing to do what you have to. Don't worry, I didn't tell her what you think I did. I wanted to, but she's too loyal to you to have agreed with me yet. Hopefully, the seed I planted instead will take root, and she'll realize which one of us is really looking out for your best interests."

Dusk flicked to the fountain, where he perched on the rim and stared into the water. "You don't understand—it's not like I don't want to. But I've worked to help this family for so long, I shouldn't throw it away now for my own benefit."

"Your benefit?" Diya muttered and flew to sit next to Dusk. "What about mine? You're dragging me away from my home while you spend the rest of your life resenting yourself for loving her. Then one day you'll be gone, and I'll be alone. Forever." He dangled his bare feet in the water, splashing them both with droplets that sparkled in the pre-dawn light.

"Diya," Dusk groaned. "Please. She's intended for someone else. Someone it seems she's set on being with, or she wouldn't have sent him the rose."

Diya pulled his feet out and curled up, holding his knees against his chest. "She doesn't want that life; you know she doesn't. She'd pick you if you asked."

"What I know is that she didn't tell me about it. She didn't want me to find out," Dusk said. There had also been the sensations he'd gotten when she thought about the prince, feelings that were much more positive than Diya implied they would be. "In spite of what you believe, she's made her choice, and it wasn't me. All I can do now is help her get what she wants."

"But is it really what she wants?" Diya asked. "Just 'cause she chose him months ago doesn't mean she wouldn't choose you now."

Dusk looked up at the dark blue sky growing lighter by the second. He had to move forward, regardless of how much Diya pestered him. It was the best thing for everyone.

"I need to go in for breakfast. It wouldn't be very proper of me to help her get ready on time, then be late myself," he said and flicked his wings, rising into the air. "I'll be back to get you as soon as I'm done, and we'll get on the boat."

Diya smiled halfheartedly as Dusk flew away, then stared down at the fountain and splashed his feet again.

"Wouldn't miss it," he muttered.

Dawn stared at the foamy bubbles in her bath and splashed at them absentmindedly. The situation with Diya was getting more complicated, and she couldn't continue pretending she wasn't right in the middle of it all. She felt horrible for not letting Dusk know immediately what Diya had said the night before, but how could she have told him about something she didn't understand? Diya had made it clear that he was angry with her, but it seemed like he thought there was something she could do to change things. And what difference did it make to him why she linked with Dusk? Was it wrong of her to do what she wanted, what Dusk wanted? No, it couldn't be.

She was startled out of her thoughts by Sarah coming into her room.

"Morning Dawn!" she chirped brightly. "Good to see Dusk got you up like he said he would."

"Morning, Sarah," Dawn greeted her a little less cheerily. She reached over to the little table for her towel and got out of the bath.

Sarah frowned as she pulled Dawn's travel dress from the wardrobe, the only remaining garment. "Everything all right?"

"No," Dawn said, sighing. "But I'll get over it."

"Who do you think will be more shocked to see you there on time, Bert or the king?" Sarah asked as Dawn got dressed, hoping to take her mind off whatever was bothering her.

Dawn played along, happy for the distraction. "That's a tough call. If Dusk wasn't in on it, I'd pick him."

"I guess I would too. You be sure to give Bert lots of attention while he's there. Don't want him feeling down," Sarah said.

"It'll be hard for him knowing you and Dusk are staying with me," Dawn agreed, sitting at her vanity. It bothered her to imagine Rob staying alone in Mantrisa while she had Sarah and Dusk to keep her company in Kirkjufell.

Sarah shrugged and grabbed Dawn's hairbrush. "It's the life he chose. But I do hope he finds a way to be happy on his own."

Dawn sighed as her hair was tugged and pulled by Sarah. If only he could stay with them, life in Kirkjufell would be all the more appealing. Living in a place as massive as the Palace was intimidating, but Rob always worked to make her feel secure no matter the circumstances. "I suppose that's the best we can hope for."

Once Dawn was ready, they hurried down the stairs. As they left the northeast tower, they spotted Rob walking down the hall away from them.

"Rah!" Dawn called, and he stopped and turned around, smiling.

"Sarah, what did you do with the real Dawn?" he teased when they reached him. "This is obviously a fake. She's never been on time for anything in her life." He winked at Dawn and offered her his arm, which she gladly took. They reached the dining hall in no time and he opened the door. "Ladies first."

There was still a place for Rob at the high table, and once he and Dawn were seated, only the fairy seat between them remained empty. Dawn tried not to worry about Dusk, an effort her mother proved very helpful with.

"I'm so proud of you, sweetie," Eleanor said, turning and smiling at her daughter once she was settled. "Doing so much for your people, helping with the Night Rise, and now going to Kirkjufell to marry and become queen someday. That's my girl." She leaned over to embrace her daughter.

Dawn blushed and hugged Eleanor back. "I'm just trying to be as amazing as you."

"You'll be wonderful," Eleanor replied, squeezing her shoulders reassuringly. "Just keep your head around Henry and you'll win him over as easily as you have Geoff."

The queen held her close for another minute, then let go and turned away. At that moment, Dawn felt Dusk coming and took a deep breath. Rob watched her with concern.

"Are you okay?" he asked quietly.

"I'm just a little anxious about leaving," Dawn answered. Her eyes darted to the door as it opened and Dusk flew in. He looked at her and she relaxed. The shimmer he sent her was soft and gentle. They smiled at each other as he reached his tiny table.

"Good morning, Robert," Dusk said as he sat down.

Rob glanced sideways at him and just barely managed not to grimace. Lately, it seemed that every time Dawn was unhappy, this fairy was behind it. The current instance was clearly no exception.

"Morning," he muttered dispassionately, and Dusk twitched in annoyance.

Dawn elbowed Rob lightly, hoping to redirect the boys in a more companionable direction. "The chocolates are delicious. Best ones I've ever eaten."

"So you tried them?" Rob smiled shyly. "I can make them for you again. I'll bring you some every time I come visit."

"I won't be able to finish them before you bring more if you do," she said, smiling. So far so good. "I've barely started on them. They're so rich!"

She felt a grateful tingle and beamed. *You're welcome*, she thought and looked at Dusk. He grinned at her and she knew he'd gotten the message.

"Only the best for you," Rob replied, eyes flicking down at the fairy. "I'm glad you're enjoying them."

"Oh, yes. I'm enjoying them very much," Dawn answered, still looking at Dusk. "I'll be happy for them in Kirkjufell especially."

Her heart thumped as it had when Dusk had given her his rose, the first one she'd pressed and sent to Geoff. It occurred to her it had only ever behaved this way—she'd only ever felt like this—for Dusk. Even the time Geoff had kissed her couldn't compare to the smallest of glances from the fairy.

"Ahh, finally," Rob said as servants placed plates in front of them, full of fruit, poached eggs, and sausage links.

Dawn speared a strawberry half and slowly ate it, focusing on the up and down motion of her jaw as she chewed. She swallowed and sliced one of her eggs, letting the yolk spill and spread over her plate. Rob gobbled his sausages, only taking two bites per link, then swallowed his eggs practically whole. He cleaned his plate and gulped his water to wash it all down.

"Are you ready?" he asked Dawn as he set his cup down, making it clatter against his plate.

"Not quite," Dawn said, indicating her half-eaten food.

"If you're done, Robert, I have a job for you," Dusk said. The last morsels of his strawberry were sliced into delicate bites.

Rob looked down at him with as neutral a face as he could manage. "Normally I wouldn't mind, but I promised the king I'd keep an eye on Dawn until we leave."

"In that case, she can come too. Leopold is lending us a chest for the lantern while we're in Kirkjufell."

"Is he?" Dawn brightened, having a guess at which chest. "Is it from his collection?"

"It is," Dusk said.

Dawn smiled and ate the rest of her food with newfound vigor until it was gone. "Let's go."

Dusk chuckled and ate his final bite, setting his silverware carefully on his plate. Rob stood and helped Dawn up from her seat, and they left together.

"So what's special about the chest?" Dawn asked. Everything in the collection was magical and rare, but the mahogany box she was thinking of didn't appear to do anything.

"It's spelled to only be opened by fae magic," Dusk explained as he led the way to the king's rooms.

Dawn laughed aloud, soliciting odd glances from the boys.

"Sorry," she said, blushing. "It's just... I've opened it before. It's too bad I never thought to ask what it did until now."

Dusk chuckled as they reached the royal suite and entered. He flitted over to a door-sized tapestry of a flying dragon and hovered next to it. "Would you like to do the honors?"

"Yes," Dawn said, smiling. She stepped up to a small painting of a fairy next to the tapestry and shifted it aside, revealing a wheel embedded in the wall. She turned the wheel and the tapestry slowly swung inward. It was a narrow storage room, cramped with a couple of shelves holding smaller items, crates full of scrolls, and larger valuables sitting on the floor.

Dusk floated into the room with Rob, and they squeezed through the space, careful not to disturb breakable vases, statuettes, and oddly shaped glass pieces. The fairy led the way to the far wall and hovered over the chest. It was plain in appearance, with brassy hinges and a basic swivel latch. The wood, while of high quality, was only finished with a standard gloss for protection, with no paint or stain to bring out the color.

"It doesn't look very special," Rob said as he tested the weight of the chest before lifting it. His arms fit around it easily, and while it was solid wood, its small size meant it was light enough to carry if a bit cumbersome.

"Exactly," Dusk agreed as they exited the secret room. "Remember what Alex said about the lantern? No one would think anything valuable is in here, and anyone who does will find a nasty surprise if they try to get in."

Dawn turned the wheel back to close the secret door and realigned the painting. She had a thought as she followed the boys out of the suite. "Did it used to be Coma's?"

"Yes," Dusk said as he led them to Dawn's tower. "Aaron salvaged it after the Great Shaking."

"Has the lantern been in it before?" Dawn asked tentatively, not sure she wanted to know.

Dusk slowed, wings going slack as he remembered. "Once or twice. Not very long, but any amount of time was too much."

"So we know it fits," Rob said, oblivious to this newest piece of Diya's misfortunes.

"Indeed," Dusk agreed, chuckling. His wings revitalized, flapping strongly again. "And the sooner we get it back in, the better."

They climbed the tower to Dawn's room and the boys loitered in the doorway as she went in.

"I need to get Diya ready. We'll meet you at the river." Dusk excused himself and wandered off.

Dawn looked at Rob expectantly, raising a brow when he didn't move. "Are you coming?"

"Oh, right," Rob said and hesitantly entered Dawn's room.

He set the chest down by her desk and fidgeted with his fingers, bending and unbending them against each other. Dawn watched him quizzically for a moment, then packed the lantern away in the chest.

"Here you are," she said as she closed the latch.

Rob took the chest again and left the room, relaxing as he did. He stood in the doorway and watched Dawn as she checked for anything that may have been missed. The wardrobe was empty, the bath table clear, and her desk looked lonely and barren without any writing materials.

Dawn closed her eyes and breathed in deeply, putting her right hand on her necklace as she did. She reached into her pocket with her left hand and felt her handkerchief and the chocolate box. Geoff's bracelet settled on her left wrist, the beads bumping into her friends' presents as she tightened her grip. After a final glance around the room, she left, pulling the door shut behind her.

21

The sun shone brightly, playfully bouncing on the ripples of the Claw River and making anyone who looked at the water blink. A triple-decker boat swayed slowly back and forth in the current, tugging gently at its anchor as it waited.

Dawn and Rob stood by the boarding ramp, watching the ship's crew scuttle around. It was past time to board, but Dawn wanted to wait until everyone arrived before getting on. Rob shifted the chest around, starting to tire of its weight when the last passengers finally approached. The fairies appeared over the castle wall and made their way to the river, with Dusk half-dragging Diya, who was trying to go anywhere but towards the boat.

"Sorry we're late," Dusk said as they paused with Dawn and Rob. "Someone wandered off, and I had to go find him."

He glared at Diya, who wrenched his wrist out of Dusk's hold and glowered at his feet. Dusk sighed and nodded his head at the chest. "Robert, perhaps we should get that aboard?"

"Sure," Rob answered, happy with the idea of not having to continue carrying it.

Dusk flicked up the ramp but turned back when he realized Diya wasn't following. "Are you coming?"

"No," Diya said, staring stonily at his friend.

Dusk groaned and glanced at Dawn. "Make sure he gets on, will you?" he said, then flew up to the lowest deck, Rob close behind.

"The chest isn't going to be difficult for you, is it?" Dawn asked once the boys moved out of view.

Diya turned to look at her, his face expressionless. "Why would it be?"

"Dusk mentioned you may have had a bad experience with it."

Diya laughed darkly. "Dusk doesn't know the half of it. The lantern was my permanent prison, but that chest was torture. If I hurt the lantern in an effort to escape, if I talked back or said anything he didn't like, sometimes just when he was angry at something else and wanted to take it out on me, in the chest I'd go. For days, or even weeks. Once for years. I never told Dusk how bad it really was—it wouldn't have helped. What I wanted was for him to forget about what happened and be the same friend he was before."

He eyed Dawn up and down a moment, then looked up at the noon sun above them. "But all my effort went to waste when you came along."

"Dawn!" Sarah waved at her from the top of the ramp. "They want you on now."

"Be right there," Dawn called back, then turned to find Diya had flown off. She looked around anxiously and caught sight of him near the mainsail. Any idea she may have had about what he wanted was ruined now that he'd simultaneously blamed her for everything *and* given her a secret she couldn't pretend she didn't have. She shook her head and climbed slowly up the ramp.

An hour later, the anchor *thunked* on the deck and the boat lurched into motion, slowly moving into the wide river and going up to the lake.

Dusk flicked around the main deck, searching for Diya among the busy crew. There were a few fairies working, and they made

Dusk's search that much more difficult. Every time he noticed fluttering wings, it was an aer fairy helping guide the sails, or a hydro fairy keeping the boat's path clear.

"Dusk!"

He turned away from the prow to see Rob jogging towards him.

"Did you need something?" he asked as the knight came to a stop.

"Well, no," Rob said, shrugging. "I just noticed you and figured I'd check in. I did a quick walk around, and everything looks good."

"Indeed," Dusk replied, cocking an eyebrow. "And did you perhaps want to ask how Dawn was doing?"

Rob sighed and looked out at the water. "She wanted to be alone when I went to see how she was settling. Thought you'd know if she's all right."

"You know her as well as I do," Dusk said. "She's trying to adjust to some of the changes this trip will bring. However she takes to Kirkjufell, she will always miss Mantrisa and the people she's leaving behind."

"Yeah," Rob said, glancing at him and almost smiling. "Just hard being the only one who has to go back."

"If she thought there was another option, I don't doubt she would do anything to change that," Dusk said.

"Yeah? Maybe I can think of something," Rob said. "Thanks, I guess, for the talk."

Dusk watched him head away, then noticed a coiled rope nearby that seemed to be twitching.

"Is that where you plan to stay until we arrive?" he asked.

The rope shifted, and Diya's scowling face appeared from between the coils. "What are you doing with that boy? You know what he's going to do now that you've pushed him."

"Is this why you were hiding, so you could spy on me?" Dusk replied, half-smiling. Leave it to Diya to meddle where he shouldn't, then get mad when Dusk tried to clean up his mess. He settled himself on top of the rope and looked down at his friend. "He shouldn't be stuck regretting that he never took the chance when he could."

"But it's all right for you?" Diya said, his voice sharp. "And what if she accepts him? What're you going to do then?"

"Be happy for her," Dusk answered. "She does care for him, and it would be a shame for him to return alone while Sarah stays."

Diya sighed and crawled out of the pile, still scowling. "Doesn't make you less of a hypocrite."

"What would you have me do, tell her I love her and I don't want her to be with anyone else?" Dusk asked and shrugged. "Put my own desires first?"

"Yes," Diya answered, looking hard at his friend. "Exactly, yes. If you put yourself first for once, we'll all be happy, but you're so damn determined to do what you think is necessary you can't see that."

Dusk shook his head. "Not everyone will be happy. How do you think Leopold would take such interference from us?"

Diya snorted. "Really, I thought you'd realize how good it will be for them too. You don't see the political value of going through with it? Leopold won't be happy about the Kirkjufells, but do you think he'll gain nothing?"

"Installing his daughter as queen of the richest kingdom in the world is far more valuable than any benefit I may theoretically provide," Dusk argued. "And you're forgetting the lantern again. Keeping it in another kingdom, away from Berniece, is highly opportune for us."

"I'm not forgetting; I just don't care," Diya said, glowering. "And the fact that you don't get that no matter how much I say it is frustrating. The only thing I want is for it to no longer be something you're hung up on."

Dusk glared down at Diya. "It would be a problem for everyone, including you if Berniece got her hands on it."

Diya glared back, his wings twitching in irritation. "I'm not saying it wouldn't be, but this isn't the only solution. Besides, even with that thing, she'd be no match for you."

"But why give her the chance to prove it in the first place?" Dusk replied, his own wings poised for striking. "Regardless of other possibilities, we've already started this one."

"Really?" Diya smirked and his wings relaxed behind him, settling into a transparent cloak. "Then why'd you give her that necklace?"

"It was for her birthday," Dusk answered tiredly. "It happens to be her favorite rose, and I thought it made a nice gift."

"It'll make a nice convertor too," Diya said. "You know better than I do what it'll require to set it up, and you gave yourself everything you need to do it."

"That was before I knew she already chose Geoff," Dusk answered. His wings fell as he curled into himself, wrapping his arms around his legs and shrinking into a ball. It was a lose-either-way situation. Don't do it and leave Diya alone forever, or do it even though it wasn't what Dawn wanted, keeping him alive but miserable with himself. "Of course, if we did decide to do it, I'd only get one attempt. What would you do if I failed?"

Diya flew up to sit next to Dusk and kicked his feet against the rope as he leaned on his friend. "I'd just be glad you tried."

Dawn stood at the back of the boat, watching the sun as it slowly crossed the sky and proceeded closer and closer to the horizon. She was joined by Dusk and Diya, who came up silently and landed on the railing next to where she was leaning.

"We'll be reaching the lake in about an hour, then it'll be time for dinner," Dusk said.

Dawn sighed. "And then I'll go to bed, and wake up in my new home."

Diya looked at Dusk expectantly, then rolled his eyes and turned away when Dusk didn't react. Dawn pursed her lips at the exchange and looked at the water beneath them.

"Dusk, I'd like to speak to Diya alone, if it's all right with you," she said.

"If he promises to behave himself," Dusk said and raised an eyebrow at the lux fairy.

"Sure, I'll be good," Diya replied, staring Dusk down.

Dusk rolled his eyes and wandered away. "I'll know if you aren't."

"So what does the Fairy Princess wish of me?" Diya asked mockingly once they were alone, sitting down next to her.

"I was wondering something," Dawn said and looked him in the eye. "You seem so unhappy that I linked with Dusk—why did you suggest it in the first place?"

Diya inhaled through his teeth and shifted his gaze to the horizon. "You won't believe me if I tell you the truth."

"Try me," Dawn said, making him laugh.

"You're pretty funny, you know that?" he said, smirking. "I was just messing with Dusk. I knew bringing up linking in front of everyone would irritate him."

"And you're certain that's the only reason?" she said.

Diya leaned back and looked up at the sky and the stars that were just becoming visible. "I wanted him to realize what he wanted and go for it, or just kill the idea for good. Unfortunately, my plan backfired and made a bigger mess instead." His eyes moved to Dawn as he spoke. "I didn't account for you wanting to involve yourself in my affairs."

"I can't help that your affairs got mixed up with my life," Dawn said, her gaze back on the sun as it just touched the river. "Dusk does what he wants, and he wants this."

Diya snorted. "Now you're starting to understand him. I just hope you figure it out in time."

"Figure out what?" Dawn turned to look at him but he was gone, floating off after Dusk. She stared out at the water again.

Why couldn't he have never said anything about linking in the first place? However she thought about it, it made no sense that Diya would want it. He'd only been telling her constantly how angry he was to be losing his friend. The bigger question, though, was why Dusk decided to. There was something important that neither fairy was sharing with her, and all she wanted to know was what it could be.

A few minutes later she heard footsteps and turned to see Rob approaching. She smiled at him and invited him to join her at the railing.

"How was your patrol?" she asked.

"Great," Rob answered, taking in the pre-dusk light and the sparkling water beneath them. "No problems of any kind."

If only the same could be said for her. "And you'll keep it that way, I'm sure."

"I'd like to," he replied softly. "In fact, I'd like to do more than that."

"Oh? Like what?" she asked curiously, glancing over at him.

Rob cleared his throat. "I want to be with you, helping you, keeping you safe, whatever you need. Forever."

Dawn's smile melted away and her stomach rolled uneasily. "What do you mean, Rah?"

"I mean, I want to give you a chance to have what you want, and so..." Rob stepped away from the railing to get down on one knee and took her hand, holding it gently between his. "Dawn Mantrisa, will you marry me?"

"Will I..." Dawn tugged her hand, but he held on firmly. Something wasn't right about this—he wasn't acting like himself. "Rah, you can't be serious."

"But I am," he said, eyes smoldering with the same intent they had all his years as a squire, striving to do what he believed in. "I'm sorry I waited until now to do something for you, but it isn't too late to go home, be where you want to be. You have a choice, a chance to live the right life for you."

"You're so sweet," she said, smiling as she carefully removed her hand from between his. "But you're wrong. I don't have a choice. I never have. Kirkjufell is where I'm supposed to go, and Geoff is who I'm meant to be with."

"No!" Rob stood and pulled Dawn close to him, holding her protectively. "Your life matters. You matter. I haven't spent my entire life trying to show you that to have you feel like this. So will you listen to me, to your heart, and stay in Mantrisa?"

Her heart? Her heart was telling her that she should stay in Mantrisa, yes, but it was also telling her something else. Something she couldn't have, someone she wanted more than anything. Had Dusk been the one to ask her to stay, she wouldn't have hesitated, and would have agreed without a second thought. But he knew as well as she did that there was no point to it. There was only purpose in Kirkjufell, in marrying Geoff.

"I wish I could," she whispered and buried her face in his shoulder. "I really wish I could."

"So I've wasted my life," Rob said as he released Dawn. "All my effort for you, the time we've spent together, for nothing."

"Rah," Dawn said, reaching up to touch his shoulder, but he shrugged her off.

"No, don't," he said dejectedly. "I don't need your sympathy." He sighed heavily and left without another word. Dawn watched him go and rubbed at the stinging in her eyes. She pulled her hand away and found it was wet with tears.

"Are you all right?" She heard Dusk's voice and laughed.

"You know the answer to that," she said as she dug in her pocket for her handkerchief.

"I do, but I'd still like to hear it from you," Dusk said gently.

Dawn dried her eyes and glared at him, hovering next to her so calmly as if her life wasn't falling apart around her. "I'm doing quite terribly, as you can see *and* feel, I'm sure. What's wrong with everyone today?"

"We're all on a journey we'd rather not be part of," Dusk said. "Though it seems to be hitting you the hardest."

Dawn shook her head and blew her nose. "It feels like everyone wants something of me, but no one is telling me anything. Yet I'm apparently expected to go along with it all without any time to consider it, or talk to anyone else, and I'm just so frustrated."

"Well, I'm here. Talk to me," Dusk said. He landed on the railing and looked up at her, waiting.

Dawn laughed. How simple he made it seem, how easily fixed. If only she could believe him. "You're just as bad, you know. Diya keeps putting ideas in my head that make me doubt if you're keeping your promise."

"Which promise?" Dusk frowned.

"That there won't be any more surprises."

"Oh," Dusk said, grimacing and looking away. "That one."

Dawn stared at him closely, trying to read his thoughts since he wasn't sharing. "Yes, that one. It isn't something bad, is it? Though I don't know what could be worse than what you've already done."

"It's nothing," Dusk claimed, shrugging. "Diya just likes to make trouble, and he's angry that he'll be losing me in what's a relatively short amount of time. He doesn't want to blame me for anything, so he's projecting all of his problems on you."

"So I'm just his scapegoat," Dawn said. She fiddled with the hand-kerchief, wiping at her eyes one last time before putting it away. "If he needs to hate me to be all right with what's going on, that's fine. It just seems like there's more to it than either of you are saying."

"Now isn't the time to worry about it," Dusk insisted, only proving her right. "You have a prince to marry and we've got the lantern to drain. Diya's holding onto an idea that can't happen, but he'll push until the window for it closes."

Dawn sighed. *There* was that important thing they weren't telling her. But had she really expected Dusk to tell her? He'd shared a story or two about the past, but when it was something in the present, he didn't say a word. "But why won't you tell me? I'm sick of only finding out what's going on after it matters."

"I don't want to force you to make a decision that isn't only about you," Dusk replied. "You shouldn't be stuck regretting it, whichever way it goes."

Dawn looked at him, his posture relaxed, but his wings flicked almost imperceptibly. Magically he was keeping his feelings hidden, only serving to assure her there was something to hide.

"Do you regret it?" she whispered. "That we aren't doing whatever it is?"

"No," Dusk said, shaking his head. He stared into her eyes for a minute, then sighed. "Yes. I'll never stop fighting with myself about it because I want it. But there are other things going on that are more important than me, and I have to see them through. By the time they're done, we won't have this option anymore."

Dawn's expression hardened. "So you're just going to regret it by yourself? Without me?"

"There's no reason for us both to suffer," he said, a firmness in his glance.

Dawn watched the sun dip itself into the river and vanish, bathing the world in the usual darkness of night.

"I want to go rest for a while. Think anyone will mind if I skip dinner?" she asked, turning away from the stern.

Dusk half-smiled. Only his gentle glow remained, and he brightened it for Dawn to walk across the deck to the stairs. "I'll have some food brought to you. Do you want company, or would you rather be alone?"

"I don't know. Both," Dawn replied after some consideration.

"Then I'll stay with you, but we don't have to talk, or even look at each other," Dusk said.

Dawn took a deep breath and sighed. "Sounds perfect."

22

"I'm going to kill that fairy," Rob said as he stomped down the hallway to Sarah.

"What'd Dusk do now?" she asked tiredly. She'd just gotten Cedric to sleep after putting some broth in him and had been hoping to relax a bit before dinner. Her father was notorious for getting seasick just looking at water, and it took all of her skills and energy to nurse him constantly.

"That bastard set me up, that's what," Rob went on obliviously, following Sarah as she headed to her cabin. "He's nothing but trouble, and we'd all be better off without him."

"You realize if you kill him, Dawn will die too," Sarah said as she opened the door. "Has to do with the link."

Rob strode in and sat down on her bed, throwing his hands in the air. "Well, that's just great."

"It's what it is," Sarah said, shrugging. "Now are you going to elaborate on this wrongdoing, or do I have to just blindly believe you?"

"Never mind," he grumbled, feeling much less like talking about it suddenly. "It's nothing."

"Really," Sarah said, arms crossed as she stared down at him.

"Yes, really," he replied, glaring back at her. "Did you bring your cards? I could use a game."

What he could use was the distraction, but Sarah felt the same way and obliged. In moments, they were sitting on either end of the bed with the cards piled between them. They took turns placing cards down, occasionally slapping the pile and adding it to their hands.

"So, how's Cedric?" Rob asked after a few rounds.

"Fine, I guess," Sarah said absently as she straightened her over-sized hand and started a new pile.

Rob watched her carefully for a moment before putting down his next card. His hand was significantly smaller. "Are things going all right with him?"

"You mean the spying?" she replied sarcastically. The additional job the fairy had given her certainly didn't help things, but she had other issues. "It's not going great, but that isn't the problem."

They were quiet for a few more rounds of placing cards, focused on the game. Soon Rob placed his last card and Sarah collected the pile.

"Want another?" she asked as she shuffled, watching the cards bridge and fall together.

"It was my fault," Rob said, also watching the cards.

"What was?"

"In the forest, when we got into that fight. It's like the fairy said: I didn't catch the signs like I should have."

"Oh Bert," Sarah said, rolling her eyes. He was so melodramatic she couldn't help teasing a little. "At least it isn't *stopping you from being a knight* or something."

"What?" Rob furrowed his brow in thought while Sarah dealt the cards out. "Are you still having issues using magic? I thought it was supposed to come naturally once you realized you could."

"My father doesn't want me to be a mage, apparently," she

answered, setting the last few cards down roughly. "Doesn't think it's safe."

Rob snorted as he grabbed his new hand. "Well, too bad for him. It's your decision what you do with yourself."

"Because you're one to talk," she replied, smiling. "But thanks."

Cards were placed, slapped, and picked up over and over. Rob watched Sarah more than the game and soon lost a second time.

"Much as I'd rather blame the fairy, you know what really was my fault?" he asked while Sarah shuffled again. She looked up at him curiously. "I proposed to Dawn, so she could stay in Mantrisa. She said no."

Sarah dropped the cards and laughed. "Oh Bert," she said, shaking her head while her body shook with mirth. "You are such an idiot."

Once her breathing was under control, she reached down to pick up her cards. They glowed maroon as she touched them, and she jumped back in surprise.

"See?" Rob said, grinning as he picked the cards up and handed them to her. "You were made to do the magic stuff."

"Maybe I was," she said softly, watching the glow flicker and fade away.

Sometime after dinner started, Dawn let Dusk out of her room to acquire a plate for her, leaving the door cracked open for his return. She curled up on the velvet loveseat and wrapped herself in a light blanket, still feeling down after the day's events. Moments later she was interrupted in her moping by an uninvited guest.

"Having a nice evening?" Diya asked, looking over her appraisingly and smirking.

"What do you want now?" Dawn returned testily.

Diya flitted over and landed on the loveseat, lying down at her feet and stretching out. "I was curious how things went with that boy of yours, and by the looks of it, you didn't accept your consolation prize. Good for you."

Dawn frowned. "My what?"

"You know, your knight," Diya answered, rolling over onto his stomach. "Dusk sent him to you hoping you'd keep him and be happy, at least as happy as you can be without Dusk. But really, I should thank you for rejecting him. One less excuse Dusk can make."

"What are you talking about?" Dawn sighed. Why couldn't he leave her alone to wallow in her misery? "He wanted Rah to do that? Does this have something to do with that idea of yours?"

Diya grinned. "He mentioned it, did he? Still didn't tell you what it is though. He's trying to give himself more reasons why he shouldn't do it. 'Look how happy she is, she's better off, it's what she really wants.' But it's all lies. He knows neither of you will ever be content with things like they are now."

"He said he'll regret not doing it, but it's better if we don't," Dawn replied, trying to convince herself, more than Diya, that Dusk knew what he was doing. "Anyway, I don't have the ability to choose anything else, especially when I don't know my alternatives."

"You don't have to know your choices to realize this is the wrong one," Diya argued.

"What's the wrong part?" Dawn asked irritably. Kirkjufell was the one right thing she was doing; the thing she'd been working towards her entire life. How could she be wrong to choose it, to choose Geoff and becoming a queen? "Because it seems like I'm doing what other people want, and whatever I don't do will be wrong in some way."

"Yeah? You're still ignoring what you want, or didn't you figure out what that is yet?" Diya asked.

"You mean that I want Dusk to be happy because I love him," she said. There it was—she loved him, she did. Crazy as it was, a human in love with a fairy, the only thing crazier would be a fairy in love with a human. She glared at Diya, daring him to push her further. "Satisfied?"

"Very," he said, grinning. "But the real question is are you able to watch him suffer alone? Or can you deny him what he thinks he wants so that he can have what he needs?"

"It sounds like I can't get it right no matter what I do," Dawn said.

Diya sat up and shrugged. "It might look that way now, but when you know what it is you'll understand."

"Then why don't you just tell me? Instead of giving me this run around again and again?"

"You'll find out after you make the right choice," Diya said. How very mysterious, and entirely unhelpful.

"Glad you're confident in me," she muttered.

"Dusk might be an idiot but he picks good people. I wouldn't be so insistent except we've got no time to do it, so we can't wait for you to reach the answer on your own."

"So you think I'm smart, but slow," Dawn said. Just how long was this timeframe? What did it correlate to?

Diya smirked. "I didn't say that. But if that's how you want to feel about yourself, I won't disagree."

"Well, he thinks we have a lot in common," Dawn said, grinning. "So what does that say about you?"

"That I'm intelligent," Diya said. "Which you'll see for yourself soon enough."

"What will she see?" Dusk asked as he came into the room.

He was followed by a crewman who carried a plate with soup and bread. The crewman set the plate down on the table next to the loveseat, then bowed and left quietly.

"I was just giving her my sympathy," Diya explained casually.

Dusk raised an eyebrow at him. "We both know you don't have any of that."

"Maybe not," Diya said and shrugged. "But at least I don't have any self-imposed torment either."

Dusk sighed and rubbed his forehead. "Would you like me to get rid of him?"

"Do you want him removed?" Dawn asked. Some of this really had nothing to do with her, and she was starting to pick up on the moments like that—now, for example.

Diya laughed and flitted up into the air. "Don't bother yourselves. I'll go." He floated to the door and paused, turning back. "Do try to have a nice time, while you still can," he sneered and left.

Dusk shook his head slowly. "He'll get over it eventually," he muttered, and Dawn thought she felt an *I hope* at the end. "He didn't bother you again, did he?"

"No more than usual," Dawn answered and started on her soup, scooping up some potato and celery. "He did refer to Rah as a 'consolation prize,' which I find a bit offensive."

Dusk joined her on the loveseat, taking the space Diya had vacated. "That's rather insulting, even for him."

"He thinks you provoked Rah to action," Dawn said as she dipped her bread in the creamy broth.

Dusk winced. "He isn't incorrect. I thought it was best for Robert and you if he realized things before you're married."

"While I agree with that, it isn't right of you to manipulate him," she said. "Especially if you did it for your own benefit, like Diya implied."

"My benefit?" Dusk scowled at nothing. "Nothing I'm doing is for my benefit. Everything is for Diya like it's always been."

"Well, he's made it perfectly clear he doesn't want what you think is best," Dawn said as she poked at the soup, not sure herself which fairy she agreed with. "And he's very keen for me to help him stop you."

"Do you trust me?" Dusk asked, looking at her pleadingly. It was an unusual expression for him.

Dawn swallowed and lowered her spoon. "Of course I do."

Dusk smiled, but it didn't reach his eyes. "Good. Then promise you won't let Diya get to you. He won't be an issue much longer, and we can all forget about this if you can hold out until then."

"How much longer?" Dawn asked.

"Promise me," Dusk insisted, holding his hand out to her.

His eyes gleamed, the same strange gleam she'd seen in Diya's in the Ruins, a gleam she couldn't refuse in Dusk. She held out her finger and touched it to his hand. "I promise."

Dawn was just setting her spoon down in the empty bowl when there was a knock on her door.

"Dawn?" Sarah said as she opened the door slowly, peering into the cabin like she wasn't sure she was welcome.

"Sarah!" Dawn exclaimed happily. "Come to say goodnight?"

"I just wanted to check on you before I went to bed," Sarah said and sat with Dawn on the loveseat. "Bert and I missed you at dinner."

"Oh," Dawn said, drooping. "How is he?"

Sarah glanced around the cabin and spotted Dusk over by the portholes. "He's better now, but he was pretty messed-up when he came to see me."

Dawn groaned and pulled her blanket over her face. "I'm a horrible person."

"You are not. If anyone can claim that title, it's him," Sarah said and nodded at Dusk.

Dusk sighed heavily and rolled his eyes. "Regardless of what he may have said about me, I had good intentions."

Sarah shrugged. "Fine, but if you harass Bert again, we'll be having a little chat."

"Wonderful," Dusk muttered, making both girls giggle.

"Well, I'll let you get to sleep," Sarah said. She gave Dawn a hug and left the cabin, leaving the door open for Dusk.

"You don't really mind her, do you?" Dawn asked as she got up. She moved to her travel trunk and pulled out her nightdress.

"Not at all," Dusk answered and fluttered over to the door so Dawn could change. "I'm glad you have her—she's a good friend to look out for you."

"The same could be said for Diya. I'm rather sorry for him that you'll leave him someday," Dawn said as they met in the doorway. Really, it wasn't fair to any of them, what would happen to Diya. The lux fairy had been through so much already; he didn't deserve to lose Dusk forever.

"I am too," Dusk said quietly, his feelings so strong he barely kept them from Dawn.

"But you're doing the right thing," Dawn said, and for an instant, she thought she felt guilt.

"Yes. It's the right thing," he said as the door closed behind him.

23

Dawn was woken up at what seemed like noon if the light coming in from the portholes was anything to go by.

"Dawn! You need to see this," Dusk said as he shook her shoulder.

"See what?" Dawn asked sleepily. She was strangely tired for it being noon.

"Up, now!" Dusk demanded, pulling her blankets away and grabbing her hand. He attempted to drag her but only succeeded in lifting her arm.

"I'm coming, just let me do it, please." Dusk let her go and she got out of bed as quickly as her tired limbs allowed. "So what is it?"

Dusk flew to the east-facing porthole. "Come look."

Dawn yawned and shuffled over. She pushed the glass open and stuck her head out. "It's the sun. Now can I get some more rest?"

"Look again," Dusk insisted, pointing at the horizon.

Dawn looked where he was pointing and squinted. She rubbed at her eyes and looked again.

"What's going on?" she asked fearfully. From up in the sky came the intense light of a noon sun, while behind the mountains was the light pink of approaching dawn. Dusk flew over to the table where Dawn had left her necklace for the night—it was sparkling.

"It would seem the Kirkjufells are currently experiencing the opposite of our Night Rise," Dusk explained. "Get dressed and come out to the main deck as fast as you can. I don't know how she'd manage this, but I think we might not be rid of Berniece yet."

A few minutes later, Dawn made her way to the prow and found Rob standing guard, facing the water. She looked around for anyone else and only saw a handful of crewmen nervously going about their work. After a final glance, she resigned herself and walked over.

"Morning, Rah," she said sheepishly as she reached him.

"Ahh, morning, Dawn," Rob stammered and turned away from the prow. "Good to see you up. Sarah is checking on Cedric, then getting some food for us, and Dusk is talking with the captain." He gave his report mechanically, grateful to have something to focus on.

"Thank you," Dawn said. The real sun was barely above the peaks. Just out of view above her was the strange, artificial sun. It seemed whatever Berniece was planning involved them reaching their destination. She fiddled with Geoff's bracelet for a moment before remembering what it was and stopped. "Rah, I was thinking."

"About?" Rob asked warily. At this point, he had no idea what was going on in her head.

"Well, it looks like I'm going to be in danger no matter where I go, as long as I have the lantern," Dawn said. Rob nodded, and she continued. "So maybe I should have someone to protect me. Someone I know I can depend on, who's always been here for me."

"Are you saying you want me to stay with you?" Rob asked, both excited and worried to hear her answer.

Dawn looked at her feet, not sure she should suggest what she was about to. Rob would want to, she knew, but was it fair to him? But was it fair not to, to make the choice for him by never saying it? "Maybe, if you wanted, you could swear fealty."

Rob lifted her chin so they were staring into each other's eyes, then knelt and pulled his sword out, holding it across his raised hands. "Dawn Mantrisa, I offer you my blade, that I might serve and protect you until my last breath."

"I gladly accept your offer," Dawn replied, smiling as she took the sword. "I declare thee Sir Robert Millner, sworn knight to myself, Dawn Mantrisa, the Fairy Princess."

She placed the tip of the sword on his right shoulder and moved it to his left. He smirked at her as he stood and she handed the sword back. "Fairy Princess?"

"It seemed the most accurate title," she replied, blushing. "Once Father comes for the wedding, I do expect you'll explain things to him."

"Of course. And *you* get to tell Sarah the bad news," Rob said.

"Bad news?" Sarah asked as she approached. She was carrying a tray of fruit, bread, and hard-boiled eggs for their breakfast.

Rob grabbed a chunk of bread and took a big bite. "What, no meat? I've sworn fealty to Dawn, so I'll be staying in Kirkjufell."

"Are you?" Sarah replied, eyeing him like she wanted to smack him but couldn't with her hands full. She noticed Dusk approaching and held out the tray. "Want some breakfast?"

"No," Dusk answered and stopped next to Dawn. "The captain didn't know anything—the boat hasn't gone to Kirkjufell for a few weeks but the crew had some information. It seems this started the same day as the Night Rise."

"That doesn't make any sense," Dawn said, frowning. "Surely we would have heard something from Henry if that were true." Ill-mannered as her mother implied him to be, the Kirkjufell king would have told Leopold what was going on, wouldn't he?

"Enough men confirmed the date to prove it," Dusk replied. "And even if they didn't, there was word from a passing fishing boat earlier this morning."

"Is it possible it's just a coincidence?" Rob asked. "I understand it looks bad, but we don't have all the facts."

"We can hope that's all it is," Dusk replied. "But I doubt we'll have room to think so once we learn more."

They went quiet as a bell rang to signal they would be docking soon.

The last wisps of morning fog reached towards the lake city, desperately trying to penetrate their usual playground. It was unobtainable since the coming of the artificial sun. The city of Kirkjufell sprawled around and on the lake, made up of floating bridges and houses, and boats that drifted around, under, and even through buildings. Mixed in with all the water-based commotion were a variety of goats being herded, shipped on special barges, and walked on leads like dogs.

A decent crowd had gathered at the docks to see the princess arrive, clogging bridges and waterways alike. A pair of palace guards shoved through the onlookers, forging a path over the lake to the palace. They wore heavy, dark grey cloaks embroidered with bright colors to represent the palace. Rob walked in front, carrying the chest, followed by Sarah and Cedric, the latter of whom was limping along with difficulty. Dawn brought up the rear with Dusk and Diya, all three smiling and waving at the enchanted onlookers.

Travel through the city was difficult with so many people pushing past in the limited walking space, and the guards shoved at the crowd with the blunt end of their spears. Every movement on the water made the bridges rock and sway in time. Adept locals kept their footing, and Rob managed well, but the others went slowly, almost shuffling to maintain balance.

The guards reached a cross-bridge and halted the procession to allow the path to clear. A herd of goats had gotten spooked and scattered everywhere, and many people were scurrying after them with minimal success at rounding them up. Dawn took the opportunity to look around the city and noticed something.

"Don't we know him?" she asked Dusk quietly, nodding to the right. Sitting at a boat tavern the next bridge over was a man in a trench coat.

"We certainly do," Dusk replied as he glanced over. "Interesting he'd end up here, though perhaps fortuitous for us." He flitted up to check how the goats were coming, then floated back down to eye level. "Diya, you let us know if we start moving, all right?"

"No problem," Diya answered and waved them off.

They pushed through the crowd and crossed a small patio to the boat tavern—thankfully anchored to the lake bottom—which Dawn was relieved to find was more stable than the bridges. The barman bowed and tripped over himself to offer Dawn a drink, and she politely accepted water. Once she had her glass, the barman shooed away the stragglers so she could sit in peace. She thanked him and chose the end of the bar, right next to the ginger haired man.

"Fancy running into you here," Dawn said, taking a sip of her water. It was spring water, chilled and subtly flavored with minerals, unlike anything she'd had before.

Zan pocketed the hand mirror he'd been using to check his teeth and bowed his head to her. "Why, Your Highness, to what do I owe the pleasure?"

"We want your help," Dusk said, landing on the bar between them.

"Ahh! And the very same fairy who came to your rescue," Zan exclaimed, face lighting with exaggerated surprise. "Why would you desire my help, Princess? It seems you've brought your best from Mantrisa already."

"It's not the best we're interested in, it's the worst," Dusk replied.

"You happen to be the scummiest man we know, which makes you well-suited for the job I have."

"Indeed?" Zan raised an eyebrow and looked at Dusk. "And what job might you be wanting?"

"What else? Information," Dusk answered and lowered his voice. "There's something going on here that we believe is connected to the Night Rise."

"So you want me to dig up whatever I can about this infernal sun," Zan said, rubbing his stubbly chin in thought.

"I want names of anyone involved," Dusk said.

"Names I can do, but they don't come cheap," Zan answered. "What're you offering in return?"

"How about not telling the guards that you assaulted the princess?" Dawn offered.

"If you think you can get me arrested that easily, you'd better look for someone else to get what you're after," Zan replied and leaned in. "As it happens, I'm waiting for a message from a friend with a big job. If you get me some payment before I leave, you can have whatever information you want."

"I can get you pearls," Dusk said.

"Pearls'll do," Zan answered after a moment's consideration. "You have a week if everything works out as it should with my friend."

"I'll have them tonight," Dusk said. "Think you'll find something that fast?"

"Fairy boy, you assume I don't already have some," Zan replied and stood. "You just have Paul show you the side entrance when you're ready, and he'll bring you to me." He finished the rest of his drink in one gulp and bowed to Dawn.

"A pleasure as always, Princess," he said. With a flourish, he straightened himself and his coat, and vanished into the crowd.

At the north end of the lake, a single mountain squatted apart from the Tail Spikes. While it wasn't particularly massive, it commanded attention with its marvelous waterfall that ran almost the entire height, feeding the lake and giving life to the city. The waterfall split near the bottom and spilled out to either side of great wooden doors, forming the main entrance to the Kirkjufell Palace.

Originally a mine, the entire mountain had been magically hollowed out by wizards, who'd smoothed ore veins and widened mineral deposits, forming an extravagant, labyrinthine living space. Peppering the outside were terraces teeming with vegetation and animals from all over the world.

As the guards reached the doors, they slowly opened inward, and the Mantrisa escort entered the palace. The entrance hall was long and wide with a high, curved ceiling; the walls were rough-textured like a cave. Most of the lighting came from special slits in the walls that were invisible from the outside while allowing a decent amount of sunlight in. At the far end of the long room was a spiral staircase that wound up through the center of the mountain. It was the only staircase that went through all thirteen levels, making it the primary method of moving around the palace.

Waiting for them at the midpoint of the hall were King Henry and Prince Geoff. Henry's features were sharper than his son's, more hardened, but neither Kirkjufell was terribly friendly. Both were strongly built as they stood at attention, though Geoff's stance was looser, seemingly able to flow into movement, while Henry was rigid.

Gold buttons and embellishments adorned their dark grey clothes. Both were practically covered in jewelry—rings with gems, necklaces of various metals—all from the palace itself. On either side of them were half a dozen wizards, several knights, and other servants, many of whom stood tensely near their royals, ready to jump at the slightest glance. The guards waved Cedric and Dawn forward, and the rest of the group to the side.

"Welcome, Princess Dawn Mantrisa," Henry greeted her. His words were crisp and emotionless, sounding rehearsed. He looked through her as though she were transparent, focusing on a point behind her. "We've awaited your arrival eagerly. How did you find your journey?"

"It was swift and without turmoil," Dawn answered, knowing what was expected. Her first time meeting the king was treated formally, a bit of a show for the staff present. What she wanted to do was talk to Geoff alone, but it would have to wait until enough effort was made to satisfy the king.

"Good." Henry nodded. "I trust the passage through our city was equally flawless. It is an incredible setting, is it not?"

"Completely breathtaking," she said. "Though I must admit I may have been distracted by the sun that has taken residence in your sky."

"Ahh, yes," Henry replied, smiling. "A humble tribute to the great dragon Solaris, whom we are currently celebrating. We understand that it would seem unusual to you, who worship fairies."

Tribute? They were meant to believe that's all it was? Anything requiring such a quantity of power was unheard of, even for the overly powerful Kirkjufells. And really, if that were all it was, why hadn't any of them heard about it before arriving?

"Forgive me, Sire, but that is incorrect," Dawn said with a slight bow of her head. Now was not the time to inquire further about the sun, and anyway, she had another point to address. "We worship dragons the same as everyone. Though we do have a greater emphasis on Nova and may seem less devout to others than we might be."

"It would seem we both have much to learn of others' customs," Henry said, a slight edge in his voice. "You may notice our modest selection of wizards. We apologize that only half are able to attend today, as the rest are needed to maintain our sun tribute."

"Yes, of course. May I present our wizard, Cedric Crawford," Dawn said, gesturing to him as he bowed. "And our most powerful fairy, Dusk." She looked over to him and he flitted next to her, also bowing.

"How amusing that you brought along your little pet," Henry said, chuckling as he studied the tiny creature in front of him.

Dusk bristled, and his frown was sharp as he looked at the king. "I am no pet, Sire, nor is any other fairy. We are free beings who happen to reside near the Mantrisas, and so we offer them our aid."

Henry raised a brow and looked at Dawn. "So they're...servants?"

"I believe what they are trying to get at," Geoff interrupted, "is that they are essentially the same as wizards and act as mages and counsellors. Is that accurate?"

"Precisely," Dusk agreed, nodding gratefully to the prince.

"In that case, perhaps a demonstration is in order?" Henry asked.

"With respect," Dawn said, tone less than respectful, "Dusk did not come on this visit to provide entertainment."

"It's perfectly all right," Dusk said, sending Dawn a reassuring shimmer. "I'd be happy to do a little something." He floated up towards the ceiling, stopping just below it.

Everyone jumped as the room went dark and only the glowing fairies could be seen. Dusk began to shimmer and sparkle until lights of every color burst forth and bounced around the hall. The lights moved faster and faster, swirling together in an intricate dance, finally joining to form a rainbow dragon, a small-scale Nova. The dragon flapped its wings and soared above the captivated audience, twisting and looping through the air. It landed on the staircase and roared, deafening everyone, then it lifted its head and blew flames that traveled the length of the hall and exploded in colorful bursts.

The dragon faded and the light returned to cheers from the

attendants. Dusk flew back down to eye level and bowed. Dawn smiled triumphantly at the Kirkjufells and caught Geoff's eye, who smirked and winked at her.

Once the room calmed, Henry spoke again. "Thank you for indulging us. Now you must be ready to get settled. The staff will show your companions to their rooms, and Geoff will take you to yours. We regrettably do not have anything prepared for your fairies, as we were not expecting their arrival. You may inform one of the servants what accommodations they need, and it will be seen to."

Dawn bobbed her head. "Thank you, but they will be residing with me in my room. They won't require anything but the ability to wander where they will."

"Then Geoff will take the three of you," Henry replied with a cocked eyebrow. "Everyone is dismissed."

24

The entrance hall cleared until only Dawn, the fairies, and Geoff remained. The prince crossed to her in two long strides, and she held her breath while he looked her over. His eyes were neutral as they scanned her, without any glint of emotion. After a minute, he held his hand out.

"You ready?" he asked.

"To go to my room?" she answered warily. It was good he wasn't angry, right? But she still sensed there was more going on in his mind than he was letting her see. She settled his bracelet on her wrist as she put her hand in his.

He jerked when they touched, throwing her hand away while he stared at his own, then grabbed her wrist and brought the hand to his face.

"What is that?" he asked, rubbing his fingers on her palm and squinting. His eyes shifted to Dusk floating next to her and the squint became a glare. "This your doing?"

"Depends what it is," Dusk answered, shrugging.

"Must be you. That's the only thing that's changed," Geoff said, and returned his focus to Dawn. "Better get you upstairs then. Let you put them away before we have some fun."

Diya flinched and flicked closer to Dusk, who took his hand and gave it a reassuring squeeze.

"Excuse me, but they are not my property," Dawn said, stumbling as Geoff dragged her to the spiral stairs. "You've no right to refer to them in such a way."

"And you had no right to link with that one," Geoff said, glancing back at the fairies as they ascended the stairs. "I told you not to. Now you get to live with the consequences of disobeying me. Won't be too harsh, though, since it seems I'll gain from it as well."

"There won't be any sort of punishment," Dusk said sharply. "If you've an issue with what Dawn has done by my choice, we can have a private discussion, but you aren't to do anything against her."

"What a killjoy you are," Geoff muttered. "You don't seem to realize how things work around here, so I'll inform you: *this is my palace*, and anyone who lives or works here does what I say, including you, if you don't want to be punished yourself."

"Thought you were just a prince," Diya said with a snort. "Aren't kings the ones in control?"

Geoff paused to smirk at the lux fairy. "Aren't you something. Didn't catch your name, though, or was it given?"

"It's Diya," he said, his blue grey eyes steely.

"Is it," Geoff said as he turned and continued going up the stairs. "If you're referring to Henry, you'll figure out fast that he has no power over me. He's only king because I allow it, for now." He shifted off the stairs at the next landing, and Dawn stopped, refusing to move.

"Aren't I staying on level nine?" she asked.

"Yes," Geoff answered, looking at her closely.

"Then why are we here? This is only the eighth level."

"Really. Didn't think you'd keep such careful track," Geoff said as he got back on the stairs. "Going to have to be a bit more creative to throw you off."

"You mean you want to get us lost?" Dusk asked, frowning.

"Precisely," Geoff said, smirking back at Dusk for a moment. "You will anyway if you try to get around without help." They reached the next level and he pulled Dawn off the stairs successfully. "But you'll have to find someone else. I'm only taking Dawn around."

He led them through passage after passage. There were so many turns Dawn didn't think she'd remember the way. Many hallways were sloped, and the widest ones had ruts in the center from wheels passing through them during mining. Dawn tried to note the wooden beams that supported the passages, wanting some form of reference, but they were so regular as to be invisible.

Eventually, they reached a small bedroom with basic furnishings and a bulky fireplace in one corner. Even Dawn's luggage was more decorative than the cold grey stone that made up the walls, floor, and ceiling. The chest with the lantern was tucked among her trunks at the foot of the bed.

"Is it to your standards?" Geoff asked.

"I'll be comfortable," Dawn said with a glance at the rough bedding and cramped vanity set.

"Good. So you're ready to play," Geoff said, and she shook her head.

"I'd really like to have a bath," she replied. She needed to talk to him, but first, some time to put her thoughts in order.

"'Course you would," Geoff said and released her hand. He went to the far corner where the rugs didn't reach and knelt by a wooden door in the floor. His fingers found the ridge along the edge and he lifted the door up. Underneath was a square of water surrounded by stone on three sides, and a stream on the fourth. The door slid down into a slot on the fourth side, cutting the pool off from the current. "There, you're set. I should warn you—it's a bit chilly."

Dawn knelt next to Geoff to test the water. It was icy cold, and she pulled her hand out quickly.

"That's all right. I can warm it," she said.

"Can you. Something the fairy gave you?" Geoff asked. He stood and glared at the fairies who were hovering by the pair of window slits.

Dusk looked over and shrugged. Dawn got to her feet and put her hand on Geoff's arm.

"If that's everything, may I please have some privacy?" she said. Not now, not just after arriving. She knew there would be some discussion between the boys, but she wanted to talk with Geoff first.

"Don't want company while you bathe? Shame," Geoff replied. "Shall I take your fairies somewhere for you?"

"We'll be all right on our own," Dusk said, settling Dawn's worry. "We'd like to go down to the city and wander a bit."

"Really," Geoff said and smirked at Dawn. "Then I'll be back to get some alone time with you. One hour." He left the room and the door slammed shut behind him.

"Will you be all right with him?" Dusk asked.

"I should be," Dawn said, still concerned by Geoff's behavior, but hopeful she could change the tone once she had some time to settle herself. "But you'll know if I'm not."

"Right. Come on, Diya," Dusk said as he flicked out of one of the glassless windows.

Diya paused on his way out and smirked at Dawn. "I'm sure you'll have lots of fun."

Geoff trotted back to the spiral stairs and descended one level, taking the steps two at a time. He expertly navigated the maze of hallways until he found the room he wanted. The door was ajar, so he stepped in.

Sarah was sorting her needlework on the nightstand and didn't notice him at first. He silently watched until she turned and caught sight of him. She squinted for a moment, about to tell him off for coming into her room, then realized who it was and closed her mouth.

"Been a while, hasn't it?" Geoff said and smirked. He crossed the room to her bed and threw himself on it, laying back on the pillows and rumpling the blankets. "Haven't done a very good job looking after Dawn for me, letting her do things I don't like."

"Do you need something?" Sarah asked, too stunned to continue unpacking. He'd barely said two words to her in all the times he'd visited Mantrisa. What possible reason could he have for coming to see her now?

"'Course, or I wouldn't be here," he said as he sat up and glared at her. "For starters, why'd you let Dawn link with the fairy? Supposed to be looking after her, aren't you? And she did that without my permission."

"It was her choice," Sarah said as she crept away from the bed. This was bad; she shouldn't be alone with him. "She doesn't do what anyone tells her, especially when it comes to Dusk."

"Wrong." Geoff stood and closed the space between them. He leaned over her and she winced away from his stare. "She does what I say, and it's your job to make sure of it. You fail again, you won't continue as her maid. Is that understood?"

"But I can't—"

"Is that understood?" he shouted, and Sarah whimpered and nodded. He straightened away from her and smirked. "Good. Now you can tell me what's going on with the fairies. Who's that other one she brought? Diya?"

Sarah forced air in and out of her lungs a few times. The worst was over, presumably. Just answer the question, and he'd go away. "He's Dusk's friend. That's all I know."

"But why did he come?" Geoff asked. He walked over to the wardrobe and touched the garments Sarah had managed to hang, rubbing the fabric. She cringed as his fingers found her mother's dress. "Dusk may have connected himself to Dawn, but the other one shouldn't be here. Why is he?"

"They haven't told me anything," Sarah said, hoping he'd get the hint. "Whatever it is, they don't want anyone else to know."

"Then you find out," Geoff said and walked back over to her. "You're the maid, that's what you do best isn't it? Find out everything and let me know. You fail to get me any information, then out you go." A strand of hair was in Sarah's face and he brushed it aside, running his thumb on her cheek as he did. "And trust me, leaving is the best punishment you can hope for around here."

Dusk led Diya away from the mountain and out over the lake. They flew high, unnoticed above the city until they were in the outskirts and drifted lower.

"So what're we doing?" Diya asked after several minutes had passed in silence.

Dusk glanced at him for a moment, then returned his focus to the lake below them. "We're getting pearls."

"For me?" Diya grinned. "Nice of you to remember."

"One for you, yes," Dusk said. "But more for Zan."

"Zan?" Diya asked, frowning. "Is that the guy you went to talk to earlier? Who is he?"

"He's a mercenary we met on the way to the Realm when we came to get you," Dusk explained. "I've hired him to find out who Berniece has working for her here. He's getting pearls for payment."

"Think it's someone in the palace?" Diya asked seriously.

"It has to be," Dusk answered. After what Henry said, what other option was there? Berniece couldn't possibly have managed this without an inside man. "Zan seems to already know something, so I'm meeting him tonight."

Diya snorted. "I have my guess who it is."

"That wouldn't happen to be Geoff, would it?" Dusk asked, glaring.

"Who else?" Diya returned, wings twitching. "There's clearly something off about him. Even if it isn't related to Berniece, we can't trust him."

"And this has nothing to do with him being in the way of what you want," Dusk said sarcastically.

"Hey, I can be concerned for Dawn's well-being too," Diya replied. "You know you don't like him either."

Dusk sighed as he remembered his first time meeting Geoff. Dawn had been so enthralled, so happy. He wanted that for her, no matter who provided it. "It doesn't matter if we like him. As long as Dawn can get along with him, they'll get married and we can move on."

"No," Diya said forcefully, hands balling into fists. "I'll still complain, and push both of you until you're dead. If you won't do it, you'll never hear the end of it from me."

Dusk slowed and looked hard at him. What Diya wanted was fair, to a point. It would mean not leaving the lux fairy but at the cost of someone else.

"I'll consider still doing it, but only after we drain the lantern," he said.

"Great," Diya said, smirking. "Now what are we going to do with that boy in the meantime? He's going to be hard to live with."

Dusk halted and floated down to the water. They had found a small sandbar a fair way outside the city that would have plenty of oysters.

"If anyone can make him easier to live with, it's Dawn," he answered. "Ready to swim?"

25

Exactly one hour after he'd left, Geoff knocked on Dawn's door and entered her room without waiting for a response.

"Oh, good, you're ready," he said, disappointment written all over his face.

Dawn set down her hairbrush and glared at him from the vanity. "I am, but you shouldn't enter a lady's room without permission."

Geoff laughed. "But this room is in my palace. I don't need anyone's permission for anything as long as we're here."

"Then maybe we should go outside of the palace, for now," Dawn said. They needed to find some compromises, clearly—and fast. "So we'll be on equal terms."

"Where's the fun in that?" Geoff grabbed her hand, yanking her onto her feet and out the door.

"Wait!" Dawn cried as she was dragged away from her room. "I need to see Rah first."

Geoff looked back at her, still moving. "Your squire? What do you want him for?"

"My knight," Dawn said. "He needs to guard my room when I'm gone."

Geoff smirked and continued leading her to the stairs. "Got some valuables in there? He's on the way. We can stop for a second."

They reached the stairs and Geoff sped up them, making Dawn struggle to stay balanced.

"I thought he was staying on level eight," she said. "Shouldn't we be going down?"

"You think you know this place so well already?" Geoff asked, pulling her off the stairs onto the tenth level. "I *told* you I'd take you to him. We'll get there."

He led her around in what felt like circles with all the twists they took. Eventually, they stopped in front of a single door at the end of a long hallway.

"Do you want to knock?" Geoff asked with his fist resting against the wood.

Dawn nodded and gently tapped on the door before he did it anyway. She stared at the wizard who appeared.

"Excuse me, it seems we have the wrong room," she said.

The wizard looked between her and Geoff and sighed. "I'm afraid you have the correct room if you were being directed by my nephew."

"Then you must be Edmond, the head wizard. Pleased to meet you," Dawn said and curtsied for him.

Edmond smiled at her and bowed his head. He had lighter, graying hair, and his features were soft, and rounder than the other Kirkjufells. His clothes were various shades of off-white with silver accents, and the only jewelry he wore was a plain gold band on his left thumb.

"I am indeed, and what a charming princess you are, Dawn," he said, the corners of his mouth turning up for a moment. "Perhaps, if we're lucky, some of your good manners will rub off on this one." He nodded at Geoff, who smirked.

"Not if I corrupt her first," he said, squeezing her hand too hard. "Which I'll be getting to shortly, but I thought we'd stop and see you on the way, maybe mention she brought some friends with her you'll want to meet."

Edmond pulled a handkerchief out of his pocket and used it to clear his throat. "Excuse me. Who might these friends be?"

"They're fairies," Geoff answered, squeezing harder, and Dawn bit her tongue to keep quiet. "One of them is quite talented, by the looks of it. Think you'll get along well with him."

"Fairies," Edmond repeated as though he was tasting the word. "Perhaps you would introduce us after dinner? I'm in the middle of something at the moment, but I would like to see them if you don't mind."

"I'll let them know," Dawn said, relaxing as Geoff's grip loosened.

"Excellent," Edmond said, stepping back into his room. "I must return to my experiment, but thank you for coming to see me, even though you didn't intend to. You be sure to let me know if Geoff gives you too much trouble, which he undoubtedly will."

"Of course. We'll leave you to your work," Dawn replied. Interesting that he would be entirely unconcerned by Geoff's behavior. Was he so used to it, he simply didn't have it in him to be bothered anymore? Whatever the reason, it didn't bode well for her that Geoff could so freely treat her this poorly.

Edmond nodded and closed the door. The instant he was out of view, Geoff tugged on her to drag her away, but she wrenched her hand out of his grip. "No more of that, thank you. I can walk myself."

Geoff shrugged and leaned against the wall. "All right, let's see you find your knight without me."

Dawn looked down the hall and grimaced. The place was sprawling and vast, difficult to get around if you hadn't been doing it your whole life. She had no way of finding anything without help.

"Fine," she said and held out her hand. "But I won't be thrown around anymore."

Geoff smirked and took her hand gently. "That's better."

After many hallways, turns, and what felt to Dawn like unnecessary switchbacks, they found the stairs again and descended two levels. Level eight was as bad as the others, and she didn't even try to keep track of where they'd gone until finally, they reached a bedroom door. Dawn looked at Geoff skeptically when they stopped.

"And this is Rah's room? Not someone else's?"

Geoff stared at her blankly, then knocked once and opened the door, pulling her in after him as he entered. They found Rob doing training exercises. He paused mid-swing and lowered his sword.

"Dawn! Is something wrong?" he asked, glancing between her and Geoff nervously.

"No, everything's fine," Dawn assured him while glaring at Geoff. "He's just showing me around, and Dusk went out with Diya, so you need to watch my room."

Rob nodded and sheathed his sword. He caught Dawn's eye, and she saw a flicker of anger in them. Anger at the prince and his behavior, anger for Dawn that she wasn't stopping it.

"Right," he said. "Any idea when they'll be back?"

"Hopefully not for a while," Geoff answered. "My plans for you don't involve any escorts." He tugged Dawn, and she stumbled into him.

Rob looked between them, anger shifting to resolve. "Maybe I should come with you instead?"

"We'll be fine," Dawn said quickly. The last thing she needed was an angry knight making Geoff any worse. "Someone has to keep an eye on things."

"What things, exactly?" Geoff asked with interest. "It wouldn't be something in that chest you were carrying earlier? That one that ended up in her room?"

"No, that's nothing," Dawn answered. How had he noticed that? They shouldn't have had Rob carry it in.

"Really." Geoff looked at her quizzically. "Then why bother carrying it special, and not sending it with your other things?"

"Because it's the fairies' things," Rob said. "We didn't want it to get mixed up with everything else."

Geoff laughed. "Well, you better get going. Don't know who might want their stuff." He pulled Dawn out of the room and turned back to Rob. "I trust you can find your own way. Don't need my help."

"I'll be fine," Rob replied, exiting his room after them. "There's a service stairway right down here that goes directly to it."

"Is there?" Dawn said, looking pointedly at Geoff.

"Of course there is. We arranged you all so you could find each other easily," Geoff explained with a grin. "In fact, Sarah is right over there." He pointed to a little turnoff that led to her room.

"And you didn't think to use those to bring me here?" Dawn asked testily.

Geoff shrugged. "I prefer the spiral."

Dawn sighed. Maybe this was going to be more effort than she'd expected. "Rah, would you check if Sarah is done with her room before you go? If she is, then take her with you so she can work on mine."

"Sure," Rob replied as Geoff pulled her away. "Take care."

"I'll try," Dawn called back to him as she was dragged around a corner and out of sight. She turned to look at Geoff angrily. "What is wrong with you? I wasn't done speaking with him."

"I was," Geoff explained. "He's a bit boring. You're better off without him."

"Enough!" Dawn jerked back, almost knocking them both off

their feet. Yanking her around was one thing, but she wouldn't let him insult her friends. "What is going on with you? Is this all because you're angry with me?"

Geoff sniffed and stepped closer to her. "You really have no idea, do you? You're wearing my bracelet like I told you, but you've got something else too, something from him. That why you sent his rose because he gave you a new one?"

"No, it's not like that," Dawn said, staring at the floor. She should have considered that and hidden the necklace at first, until she'd smoothed things over.

"Really." Geoff pulled her chin up so she couldn't avoid his eyes. "You forgot who you belong to, didn't you? It's always been me, but you didn't listen when I told you what to do, what I wanted. Now you've brought him here, to me, and if he doesn't behave himself, it's on you."

"Please, leave him out of this," Dawn whispered. "I came to be yours, and he won't interfere if you don't bother him."

"Wrong," Geoff growled in her ear. "He got involved with you. That means he's a problem for me. You really want to prove something, you'll send him back."

"I'm sorry, I can't," she said. Maybe alone time wasn't such a good idea. "He wants to be here and won't be ordered around."

"Like I care?" Geoff asked. "If you really give a shit about him, you'll send him back. Otherwise, anything I do to him is your fault."

"I'll talk to him," she whispered. "But I can't promise anything."

"Can't promise at all, or can't promise me?" Geoff asked. He turned away from her and dragged her down the hallway. "Better not be the latter, or I'll be angry."

They went through several more hallways and twists before Dawn had enough of uncomfortable silence. Even if talking was tricky, she needed to try. The real Geoff was still there, somewhere. She just had to find him, coax him back out. The same gentle approach she'd used with the dog in the Ruins could work here, simply adapted for an unruly human.

"Where are we going?" she asked.

"The lift," he answered. "Since you're already tired of the stairs."

He led her into the servant passages and headed to a small alcove. Inside were a pair of ropes that moved up and down opposite each other. Attached to the ropes at regular intervals were platforms that were just the right size for a single person to fit comfortably as they passed through the levels.

"How does it work?" she asked, intrigued.

"It's water-powered," Geoff explained. "There're wheels at each end that turn as the stream moves over them."

This felt like progress. If she could keep the conversation civil, they just might manage. "Does it go through all the levels?"

Geoff shook his head. "It only goes down to the seventh level. Ready to ride it?"

"I think so," Dawn said, nervous, but excited.

Geoff smirked and stepped over to the side that went up. He waited until the approaching platform was still several feet below the floor they were standing on and jumped. Dawn gasped as she was dragged after him and they crashed onto the platform together. They clambered to their feet with difficulty, trying to avoid bumping each other and getting thrown off as they rose to the ceiling. Eventually, they straightened themselves, and Geoff held her close.

"Sorry it's so slow," he said with his mouth practically touching her ear. "I keep suggesting to Ed that he should make it faster, but he never listens."

"Getting off isn't as dangerous, is it?" Dawn asked softly.

"It could be if you want it," he said, then laughed when she grimaced. "I guess that's a no. Fine, we'll do it correctly, just for you."

"And where are we getting off?" Dawn squirmed a bit so she wasn't breathing on his neck.

"At eleven," Geoff answered.

"Your level?" Dawn asked. This could be good, right? "What are we going to do there?"

Geoff squeezed her a little as they passed through another floor. "I could show you my bedroom, but you're too polite for that. So instead we'll go play with the girls."

"Are they ready to meet me?" It was a better option than the other suggestion, at least. And assuming they were as well-trained as Geoff claimed, they would be fine.

Geoff laughed as they passed through another level, watching the platform above them.

"Get ready," he instructed as the platform approached the eleventh floor. He shifted his grip around her waist and tensed, then hopped off as the platform became level with the floor.

"Better? We'll do it from higher up next time." Geoff winked and let go of her waist to grab her hand again.

He dragged her through many more passages, then through large double doors that opened out to one of the palace's terraces. Most of them were open to the sky, but this one was covered with a great glass dome. The terrace was filled to bursting with plants, trees, and animals—all from faraway places Dawn had only seen pictured in books, if at all.

Sunlight filtered through the dense tree canopy, giving everything under it a shadowy green tint. Orange and yellow striped hibiscus climbed the tall trunks, providing a ladder for crawling insects. A carpet of creeping vegetation covered the ground, with tiny flowers speckled in the leaves like a hidden rainbow. The blanketing warmth of late-summer evenings was stirred by a gentle breeze, carrying a heady burnt-cedar scent.

A bird called from deep in the trees, a crackling cry that

immediately was repeated. Moments later a flock of black and white birds with heavy orange beaks burst from the canopy in a flurry of wing flaps. They cawed as they flew overhead, long tail feathers flowing behind them, then went up and away into the farthest reaches of the massive terrace.

"You like it," Geoff said.

Dawn nodded, still gazing at the flowing vines that hung off the towering jungle trees. "It's beautiful."

"It's not bad," he remarked and tugged on her to bring her farther in. "You'll get your own terrace, and you can decide what goes in it."

"And can I decide who gets to enter?" Dawn asked, craning her neck to take in as much as she could while he pulled her along. She caught a lively colored bird hiding in the leaves above her, and some sort of marsupial dangling from vines.

Geoff laughed. "Yes, except for me, of course. Terraces are part of the palace."

"Oh, wonderful," Dawn remarked less-than-happily. At least it would be something of hers, though. She could plant roses, and maybe Dusk would be willing to grow another Heart of Dusk bush.

They walked in silence for several paces until Geoff stopped under a grove of trees, staring up into the branches. "There they are. Jewel, Crown, come meet the new princess."

Dawn followed Geoff's gaze and saw two pairs of yellow eyes looking down at her. One blinked and jumped down, landing quietly on four large paws. The other followed, and Dawn stared at the pair of cougars that crept up and sniffed her curiously. She slowed her breathing and held still while they inspected her. Satisfied, the cats curled around her and rubbed against her, purring happily. Dawn pet one of them with her free hand, scratching under her chin.

"Told you they'd like you," Geoff said. "More than I thought they would, though." "Were you expecting some hostility?" She eyed him as the cougar started purring. Hadn't he introduced the roses to them with the intention of helping this initial meeting? Or perhaps he'd had another motive, but it had worked out in her favor after all.

"Some wariness, at least," he said, shrugging. "You traitors. Should have made her work for the affection. Hopefully, they'll do better with your fairies."

"I'm sure they'll like each other," Dawn said, returning her attention to the cougar who bumped her hand with a furry forehead. "Fairies tend to be good with animals."

"Unless I tell the girls they're enemies," he said, smirking. "Won't be very nice to them then."

A few hours later, Rob and Sarah were playing card games in the doorway of Dawn's room when Dusk and Diya returned, entering through a window slit. They were carrying a kelp net laden with pearls between them.

"What've you got there?" Rob asked, looking over as the fairies floated to the vanity.

"Nothing for you to worry about," Dusk replied.

He and Diya set the pearls in front of the mirror, carefully arranging the net to keep them together. Sarah watched the fairies, then gave Rob a pointed look.

"Talk to him," she whispered.

"You told me you'd explain more, especially if it pertains to Dawn," Rob said. How were they supposed to work together if Dusk constantly kept him in the dark? He may not be linked, but fealty meant something, even to fairies.

Diya laughed as he leaned back on the mirror, watching Dusk with mirth. "So it's only promises that stop my plans you'll keep."

Dusk glared at him, then looked at Rob. "Sorry. Dawn and I ran into a friend on the way here who's going to help us. That's his payment."

"What friend? And payment for what?" Rob asked.

"The mercenary we met in the forest," Dusk explained. "He's getting information about this artificial sun of theirs."

Sarah gasped, dropping her cards as she brought her hand to her mouth. "Is that really a good idea?"

"I understand you'd be cautious about his involvement. That's why I didn't want to say anything," Dusk said. "But we need all the help we can get if we want to keep Dawn and the lantern safe."

"Then let me come too," Rob said. This was exactly the sort of job he should do, as Dawn's sworn knight. Not to mention he could find out about that boy once and for all.

"You'll only risk us being noticed. I've no need of your help," Dusk said. A flimsy excuse, but the best he could manage.

"But I want to give it," Rob replied, lifting his gaze to Dusk. "Please, I only want what's best for Dawn."

Dusk tried to say no, but Rob's eyes were very persuasive and wouldn't let him. He shook his head and sighed. "All right, if you feel you must."

Rob grinned and returned his attention to the cards. Sarah glanced between the boys for a minute, then cleared her throat when it was clear Rob wasn't going to continue the conversation. "Well, speaking of helping, Rob and I feel that Geoff is a danger to Dawn, and we need you to help us protect her."

Diya smirked at Dusk. "See? I told you he was bad."

"So you already know what we're dealing with?" Rob asked, looking up at Dusk again. "What do you think? You can't be all right with Dawn marrying him."

"While I don't find him appealing, I believe we should give Dawn a chance to work on him before we interfere," Dusk said. "If she can live with him, it isn't for us to get involved."

"I don't think she's safe with him," Rob explained. "He was rough with her when I saw them, and she didn't stop him."

Dusk frowned. "He didn't hurt her, did he?"

Rob shook his head. "Not *this* time."

"He will, though," Sarah said. "Maybe not on purpose, but it'll happen sooner or later. Sooner if we do nothing."

Dusk flicked his wings and sped through the doorway, buzzing down the hallway and out of sight, without so much as a backward glance.

26

In the heart of the jungle terrace, the dense trees and under-growth thinned around a modest pool. Rocks were stacked on one side and a small rivulet traced the gaps as it trickled down. Long-legged water bugs skipped around the surface, occasionally drop-ping into the shallow pool. Hiding in the foliage around the edges of the water were several of Geoff's grass creations: a goat like the one he'd given her, a snake that flicked its tongue, and a cougar that stretched.

Dawn sat a little way from the pool, quietly watching the scenery. She glanced beside her at Geoff, who was sprawled on the mossy ground, sleeping. Shortly after showing her the cougars, he'd decided he wanted to lie down and had dragged her over here. He'd fallen asleep almost instantly, still clasping her hand. She tugged it gently, and he tightened his grip and shifted around her arm, hold-ing her in place. She was just starting to wonder how much longer she'd be stuck when she felt a shimmer and smiled.

"About time you got here," she said quietly as Dusk approached. "He's been out for hours."

"Indeed." Dusk glanced over the sleeping boy appraisingly as he landed next to them. "Sorry I didn't get back sooner to keep you company then."

"That's fine," Dawn said. "It's been nice, actually. I rather like him like this."

"Like what?" Geoff opened his eyes and sat up on his arm. "Quiet? Harmless? Vulnerable?" He smirked, then glanced over at Dusk and frowned. "How'd you get in here?"

"There are doors," Dusk answered.

"I'm aware of that. Didn't realize you'd be able to manage them. I'll have to lock them next time."

"Still won't keep me out," Dusk said, half-smiling.

"No?" Geoff sat up fully and pulled Dawn onto his lap. "Is that true?"

"If he says it is, then yes," Dawn answered.

"I'll figure out something to keep you apart. Can't have fun with you if he's always here to watch. Unless you like that sort of thing." Geoff looked over at Dusk questioningly.

"What I'd like," Dusk said crisply, glaring, "would be for you to treat her with respect. And until you do, I'll be around."

"And what will she do if I don't?" Geoff asked, smirking. "You want to stick around, I can leave you both here with the girls. Won't be going anywhere without my say-so then."

"Actually, I can get around just fine," Dusk said. "And in a moment, Dawn will be able to as well." He flitted closer to them and held up his hand. Dawn touched her hand to his and he placed his other palm on the ground.

Dawn felt a tingle of magic, then gasped as the entire palace layout formed in her mind. She saw all thirteen levels—each room, stairway, hallway, terrace, *everything*. There was the stream running through various rooms and terraces, and the basin above them that fed it. Larger furniture, like beds, tables, and shelves, marked what each room's purpose was—bedrooms, kitchen, library—though she couldn't make out finer details. If she concentrated she could just pick out life forms as they wandered and worked, able to guess what sort of person each was by their behavior—guards patrolling, knights swinging weapons, wizards keeping the artificial sun alive.

"I see you were telling the truth about the lift—it runs from the seventh level to the twelfth," she said with a look at Geoff. "But you didn't mention there's another one that goes through the lower half."

Geoff glared at Dusk. "If I'm not allowed to know anything about you, then you don't get to show her my palace. But since you've gone ahead and done it, there better be some answers for me about you two."

"What did you want to know?" Dusk asked, fluttering his wings casually.

"I want to know what the hell you're doing in my kingdom. You weren't supposed to be here interfering with my plans, so explain yourself."

Dusk climbed onto Dawn's hand and she lifted him up to eye level. "I am part of Dawn's escort. My presence here is no different in purpose than her knight or maid."

"Liar," Geoff said and laughed. "You're more than an escort, aren't you? Or at least you want to be. Doing what you can by linking, anyway. I get why you'd want to come, but not your friend. You've got something planned, haven't you? And you don't want me to know, but I'm getting in your way, trying to get Dawn to myself like I am."

"I assure you there is nothing to get in the way of," Dusk replied quickly. "Diya is my companion, that's all."

Dawn felt an anxious tingle and pursed her lips. Being questioned by Geoff was enough of a concern on its own, but to also be pressed about Diya was too much for Dusk. She took a steadying breath and tried to send him something reassuring through the link.

"Highly irregular for an escort to come with an escort of his own," Geoff said. "So much so that it basically gives you away as being up to something. And that's fine as long as you stay out of my business, but you're not, so I'll ask you again. Why. Are. You. Here?"

"You want answers, you can tell me something first," Dusk said. "What's the real reason your wizards are keeping up that sun? I heard it started the same day the Night Rise did, and I'm wondering where they got the power to get it going in the first place."

The anxiety from Dusk subsided as he shifted to a new topic, and Dawn focused on the now comfortable presence of the link. If Dusk was calm enough to keep his feelings under control, he wasn't overly troubled by Geoff. And if Dusk wasn't troubled, she should try not to be either.

"You think we took your light?" Geoff shrugged. "Maybe we did, I don't know, but what of it? You put a stop to it anyway. Talk to Ed if you really care—he's in charge of it."

"But why are they doing it?" Dusk asked, wings twitching in annoyance. "I may have been in the Mantrisa kingdom in more recent years, but I was in the Sky Forest for the majority of my life. This artificial sun—for 'celebrating Solaris' if Henry is to be believed—is entirely unheard of."

"Fine, you caught me," Geoff said and frowned. "I told Henry it was a terrible excuse, but he thought it would work. Doesn't know anything about fairies, but I like it that way. Something I can use against him. You try to tell him you don't believe it though, he'll never admit it. As for why, you'll see soon anyway, when it's too late."

"Too late for what?" Dawn asked softly, catching a tint of menace in his words.

"Too late to matter," Geoff answered. "There, I gave you something. Now it's your turn."

Dusk shook his head. "You've given us nothing, other than the knowledge you know more than you're telling. As far as I'm concerned, we're even."

Geoff tensed, tightening his grip around Dawn. "Except it's not even. You'll learn what you want to know. It can't be helped. And what do I get? Least you can do is give me some damn privacy with the princess."

Privacy? And what had he done with that all day? Dragged her around, and found as many other people—or cougars—to see as he could. And it was only because Dusk was here that he wanted more. At this point, Dawn would love some privacy—away from Geoff.

"You've had plenty of time alone with her for one day," Dusk replied coolly, echoing Dawn's thoughts. "It isn't my fault you slept through most of it."

"Not my fault either," Geoff said, shrugging. "Sun's been keeping me up at night, among other things. I was thinking I might invite Dawn to help me get more sleep tonight."

"You will do no such thing," Dawn said, appalled by the idea. Even if she were ready for such things, it was entirely inappropriate before they were officially wed, a fact that her family, at least, would care about. "I won't be engaging in anything so improper."

Dusk smiled up at her. "Seems I was right that you'd be able to handle him."

"Great, does that mean you'll go away?" Geoff asked, eyes smoldering with angry mirth. "I suggested to Dawn earlier that she keep you in her terrace when she gets one, but she seems to think you'll be more comfortable staying with her. Unfortunately, there's no place for a fairy in my rooms, so you'll have to figure something else out once we're married. Better enjoy sleeping with her while you can."

"For someone who claims to know anything about fairies, it's odd you'd think I sleep," Dusk said, matching Geoff's amusement.

"Oh, I know you don't," Geoff said and shrugged. "I also know you don't need to eat, but one of you always does with the Mantrisas. Just funny that actually helping me sleep would be improper, but you and your escort living in her room is fine."

Dawn glared at him. "That's different. I know them, and they know how to behave themselves."

Geoff laughed. "They do, do they? Is that what keeps them out of trouble? Anyway, I thought the whole point of you coming here was so we could get to know each other."

"Not like that," Dawn said, pushing him away slightly. "Maybe not ever if you keep this attitude. You're moving too fast."

"Fast? You think it's too fast?" Geoff laughed again. "Maybe for you, since you've obviously been avoiding thinking about living here. But I've been waiting for you for years. If it weren't for Isabella, we'd have been married by now and working on children."

"You've waited this long, you can make it a few more days at least," Dawn said. She was in no position to take longer than Geoff wanted, but still, he was asking more than he knew. "I need time to adjust to everything. If you can be good until I am, then we can get married."

"If I can be good," Geoff repeated mockingly. "And who's going to make sure I do? Your boyfriend? If he really wants to help, he'll give us some space and go back to your little kingdom."

That was enough. She could almost forgive Geoff being angry when she went against his wishes. And some of his behavior, she was sure, was nothing more than lingering effects from his sickness. Those she could help with, discussing with him fully about decisions, and her abilities from linking could almost certainly improve him. But the constant ridiculing of her friends and threats against Dusk were unacceptable.

"I can make sure you do, even if Dusk were to leave," she said. She concentrated on the ring that she felt pressing against her waist, focusing her magic to heat it. Geoff looked at her quizzically for a moment, then jerked his hand away and shook it.

He winced, then glared at her. "You made your point. Got any other tricks I should know about?"

"If she wanted to, she could destroy your precious palace," Dusk said, shrugging like it was nothing.

"You wouldn't try anything like that though," Geoff said, pulling Dawn back against him. "It wouldn't be proper. If I give you time, you'd better be willing to give me more than you are now. You could at least pretend to be making an effort."

Dawn glared at him. What was she doing, then, if not making an effort? "I am trying. You're what's being difficult."

"No, he's right," Dusk said, and her heart dropped. "You've proven he can't get away with mistreating you. Now you need to accept him as he is."

"Well said, fairy. Didn't think you'd be on my side," Geoff remarked, smirking. "Maybe you can set a good example for her, and leave us alone now?"

"You don't have to, Dusk," Dawn said. If he did what Geoff wanted now, it would be all the harder for him later when they were married.

"I don't, no," Dusk agreed, and fluttered up off her hand. "But I'm going to. It's almost time for dinner anyway."

"You aren't coming with us?" Dawn asked.

Dusk shook his head. "There won't be a place for me. And I should really stay with Diya for now, help him settle."

"Right." Dawn nodded sadly. She wasn't in Mantrisa anymore, and the sooner she got used to her new home, the better. "Well, you have an invitation after dinner to see Edmond, if you're willing."

Dusk raised an eyebrow. "Do I? I suppose I'll have to accept."

"He just wants to meet you and Diya," Dawn said, hopeful Dusk would like the wizard. He was, of the three Kirkjufells, the best gentleman, and the most learned about magic. Exactly the sort of person Dusk would get on with. "I'll take you there once I'm done eating."

"All right, we'll go. As long as he doesn't keep us too long," Dusk said.

"Oh? Got other plans for tonight?" Geoff asked with interest. "Since you aren't up to anything, is it some fairy thing? Ed would love to hear about it if it is."

"If he's curious about us, he can ask himself," Dusk replied crisply. "And I thought you were keen for me to go."

"Oh, yes, you're right. But it seems you managed to stall long enough that we need to get moving ourselves or we'll be late for the feast," Geoff said as he got to his feet, pulling Dawn up after him. "The sooner we get there, the sooner you can take your fairies to Ed. And while we're there, I know Henry would love to hear all about what a great time we're having."

"And I suppose you want me to tell him I'm happy here," Dawn said. Even if she weren't trying to adjust to the palace, she didn't know how she could pretend there was nothing bothering her. Geoff's attitude, the sun Dusk believed was connected to Berniece, Henry's rude comments about fairies... There was a lot to be un-happy about.

Geoff winked at her. "You just smile and agree with anything he says and he'll never know you aren't. Hell, you could tell him the truth and he wouldn't care. In fact"—he leaned over her and lowered his voice—"he'd probably tell you it's your own fault for not giving me a chance. You think my suggestions are bad, just wait until you hear some of his."

"So you think it's best if I lie to him," Dawn said, frowning. She wasn't keen on doing the exact opposite of what her mother advised with Henry, regardless of what Geoff thought. Or maybe, consider-ing his behavior, *because* of what he thought.

Dusk fluttered close to her and put his hand on her cheek. "Be as honest as you can manage. Just focus on what you genuinely enjoyed. I know today has been difficult, but I felt a few happy moments."

"All right." Dawn smiled at him, feeling at ease from his touch. "I can do that much."

"You felt?" Geoff asked, glaring at Dusk. "The hell does that mean? So I can't do anything to either one of you without the other knowing. How is any of this supposed to work, then? I just go along with what you want because if I don't, he'll hear about it?" He squeezed Dawn's hand, making her wince and Dusk twitch.

"You really didn't consider me ever, did you? Just went your whole life playing with fairies and ignoring where you'd end up, who you'd end up with, while I thought about you every day, waiting for you to come and give me what I want. Then you finally arrive, and you give me more than that, and nothing at the same time. Because you decided to fall in love with someone else, someone you couldn't be with even if you weren't intended for me."

With her free hand, Dawn pulled her hair over her shoulder, running her fingers through it. Why did he have to be so observant? Had he noticed this over the years they'd been writing to each other? Or only guessed it, then when Dusk came with her, he knew. Either way, how dare he figure it out so easily, so certainly, when she had struggled with her emotions for years. Yes, years. She'd loved so long and so deeply it wasn't right for Geoff to condense it so flippantly.

The fountain trickled behind them as the seconds stretched into minutes, the three of them silent, staring. Dusk looked past Dawn's shoulder at some birds in a tree. Geoff's eyes flicked between the fairy and Dawn's hand in his, dissatisfied with both. Dawn looked down at her feet, sniffling as her eyes filled with tears.

Geoff used to be kinder, gentler, and able to speak with others cordially. She wanted that version, the version she'd idolized when she was young, dreamt of being with someday. As he was now, the prince wouldn't alleviate any sadness she had at not being with her real love.

"And what about you?" she whispered. "You aren't the same as before, how I remember you. Maybe, if things hadn't changed, they would have gone how you wanted. But they did, and I can't help that, no matter how much I want to." She looked up at Geoff, eyes stinging. Even though they weren't married yet, it was already too late for her. "But I promised to do this, and I intend to. It's the least I can do."

"The least for who, you or me?" Geoff asked with an edge in his voice, then fixed his gaze on Dusk. "Bastard. Making her yours, then telling her she should still marry me. What are you playing at? What do you get from all this?"

"It's none of your damn business what I get," Dusk said, glow flickering.

Geoff laughed darkly. "Just like everything else about you. Go on, get back to your little friend. You don't have to be around to know how I'm treating your girl anyway."

Dusk didn't say anything, just looked at Dawn for a moment before he turned and flew away. Dawn wiped at her tears as they rolled down her cheek and felt a warm, comforting shimmer. She let it flow through her until the tears stopped and it faded. Geoff watched her as she dried her eyes with her handkerchief, then wordlessly pulled her back into the palace.

27

Diya was alone when Dusk returned to Dawn's room; Rob and Sarah had left already to go to dinner. The lux fairy was sprawled on a pillow and looked up as Dusk entered.

"How're the lovebirds?" he asked.

Dusk closed the door and glared at him, his eyes shining. "Stop it."

"That bad, huh?" Diya stared at him for a moment, then fluttered over. "Having second thoughts about going through with it?"

"No," Dusk said and went to a window slit to land, avoiding looking at his friend. "However hard it'll be, I have to take care of you."

Diya snorted and followed him, landing in the window slit with him. "Yeah, so you keep saying. But who'll take care of me when you're gone? And don't say I'll have to look after myself; I either need you or I don't. You can't have it both ways."

"Fine, you don't need me," Dusk said. "I'll just forget the lantern and Berniece and we'll all live happily together for the rest of time."

"Exactly," Diya said, grinning. "That sounds nice, doesn't it? She'd like it too, you know. Then I'll have two friends, which would be great since you can be an ass sometimes."

"Not as much as you," Dusk replied with a chuckle. He pictured it for a moment, then shook his head and sighed. "It certainly would be nicer than this, but she's determined to marry him now. I won't undo what I've started."

"Why not?" Diya frowned. "You'd really rather she be his her whole life? You know she loves you. If it were anyone else you wouldn't get in the way, but you won't let yourself have it."

"It's not like I'm losing her. We'll still be together like we've been until now," Dusk said. "All she wants is to keep her friends close."

"But you're not just a friend anymore," Diya said. "You can't be the same, not since you linked. You knew that when you did it, but she had no idea. Now you want to pretend nothing's different, but she's realizing that's not the case—and you can't stop her."

Dusk shook his head. "She never had the luxury of choosing love. Linking with her is as close as she can get to what she really wants, and she'll be happy for it even while married to Geoff."

"But she can't marry him," Diya said, grinning impishly and leaning into Dusk. "Technically you're already married to her."

"Linking is not the same as marriage. No humans would acknowledge it," Dusk replied, shoving his friend back.

Diya glowered at him and leaned against the sill. "It's the fairy equivalent, and you know perfectly well they'd have to recognize it as such if you said so."

Dusk raised an eyebrow. "Since when were you such an expert in human matrimony laws?"

"Hah. So it's true," Diya said, grinning.

Dusk rolled his eyes. Only Diya could bullshit his way through something so blatantly made-up, and still end up in the right. "I see you've run out of ideas to convince me if this is what you're going with now."

"Maybe I have, or maybe I'm just distracting you while my real plan continues on its own," Diya replied as he sat down, swinging his feet over the edge of the window slit. "But hey, if this worked I wouldn't complain. Might laugh, though."

Dusk chuckled and sat with him. The lake glittered to their right, brightly reflecting the artificial sun. Shouts drifted up from the city as people hurried home for the evening, shoving past each other on the limited bridge space. "I'd give you that one. Think I'd have to laugh at me too."

Diya stopped smiling and brought his knees up, curling in on himself. "But you're fighting dirty. How'd you convince her to keep her knight?"

"She decided to on her own," Dusk said, avoiding Diya's eyes.

"Don't lie to me. If you're going to claim this is for my benefit, then the least you can do is be honest."

Dusk leaned against Diya, resting his head on his shoulder. "Fine, I influenced her. And I'm glad I did because we need his help here. You don't want to be stuck watching the lantern on your own if he were to leave."

"And what if I didn't have to be?" Diya asked. He wiggled himself under Dusk's arm and clung to his friend's waist. "What if we did something else with it? Or rather, let someone else deal with it for us."

"Who would?" Dusk asked. "Because I'm fairly certain the only people who can are people we don't want to give the lantern to."

"Maybe," Diya said, nodding. "But what if we taught someone how to use it? Someone we know we can trust to look out for Dawn, who's already shown an aptitude for magic, who wants to go home as much as I do."

Dusk stared at him blankly. "You want to give the lantern to Sarah."

"Why not?" Diya asked. "She'd take good care of it, we know we can trust her, and she's ready to do more magic, you've said as much. She just needs a teacher, might as well be you."

His immediate thought was the obvious reason: Sarah wasn't a mage. But when he considered it, she had the potential that no one else did. And from what he'd seen, it didn't seem she would need long—a few months at most—before she could do the basic task of moving magic between capacitors. It was actually so sensible, Dusk was surprised he hadn't thought of it himself. He gently removed Diya's arms from his waist and stood up to think.

"It's not a terrible idea," he said after a few minutes. "On the one hand, we don't want to waste any time getting it drained; on the other, I'd prefer it if Dawn and I didn't have to be the sole users. It would be better if someone else who has more time for it could help out, and I could easily rework your circlet so Sarah could store power in it but not take it out."

Diya flicked his wings impatiently while Dusk pondered the idea. "So? You like it?"

"I do," Dusk said. "I'll teach her to read spells and manipulate magic until she can work on it for us. At the very least, I'd prefer not to have it in Geoff's rooms, so putting it somewhere else would be ideal."

"Geoff's rooms," Diya repeated, and his wings drooped. "So it's not about the lantern then. You just don't want to be happy."

Dusk sighed and watched a runlet of water from the Tail Spikes. It churned and splashed where it met the lake, disrupting the passing boats. "Enabling Sarah to use the lantern is helpful, but it doesn't change everything else Dawn is doing. You can't invent something to stop her from being a princess."

"I see. It's really not for me after all," Diya said as he got to his feet. He flicked over to the bed and shoved his way under the covers.

"Diya," Dusk called after him wearily.

"No," Diya replied sharply. "You keep saying you're doing everything for me, but you won't do the one thing that actually is for me because you think it'd be selfish."

"You don't understand humans and their needs," Dusk argued. "Everything they do is for the betterment of their families, their children. They don't live long and can't worry only about their own wants."

Diya poked his head out of his nest and glared at Dusk. "So you care more about their little kingship than me, just because it was Aaron who helped me. If I'd never been in the lantern, you wouldn't care about any of them."

"No, I wouldn't," Dusk agreed. "And I wouldn't hesitate to give her up to change what happened to you. But as it is, the best thing I can do is ensure her family's rule, and be here for her while I do."

"No," Diya said. "The best thing you can do is what I keep saying you should do so you can stay with both of us. Use that necklace you gave her to turn her into a fairy, and the three of us will be happy."

Dusk flew to the bed and sat next to Diya's pile, scrunching himself up and staring at his lap. "It's never been done before. Coma tried for years to turn humans into fairies, and it always failed."

"You don't have to tell me about it," Diya said, shuffling himself closer to Dusk and leaning against him. "I saw enough of his attempts. But he wasn't linked to any of them, and she has a fairy alignment. You could do it—you're better than he ever was anyway."

Dusk shook his head. It was more complicated than Diya made it seem, no matter how much he wanted to try. "It would take more power than even I have. At best I could work on it over time, but she'd have a family of her own long before I could finish."

"You can use the lantern," Diya said nonchalantly. "Really, it's got plenty, and I don't care about it anyway."

"You'd really be fine with that?" Dusk asked, looking at his friend's face. The magic wouldn't fix anything, but it might at least help the lux fairy feel like his old self. Certainly not something to give up so easily.

"Are you honestly asking if I'd rather have magic or you?" Diya snorted. "You wouldn't even need that much. We have the same alignment. Super efficient."

Dusk smiled. Of course Diya would be logical now, when he'd made such a mess of things they couldn't get out one way or the other. If only Dawn hadn't chosen Geoff and sent the rose, or if she'd mentioned it before they linked and he wouldn't have thought he had a chance in the first place. But, it wasn't fair of him to act out of his own insecurities, without regard for what he was doing to Diya.

"We can't simply do it," Dusk replied. "Not while we're here, anyway. Dawn still wants to make things work with Geoff, and she might choose him. I don't want you to say anything until after she decides, all right?"

Diya crawled out from under the covers and sat in front of Dusk.

"And afterward, you listen to me the first time," he said, then spat on his hand and held it out.

Dusk smirked, spat on his own hand and they touched their palms together. "Deal."

Footsteps echoed in the stone hallways as Geoff led Dawn to the dining room. He was silent, and Dawn couldn't decide if it was better or worse than listening to him. At least if he were talking she'd know what he was thinking, partially. Every so often he would glance down at their clasped hands like he thought she would break away from him again if he didn't check on her. She wondered if she would—or could.

Dawn followed their path in her mind, seeing all the possible ways they could take and noting that this was one of the quickest routes. Geoff wouldn't attempt to get her lost again. They went down the spiral stairway, and she almost giggled. He looked at her as she stifled the sound, and she blushed and watched her feet.

He snorted and looked ahead. "Something the fairy did?"

"No," Dawn answered quietly.

"So you're laughing at me then," Geoff replied. "Think it's funny, what you're doing?"

"It's the stairs," she said, glancing at him. "You had said you like them more. I thought it was sweet."

"Sweet?" Geoff stopped for a moment to look at her. "That I actually like something, you mean? As if I'm human, and have feelings too. But you can't feel mine, don't care about me."

"I've always cared," Dawn replied. "I can give you what you need. I'll learn to if you help me."

"You had your whole life to learn," he answered. "But you spent it playing with fairies. Used up all your cares on them, now I get nothing."

"But you do get something," Dawn said, thinking quickly. When he'd first taken her hand after they arrived, that was proof her theory was right, that she could heal him. And if she could do that, maybe things weren't hopeless. "I thought I'd be able to help you if I had Dusk's magic. And you said yourself it would benefit you."

He pulled her hand up to his face, almost touching it to his cheek. "I do get this. But you aren't doing it on purpose, so it doesn't count. And even if it did, you'd have to be touching me at night for it to really help."

Dawn blinked slowly while her mind churned. What was different about night? Why was it special? Considering what was going on here, only one thing made sense. "At night, when it's dark? But it isn't dark here because of your wizards."

"Think you're onto it, then? Figured out the secret?" Geoff pulled her off the stairs and into an alcove. He pressed up against her and spoke quietly in her ear. "It's for me. They're trying to help, but it's worse like this. Henry doesn't care what happens to me as long as you don't find out until after we're married. Then the sun will go away and you'll see my curse."

"And then it won't matter," Dawn whispered.

He nodded, a dark curl falling on his forehead. "Then you'll know everything, and I'll still know nothing."

Why was he telling her this? Such a personal thing to share, that could easily destroy his chance of keeping her. Knowing Geoff, it must benefit him somehow. The real question then, was what did he gain? Certainly not her sympathy, she had plenty of that. Was it possible he actually cared about her? Wanted her to know what she was marrying, to keep her safe?

Dawn pressed her ear against his chest and listened to his heart beating, making him snort.

"See? I told you I'm human," he said.

His heart thumped the same as it had when she'd listened to it years ago. Strong, steady, going in its own rhythm.

Dawn lifted her head and looked at him. "It's nothing to do with you, what they're doing here. It isn't even to do with me either. Dusk just needs me so he can help Diya."

"So he's using you? And that's better than being with me?" Geoff asked. "I'll be using you too, but at least you'd be doing something for your family. And I can take care of your physical needs, give you what he can't."

"It's a magic thing. He needs to be linked with a human to be able to do it," she said. "It was his choice."

"Funny, that," Geoff remarked. "I chose you too, and you don't love me."

"I tried to love you, and I almost did before," Dawn replied. The feelings she'd had when he visited her were childish but could have blossomed into more. Would have, she believed, if another hadn't taken her heart already. "If we'd really been friends first, I might have succeeded."

"All right, we'll start with that," Geoff said and pulled her out of the alcove. "We'll be friends today, and then we can step up to something else tomorrow."

"We'll start with being friends," she said, liking the idea. Had their rough conversation with Dusk actually helped? This was closer to the Geoff she missed. Now to keep him here, and bring him back further. "You tell me how it goes tonight. Maybe spending time with me today will make it easier. Then we'll see where we are."

"It'll get easier if you stay with me. But since you won't, I'll manage, like I've been since it started." They reached the dining room and he paused to smirk at her before entering. "Ready for Henry?"

Dawn nodded. "No, but I may never be, so we might as well get on with it."

"Good answer," Geoff said and pulled her through the doors.

The dining room was uneven and shapeless with rough, rounded walls. It had been a natural cavern, and care had been taken to preserve the feel. Above them were stalactites of varying sizes, some glowing to light the windowless space, all sharp and toothlike.

In the center of the space was a single long table, the Kirkjufell brothers sitting on either end. Geoff sat Dawn down in her seat on Henry's left, then went around behind Henry to sit across from her.

"You're late," Henry said as Geoff settled.

"I was showing Dawn the cougars and we lost track of time," Geoff explained while holding Dawn's gaze. She felt his foot bump against her calf and then hook behind her ankle to pull it closer to him.

"Ahh, getting straight to it with this one, are you?" Henry said and turned to Dawn. "And how did you like them? Quite majestic, aren't they?"

Dawn smiled politely and tried to ignore Geoff rubbing against her. "I enjoyed them. They were very impressive."

"They were wild, you know," Henry continued. "Geoff found

them when he was a small lad, brought them home, and tamed them. He has quite the way with beasts."

"Does he?" Dawn replied, avoiding meeting either Kirkjufell's eyes. She was saved from further conversing as servers arrived with dinner.

Heaping trays were placed along the table, with roast goat in cheese sauce, nut and berry bread, and a variety of fish dishes. Dawn looked at what seemed to be raw fish cut in chunks and wrapped in kelp with interest. Geoff noticed where her attention was and smirked. He reached across the table to grab her plate and put some of the kelp fish on it.

"Ever had raw fish before?" he asked as he set her plate back down, then filled his own plate almost exclusively with it.

"No, I haven't," Dawn said, cutting herself a tiny piece. She chewed slowly, not thrilled by the texture, but enjoying the flavor. Geoff watched her until she swallowed, then worked on his own food, practically inhaling it.

They continued eating in silence, giving Dawn a chance to glance down the table at Edmond. He was flanked on either side by a total of seven wizards, six of theirs and Cedric. Five empty seats were between the two halves, marking where the other Kirkjufell wizards would be if they weren't busy.

"They're quite dedicated to their work," Henry said, nodding at the empty seats. "My brother does a good job leading them."

"We met him earlier. He seems quite studious himself," Dawn said.

"Yes, he's a skilled wizard," Henry agreed. "Always working hard taking care of his charges, not afraid to make sacrifices when they're needed."

"Just the sort of person a great leader needs under him," Dawn said. Geoff twitched against her as he tried not to laugh, and she grinned at him.

Henry looked at his son seriously. "You don't let this one get away from you. She's got a sharp mind in that pretty head of hers."

"I don't plan to," Geoff replied, smirking. Dawn tried not to squirm as he worked his foot under her skirts and touched her bare skin.

Henry returned to eating, and Dawn tried to focus on her own plate. Geoff returned his attention to his fish, then looked up at her and frowned. She jumped as he reached across the table and grabbed her necklace.

"I see the rose retained its effect after he put it in glass," he said, then held the glimmering pendant in front of his father. "You see this?"

"Quite interesting," Henry said. "Something special?"

"Yes," Dawn answered, watching Geoff carefully. "It's magic. It only sparkles at dawn and—"

"Dusk," Geoff finished for her. "How very poetic."

He let go of the necklace and slumped back down. His plate was almost empty, and he grabbed more of the kelp-wrapped fish. Dawn felt him twitch against her until he took another bite, then calm slightly. She reached under the table and placed her hand on his knee. He looked at her, then put his hand on hers and squeezed it gently. She left her hand in his for the rest of dinner.

28

Once Geoff cleared his plate a second time, he excused himself and all but sprinted from the dining room. Dawn watched him go with concern, wondering what he had that she inadvertently helped with.

"So, what do you think of my boy?" Henry asked her after Geoff disappeared.

"He's something," Dawn answered. Overall the day had been rough, with him insulting her friends, yanking her around the palace, and arguing with Dusk. But mixed in with all the bad were a few moments that showed her a real human. The surprise he'd shown when he first touched her hand, the joy he couldn't help but have when they saw the cougars, and his sleeping face almost childlike in its innocence.

"That he is," Henry said, giving Dawn a hard look. "But something good, that you like the idea of, or something you aren't too sure about?"

Dawn brought her thumb to her lips while she considered. The good moments were pleasant, but they didn't outweigh the tough ones. "I'm not sure, no. He'll take some getting used to if I'm honest."

"Then you'd better start getting used to him. Perhaps I should have someone take you to his rooms, and you can continue getting familiar with each other?" Henry beckoned one of the servants over, a young boy who was a year or so away from growing into his gangly limbs. Dawn bit her tongue to keep from making a sound as she recognized him. "Paul, I need you to take the princess up to Geoff."

Paul bowed, giving no indication that he also recognized her. "Of course, sire."

"No, that won't be necessary," Dawn said, relieved that Paul knew how to act. "With respect, Sire, I would prefer to go at my own pace with him, and take a little more time."

"Nonsense," Henry said, waving the idea away. "You're going to be his wife soon; you may as well know who you're marrying. You know what they say about trying the milk before you buy the goat."

Dawn blushed and gaped at him. "I am not a goat, Sire, and I will not be visiting the prince in his rooms until after we are married."

"So you do mean to wed him," Henry said, smiling. "Just make sure you get to it. He's waited long enough for this without you wasting more of his time not giving him children. We have a royal line to think of."

"I'll keep that in mind," Dawn said. She looked at her plate and decided she'd eaten enough. "I'd like to be excused now, please. Edmond was hoping to meet the fairies tonight, and I'll need to take them."

Henry looked across the table at his brother, who was finishing up and standing to leave. "All right, then. Paul can help you get around."

Dawn almost said she didn't need help, but caught herself. "That would be perfect, thank you."

"Well, off you go. Don't want to keep him waiting," Henry said and waved her on.

Dawn smiled politely and followed Paul out of the dining room. She leaned back on the heavy wood door for a moment, eyes closed.

"Are you all right, Your Highness?" Paul asked nervously.

"I've been better," she remarked, giving him a stern look as she straightened and followed after him. "Of course, I can't help but remember our last meeting."

"Oh," Paul said, then flashed her a toothy grin. "But you have to admit, I was right about you."

Dawn laughed, unable to help feeling at ease with his boyish charm. "I suppose I must. Just no repeats, all right?"

Paul's grin broadened and they reached Dawn's room quickly. As they turned the last corner, they saw Rob leaning on the wall next to her door. He turned his head and instantly was standing ready to fight, hand on his sword hilt.

"You!"

"Me," Paul said, flashing his teeth at Rob. "You kept my mark, I see."

Rob rubbed at his cheek and glared at the boy. It had finally healed enough not to bleed if he scratched it, but it would be an angry red color for another week or two.

"Paul will be assisting us this evening," Dawn said, raising a brow at Rob. He frowned, but relaxed. She smiled and walked past him into her room.

Dusk was sitting in a window slit, staring at the sky. He flicked his wings and floated over, looking at her with concern. "How was dinner?"

"Better than expected," she said, gesturing out at Rob and Paul, who were making faces at each other. "I did manage to find Paul."

"Wonderful," Dusk said, perking up. "Well, we'd best get moving. Come on, Diya."

Diya looked up from the bed where he was lounging and scowled. "Time to see the wizard?"

"The sooner we get there, the sooner we'll be done," Dusk replied, and Diya snorted and took his time getting up and airborne.

"Or we could put it off forever and never see him," he muttered as he followed the others out of the room. "He's human—he'll die eventually."

Dawn followed Paul's path to Edmond's room in her mind, noting it was a short, direct path without Geoff as the guide. She took a deep breath as they reached his door and she knocked, somehow more nervous now than when Geoff had brought her.

"Dawn," Edmond said, smiling as he opened the door to invite her and the fairies in. "Lovely to have you back. Thank you for bringing them."

Edmond's sitting room was small, with a pair of armchairs in the center, sitting on either side of a low, round table. On the left were a fireplace with a cozy fire crackling away and the first real window Dawn had seen in the palace, a large picture window that faced the mountains and the east side of the lake. A writing desk squatted on the wall opposite the window, covered in loose papers and beakers haphazardly thrown about.

Dusk floated into the room after Dawn, but Diya hovered in the doorway, making Dusk sigh and flutter back to pull him in.

"Just a quick hello, then we'll leave. You'll be fine," he whispered.

"Everything all right?" Edmond asked. He sat in one of his armchairs, and Dawn settled herself across from him.

"Perfectly," Dusk said as he and Diya landed on the arm of Dawn's chair. "Just a bit tired from the travel. Diya always did have trouble with boats."

"Understandable. Is there anything I can offer to help, Diya?" Edmond asked, saying his name as if it were a sweet he'd eaten before but had forgotten the taste of.

Diya spasmed and glared at the red velvet armrest he was perched on. "No."

"If you're certain," Edmond replied and slid his gaze to Dusk. "My nephew mentioned one of you was rather talented. May I presume it to be you?"

"It would be me, yes," Dusk said and held out his hand.

Edmond glanced at the hand curiously, then saw Dawn signaling and held out his finger in return.

"How quaint," he remarked as they shook. "I'm very sorry I wasn't able to see your presentation earlier, but I've been busy recently. Perhaps you would be willing to come again, and we can show each other what we know?"

"Perhaps," Dusk said. "Quite a lot of effort to keep a sun going. Must be rather difficult for some of your wizards."

"Indeed it is," Edmond agreed, sitting back in his chair. "But Henry insists it be present, so we will maintain it. They're on a rotation to ensure its strength while allowing them rest when needed, and I paired them so they balance with each other."

"So the strongest with the weakest, and so on?" Dawn asked. So far, so good. If Dusk got on with Edmond, they all just might manage to be content here.

"Yes, they work well together in this fashion," Edmond replied. "There are a few nuances to the system, of course, so I am required to supervise every transition, and we have servants ready to help if anything happens."

"That's a lot of effort for a tribute I'd never heard of until today," Dusk said, in the tone Dawn knew meant someone was walking a thin line.

Edmond shrugged. If someone was in trouble, it wasn't him. "It's a newer idea Henry came up with."

"So new, none of his people seem to be aware of the reason," Dusk replied with a cocked eyebrow. The wizard wasn't getting off that easily. "As if there is another purpose for it?"

"Do you suspect something?" Edmond asked with interest. "It's possible my brother has another intention, but it isn't for me to discuss."

"Geoff knows what it's for," Dawn said without thinking, then mentally kicked herself. He'd said something in confidence, and she shouldn't reveal what she knew. "Though he didn't elaborate."

Edmond chuckled. "And he won't unless something changes his mind, which is rare."

Diya fidgeted and bumped his elbow into Dusk, who cleared his throat.

"Forgive me for the short audience, but Diya needs to rest, as you can see," he said.

Edmond coughed into his handkerchief and nodded. "Of course, don't let me keep you. Please come by anytime and we can talk about magic."

"We'll be sure to," Dusk said and helped Diya into the air.

Dawn smiled at Edmond as she stood. "Thank you. It's nice to know at least one Kirkjufell has good manners."

Edmond grinned and followed them to the door. "Like father like son, aren't they? Finding both of them a bit tricky?"

"Very," Dawn said. Tricky was an understatement—the pair was as bad as the palace to navigate.

"Then it's a good thing I'm here to help you with them," Edmond said as he closed the door.

The way back to Dawn's room seemed faster, with the fairies, and even Paul, feeling relieved to be away from the wizard. Dusk took a moment to carefully arrange the net of pearls into a pouch he could carry alone, setting one pearl on the vanity for Diya's circlet. Once ready, he followed Paul with Rob.

"Take care," Dawn called softly after them. She felt a tug and smiled as they disappeared, then closed her door quietly. Diya was settling himself in the center of her bed.

"Am I going to have to find somewhere else to sleep?" she asked.

Diya indicated the space around him. "I don't take up much space. Plenty of room for you too."

"We'll see what Dusk has to say about that when he gets back," she said, laughing.

"He can share too," Diya said. "Not like he can stargaze tonight."

"From what Geoff told me, they plan to keep doing it until we're married," Dawn said as she pulled her nightgown out of the wardrobe.

"And how long will that be, then? I don't like the never-ending daylight, but this requirement to get rid of it isn't great either," Diya said, sitting up to watch her.

"And what do you have against it?" Dawn asked. "As far as I can tell, it doesn't affect you any."

No more than moving to Kirkjufell, anyway. He would still be with Dusk as much now as ever. More even, with Geoff taking her time away from the fairy. If anything, this change was only positive for Diya, who was content enough to make jokes and flick around curiously like he had in her room at the castle.

"Not me, no," Diya said, shrugging. "But you already know how it'll be for Dusk. He was in rough shape when he got back from checking on you. Lucky I know how to work him, or he'd still be a mess."

Dawn winced. Considering how the situation had upset her, she could only imagine what it had been like for Dusk. "I don't want to put him through any more of that, but I can't prevent it. Geoff knows too much, and likely won't change how he treats Dusk."

"You're the only one who can do something about it," Diya argued. "It doesn't matter what Geoff does if you choose something different."

"If I choose what?" Dawn asked. She wanted to choose Dusk, she did, but how could she? Sure, he could become human, but she'd have the prince to marry regardless. Otherwise, there was no option that allowed the two of them to be truly together. "There are no other choices. There's only Geoff."

"You've got another choice—don't pretend you don't know," Diya said. He flicked his wings and went to the window slits, landing in one and watching the city beneath them. "Why'd you keep his rose so long? If you really wanted to give it to Geoff, you'd have done it sooner, wouldn't you?"

"I would have," Dawn said. She held up her pendant to study the rose, and the bracelet caught her attention from the corner of her eye. "I didn't want to send it, but my father found out I hadn't and told me I needed to. He was worried I might lose the engagement if I didn't."

"But you didn't want to," Diya said. His eyes had the same strange gleam they had in the Ruins when she'd lit a lamp with fairy magic. "That's what matters. You want to choose Dusk, and you should. It'll be worth it, I promise."

Paul darted along the brightly lit hallways of the palace, his senses focused on any sign of people crossing their path. Occasionally he would stop and backtrack to an alcove or around a corner, signaling for Dusk and Rob to hide with him until the way was clear.

They made it down and out of the palace without notice, and Paul directed them to nearby stables. Horses paced and kicked at their doors, tired from bright nights keeping them awake. Several whickered as the boys passed them, looking out of windows with burlap wrapped over their eyes.

Paul led them past three stables, turning at the fourth where Zan was waiting on the far end. The mercenary was leaning on the side of the stable, arms crossed, one knee bent, with his fox, Mina, curled up under him. He brushed some dirt off his shoulder and stood as his visitors approached.

"Nice work, Paul," he said and tossed the boy a coin. Paul smiled as he caught the gold and trotted off. Zan watched him go, then shifted his eyes to Rob. "Nice to see you again, boy."

"That's 'sir,'" Rob said, gripping his sword hilt.

"So I see," Zan said, giving Rob an approving nod before addressing Dusk. "Well, fairy boy, you got my pearls?"

"You have my information?" Dusk asked and pulled a pearl out of his pouch, holding it up.

Zan took the offered pearl and looked at it closely as he rolled it between his fingers. He brought it to his mouth and rubbed it against his teeth, then nodded. "Good quality you've found. A rare variety. Should've guessed you'd be good at pearl-hunting. Sun's being controlled by the palace wizards—nothing special."

"Yes, so Henry claims," Dusk agreed. "His brother is in charge of it, but he didn't let on what it's for."

"So you spoke to Edmond," Zan said, nodding. "And he told you about Geoff? And the visit they had from a witch right before all this began?"

"No," Dusk said and handed over another pearl. "But you'll enlighten me, won't you?"

Zan smiled as he pocketed the second pearl. "Story is that she came to look at Geoff because he was getting some symptoms similar to his mother's before she died. Wanted someone to look at him and make sure he didn't have the same illness."

"They never discovered what she had, did they?" Rob asked.

Zan waited as Dusk handed him another pearl. "They didn't, no. Edmond searched for a cure. Didn't find anything. That's why they went to someone else now for the prince. Witch came in and the symptoms left, but something else replaced them."

Dusk sighed and gave Zan the entire pouch. "Out with the rest of it."

Zan counted the pearls, slowly dropping them one by one out

of the pouch into his palm, then nodded as he tucked them away in his coat.

"No one knows what he has, or they won't say if they do. Henry's paying enough to keep everyone quiet. But after the witch saw him, some strange things happened in the mountains, things even the king can't hide. Animals went crazy, gathering and howling like never before. Whole herds of goats gone. Then the sun came, and it stopped again."

Rob paled as he imagined any number of terrible things that could be going on. Could it be the People of Ice in the north he'd heard stories of? Or magic from the mages here gone wrong? Or worst of all, what if something happened to the Circles? The magical prison sealed by the first-degree dragons themselves was nearby, watched over by the second-degrees in the Sky Forest. It was impenetrable, locked forever, but what if the creature inside had gotten out?

"What would cause something like that?" he whispered.

"And the witch?" Dusk asked calmly, as though he hadn't heard the same news as Rob. "What was her name?"

"Didn't have one," Zan said and shrugged. "Everyone knows her as the mountain witch since she lives up in them somewhere."

Dusk glowered. He knew what this meant, and he liked it as much as anything else in Kirkjufell. "What else does she do, besides heal mysterious illnesses?"

"Comes down occasionally to sell potions, and a lot of poor couples'll go to her when they're with child," Zan said. "Apparently she'll take alternative forms of payment if you don't have money, but no one ever reveals what they've given her."

"Anything else we should know?" Rob asked, hoping there wasn't more.

"Only that the witch and Edmond were a bit personal, if you know what I mean," Zan said. "It's no secret he's after his brother's throne. Anyone with sense would tell you he's finally making his move with her help."

"I had a feeling he was up to something," Dusk muttered. "Another wizard she's hired to help her. All so she could hide here and not do any of the work herself."

"Could be," Zan said, raising an eyebrow. "Seems like there's more to this than you're telling me, though. You want the full story, you gotta share what you know. Then I can get more details for you."

Dusk shook his head. "If she is our witch, then she's our problem. We'll figure out the rest ourselves, but you can keep your change."

Zan smirked. "Sure thing, Fairy. Paul'll help you out again if you need it. You're good for another story if you change your mind, but I'm not going out of my way for it."

"I wouldn't expect you to," Dusk replied with a grin. He offered his hand and Zan gave him his pinky to shake.

"'Til next time, kid," Zan said as he shook Rob's hand. "And thanks."

"For what?" Rob asked, frowning as he dropped his hand.

"Keepin' that scar," Zan replied, pointing to Rob's cheek and half-smiling. "Means something to the boy, that you were a worthy opponent. Keepin' it shows him you feel the same."

Mina got to her paws and rubbed against his leg, and he smiled at her. He bent down to scratch her ear, then straightened and sauntered away with her skipping along beside him.

29

Dawn awoke to the soft glow of sunrise that slowly crept into her room under Dusk's control. She looked up as Sarah knocked on her door and entered.

"Morning," Dawn said, yawning. "Did you sleep well?"

Sarah shook her head, rubbing at her bleary eyes. "I don't know how anyone could with this nonsense, though it seems you had some help."

Dusk smirked from the window slit where he was watching the real sun as it rose above the mountains. "Only a little. But depending how things go we may be able to help you out as well."

"Oh?" Dawn asked as she stretched and worked on getting up. "You aren't thinking of abandoning me, are you?" She felt a shimmer jab at her and she grinned.

"We've discovered that Berniece is here, and we want to consider other options for the lantern," Dusk said. "Diya's had an idea for it that we need to go over with you."

Sarah raised an eyebrow at Diya, who was stretched out on the mantle. He grinned at her and she turned to Dusk. "Well, let's hear it I guess."

"How would you like to use the lantern for us?" Dusk asked.

Sarah blinked at him slowly. "How would I like to what?"

"Handle the lantern," Dusk repeated. "Diya wants to entrust you to drain it for us, and I can teach you how to read spells and manipulate magic so you'd be able to. We need to maintain access to it for now, but we don't want to put it closer to Geoff when Dawn moves. Diya can stay in your room in the meantime to help you sleep, and if you have questions beyond what I teach, he's very knowledgeable in human magic."

"You are?" Sarah asked, and Diya shrugged. She rolled her eyes and turned to Dawn. "What do you think?"

"If you want to help, it's certainly a good opportunity," Dawn said. Learning from Dusk would not only help Sarah become the mage she'd always wanted to be, but would also help the two of them develop their own friendship, apart from her. But there was an important point to consider. "Will it be safe, though?"

"Perfectly," Dusk answered. "I won't have you do anything with the lantern until you've proven your ability to work on it, and I'll always supervise when you do. You're ready to do more with magic —you just need someone to direct you."

"If you say so," Sarah said and smiled. "It all sounds good to me; I'll do it."

Dawn hoped it was merely excitement at learning that made Sarah so quick to agree. Normally her friend would ask more questions, be less willing to take Dusk at his word. She wasn't doing this for something else, was she? Like to spite her father?

"Great," Dusk said and flew over to open Dawn's bath, lifting the heavy door with magic. "You let me know when you have time and we'll get started teaching you."

He flicked to the windows and Diya joined him, leaving the girls behind.

"Well, this is exciting," Sarah said as she pulled a dress out for Dawn, then frowned as she set it on the bed. "Though it's also concerning about Berniece. I'll keep a close eye on Father for you."

"Thank you, I'm sure Dusk will appreciate that," Dawn replied, undressing to bathe. "Although I hope you can enjoy spending time with your father before he goes home."

"I guess," Sarah said, dropping her gaze to the floor. She exited the room and almost walked into Rob standing just outside the door. "Bert! What are you doing here?"

Rob looked at her with red eyes, having slept about as well as her. "I'm guarding the room like I'm supposed to."

"I'm pretty sure they're all right while Dawn is still there," Sarah said.

"Maybe, but they'll need me soon while she has breakfast," Rob replied, crossing his arms and leaning on the doorframe.

"Suit yourself, I guess," Sarah said as she rolled her eyes. "But just so you know they're planning on moving it to my room later, and I don't want you hovering around all the time."

"Your room?" Rob repeated and furrowed his brow. "Why would they want to do that?"

Sarah shrugged. "They think it'll be safer with me, and Dusk is going to teach me to use it so Dawn doesn't have to."

"Really?" Rob replied, less-than-enthusiastically.

"Do you think I can't?" Sarah asked and crossed her arms.

"I know you can," he said. "Which is why I'm worried. Did you forget you're being watched?"

"Not as much as Dawn is," Sarah said, shuddering a moment as she recalled Geoff's visit. But, all the more reason she wanted to help, to be there for Dawn. "Look, Dusk wants to do it, and you know how he is with the lantern."

Rob snorted, not liking it, but unable to out-logic Sarah. "Oh, all right then. As long as *he* says so, it must be the best thing."

"Get over it already, Bert," Sarah said, rolling her eyes. "He helped us, didn't he? Dawn is fine, and she'll remain fine with him around. And you know it's better if the lantern stays somewhere away from Geoff."

"And what lantern might that be?" Geoff asked from behind them. He smirked as Sarah jerked in surprise and turned to face him.

"Not something you need to worry about," Rob said, glaring at the prince. So much for keeping Sarah out of this—now he'd have to think fast to keep things from getting any worse for Dawn.

"No? Then it's something to do with the fairies, isn't it?" Geoff crossed his arms and leaned back on the wall across from the doorway. "So what does it do?"

"It doesn't do anything," Sarah said and shifted nervously.

"It must do something if they don't want me to get it," Geoff said, smirking. Sarah's inability to lie wasn't lost on him. "That's what's in that chest, isn't it? The one with the fairies' things. Now, are you going to tell me about it, or am I going to have to ask Dawn?"

He moved off the wall and stepped over to the door. Rob placed himself between them and put his hand on his sword hilt.

"She isn't available currently," he said, eyes hard as steel.

Geoff slid his eyes up and down the knight, deciding where to strike first. "Then you'd better get talking."

"It's a magic capacitor," Sarah answered softly. "That's all we know."

"A capacitor," Geoff repeated, gaze shifting to her. "And what are they doing with it? Must have a lot of power if they want to keep it hidden. Enough to get up to all kinds of trouble."

Sarah pursed her lips, her eyes glancing between the boys. Any information was too much, but none could be worse. "They're emptying it."

"Obviously," Geoff said with a snort. "What else would you do with a capacitor, besides fill it? The question is what are they doing with the energy? Or didn't they tell you about it?" Sarah winced and he laughed at her. "Guess not. Great friend you've got, never telling you anything while she runs around with fairies."

Rob moved in front of Sarah, knuckles white as he gripped his hilt.

"She's the greatest," he said. "Maybe you'd realize that if you weren't so busy harassing us and yanking her around like an object. If you don't stop treating them like you are, you'll answer to my blade."

Geoff leaned over him and sniffed, a hunter assessing his prey. "Idle threats don't scare me. You won't be wetting that with my blood, though I'd like to see you try. It'd give me a reason to rip you apart."

"Are you challenging me?" Rob asked through gritted teeth. Just barely, he started pulling the sword out.

Sarah's whisper was sharp. "Bert, put that away." Rob glanced at her and complied, making Geoff laugh.

"Not as tough as you pretend, are you?" he said. "Letting a maid tell you what to do. My knights only follow my orders. Of course, my maids would never try anything like that. They know their place."

"Then it's a good thing I'm not your maid," Sarah replied. "I won't stand by and let you torment my friend."

"Think pretty highly of yourself, don't you?" Geoff asked. "You must have gotten special treatment in Mantrisa, being the personal maid of a princess. Don't think that'll continue here. Now, do your job and get Dawn ready so I can see her."

Sarah turned pink and entered the room, closing the door behind her.

A few minutes later Sarah returned to the hallway. Rob was staring stonily at Geoff, who was leaning on the wall next to the door and cleaning his fingernails.

"She's ready," Sarah said, fixing her eyes on the wall next to Geoff's shoulder.

"Good girl," Geoff said. He grabbed Sarah's chin and pulled her closer, leaning over to whisper in her ear. "Don't forget our little arrangement if you want to keep it that way."

Sarah trembled as he put his nose on her neck and inhaled deeply. He sighed, then pushed past her to the room.

Dawn was just finishing drying her hair, testing some aer magic as she ran a brush through the damp waves. Her eyes found him in the mirror from where she sat at the vanity.

"How was your night?" she asked.

"Terrible as ever," Geoff replied as he crossed the room to her. "Worse actually, since I had a taste of you yesterday. What's the capacitor for?"

"It doesn't affect you," Dawn said, turning to face him. "We aren't using it for anything you'll ever see."

Geoff snorted. "Then why not tell me? Sarah said you're emptying it. Didn't explain what you'd want to do that for, though. If it's really nothing, why do you want to keep it away from me?"

"There's a witch after it. We're moving the energy somewhere else to make sure she can't have it."

"Where to? And how exactly does that prevent her from getting it?"

"It's complicated," Dawn said. Not to mention personal. Neither fairy wanted the story given away to anyone who asked. "The lantern is dangerous, so we're going to disable it from holding energy at all. Where we're putting it isn't your business."

"Dangerous. To who, you or the fairies?" Geoff asked. She pursed her lips, and he smirked. "I want to see it."

"You really shouldn't try that," Dawn said as he stepped over to the chest at the foot of her bed.

He ignored her and attempted to turn the latch. There was a flash and a bolt of energy went through him, throwing him backward.

"Fancy chest you've got," he said, glaring at her. "What's the trick to it?"

"There's no trick. It just requires fae magic to open it," Dawn said.

"Does it. Awful lot of effort for a witch. Why are you so afraid of her? Unless it's not you that's afraid, but your little boyfriend."

Dawn closed her eyes and pictured Dusk. *Geoff, help,* she thought at him, then opened her eyes and looked at Geoff. "He's not afraid," she said. "The witch is powerful and she's got people after the lantern, so we're keeping it secure."

Geoff raised an eyebrow. "Must be people here or you wouldn't go out of your way for it. So, who is it? Who wants it?"

"Who wants what?" Dusk asked as he arrived through a window slit with Diya. He fluttered over to Dawn and looked at Geoff expectantly.

"Your capacitor. Dawn was just about to tell me who's interested in getting it," Geoff said.

Dusk scowled at him. "Why would we tell you anything? We know you're part of the plan. Maybe you're also getting something out of it."

"Paranoid little thing, aren't you?" Geoff said lazily. "If I am involved, no one told me. I don't appreciate being manipulated, so if they *are* using me somehow, I'll see to it that they fail."

Dawn chose her words carefully. "You mean you'd help us?"

"That's what I said," Geoff replied.

Not in those exact words, maybe, but Dawn knew he would follow through on his intention. Whatever he wanted to do with the witch would likely be beneficial for them, and that was all that mattered.

"Then why don't you help by telling me about the mountain

witch who saw you recently?" Dusk said. "Right before Edmond put a sun in your sky to stop something that happened to you."

"I see you told him what I said last night," Geoff said, glaring at Dawn. "Though I don't know where you heard about the witch seeing me. I never mentioned her."

"She didn't tell me anything," Dusk said. "I have other sources. Now tell me about the witch, and if I like what you give me, I'll share something in return."

"It's about damn time you did," Geoff said. "I don't know much about her—just that she's supposed to be able to cure anything. No one mentioned that she was equally good at cursing. Found that out when she did it to me. Never should have brought her in, but Henry insisted. Now the sun's destroying my city to keep the curse hidden while Dawn takes her time deciding if she can put up with me. What I'm cursed with doesn't matter, but if you think the witch that did it is after your lantern, I want to help you get her."

Dusk nodded. "From everything I've heard, your mountain witch is our Berniece. If my information is correct, she and Edmond are planning something together. What they want with the lantern we can only speculate, but it seems Edmond is after your father's throne."

"Is he," Geoff muttered darkly. "We'll be stopping that, then. He's not taking what's rightfully mine."

"But he was kind to us," Dawn mumbled, not wanting to believe the man who'd been so friendly would be working with Berniece.

"What, did you think you'd found an ally?" Geoff asked, laughing. "That he was such a gentleman, he couldn't possibly be conspiring against you? He might know how to act in polite company, but he's still a Kirkjufell."

Diya snorted from Dawn's bed where he'd made himself comfortable in the bedding. "He's a wizard. What else do you need to know?"

Geoff laughed again. "You have problems with yours? That why you brought him too, so you could keep an eye on him?"

"As it happens, Cedric is the entire reason we found out about the witch," Dusk said. "Whether or not he knew what he was getting into, I couldn't say."

"From what Sarah tells me, he was only following orders," Dawn said. It certainly wasn't anything malicious on his part.

"So they're in on it together, are they?" Geoff asked. "Didn't think Ed had any friends outside of the palace, and I certainly wouldn't pick Cedric. He's not too impressive. Bet he's no good at magic. Why would the witch use him, though? Ed at least is highly skilled, part of the royal family. Valuable. Only thing Cedric has is being your singular wizard, which isn't worth much."

Dawn gasped and reached into her pocket for her handkerchief, grasping it tightly. When Cedric first came to Mantrisa, her parents were skeptical about the need for a wizard, but something else had made up their minds. "He has Sarah. The reason we took him in the first place was because of her, so she could be my companion."

"Think the maid's part of it too?" Geoff asked and smirked. "Still want to give her the capacitor?"

"Her role in this is completed," Dusk said with finality. "Likely she was only a means of getting into the castle, and a convenient way to fetch the lantern when it was time."

"And how close is she to Cedric? Think she'd help him if she knew what was going on?" Geoff asked.

"She already knows most of it," Dawn said. "And while she's tried to deny Cedric's intentions, she's remained faithful to me. I don't trust anyone else more."

"Better hope you're right," Geoff replied. "Things might change once we find the witch. We know what Ed's getting from helping her, but what about Cedric? If it's something Sarah wants too, she might betray you."

"I don't feel that she would, from what I've seen," Dusk said. "Regardless of what Cedric wants, I think she'll make the right choice."

"She told me she'll watch him for us," Dawn said. "She wouldn't do that if she weren't firmly on our side. I can talk to her later and make sure."

"All right," Dusk agreed. "In the meantime, we need to start working on Edmond. Find out his next move, so we can prepare a counterattack. I presume you'd like to handle your uncle?"

"You presume correctly," Geoff said. "I can get him talking; he won't stay quiet for long. Especially not against my secret weapon."

"And that is?" Dawn asked.

Geoff smirked and grabbed her hand, pulling her out of the chair and into him. "You."

30

"It's simple," Geoff explained as he led Dawn to breakfast. He brought her along a straightforward path that used the spiral stairs. "I can get anything I want out of Ed if his guard is down. That's your job. You distract him with your pretty words and he'll be easy prey for me."

"If you say so," Dawn said tentatively.

"Still like him, don't you?" Geoff asked, looking back at her. "Think he's better than Henry, anyway. Wouldn't mind if he were king instead. But what would that leave me? You won't stay if Ed wins."

"The only way it makes sense for this all to be connected is if Edmond did take my kingdom's light," she replied. As sorry as she was to consider it, she couldn't refute the evidence against Edmond. "If that's true, then he's my enemy as well."

"He's your enemy because he's after my throne," Geoff said. "Or did you forget you're here for me?"

"We haven't officially become engaged yet," Dawn said. "Maybe I should just go, get the lantern out of here, and leave you alone to deal with your uncle."

Geoff spasmed, jerking her. "But you wouldn't leave me, not now that we're friends. Unless you changed your mind about wanting to care."

"No, I still want to," she said. It bothered her that his own family didn't seem to care about him, only spurring her to continue trying. The better he was, the happier she could be as well. "I'm sorry last night was worse. I wish it had been better."

"I told you it would only get better if you stayed with me," Geoff said. "But maybe I can convince you to come tonight. I've got something to show you after we chat with Ed that you'll like."

"Something like the lift, or the cougars?" Dawn asked warily.

"You did like them," Geoff answered with a smirk. "But this is better. No clues, though. Don't want to ruin the surprise."

"I can't wait," Dawn remarked quietly. All of Geoff's plans so far had been exhausting, and at this point she wasn't sure how much more she could put up with. If he wasn't going to let her opt out of anything, she didn't know if she could muster any new enthusiasm.

Geoff laughed as they reached the dining room, pausing at the doors. "In that case, maybe we should skip breakfast and go there right now. Won't have to see Henry that way."

"That is tempting," Dawn said, briefly considering saying yes. "But Edmond is important enough to take care of first, and I'm hungry."

Geoff laughed again as he pushed open the doors. "You do have your priorities, don't you?"

A couple of servants were milling about, cleaning up breakfast. Henry was alone at the high table when Dawn and Geoff joined him. The king watched his son with a raised eyebrow as he sat down.

"You're late again," he said.

Geoff smirked as he started filling his plate with the same raw fish from last night.

"Took longer to collect the princess than I expected," he said and bumped her knee with his. "One of her roommates is very chatty."

"I see," Henry said with a frown and looked at Dawn. "You aren't going to continue making my son late to everything, are you? Any sufficiently appropriate behavior shouldn't keep you."

Dawn blushed and focused on the berries she was adding to her plate. "Perhaps if Geoff didn't feel he needed to personally take me everywhere, he'd be on time."

"Ahh, but then you wouldn't be getting used to him, would you?" Henry replied. "Now, you'll be making some progress with that today, or I'll have your things moved to his level."

"I told you it was her fairy's fault," Geoff said, choking on a laugh. He got his foot under Dawn's skirt and rubbed against her leg. "You'll have to find them somewhere else to stay if you move her in with me."

Henry nodded and stood. "If they're too much of an issue, they'll be removed from the palace. You'll tell me your progress at dinner. Be on time."

Dawn watched the doors close behind him, then shoved Geoff away.

"Stop that," she exclaimed angrily. "It's no wonder you're so rude, with a father like him." She sighed with frustration and bit into a strawberry.

"He'll stop once you give me a son," Geoff said. "Might want to be more willing to start on that if you're already tired of him."

"He'll have other things to worry about if we don't stop your uncle," Dawn said. "I'll think about it after that."

Geoff snorted. "Sure are finding plenty of ways to stall. Don't want kids either, do you? Just unhappy with everything you've been given."

Dawn opened her mouth to protest, then stopped as she thought of Dusk. He wasn't supposed to be part of her life, but he was the best part of it. The only part she truly wanted. She loved her friends, but if she didn't have Dusk, she couldn't be happy here, or anywhere. He'd made himself part of her life, and all she wanted was for him to stay.

"I'll get over it," she said quietly. "This is my life, and it'll continue whether I'm happy or not. I'll be ready to do what you want someday if you remain patient with me."

"And what am I supposed to do until then?" Geoff asked. "I'm not going to wait around while you figure out you'll never be happy because you can't have your fairy. Best thing you can do now is what he told you. Accept your new life with me, and everything it includes."

"Well, right now it includes a conspiracy to steal my lantern and your kingdom," Dawn said, glad for something else to focus on. "But I suppose that's as good a place as any to start accepting things."

Geoff looked satisfied as he finished the rest of his fish. He fidgeted while Dawn cleared her own plate, then stood and grabbed her hand.

"Ready to see the wizard?" he asked as he pulled her out of the chair.

Dawn tried not to stumble as he practically ran with her. "Even if he is bad, I still would rather talk to him than Henry."

Geoff laughed, practically dragging her into the hallway. "Would you. We'll see how you feel after I've worked him. You may realize some things that change your mind."

"Like what?" Dawn asked with concern.

Geoff winked at her and smirked. "You'll see."

After breakfast, Sarah was shown to the balcony above the waterfall. A dense mist hung over the space, fat water drops that were flung up from the fall and landed on the balcony. The stone was textured and inset with grainy wood at regular intervals, but the incessant water made slipping a constant threat. A white marble wall curved along the open side, more ornamental than practical, though it succeeded in preventing falls.

Sarah pushed damp strands of hair off her cheeks that were bright red from the cold water hitting them. At least the water was clean—it was treated magically when it was pulled into the basin that fed the waterfall—and made the air fresh.

Edmond and his twelve wizards were gathered at the edge of the balcony. Six stood in a line, some with closed eyes, others waving their arms as they fueled the small sun above their heads, the noise of the waterfall drowning out any thoughts that might distract them. Behind them, the other six wizards were waiting in a cluster, readying their magic to take over. Four of them were muttering spells to start the channeling. One of them, a bard, was tuning her flute, and the final wizard stood perfectly motionless, eyes closed as he mentally worked.

Sarah passed behind Edmond as he stepped into the line of six, helping them hold the magic while they switched out one by one. He all but shouted to be heard over the roaring water, and Sarah couldn't make out more than a couple of words as she continued past him.

Cedric was standing where the marble wall met the outside of the palace, observing. He glanced at his daughter as she stopped next to him, giving her a knowing look. "Rather inspiring, isn't it?"

A frail wizard with white hair trembled as he stepped away from the line, looking ready to fall over at the slightest breath of wind.

"It does look rather hard on them," Sarah replied. A servant approached the old wizard and helped him slowly limp back into the palace.

"Exactly why I feel as I do," Cedric said, smiling like he thought he'd won. "This is what becomes of those who choose to study magic. I only want better for you."

"Then why are you a mage?" Sarah asked, watching the fresh wizards settle in for their shift. Even rested, they were gaunt and pale from overworking.

Cedric stammered for a reason, finally relaxing as Edmond approached them.

"And this must be Sarah," he said, smiling. "If you aren't the exact image of your mother. I'm very pleased to finally meet you."

Sarah nodded and curtsied. "Pleased to meet you as well."

Edmond chuckled. "Why, you're just as polite as Dawn. Must be something about living in Mantrisa. Now, I heard a rumor that you recently discovered sorcery. That is most exciting."

"It is," Sarah said, smiling at Cedric. "In fact, the fairies are planning on teaching me more." Her father's face darkened, and she almost felt sorry for him.

"Very generous of them," Edmond said. "They must think greatly of your natural talent."

Sarah blushed. "I guess so."

"I'd also be happy to help you cultivate your skill if you'd like," Edmond said. "Perhaps they would be willing to teach you in my study, and we could observe each other."

"If you want to," Sarah said, then turned to her father. "I need to go meet some of the servants and get a tour. I'll see you later." She bobbed a quick curtsey to Edmond and skipped away back into the depths of the palace.

"Quite the girl she's become," Edmond remarked, staring after her.

"You aren't thinking of using her to get to the fairies, are you?" Cedric asked.

"You didn't offer anything better," Edmond said. "And after your blunders, it's the least you can do."

"My daughter is not to be part of this," Cedric said.

"She's already been part of it," Edmond replied with a laugh. "The only part you managed to do correctly. We've done everything flawlessly over here, while you did nothing but screw up. Letting me use Sarah a bit more won't kill you."

"Why not use Dawn?" Cedric asked. "After all, she has the link with one. She would do the job much more nicely."

"She is closer to them, and that's why we can't use her," Edmond said. "She might realize what I'm up to. Besides, Geoff's keeping her busy running around the palace. He's not interested in sharing her, so I wouldn't get her as often as I'd like."

"I don't want any harm to come to Sarah," Cedric said. "That would include you. If you don't feel there's any other way to catch the fairies, then do what you must, but no more."

"I promise I won't touch her beyond what is required to get the fairies," Edmond said. "Though a sorceress is a precious commodity. You'll need to be careful if you don't want anyone to take her from you."

Cedric sighed. "Once Berniece is satisfied, I can take her away, out into the country, and we'll live quietly. There, I can keep them both safe."

"Assuming she still gives you your reward," Edmond said. "Which she'll only do at this point if we do succeed in giving her the fairy."

"And you're certain she wants Dusk?" Cedric asked. "I understand she'd be attracted to his skill, but the other has been caught before."

"Making him less likely to be captured again," Edmond countered. "She's very interested in the link, and would like to have a specimen for study in addition to his superior talent."

"And you wouldn't mind giving the princess a reason to remain in your kingdom," Cedric said.

Edmond smirked. "I wouldn't mind that, no."

"It's ready," Dusk said as he finished setting the pearl in Diya's circlet and held it up. "How's it look?"

Diya grinned and stopped bouncing on the end of Dawn's bed. He floated over to the pillow where Dusk was sitting and inspected his work.

"Perfect," he said and knelt.

"Would you just take it?" Dusk asked. Diya smirked at him and he sighed. "Fine. I dub thee Diya, the Fairy Prince." He placed the circlet on Diya's head dramatically and bowed. "Does it please you, Your Majesty?"

Diya grinned again and flew over to the vanity to look at himself in the mirror. "His majesty is very pleased, thank you, Sir Dusk. Really, though, it's great. Maybe you should think about going into jewelry-making full time."

"Maybe," Dusk said, half smiling. "After we deal with Berniece. It's quite cheeky of her to hide out over here and hire wizards to get the lantern for her. Rather well thought out, except for us."

"We do have a history of ruining schemes," Diya said with a grin. He fluttered his wings playfully, then dropped both them and the smile. "Although I think they messed up with the boy. You know what he is, right?"

"Only one thing it could be, considering," Dusk said, grimacing. "Not a smart move to give someone like him that kind of power."

"Are you going to tell Dawn?" Diya asked seriously.

"It isn't for me to share," Dusk answered. "Just as it wasn't for me to explain the lantern without your permission."

"But this is different. Her friends are worried about her for good reason," Diya argued. "Saying nothing might be worse. I could lose both of you if anything happens."

"Nothing will happen as long as Edmond maintains the sun," Dusk said. "And Geoff will likely get angry if I do tell Dawn, putting her in just as much danger."

"And if they do get married?" Diya asked. "What then? They'll stop trying to cover it up and let her see. They don't care about her safety as long as she does what they want. And I doubt she'll be happy with you if she finds out you knew but didn't tell her."

"She's a smart girl. She may figure it out herself before we have to worry about that possibility," Dusk said.

Diya snorted. "She hasn't figured out what you need yet—she won't realize this until he shows her what he is."

"She'll figure it out," Dusk said. "Even if she doesn't, I have a feeling she's much safer than you think. You remember what happened when we first arrived, when he touched her?"

Diya raised an eyebrow. "You think she's placating him?"

"Passively," Dusk replied. "It is one of her abilities."

"You've never tried it on his kind before, but I guess you know more about it than I do," Diya said, then laughed as he thought of something. "Actually, she was already pretty inclined to this before you linked. Might have done all right without you."

Dusk smiled. "I'm sure she would have."

31

"Ed!" Geoff shouted down the hallway at his uncle, catching him just before he reached his rooms.

Edmond stopped and turned around. His nervous expression melted away when he saw the prince wasn't alone. "Ahh, Geoff. Bringing Dawn back to visit again?"

"Something like that," Geoff replied as he and Dawn caught up to the wizard.

"Well, at least you've come when I'm not busy. Why don't you wait here, and I'll send for a tea service," Edmond said.

"That would be lovely," Dawn replied, smiling as naturally as she could. Whatever Geoff intended with the wizard, she wasn't thrilled to be part of it. Why couldn't he talk to his uncle without her? "I was hoping we could chat for a bit."

"Of course," Edmond said. "I've just finished overseeing another transition, so I have plenty of time to talk."

"Good, then we'll just be in your sitting room," Geoff said and pulled Dawn towards his door.

"Please, I would rather you wait for me," Edmond exclaimed. "Dawn, you'll keep him under control, won't you?"

"I'll try," Dawn said, looking at Geoff skeptically. "But I think you know better than I do how difficult that will be." Geoff winked at her.

"I suppose I do," Edmond mumbled. He took a moment to pull out his handkerchief and coughed into it. "Perhaps we won't bother with the tea, then."

"Don't be like that, Ed," Geoff said. "If it means that much to you, I'll go fetch it."

"If the princess would like to have tea, I do feel that would be better," Edmond said. His eyes cried for help in spite of his effort to keep his face neutral.

"Yes, tea would be nice," she said.

Geoff squeezed her hand and let go as he went back up the hallway. "I'll be right back. Don't get too cozy without me."

"I wouldn't dream of it," Edmond muttered, making Dawn giggle. "You seem to be getting on better with him now." He opened the door and ushered her to an armchair.

"I'm getting used to him," Dawn said as she watched Edmond hurrying about for a few minutes, clumsily trying to hide some of his things. Paper and equipment were scattered everywhere— he clearly wasn't prepared for company now. "Please, don't trouble yourself on my behalf. I understand some clutter has built up with all the work you've been doing lately."

Edmond stashed a pile of letters in a desk drawer and settled in the chair across from her. "Thank you. I would still rather have things be a bit more presentable for you if you could warn me before your next visit."

"Oh, of course," Dawn replied. "It was Geoff's idea to jump on you like this, as you may have guessed."

"Yes, that is, unfortunately, his style," Edmond said. "You'll find very few escapes from him, I'm afraid. I hope I can provide one for you when he's particularly ornery."

"Perhaps you could do the same for Henry as well?" she asked.

Edmond smirked. "I certainly can help with him. As his younger brother, I know a thing or two that you'll find useful."

"At least I understand Geoff a little better," Dawn said. Her interactions with the king had been the least pleasant so far, hinting at the difficult life Geoff had always known. "Henry's not going to be easy to live with."

"No, he's never been that," Edmond said. "Bit harsh of a ruler too, if I may be so bold. Too much concern for power, not enough for his people."

"So exactly like you," Geoff remarked as he entered the room. Edmond colored slightly, and Geoff smirked as he placed himself on the arm of Dawn's chair. "Didn't miss me too much, did you?"

"We were just fine," Dawn said, leaning back to give him more room.

Geoff nodded and shifted his weight around a bit, getting comfortable. "Tea'll be here in a few minutes. Until then, why don't you continue sharing your opinion on how Henry handles the kingdom?"

"Well, you can't disagree that he's inclined to power," Edmond said.

"I wasn't disagreeing," Geoff replied. "Merely pointing out that you're the same as your brother, no matter how much you like to think you're not. Regardless, how he takes care of things shouldn't be any of your concern. It'll be mine when he's gone, and you know better than to mess with my things."

Edmond pursed his lips. "Enough people have been sent away for doing so, particularly in recent years. I won't be contributing to the number."

Geoff laughed. "And how many wizards have left, or gone missing under you? Probably more than those who've crossed me—you've been around longer."

Could he really be mistreating the wizards? It was common

knowledge how dangerous the work could be, and with thirteen wizards it wasn't surprising the Kirkjufells lost some here and there. But to insinuate that Edmond pushed them, knowingly forced them into things that would lead to their death... Even with all the wealth in the world, it was unbelievable what the Kirkjufells seemed able to get away with.

"They know what they're getting into," Edmond said. "It's a risk every wizard takes when he performs an untested spell."

"Really," Geoff replied. "Dawn, is your magic safe, do you think, or are you risking your life when you try something?"

"I'm all right," Dawn answered quietly. "But I'm sure it's different for me."

"Right, because you are learning under a fairy who cares about you. The wizards here are under someone who's 'willing to make sacrifices,' as Henry put it," Geoff said.

"Human magic is not the same as fairy magic," Edmond argued. "Nothing's safe when you don't know your own alignment, regardless of who is in charge. Fairies have it significantly easier."

"Interesting theory," Geoff replied. "But it lacks factual support. Until yesterday, you'd never even seen a fairy."

"You don't have to see them to have an understanding of how they work," Edmond said. Carefully, measured, like he knew Geoff was leading him but didn't know where, or why.

"But why bother learning about them?" Geoff asked. "The fairies who came here weren't meant to, and there's no other reason for you to have cared. I learned about them because I'm marrying a princess who lives with them. Gives me more control over her kingdom once that alliance is made. Why are you interested?"

"I'm merely curious about all forms of magic," Edmond said. And curious about what Geoff was getting at. "Many mages are, for simple educational purposes."

Geoff smirked, having put his uncle in the corner he wanted. "Then why aren't you studying my curse?"

Edmond jumped out of his chair as there was a knock on the door. Dawn looked at Geoff and tilted her head at the drawer with the letters. Geoff glanced at it, then winked at Dawn. Edmond returned a moment later with a tea tray, his shaking hands making the saucers and cups rattle as he set it down on the table between them.

"I don't know what you mean," he fumbled as he sat down again.

"You know exactly what I mean," Geoff said. He filled a teacup and handed it to Dawn. "Careful, it's hot."

"Thank you," Dawn said quietly as she accepted it. Considering how easily he'd told her about being cursed, was it really surprising he'd use it now, to shock his uncle?

"You thought I wouldn't tell her, didn't you?" Geoff asked as he poured himself a cup. "But you know better than to expect me to follow your plan. So explain yourself, or I'll tell her what you want to do with her."

Edmond scowled. "I don't know what you're implying, but you won't be putting foul ideas in her head. Please, ignore him."

"I didn't say anything about foul," Geoff said, frowning. "Did I say that?"

"No, not specifically," Dawn answered.

"See?" Geoff grinned triumphantly. "Now talk. You cursed me, didn't you?"

"Of course not," Edmond said, glowering. "You accuse me with no evidence and attempt to blackmail me into admitting to something I'm innocent of. I'm sorry, Dawn, but it seems he is determined to sully my reputation."

"But we do have evidence," Geoff said as he got to his feet and moved to the desk drawer. "That's what you've got in here, haven't you?"

"Don't touch that!" Edmond shouted. "You may be the crown

prince, but even the king himself would not be permitted to go through my things without permission."

"Except I don't need permission," Geoff said and paused with his hand on the drawer. "Where are we?"

Edmond frowned. "We are in Kirkjufell, but I don't see wha—"

"Wrong answer," Geoff said. "Dawn, perhaps you'd like to tell him?"

"We're in your palace," Dawn replied softly, not looking Geoff in the eye. Now that he had Edmond where he wanted, why didn't he leave her out of anything more?

Geoff nodded. "Very good. And do I need permission for anything while we're here?"

Dawn shook her head. "No."

"There you have it. So do you want to tell me what you're doing, or am I going to find out when I look in this drawer?" Geoff asked.

Edmond gaped at him, then looked at Dawn and sighed. "I suppose you leave me with no choice. If you'll sit, I'll give you an explanation."

Geoff smirked and resumed his spot on Dawn's armrest. Edmond took his time clearing his throat and preparing himself a teacup. After several minutes of stalling, he sat back in his chair and looked at his nephew.

"It was the mountain witch who did this to you, you know that."

"I do," Geoff replied darkly. "But I also know you brought her in. You're the one who suggested her to Henry, and ordered everyone to do exactly what she wanted while she was here."

"I didn't realize what she would do," Edmond said. "I only recommended her because I've heard enough good things about her. I only wish I had met her myself first, then perhaps this could have been prevented."

"Goatshit," Geoff exclaimed. "You knew exactly who she was."

"I assure you I did not," Edmond said, frowning.

"No?" Geoff smirked. "Then who came to see you when my mother died? You had a visitor then, a secret one that Henry didn't know about. But I saw her, I remember."

"And who's going to believe the delusion of a child, who was wrought with sadness at the loss of his mother?" Edmond asked.

Geoff laughed. "I wasn't distressed by her death—I barely knew her. You know Henry didn't let me have any sort of relationship with her. I may have been young, but I know what I saw, and that was the mountain witch stealing out of your rooms in the dark of night."

Edmond scowled. "And what were you doing near my rooms at such an hour?"

"Couldn't sleep," Geoff said with a shrug. "I wanted to ask you for something to help but saw you were busy. Forgot about the witch until she came back, then it took me a few days to realize why she was familiar."

"You can't prove anything," Edmond hissed.

"No," Geoff said. "But I don't need to. Dawn believes me, don't you?"

Dawn nodded and took a long drink of tea.

"As if that matters," Edmond scoffed. "You aren't giving her any more choice in this than you are me. You just wait, and as soon as you let her out of your sight, she'll run from you."

"She won't be trying anything like that, will you?" Geoff asked. Dawn shook her head and he smirked. "Only been here a day and I've already got her better trained than Henry has you. That'll change once I'm king. You'll either do as I order, or we'll find somewhere else for you to serve me."

"In that case, I won't see you become king," Edmond said. "I'd rather leave of my own accord first."

"Or maybe you'd rather be the one on the throne," Geoff replied. "Of course, I'm only speculating. Wouldn't be much of a Kirkjufell if you didn't want it. Fine line between wanting it, though, and actively vying for it. Better think real carefully which side you're on."

Edmond coughed. "I only want what's best for this kingdom."

"And would that be with you in charge?" Geoff asked. "Dragons know you don't think I'm good for the kingdom. Funny, really, since I actually care more about my people than Henry. Nothing to rule if they aren't taken care of. And they turn on kings easily enough if they aren't kept happy."

"And how do you intend to manage that?" Edmond said. "You rule your servants with fear, not a hallmark of a great leader."

"Servants are different," Geoff said. "People are all tools to be used for the task that suits them, and in a way that fits. Servants should follow orders, the general public should love me, and you should do as I say."

"You may be successful with the servants, but you won't win over the people as you are now," Edmond said. "It would take a real man to lead them. Something my brother isn't, nor you."

"And do you believe you are one?" Dawn asked. Was she wrong? Was Edmond really as bad as Geoff wanted her to believe? Maybe not, but certainly from what she'd heard so far, neither was he as good as she wished.

"Why, he truly has corrupted you," Edmond said, shaking his head slowly. "You would ask me such a thing? That puts me in a poor spot no matter my answer."

"Not answering says plenty itself," Geoff said. "You see where her loyalty is, and it's not with you like you were hoping. Of course, she's a bit sore with you because you had your wizards steal her kingdom's light. Not the best way to get on someone's good side."

"You—I wouldn't... How can you accuse me like this?" Edmond sputtered.

"Would you swear it wasn't you?" Dawn asked softly. The answer was obvious, but how would he respond to her asking? That was what she needed to know. "Are your wizards powerful enough on their own, that they wouldn't need to take light from somewhere else? If you swear to me it wasn't your order, I'll forgive everything else Geoff is trying to prove against you. The only thing that matters to me is what happened to my kingdom."

Edmond drooped in his chair dejectedly. "I wish I could lie to you, and say they didn't, or that I hadn't commanded it. But in spite of my nephew's effort to turn us against each other, I can't bring myself to attempt such things. I did orchestrate the Night Rise, but it wasn't my idea. It was the witch—she ordered it."

Dawn looked down at her empty teacup and rubbed her thumb in a circle on its side. "So you are with Berniece."

"You wound me, Princess," Edmond said. "I'm making an effort to be honest with you, that we might be able to help each other, and you still believe everything Geoff has poisoned you with. You accept his narrative of me."

"Your actions fit the description, or she wouldn't," Geoff said. "Should have considered that before you colluded with a witch, made a plan to get something of hers. And I don't mean her kingdom's light. But you didn't count on her learning anything, having fairies to help her, or listening to me. Why would she? She's just a princess. Isn't meant to think and do things, just here to be another tool, but for you instead of me."

"I would never think of her as a tool," Edmond said. "That's something you do, and we are nothing alike."

"Quite the compliment! I didn't know you thought so highly of me," Geoff jeered. "Really, though, you expect her to believe that? You know he used you in his plan, don't you Dawn?"

"Ridiculous," Edmond said. "What role could I have given her?"

"But you did use me," Dawn said. "At least, the witch did. She needed a Mantrisa to recover the lantern, and I was the best target.

Ignorant of its history, and lacking the ability to use it myself, it would easily have been handed over to Cedric and delivered to her."

"Lantern?" Edmond snorted. "What are you on about? Perhaps I have misjudged you if you're able to create such interesting untruths as easily as Geoff."

"No," Dawn said as she set her cup on the tray. "I'm the one who misjudged you, it seems."

Edmond winced and stared into his tea.

"Well, Uncle, it's been fun, but I'm getting tired of this game," Geoff said as he got to his feet and helped Dawn up after him. "You're welcome to forget we were here, tell the witch she lost, and pretend you were never after anything. Just go about your business, and we'll go about ours."

"Thank you for the tea," Dawn said softly as they left the room.

Edmond waited until the door latched behind them, then emptied his cup in one long draught. He went to the desk drawer and pulled out the letters They were his direct correspondence with Berniece over the last two decades, outlining their entire plan in more than enough detail to prove everything Geoff knew and more. He glanced through them briefly, then took them to his fireplace and threw them in. With a snap of his fingers, they ignited and slowly burned away out of existence.

Satisfied the letters were no longer a liability, Edmond pulled his mirror out of a desk drawer and wrote two words on the reflective surface.

Geoff knows.

He crushed a dried begonia petal over the mirror, and the dust and message disappeared. Several minutes later the mirror glowed a pale orange, and he stopped pacing to read Berniece's reply.

Kill him.

32

"So, what do you think of Ed now?" Geoff asked Dawn as they walked away from the wizard's rooms to the spiral staircase.

Dawn considered the conversation they had just finished and grimaced. "I still like Henry less, but I don't care for Edmond either."

Geoff laughed. "Good, but more importantly, do you like me better?"

"I'm still on the fence about you," Dawn said. He was difficult, but between his family and a curse, the blame wasn't entirely his. The issues that *were* his though, were too major to excuse.

They reached the stairs and Geoff paused to look at her. "You'll know soon, once you see your surprise. Close your eyes."

"What for?" she asked as he pulled her onto the stairs and they started going up.

"I don't want you to know where you're going," Geoff replied. "It'll make me angry if you figure it out with that map your fairy gave you, and I'd rather not get angry before this. It'd spoil it."

"I won't peek," Dawn said, smiling at his answer. Here, at least, was an echo of his previous self. Maybe she was making progress with him after all.

They climbed for what felt like several levels, but Dawn couldn't be sure how many. Eventually, Geoff pulled her off the stairs and down a few hallways. She didn't see him glancing back at her every few paces to make sure her eyes were staying closed.

Finally, they went through a door, and Dawn felt a cool breeze on her cheeks.

"Are we on a terrace?" she asked.

"You can look now," Geoff replied, and she did.

They were on a terrace, as she had guessed. Unlike the first one he'd shown her, this one was open to the sky, with only a low fieldstone wall along the edge to keep them safe. It was artfully filled with leafy ferns and a small selection of fragrant flowers. A few more of Geoff's creations were tucked in the foliage: a rabbit hopping, a frog croaking, a unicorn prancing. Down a small path, she could see water rippling, and steam coming off the spring in delicate wisps.

Geoff watched her and smirked.

"Knew you'd like it. Come on, there's more," he said as he pulled her along the path to the spring.

They stopped at the edge and Dawn knelt down to test the water, intrigued by its warmth. The main pool took up the majority of the small terrace and had many plants happily drifting on the surface. Along the water's edge were smooth stones that reminded Dawn of the pool in the Fae Realm. Off to one side, out of sight, she could hear a stream burbling.

"Is this one yours too?" she asked as she stood.

"It's yours," Geoff answered. "Thought you'd like the hot spring since you're so fond of baths."

Dawn stared up at his face for a moment, then put her ear on his chest to hear his heart again. Strong, steady, solitary. "Thank you."

Geoff wrapped his arms around her and buried his face in her hair, breathing in deeply. After a moment he pulled back to look at her. "Ready to swim?"

"With you?" Dawn asked with worry. The water was tempting, but she wasn't ready yet.

"I have to show you the best part," Geoff replied. "Or did you think it was just the spring?"

"It's nice enough on its own without us disturbing it," Dawn said, turning her head and watching a lotus float past. "You don't need to show me more."

Geoff frowned. "But it's the whole reason I picked this terrace. Wouldn't be very nice of you to not come see what it is."

Dawn shook her head. "That's sweet of you, but it's fine, really."

"Wait, you know how to swim, don't you?" Geoff asked. She pursed her lips and he laughed. "I see. You'll need to learn, then. Can't live on a lake if you can't swim. The spring's not very deep; you'll be fine. And if anything does happen, I'll be with you."

"All right, I'll come," she said with a smile. She couldn't argue with that.

Geoff squeezed her, then released his grip and pulled his shirt over his head, turning towards the spring. His back was covered in scars, fine white lines that crisscrossed across his shoulder blades. Dawn blushed and looked away as she untied her dress. She heard a splash and looked behind her at Geoff, who was casually kicking around in a little circle while he waited for her.

"Don't watch," she said.

Geoff smirked and swam up to the edge of the spring. "And why not? It's the fun part."

"I won't get in the water if you're watching," Dawn said. She let the ribbon fall behind her as she brought her hands in front of her.

"Fine." Geoff stopped smiling and drifted farther into the pool. "Just don't take too long, or I'll get bored and forget."

Dawn sighed as he dove and swam off, then finished getting out of her dress, keeping her underclothes. She tenderly placed one foot in the water and sighed. It was the perfect temperature. She stepped farther in and submerged herself for a moment before wading after Geoff, who'd wandered over to the stream. He stopped swimming around and drifted to her when she approached.

"Ready?" he asked with a grin. Dawn nodded and he grabbed her hand. He led her across the spring to the edge of the terrace, and a break in the wall that was almost level with the water. "Look."

She stepped up to break and looked out at the mountains towering above them, and the luscious landscape full of rippling tributaries beneath. In the distance, she could make out the highest peaks of the Sky Forest—and saw something flying between them that could have been a dragon.

The real sun was high above their heads, making the waters below sparkle as they flowed along to the lake. She watched as an eagle flew over them and landed on an evergreen to rest, perching on the highest branch. It turned its head and looked at her, then preened itself.

"Just think how it'll look in the morning," Geoff said beside her. "With the sunrise casting shadows and painting it every color that exists. You'll be able to see it every day."

He pressed up against her back and looked out over her shoulder. She turned towards him, and he put his mouth on hers, kissing her hungrily. Their lips moved against each other and he slid his tongue past them into her. She shivered and pressed closer to him, feeling their hearts pounding against each other, trying but failing to melt into one.

She entwined her fingers together behind his head, pulling herself closer still. Geoff groaned and his fingers found her waist under her camisole and touched her skin, burning her with pleasure. They worked their way around to her back and rubbed up and down, reaching farther and farther, exploring as much of her body as possible.

Suddenly one hand reached too far down and Dawn jumped, breaking away from the kiss.

"No," she breathed.

Geoff stared at her with empty eyes, then blinked slowly and came back to reality. He licked his lips and let out a shuddering breath.

"Don't do that," he said quietly, the slightest tremor in his voice.

Dawn glared at him. "Me? What did I do? You're the one trying to get something from me I'm not ready to give yet."

"No, you did something," Geoff said fiercely, returning to himself. "I wasn't in control—you were. This thing that you do, making it go away, making me think you're helping. But really you're controlling me, pacifying me. You need to stop."

"I don't know what I'm doing," Dawn said, shrinking away from him. "You said so yourself. I can't stop anything."

"Then don't stop me," he said as he gripped her waist and pulled her back against him. "Let me have everything." His fingers twitched and started creeping along her, stretching to where they'd tried to get before while his mouth found her neck.

His touch burned again, and Dawn shoved at him with all her strength, pushing them both underwater. She flailed as her lungs screamed at her for the sudden intake of water. A hand clamped onto her bicep painfully and she made herself relax, allowing Geoff to pull her up.

"Idiot," he spat as they broke the surface. "Are you trying to kill us?"

Dawn watched the ripples around them move away, shrinking into nothing. "I'm sorry, I didn't mean to."

Geoff scowled and yanked her arm closer to him, looking it over where he'd grabbed her.

"Great," he muttered. "That's going to bruise, and your damn fairy is going to think I'm hurting you. Like I don't have enough issues with him."

"I'll tell him what happened, that you saved me," Dawn said.

"You going to tell him how we ended up underwater too? Bet he'll love that," Geoff muttered and shoved away from her.

Dawn hugged herself and glanced down at her arm. It was slightly darker where he'd grabbed her, a shadow of what would come. "Fine, I won't say anything if you don't want me to, but he might know what I'm doing. Maybe he could help."

"And maybe he could control me through you," Geoff said. "No thanks. He's not going to hear about it."

"How was I controlling you, anyway?" Dawn asked. "You were the one getting ahead of yourself."

Geoff snorted and swam back to her. "Except I wasn't. If we were going at my pace, we'd have gotten to the best part. You wouldn't let me. But you did want it, or I wouldn't have gotten as much as I did."

"I don't want anything from you," Dawn said.

"Not from me, no," Geoff said and shrugged. "But from someone. And I happen to be available to provide, unlike your little boyfriend."

"I think we should go back in now," she said, avoiding looking at him. Her body may have responded, but the more she thought about it, the more she wished it wasn't Geoff she was with.

Geoff smirked and swam around her to lead her back. "Don't want to risk it getting further yet? It'll happen, though. You can't put it off forever. But you tell that fairy to stay out of it next time."

"What do you mean?" Dawn asked as she struggled to keep up with him. "I thought you didn't want me to tell him anything."

"Not about you controlling me," Geoff said, slowing as he glanced back at her. "But when you jumped, I don't think it was entirely from you."

"When I jumped?" Dawn repeated softly. She went over what

happened in her mind, trying to get past the kissing and touching to focus on the instant she'd broken away from him. There had been a tingle. With everything else going on she hadn't noticed it, but the reaction was fueled by Dusk, as Geoff implied.

"He stopped us," she whispered.

"I'll allow it for now," Geoff said. "While we aren't married. But it better not happen once we are, or I'll punish both of you."

Dawn pursed her lips. Her being with Geoff was going to be difficult for Dusk, but what choice did she have? "I'll talk to him."

They made it to the edge of the spring where they'd left their clothes and Geoff hopped out of the water.

"Wait here a minute," he said as he disappeared into the ferns.

He returned with one towel around his waist, and another that he offered to her. Dawn gingerly took the towel and covered herself as she got out. Geoff dried and started getting dressed, facing away from her as he did.

"Ready to tell Henry we're engaged?" he asked.

In a sense, they had been engaged ever since his last visit to Mantrisa. She had kept it secret, not wanting to say anything until it was official, or so she believed. But being in his kingdom, hearing him say the word, she couldn't avoid it any longer. She didn't want to be chosen, didn't want to marry the prince and be a queen, but she was in too deep now to escape.

"There's one more thing I want before we do," she said.

"Still stalling, then? Just saying we're engaged won't hurt," Geoff said, fully clothed. He gathered his jewelry and watched Dawn dress while he slowly replaced everything. "You'll get a few more days until the wedding once we do. Plenty of time to tell your fairy he should leave and get over not having him."

Dawn straightened her dress, struggling with the back lacing she couldn't reach. If she was stuck, she may as well know everything she was stuck with. "I want to know what your curse is."

Geoff clasped his last necklace and stepped over to her, grabbing the ribbon and tugging it. "If I tell you, that's it, no more stalling. You give up and be mine."

Dawn winced as he pulled too tight. There was no going back now. "You tell me what you're cursed with, and I'll be yours."

"All right," Geoff said and tied her off. "But we're doing it my way. I'm not going to tell you, I want to show you. Tonight."

"I thought you couldn't, because of your uncle's sun," Dawn replied skeptically, turning to look at him.

"Right, so we'll have to get rid of it. Just have Dusk do that fancy little trick of his to darken the sky, and we're good. You see what you want; I get what I want." He put his arms around her again and pressed them together. "And what do I want?"

Dawn took a shaky breath before answering. "Me."

"Good girl," he replied softly and kissed her.

33

"Seventy-seven...seventy-eight...seventy-nine..." Rob counted repetitions as he practiced his sword work, slashing and blocking the air. He'd finished his entire routine and still had half the day to stand outside of Dawn's room, so he worked his way through the exercises again.

His frustrated sigh cut through the empty hallway as he missed a swing. "Damn it. Why won't you leave me alone?"

"Sorry, I can come back later," Dusk said from Dawn's doorway.

Rob sheathed his sword roughly. "No, not you. I can't stop going over what happened with Geoff this morning."

Dusk frowned as he closed the door, easing it shut with magic. "What happened with Geoff?"

Rob just glowered. "What are you doing? Need something?"

"I came to talk to you," Dusk answered. "Diya thought I should tell you about the conversation we had with Geoff, to keep you informed about what we're doing."

"Oh. Well, thanks," Rob said and sat down in front of the door. "And sorry. He only found out about the lantern because Sarah and I were talking about it."

Dusk nodded and landed in front of him, crossing his legs as he sat. "I guessed it was something like that. It's not your fault. I take it you didn't mean for him to find out."

"No," Rob said, the corner of his mouth lifting in the tiniest smile. "He's surprisingly good at sneaking up on people, and I don't know about you, but I'd rather not live with that for the rest of my life. I think we should try to get Dawn out of here."

Dusk sighed. "She's still giving Geoff a chance. It's her decision alone."

"No, it's not," Rob replied, shaking his head. "I promised to protect her, to keep her safe, so it's my choice too. Going home would be the best thing for her, but she won't listen to me. If you told her to, though, she might."

"She would," Dusk said and smiled sadly. "But I don't want to make any more decisions for her than I already have. And especially not this one."

Rob stared at the fairy, suddenly aware of what was really going on. "Why not this one? It's the one I would make, and I love her too."

"You finally figured it out," Dusk said, chuckling. "Diya will be pleased. He thought you'd notice sooner."

"You know, I wanted to let her live the life she wants," Rob said, leaning his head back on the door and closing his eyes. "She never wanted to rule, or have responsibilities, or anything like that. Just wants to enjoy being, like she thinks fairies do. But I think, maybe you're the only one who can make that happen for her."

"No," Dusk said, tucking his legs up and hugging his knees. "I'm the worst option she has. At least if she has you or Geoff, she gets a normal, human life. With me, she has to give up everything."

"If that's what it would take to get the life she wants, it'd be right for her," Rob said, looking down at the fairy. "Let her decide what's best for herself."

Dusk sighed and put his head on his knees. "But she already

chose, and it was what's best for everyone. It's right for everyone but me."

The Kirkjufell palace was a quiet, lonely place as Dawn walked through the tangle of hallways. She'd asked to go to her room alone, and Geoff conceded, having his own things to attend to. The hot spring was on the twelfth level, so she made her way to the spiral stairs to go down. She followed her map to her room and smiled when she turned down her hallway.

"Look at you boys, getting along without me," she said.

"Dawn!" Rob exclaimed and hastily stood. Dusk flitted up to eye level after him. "How was your morning?"

"Long," Dawn replied and hugged him. "I need a little break from the Kirkjufells."

"Well you can always find me when you do," Rob replied, hugging her back.

There, a sense of normalcy. Just what she needed after the day she'd had so far, and to prepare herself for the rest of it. She took a deep breath and put her head on Rob's shoulder. "What would I do without you?"

"I don't know," Rob answered and squeezed her tightly.

"Ahh!" She flinched as he put pressure on the bruise.

Rob let go, holding his hands away from her to make sure he wouldn't do anymore. "Sorry!"

"What happened?" Dusk asked, hovering near her arm. He'd felt the pain in his own arm as though the bruise was his, shocking him.

"It's nothing," Dawn said. "Really, I'm fine."

Dusk looked up at her and frowned. "Tell me what happened."

"Please, Dawn," Rob said. "It was Geoff, wasn't it?"

Dawn bit her lip and stared at the floor, avoiding their eyes. She couldn't convince either of them she was fine in normal circumstances; she had no chance against the both of them together. "It was Geoff, but he didn't mean to, really."

"Show me," Dusk said and grabbed her sleeve to pull her into her room. He looked back at her when she didn't follow. "I want to see what he did, and heal it for you."

Dawn gave in and let him lead her into her room.

"What's up?" Diya asked, looking over from the bed where he was lounging.

"Geoff hurt her," Dusk said and started helping her unlace her dress. "I'm having a look at it."

"Did he?" Diya replied. "I told you he was dangerous. Now will you tell her?"

"Tell me what?" Dawn asked. The lacing was loosened and she pulled the dress over her head, leaving her arm bare. "See, it's just a bruise."

"A bruise in the shape of a hand," Dusk said. He traced the outline that was starting to appear and Dawn felt a warm tingle follow it. "Why did he grab you?"

"We were underwater, and he was pulling me out," Dawn said. "He didn't mean to hurt me."

"They never do," Diya replied. "Really, Dusk, she needs to know."

"What do I need to know?" Dawn asked again.

"He thinks I should tell you what Geoff is cursed with," Dusk said as he finished tracing and cut the magic. "But I feel he would be equally dangerous, possibly more so, if I made him angry by revealing his secret."

"It doesn't matter anyway," she said. As frustrating as it was that Dusk was insisting on not telling her what he knew, she was finding ways to get information on her own. "He wants to show me what it is tonight."

Dusk frowned, more concerned than surprised. "How is he going to manage that?"

"Well, he wants you to help us," Dawn replied. "You can make the sky dark for him."

"Technically, I suppose I could," Dusk said. "But I don't have enough capacity to hold that much energy for long. We'd have to put it somewhere."

"You can't be seriously considering this," Diya said, sitting up. "You want her to be in that position?"

"It'll be safest if I'm with them," Dusk replied. Diya scowled and didn't say any more.

"So you don't mind?" Dawn asked. "You'll help us?"

Dusk sighed. "If this is what he intends to do, I doubt if I have much choice. He really wants to reveal it before you're married?"

"It's my requirement for him to become engaged, officially," Dawn replied. "I've agreed to it, once he shows me."

"No!" Diya stood up, his face red and his eyes sparkling. "You can't. It's the wrong choice—you can't! I've worked too hard for you to do this to me." He flicked his wings and raced to the windows.

"Diya!" Dusk called after him as he disappeared. "Damn it Diya, get back here." He followed after his friend, leaving Dawn alone.

"But what other choice do I have?" she whispered and looked at her arm.

The bruise was still there, but it didn't hurt anymore and was fading, returning to the shadow it was before. She pulled her dress back on, grimacing at the lacing she couldn't do, then went to her door and opened it. "Rah, would you help me?"

Rob jumped and blushed as she turned around to show him her back.

He started tightening the ribbon. "What happened? It sounded like the fairies were shouting at each other."

"Diya got upset and ran off," Dawn said. "Dusk went after him."

"Oh," Rob replied. He tugged on the ribbon gently, not wanting to make it too tight. "Why'd he get upset?"

Dawn sighed. "I told them Geoff and I will be getting engaged tonight."

"Tonight," Rob repeated like he didn't understand the word. He tied the ribbon and she faced him. "That's so fast. Are you sure?"

"No, I'm not," Dawn said. "I'll never be happy, but I don't exactly have any choice. Geoff wants to get married now, so that's what I'm going to do."

"But you do have a choice," Rob said. "You don't have to be with him if it'll make you unhappy forever."

As if there really was something. What would happen here, with the Kirkjufells? Her family wouldn't be happy with her, and she had no idea how they might react. Would she be allowed to live at the castle if she chose Dusk? But what could she do, how could she contribute to her family that way?

"That's what Diya keeps telling me," she said. "But he doesn't answer me when I ask him what choice. What do you think I can do?"

Rob grabbed her hands and looked down at them.

"I offered you another choice, but you said no," he said and rubbed his thumbs on her palms. "But there's someone else you could choose; someone who heals you instead of hurting you. I don't like him much, but you do, and I know he feels the same. Dusk can get you out of here, you just have to let him."

"But he can't," Dawn said and sniffled as her eyes brimmed with tears. "No one can. They won't let me go, and if I tried it would only put you and Sarah in danger too. I want to choose him, I do. But I can't endanger everyone else."

Rob wrapped his arms around her, being careful of her arm this time. "We're pretty capable on our own. I'll fight my way out if I have to and make sure Sarah's safe too. She might even help if she can do that magic stuff again."

Dawn sobbed into his shoulder. Even if she tried, what then? She couldn't just go home and do nothing with her life. Since her brother would rule the Mantrisa kingdom in time, there was only one real option available to her if she wanted to do something useful. But still, there was only one thing that she truly wanted, and it wasn't to marry Geoff.

"I wish we'd never come here. I miss home," she said. Even with her favorite people here, it wasn't comfortable, warm, safe, or happy like her real home. It felt like her real life had stayed behind.

Rob smiled and placed his cheek against her forehead. "Me too."

"Diya!" Dusk shouted as he chased after him. "Please, will you stop and talk to me about it?"

"Why should I?" Diya shouted back and sped up. He zigzagged sporadically around the outside of the palace, trying to throw Dusk off. "You didn't want to talk to her; now I don't want to talk to you. See how you like it."

"Don't make me do it," Dusk warned.

Diya slowed for a split second and glanced back. "You wouldn't do that, not after what happened last time."

"No?" Dusk asked and the air around them started crackling with energy.

"Fine, I'll stop," Diya said and froze. "But I still don't want to talk."

Dusk let out a breath as he stopped his magic and closed the gap between them.

"We agreed we'd let her decide," he said.

Diya snorted and scowled at the mountain under them. "But it wasn't a fair decision. You didn't tell her what she's giving up."

"I thought you didn't want to talk," Dusk said, half-smiling. "It wouldn't have been fair if I had. You know that."

"But you went out of your way to tell her to choose him, even after you learned what he is," Diya argued. "You've been using the advantage you have to all but make the choice for her, then pretend that *she* made it. Is that fair?"

"I don't want her to give up everything just for me," Dusk explained. "As much as I'd like her to, it wouldn't be right."

"No, letting her marry Geoff isn't right," Diya said. "Today might have been an accident, but it won't always be. And you saw how she defended him as if she's afraid of what he'll do if she says anything against him."

"She's not afraid of him," Dusk said. "I saw how she handles him, and I still think she'll be fine with a little time to adjust."

Diya scowled. "But she isn't getting time, or can't you see that? It's not long from engaged to married, not nearly enough time for either of you to grow comfortable with what comes next, even if Geoff wasn't dangerous."

Dusk twitched as he relived how he'd felt when Dawn was with the prince. "She'll be fine."

"So fine you messed yourself up," Diya said. "Or do you think I didn't notice how you were acting earlier? Whatever she was doing with him really bothered you, and based on how he is, I have my suspicions what it was."

"All right, it was harder on me than I was ready for," Dusk said, grimacing. "But I'll manage better next time, I'll block her feelings again if I have to."

"Hah! That's how she got hurt," Diya said. "You weren't paying attention to her and didn't know when he gave her the bruise. You going to keep patching her up every day? Because I have a feeling that's how often it'll be if you aren't watching out for her."

"We can't stop her now," Dusk replied. "If she changes her mind right after agreeing to marry him, it'll be worse. We have to at least let her see the curse."

"Do you even hear yourself?" Diya asked, clenching his hands into fists. "There are no options that keep her out of danger, fine. But putting her alone with him like that is really the thing you want to go with?"

"She won't be alone with him, I'll be there too," Dusk said.

"This time," Diya said. "But not the next time, or the time after."

Dusk sighed heavily and put his face in his hands. "This is her choice. It doesn't matter what I want as long as it's what she wants."

"Lies," Diya said. "Aside from you being completely wrong about your desires mattering, it isn't what she wants. She didn't want to give him the rose, you know—she wanted to keep it."

"How do you know that?" Dusk asked, lowering his fingers so he could see his friend.

"She told me," Diya said and shrugged. "You didn't think to ask, so I did. She wanted to choose you."

He spasmed as Dusk jumped at him and held him, barely avoiding throwing them into a freefall. Diya wiggled his arms around so they were holding each other until Dusk sighed and let go.

"You're sure," he said quietly. "She'd really be willing to give up everyone else for me?"

"What're you asking me for?" Diya snorted. "You're the one who knows how she feels."

Dusk half-smiled and turned to go back to the palace. "Then I suppose it's past time I talk to her myself."

34

"Come on, girls, time to eat," Geoff called to the cougars as he walked through his jungle terrace, waving a chunk of raw meat in front of him. "Get your steak before I have it all."

Jewel and Crown appeared from the undergrowth and stalked up to him. He tossed them each a steak from the platter he was carrying, then licked the blood off his hand. The cougars fell on their dinner, and he watched them for a minute before sitting down and grabbing himself a smaller chunk to eat. When the cougars were done, he threw over another pair of steaks, saving the last cut for himself.

"Good girls," he said between bites. "You leave me a bone this time, though. I've got to stay occupied for a few hours until I show her. But once she knows, I won't have to steal your dinner. She'll satisfy me."

Jewel finished her food and licked her chops, then walked over to Geoff and rubbed her head against his arm.

"Don't worry, I'll still spend time with you," he said as he pet her head. "We'll do the fun stuff, hunt together like we did before this damn sun. You miss the dark, don't you? We'll get it tonight. The fairy's good for that much, at least. Afterward, though, we might need to do something with him. Maybe you'd like to know what a fairy tastes like?"

Crown yawned and stretched before wandering up to him. Jewel licked Geoff's ear, then both cougars laid down next to him.

"Think I'll be having some wizard soon," he continued. "Have to teach Ed a lesson. Maybe some knight too, if that boy wants to try anything. I hope he does."

He finished his meat and laid back on Jewel, who purred under him. Blood covered his hands, and he sucked on his fingers.

"That's better," he breathed once they were clean. "Not as good as her, though. Nothing is anymore. But I'm getting her tonight if I can make it until then. A few more hours, then I'll finally get what I want from her."

He sat up and grabbed one of the bones the cougars had left, then settled back on Jewel. Crown put her head on his stomach and he pet her while he gnawed the last of the flesh off the bone.

Just as Dawn finished crying she got a shimmer from Dusk, so she pulled away from Rob's embrace.

"Dusk needs me," she said, and Rob nodded and resumed his guard position by her door as she went back into her room.

She waited by the windows to watch the fairies return, surprised when only Dusk appeared.

"What happened?" she asked as he reached the window slits and landed in one. "Is he all right?"

"Diya is fine," Dusk said, half-smiling. "He wants some time alone, and we could use a moment to ourselves to discuss something."

Dawn looked at her feet, unable to hold his gaze. "Something about Geoff?"

"No," he said and flicked into the air, hovering next to her face so she couldn't avoid seeing him. "While that is relevant, I need to explain things to you. Perhaps you'd like to sit down?"

"Oh, yes," she replied, crossing to the vanity. It was about Geoff, clearly—or rather, what she had been doing with Geoff. Maybe he was going to tell her he couldn't stay after all, once she was married, that he was worried Geoff would send him away. But if being with Geoff meant losing Dusk, she couldn't do it. "He wasn't angry, about earlier. I think if you can find a way to not interfere again, he won't do anything. You don't need to worry he'll send you away."

"Send me away?" Dusk frowned as he landed in front of the mirror, then lifted his eyes to hers. They burned into her, as deeply felt as the link they shared. "Dawn, there is nothing Geoff, or anyone else for that matter, can do to keep me away from you. The only opinions that have any bearing on us are mine and yours."

He closed his eyes and perched on the edge of the vanity, so close to her heart his breath caressed the pendant hanging over it. "And to that end, you need to know what choice you have."

"No," she said, blinking quickly as her eyes brimmed with tears. She knew, now, what he was going to suggest. It was tempting, but it couldn't be what Diya wanted, and anyway, she had already agreed to be with Geoff. "I know we could, but it's not worth the risk. And what would we do after? How would Diya manage?"

"I should think he'd be better for it," Dusk replied, opening his still smoldering eyes to look at her. "He's quite excited to have another friend, honestly."

"But then you won't be able to care for him properly," Dawn said, furrowing her brow. There was no logic to this decision, only shallow reasoning at best. "And really, I'm rather disappointed you believe he'd want this. I don't see any benefit for him if you were human."

"If I were..." Dusk laughed, and Dawn felt a warm shimmer. "I see you've already put a lot of thought into this, and it's good to know where you stand on that point. What I am actually offering will make Diya and me very happy. And hopefully you too."

He stretched on his toes to place his hand on her cheek, and she felt a tingle of what she might have thought was nervous energy if it had come from anyone else.

"Would you like to be a fairy?" he asked.

"A fairy," she breathed, barely hearing herself. So this was Diya's plan, what he'd been trying so hard to accomplish. It was impossible, surely, at least as impossible as her having a fairy alignment. Could she really give up on Geoff for this chance? But more importantly, how could she marry him, knowing this was an option?

Before she got excited though, she needed confirmation that it *was* an option. "And I suppose you wouldn't offer if this wasn't what you wanted."

Dusk pulled his hand away and stepped back, half-smiling. She felt a tingle from him and knew this time it was nerves, the same nerves she had herself.

"When I lost Diya, I felt the worst pain I've ever known and came the closest to what I imagine death would feel like. The day he returned I became whole again, reunited with all the parts of me that were missing. And then I met you. You showed me how much more there could be in life, how much more I could still be, and I want to spend the rest of eternity discovering everything with you."

Dawn almost laughed, hearing him describe how he felt as though he were sharing her own feelings about him. Her entire life she'd loved watching fairies, wondering about their lives, wanting to be a part of it, and Dusk was the most interesting of all, the one with the most to discover. She took a deep breath and smiled at him.

"That's exactly what I want, too."

The jungle terrace was quiet as Geoff and the cougars digested their meal. The cats took their time cleaning their claws and stretching before curling around the prince for a nap.

Once Geoff was bored of chewing bone, he closed his eyes and relaxed against Jewel to rest. He was just fading into sleep when he sniffed and sat up quickly.

"The hell are you doing here?"

Diya smirked and landed on Crown's back, who looked at him curiously.

"What, you weren't expecting anyone to come tell you off for what you did?" he asked as he scratched Crown's chin. "Good kitty, you're real sweet, even with this bastard for a master. Least he feeds you, although it's kind of weird he helps himself to your scraps."

"You have five seconds to get out of my terrace, or I'll help myself to something else," Geoff said, glaring at the fairy.

Diya snorted. "Yeah? You really think you can get me? I know what you are. That tough act isn't going to work on me. Won't work on Dusk either, if you're thinking of trying. Course, I highly recommend leaving him alone if you actually like Dawn, like I think you do."

"The hell does she have to do with it?" Geoff growled in his throat. "You aren't going to convince me not to get rid of him, so maybe you should try getting him out of here before I kill you both."

"Really, like it's so damn simple," Diya said and flicked up in front of Geoff's face, icy eyes blazing. "You want me dead? Fine, whatever, you're not the first. But wanting Dusk dead is a whole other issue. See, if you kill Dusk, you kill Dawn. And I don't think you want that, wolf boy."

"Then how do I get rid of him?" Geoff asked sharply.

"You don't," Diya said, smirking. "Ever. As long as you have Dawn, you have Dusk. And if he's around, so am I, and I'm not gonna sit here and let you hurt either of them. I don't like you, and I don't care what you try with me. But I'll be more than happy to show you what I can do if you try anything else like what you did today."

"You can't stop me," Geoff said, smirking. "I'm only giving her what she wants. So you know what we were doing, so what? He tried to get in the way but he didn't stop us before she realized how much she wants it. Now she's going to be with me tonight, and there's not a damn thing either of you little fairies can do to stop me having her."

"And what if she sees you and changes her mind?" Diya asked. "Or if you can't control yourself and hurt her? What if she doesn't want you?"

Geoff laughed. "She already doesn't want me, but she knows she doesn't have any choice. Besides, it's more fun that way. A little torment is too good to pass up."

Diya spasmed and his wings faltered.

"But she does have a choice, she always has," he said, glaring at Geoff. "And right now, Dusk is finally letting her know about it, and I'm betting she's already chosen him."

"So what? He's going to tell her he loves her, and they'll just run away together?" Geoff laughed. "Stupid fairy. She's a princess; she has a job to do. And it isn't playing with her little boyfriend forever while her kingdom suffers because she didn't get married like she's supposed to. You really think her family would let her go back? They want her here, so they can share some of my power. Rather unfortunate that really I'm the one who's getting something, but they can believe whatever they want to justify giving her to me."

"She's not going to be yours," Diya muttered darkly, wings slicing the air. "Even if Dusk didn't come around, I won't allow it. We'll all get out of here, and leave you alone to rot in your prison."

"You've got no right calling my palace that," Geoff growled. "It's only a prison if you let it control you like Henry does. I use it to my advantage, and it's never let me down. Except for when Dusk decided he didn't like me doing it, and used it to make a point. But it's not his, or yours. It's mine. Just like the mountains are mine, and the city, and soon Dawn."

"Yeah? Is that how it works?" Diya snorted. "You can be in charge of people, and claim to own the land they live on, but no one *belongs* to you. Doesn't matter if you keep her here, lock her up forever—she'll never be yours."

"You're taking this pretty personally for being the escort of her escort," Geoff said. "Been someone else's before, haven't you?" He smirked as Diya flinched. "Didn't want to be, though, just like her. Think you know how she feels, then? Think I'll break her like they broke you? That's why you're so dim, isn't it? You don't even try to hide it, just let it remind you constantly about whatever they did to you. Wish it would stop, just leave you alone to your sorry life, but it doesn't. You're stuck with it forever."

Diya shuddered and floated down to the mossy ground where he crumpled. Crown sniffed him and nudged him gently with her nose.

"Thought so," Geoff said. "Pathetic. Now you be a little smarter, and stay out of my life."

"Yeah, that's what we're trying to do," Diya said, rolling over to glare at Geoff. "Only thing we want from here is to get rid of your witch; something you want too."

"And I'll get her just fine," Geoff said, watching his hand as he flexed his fingers, squeezing them over and over. "Also get you and your little friend. I've been trying to figure out what's going on with their capacitor, and I think you've solved it for me." He clenched his hand and flicked his eyes to Diya, smirking.

"It's really yours, isn't it? That's what happened to your magic, and it's why you don't have any now. So the witch who cursed me also ruined you, made you useless. I'm pretty sure Dusk'll want to do something about her no matter what I do. But once she's gone, and Ed's been dealt with, I won't need him. And you've given me the answer to ridding myself of him."

"You wouldn't risk trying it though," Diya said with newfound strength, his own difficulties forgotten. "Even if you could manage to put him in the lantern—which you won't—but if you did, there's no telling what it would do to Dawn. If you break his magic, you might just lose the thing about her that you like the most."

"You think that's what I like the most?" Geoff laughed. "Sure, it's nice. With the sun making me itch to change, she's helpful. But I have other ways of dealing with it, and once the sun is gone, it won't matter anyway. It's not magic I want, it's her, and I always get what I want."

Diya flicked his wings and moved to Crown's back to lay down.

"That's better," he said as he scratched the cougar under him. "Good girl. He healed that bruise you gave her, so you know. He wasn't too pleased about it either."

"I didn't mean to do it. She's the idiot who pushed us underwater when she can't swim," Geoff growled. "Would you rather I let her drown herself?"

"Except she wouldn't drown," Diya replied with a shrug. "She can manipulate water and air. If you'd left her, she would have saved herself. She doesn't need you—she already has everything."

"Everything except a man," Geoff said. "And that's something she needs, no matter how much she wants to believe she doesn't. He can't give her that. Only I can."

Diya snorted. "He tried to get around that. Didn't quite go how he wanted, but he has another solution—*my* solution to all of our problems. If you're lucky, we'll even do it before we leave, everything else be damned. Then you'll be sorry."

"I've never been sorry for anything in my life," Geoff said. "And I won't be starting now. You're all so concerned for each other's feelings you can't see what's happening around you, and that's me getting everything like I always do. Whatever you want to try, I'll get what I want in the end. You just wait. I'll leave you until then, so you can regret your entire existence before I kill you."

"Like we're so scared of something we've seen before," Diya said, rolling his eyes. "You're not special, but Dusk is, and whatever you do, Dawn wants him. She'll run from you to be with him."

Geoff shook his head and laughed. "You think you know her better, or that he could get her away from me, but you're wrong. She may want to choose him, but I've got her under my thumb and she won't budge if I tell her not to. He's too nice, won't push her in a way she doesn't want to go. Because he cares about her, loves her, but I don't, so I'll push her anywhere, and harder. He can't beat me."

"Yeah, whatever. Believe what you want," Diya said, stretching as he stood up. "Well, I think I've said everything I came to, so I'll leave you to your snack."

"Are all you fairies so delightful to chat with?" Geoff snorted. "Might have to change my plans for your kind once I own Dawn's kingdom. Go on, leave. You ever bother me again, you won't get the same chance."

Diya rolled his eyes as he floated up into the air. "As if I'd make the same mistake twice. Sorry, kitties, I can't do anything for you. You'll be his only company again soon."

Geoff glared at the fairy as he flew away and out of sight, then laid back on Jewel and closed his eyes.

"Good riddance," he said to himself as he fell asleep.

35

Early afternoon wore on into late evening, though it was hard to know with the artificial sun preventing the usual tells of shadows growing longer and light slowly disappearing.

Dawn sat at the vanity in her room, writing to fill the time. She glanced at Dusk sitting next to her inkwell and smiled. He was focused on her necklace in his lap, working to make it into an ethereal convertor. She watched his hands move over the glass pendant, expertly weaving spells that would turn her into a fairy.

As she returned her attention to her journal, the bracelet on her wrist caught her eye and she frowned. She didn't feel right keeping it on, now that she was following a different path, and took it off.

"Not going to keep that, then?" Dusk asked, eyes never leaving his work.

"I wasn't terribly fond of it to begin with," she replied, shrugging as she set it on the vanity. "It's almost a shame, though. He meant well enough to make it for me."

"I doubt he'd use it to make you into a fairy, though," Dusk said, half-smiling. He glanced up at the lantern sitting across from him and inclined his head to it. "You might put that away now. We're well past the point of my needing to borrow more energy from it."

Before Dawn could respond, Diya fluttered in from a window slit and landed on her journal.

"How's it going?" he asked. He glanced at the lantern, and the necklace in Dusk's lap, and grinned. "You doing it, then? Finally doing what I want?"

"Dawn's not marrying Geoff, if that's what you mean," Dusk replied. "Although we aren't doing anything yet."

"I know, we have to make sure Berniece doesn't get the thing first. But then we're doing it? I win?" Diya asked, wiggling in place.

"All right," Dusk said and stood up with the necklace, holding it out to Dawn. "It's as ready as I can make it for now. All you have to do is wear it, and I'll take care of the rest."

Dawn accepted the necklace and hung it around her neck. "And what if something happens tonight while we're with Geoff? Should I leave it somewhere safe until we're ready to use it?"

"No," Dusk said, shaking his head. "If anything goes poorly with him, the conversion process will protect you. Just keep it on, and you'll be safe."

"All right," she replied, smiling. "I trust you."

Diya bounced on his heels and grinned up at Dawn. "Gonna have to learn to trust me too. Dusk's an idiot, but if he listens to me, he does good. Now that you're both doing what I want, it's gonna be great."

"If I knew it would make you so happy, I'd have done it sooner," Dawn said, giggling at the lux fairy.

"To make him leave you alone, you mean," Dusk muttered.

"She chose you. Now you're both stuck with me forever," Diya said, fluttering his wings playfully.

Dusk grimaced and looked at Dawn. "Still sure about this? It's not too late to change your mind."

"I've never been more sure of anything," Dawn said, unable to stop smiling.

"Sure of what?" Geoff asked as he came in unannounced. He smirked as they all jumped, then his eyes found the lantern. "Is that it? Doesn't look like much."

Dawn moved fast, but Geoff moved faster. She grabbed the lantern and raced to the chest to put it away, and found Geoff blocking her.

"Let me see it," he said.

"No," Dawn said and stepped back. "You don't need to. Let me put it away."

Geoff yanked it out of her hands.

"That's quite impressive," he said, turning it slowly while he checked what spells had made it. "Your witch did this? Much better than what she put on me, anyway. Less crude. Lot of power in it, more than I guessed. The fairy must've been in it a long time for it to have this much. And you want to disable it?" He shook his head sadly. "Such a waste." He handed it back to Dawn and moved over so she could put it away.

"You're early," she said as she latched the lid and turned to face him.

Geoff shrugged. "We were late before, remember? Henry wants us on time so you can tell him how excited you are to be getting engaged tonight."

Dawn winced and looked at Dusk, who smiled and sent her a little shimmer.

"I'll tell him that's your plan, but I won't pretend to like it," she said.

Geoff looked at the vanity and scowled. "What are you up to?"

"I don't think I'm up to anything," Dusk said, shrugging.

"No, you've got something planned," Geoff said. "Your little friend seems to think you do, anyway. I don't want either of you messing up my plans more than you already have, or all of you will regret it."

Dusk flicked his wings and flew up to Geoff, looking him in the eyes. "I hope you don't mean to imply that you'll hurt Dawn on purpose if we do. Because that's what it sounds like you mean."

"That's exactly what I mean, fairy," Geoff spat. "You think that little bruise was something, wait until you feel what else I can do to her. What I will do even if you cooperate, just to teach you a lesson. I already gave your friend some advice, but it looks like he failed to deliver the message, so I'll give it again. Get out of my palace while you can, because if I have to get rid of you, I won't play nice."

"Geoff," Dawn said quietly, and they all looked at her. "You can't do anything to them. You need Dusk to help us tonight, don't you? And they both need to be here to make sure Berniece can't get the lantern and use it to help your uncle."

Geoff laughed. "I don't need anything I can't get on my own. Dusk would be easier, but I can find another way to get rid of the sun that doesn't use fairies. Same with the witch, although I do find your commitment quite comical."

"Then you don't need Dawn," Diya said, hands clenched. "You can't get her so easily, so you might as well let us go home now."

Geoff glared at Diya for a moment, then grabbed Dawn's hand and dragged her out of her room and down the hallway.

"What the hell is he talking about?" Geoff asked as he stopped and yanked Dawn in front of him. "You didn't change your mind about things, did you? Because last time I checked, you already agreed to be mine."

"I did," Dawn said. "Promise to be yours, I mean. That's all you need to worry about, and what we'll tell Henry."

Geoff leaned into her and sniffed. "Don't lie to me. You're thinking of breaking your promise, aren't you? Don't try to tell me you're not. I saw my bracelet, saw that you took it off but kept the fairy's necklace. Going to try to leave me after everything you've already done, after what I've given you. I did everything you asked, gave you time, didn't push you more than you were willing, and this is how you thank me?"

"I don't love you," Dawn whispered. "I'm sorry, but I can't be with you. It wouldn't be fair of me to marry you and never give you an heir."

"So what are you going to do?" Geoff asked. "Tell Henry the truth? Think he'll just let you go? You know you're stuck here, and I thought you'd decided to make the most of it and give in to me. You can choose not to, and fight me forever instead, but it'll be worse for you when I get my heir in spite of your efforts to prevent it."

"If you try anything I don't want, I'll just stop you again," Dawn said.

"So you'd throw away my friendship, and everything else without a second thought," Geoff said and she winced. He started moving again and dragged her after him. "Come on, we need to get to dinner or we'll both be in trouble. You don't want to see Henry when he's angry."

"We're not leaving until we help you with Edmond," Dawn said, hoping to improve his mood. Maybe thinking he still had a chance to win her over would help.

Geoff snorted. "Damn right you're not leaving before we stop Ed, not when you're the one who tried to stall with it before."

Or not. "You don't have to show me the curse if you'd rather I not know," she said. "There's no reason to, now."

"No, I'm showing you. Unlike you, I keep my word." They reached the dining room and Geoff paused outside the doors to sniff, then grinned toothily. "Perfect."

He pulled her into him and kissed her.

"Ahh, I see you've made quite a lot of progress," Henry said as he turned a corner and saw them. "And you've even made it on time for once."

Geoff pulled away and smirked at Dawn. "We didn't want to disappoint you."

"Indeed," Henry said as he led them in and they got seated, the first diners to arrive. "So, do you think we're ready to announce the wedding?"

"Not quite," Geoff said. "We've got some plans for tonight, though. Should be able to after that." He bumped against Dawn under the table and she bit her tongue to keep from saying anything.

"Good," Henry said, then looked over at the doors as they opened. Dawn followed his gaze to see Edmond enter, followed by six very drained wizards. He caught her eye and looked pointedly away.

"Something bothering Edmond?" Henry asked softly.

"Plenty," Geoff replied. "But I doubt he'd be willing to tell you about it."

Henry nodded and leaned back in his seat to watch his brother. Cedric snuck in moments later and the food was presented immediately after he was seated. Dawn relaxed as both of her dinner companions focused on eating. She would have entirely enjoyed the meal if not for Geoff's continued effort to get under her skirt. The prince worked through his food quickly, but Dawn took her time, trying to put off the inevitable as long as she could.

Minutes before Dawn's necklace would mark the start of dusk, Edmond finished his meal and walked over to their end of the table.

"Evening Henry, Geoff." He nodded to them, then looked at Dawn. "I was wondering, Princess, if you'd be willing to come visit again this evening? In light of our earlier interaction, I believe I have a few things to tell you and your fairy companions, should they also wish to hear them."

"She's not doing anything with you," Geoff said before Dawn

could open her mouth. "Your bad behavior aside, she's going to be a bit busy with me."

Edmond frowned for a moment, then seemed to realize something and softened. "I see. Well, in that case, I'll leave you to it."

He took a moment to cough into his handkerchief, then walked out of the room. Almost as soon as the doors closed, Cedric left also, leaving most of his food untouched. Henry watched the wizard go, then scowled at Dawn.

"Do you want to tell me what the hell is going on?" he asked.

"Don't worry about him. We're taking care of it," Geoff said.

"I didn't ask you," Henry growled. "Keep your mouth shut for once in your damn life and let her answer my question. What is your wizard doing with Edmond?"

Dawn shrunk under his glare. "I don't know."

"Then why did he want to speak with you and your fairies?" Henry asked. "You clearly know something, and if you don't want me to beat it out of someone, you'd better explain."

"Damn it, Henry,"—Geoff slammed his fist on the table—"I told you I'm taking care of it. Leave her alone."

Henry glared at his son and his face darkened. "I thought you knew better than to say such things to me, but perhaps some lessons need to be relearned." He grabbed Geoff's collar and yanked him closer. "You want to act like a naughty child, then you can be treated like one."

"What are you going to do, hit me?" Geoff asked. "Like it'll do anything now."

He glanced over at Dawn's necklace and smirked as it sparkled. Henry looked over slowly and scowled. He pushed Geoff back and stood.

"I'll be sending Leopold a message in the morning. Hopefully, it will only be good news," he said and walked away stiffly.

Geoff watched the doors close behind him, then turned back to Dawn, lounging with his arm over the back of his chair. "Ready?"

Dawn blinked at him, feeling much less at ease than Geoff appeared. "Are you all right?"

"That was nothing. Told you that you didn't want to see him angry," he replied.

Dawn gulped down some spring water and carefully set down the half-empty cup. "I'm ready."

Geoff took her hand to lead her out, and she followed him quietly until they reached the spiral.

"Thank you," she said softly.

Geoff glanced back at her. "For what?"

"Well, I mean with Henry," she said.

"It was nothing," Geoff said. "I'm used to him, and he knows he can't do anything to me, especially not after dusk. Not unless he wants me to return the favor."

Dawn looked down at his hand holding hers.

"You're stronger," she said, noticing the grip wasn't tighter but seemed to have more behind it.

"Among other things," Geoff replied. "But you'll see soon, once we grab your little boyfriend. Then I can finally change." He shivered with anticipation and sped up as they got off the stairs.

"You like it," Dawn said. "Being cursed. You want to be this way." No wonder everything she tried was so ineffective. She couldn't force him to accept help he didn't think he needed.

Geoff stopped and looked at her. "Why wouldn't I? You saw how Henry acted, soon as he realized. It's good, being like this. Being kept from it is the problem. That's when I can't think, can't control myself. We're getting rid of the light. Then I'll be free again."

He shivered once more and continued moving.

"No wonder they're so worried," Dawn remarked softly.

Geoff laughed and threw her against a wall, then pressed up against her.

"They should be," he whispered in her ear before smashing his mouth against hers and shoving his tongue down her throat. He choked her, then bit her lip as he pulled away. "Everyone should be."

36

"Diya," Dusk said calmly, staring at the open door Geoff had just pulled Dawn through. "Would you care to explain how he knew about the lantern?"

"I thought we already went over that," Rob said from the hallway. After the arguing and Geoff shoving past him, he was more than a little concerned. "I told you it was—"

"Excuse me, Robert," Dusk said sharply and turned to the lux fairy. "I asked someone else. Diya, what did you do?"

"I talked to him," Diya said, shrugging.

Dusk sighed heavily and rubbed his forehead. "And why would you do that? Were you trying to make things worse? Because that's what's happened. How am I supposed to get us out of here, get her away from him, with things how they are?"

"Wait," Rob said. "Are we leaving then? She's not going to marry Geoff?"

Diya scowled. "I was just trying to make sure he didn't think he could get away with anything else. He shouldn't do things like that and not be told off."

"If you'd left it alone he wouldn't know anything!" Dusk cried, his glow flickering like fire. "Now he's angry *and* he knows what we're doing, that we're taking Dawn away. Damn it, Diya! You act before you think. You let your emotions talk for you and get you in trouble. Only it isn't just you that's going to be punished for this, it's all of us."

"I was looking out for her!" Diya returned, clenching his fists and shaking. "You'd let him do anything with her, but I wouldn't. He wants to own her, treat her like property. I couldn't say nothing. You know I couldn't."

"Diya, if you'd just waited, everything would be fine," Dusk said, relaxing slightly. "You should have said something to me first, then we wouldn't be in this mess."

"I shouldn't have to tell you. You already know," Diya argued. "Really, though, I've done nothing but tell you how I feel, and you didn't listen until what? Until you knew you had to do something to keep her safe, and you finally realized what I've been saying ever since you linked, which is that your plan was terrible for everyone. I didn't want him of all people to decide what the rest of your life would be like. You deserve better than that."

"Will one of you please tell me what's going on?" Rob asked, his eyes darting between the fairies.

Diya snorted and fluttered over to the window slits. "You tell him. I've apparently said too much."

Dusk dashed to the window as Diya disappeared. He gripped the sill and leaned out, his whole body tense.

"Stop leaving me!"

He waited for several minutes, wings twitching anxiously, then sighed and moved out of the way as Diya reentered. "I'm sorry. I won't forget again."

"Promise?" Diya asked seriously.

"Promise," he replied, hugging his friend tightly. After a minute he let go and fluttered over to Rob. "Why don't you get yourself some dinner? You likely won't get a chance later."

"Right," Rob said and hurried away, more than happy to leave the fairies to their business.

Dusk sighed and rubbed his forehead, then landed on the bed where Diya was busy burying himself in the blankets. "Do you forgive me?"

"Depends," Diya said. He squirmed around in his nest until he was looking out at his friend. "Are you done being an ass?"

Dusk laughed and sat next to the nest. "I can't guarantee I won't be again, but for now I'll try to do better."

"Then for now I forgive you," Diya said and crawled out of the blankets to sit with him. "And I'm glad I'm not losing you."

Dusk smiled and wrapped Diya in a hug.

"Me too," he replied and softly kissed his friend's cheek.

Edmond walked to his rooms slowly after dinner, allowing Cedric to catch up.

"You couldn't have waited longer?" he said when the other wizard reached him.

"I didn't realize you wished me to, or I would have," Cedric replied. "Is Dawn going to come, then?"

"Apparently she's going to be with Geoff," Edmond answered. "It would be better if we could ensure the fairies' location while we do this, but at least she'll be the distraction we need."

Cedric gaped at him. "You can't be thinking of going through with it now. You'll endanger her life, and lose the chance to secure both fairies at the same time."

"Berniece doesn't care about the fairies anymore," Edmond scoffed. "As long as the original plan isn't further disturbed by my nephew. We must act now before anything more can go wrong."

"And what do you want me to do? Since my task of lifting the lantern while they are all accounted for isn't going to be possible," Cedric said.

"I suppose you can tag along and try to keep Dawn safe while I kill him," Edmond replied, rubbing his chin in thought. "If such a task suits you. For now, we need to contact Berniece and update her, then we'll wait for my informant to let us know when he's in his rooms."

They arrived at Edmond's door and he invited Cedric into the sitting room. Cedric placed himself in one of the armchairs while Edmond gathered his mirror and quill.

"And you are certain you can trust the boy?" Cedric asked, watching Edmond dip the quill in ink. "It is a rather important task to leave to one with a tendency for disappearing."

"All the more reason I trust Paul," Edmond replied as he wrote on the mirror. "One who can disappear is one who can keep secrets. He won't ask questions I don't want asked."

"Or perhaps he sees more than he lets on," Cedric said, clutching his hands together until they turned white. "It would be a poor end for us to be done in by a child."

"Like how you were revealed by your own daughter? Lucky for you I'm in control here, and I've no intention of letting anyone stop me."

"My daughter..." Cedric whispered, shaking his head sadly. "She was only doing right by those who have earned her trust."

Edmond raised a brow at him, then sprinkled begonia dust on the mirror and sat across from the other wizard as the message faded away.

"Geoff," Dawn breathed as he leaned over to kiss her again. The stone wall was cold behind her back and she shivered. "Shouldn't we be going?"

"We'll go when I'm done with you," Geoff said. His mouth found her neck and sucked on her while his hands gripped her waist and pulled her closer.

No, not this time. It didn't matter how angry it might make him, Geoff wasn't allowed to do this anymore. Dawn felt a tingle run through her, and he jerked back like she'd shocked him.

"I thought you told him to stop," he growled, then sniffed and looked over as Dusk and Diya came into view, racing up the hallway to them. "Great, you brought the other one. Think he can help you against me?"

"Dawn!" Dusk flew up to her, searching her face. When he found no signs of harm or distress, he relaxed. "You're all right."

"Of course I'm all right," Dawn replied, then looked at Geoff. "It wasn't him this time. I said I could stop you."

Geoff glared at her and shivered.

"Fine. That's how you want to be, I won't touch you," he growled, then grabbed her wrist. "Yet. I still have something to show you. Come on, fairy, you've got work to do. But leave the broken one, I don't want him around."

"Diya's coming," Dusk said, taking his friend's hand as they followed the humans. "I need somewhere to put all the energy you need me to get rid of."

"Too small for the job, then?" Geoff glanced back at the fairies and snorted. "In that case, use your capacitor. Give it something to do before you destroy it."

"Don't do that," Diya said. "Just take the circlet with you, it'll be safer."

"I said he's using the lantern," Geoff growled. "It's either that or I'll break her." He squeezed Dawn's wrist and she flinched.

"Then I have to help him," she said. "You'll have to let go of me so I can."

"Fine. When we get there," Geoff said. They reached her room and Rob stood nervously aside while Geoff pulled her in and to the chest. "Get it."

Dawn opened the lid and reached in to take the lantern, but Geoff shoved her hand out of the way and grabbed it.

"Good girl. Now we're almost ready," he said and dragged her back out, almost running with her back to the stairs.

"I'll send Diya for you soon," Dusk whispered to Rob as he flew by.

Rob waited until they vanished, then walked the other way, to the stairs that led to his and Sarah's rooms.

"And I'll grab Sarah in the meantime," he mumbled to himself. Sarah barely forgave him after the dinner incident, when he'd run off with Dawn and left her behind. It took a week before she acknowledged his existence and a full season before she stopped giving him the silent treatment. If she was that upset after a minor antic, Rob didn't want to imagine how she'd act if she missed anything tonight.

37

Geoff ran as fast as Dawn could manage to stumble after him, until they reached his jungle terrace and he stopped to open the doors.

"We'll do it here so the girls can enjoy with us," he said.

Dusk nodded to Diya as he followed Dawn in, and Diya flicked away.

Geoff led them through the terrace to the pool, then handed the lantern to Dawn. "Now do it."

Dawn accepted the lantern and relaxed as he released her. She held her hand out for Dusk and he landed on her palm. He took a moment to secure the connection to the lantern, then looked up at the sky. Geoff shuddered as the sky began to darken ever so slightly.

"Faster," he demanded.

"I can't," Dusk said calmly. "This is the fastest I can go without endangering us."

Geoff scowled at the sky changing too slowly for him. "Dark! Give me the dark!"

"It will take a while," Dusk said slowly. "I have to pull more energy than the wizards put into it. Why don't you find the cougars and come back?"

"No," Geoff growled. "You'd like that; like it if I left. I'm not going away. Not now, not ever. You're the one who'll leave, once you give me my darkness." He twitched and started pacing, glancing up at the sky and growling at it.

Dawn watched him nervously. "Geoff, why don't you talk to me? Tell me about something that makes you happy."

Geoff looked at her with wild eyes and laughed. "Like what? I've shown you all my favorite things, all but one. What I'm about to show you. I want it; now give it to me."

"We're getting there," Dawn said patiently. "Just stay with me until then. The cougars. You've had them since you were little."

Geoff slowed slightly in his pacing and stared at his hands, holding them up to his face and making shapes with them as he spoke. "I found them. They were kittens then. I took them, brought them home. Henry let me keep them."

"Good," Dawn breathed. "What else?"

"We learned to hunt together," Geoff continued. "I could before like a human, but they showed me how to stalk prey—how to use my own strength to take life. They showed me the beauty of killing."

Stars were just becoming visible above them.

"Not long now," Dusk said softly.

"Do they swim?" Dawn asked. "Have they been to the other terrace?"

Geoff stopped pacing and glared at her.

"Your terrace. Where you promised me something you won't give me now," he growled. "Where you stopped me having what I want, what I need. Now you won't give me dark so I can change. You hate me—you want me to suffer." He shuddered and growled, then stepped closer to her.

"I don't hate you," Dawn said, trying to keep her hand steady for Dusk. "We can be friends still. I'll stay in Kirkjufell, even. Anything you want."

"Except one thing," Geoff said. "The one thing that matters, the one thing I need, the reason you're here at all. You'll stay—I won't let you go. And you'll regret not choosing me. Fairy! I want my dark!"

Dusk looked at Dawn, and she nodded.

"Have your dark," he said.

He pulled the light faster, and Geoff shivered and smirked.

"That's better," he said as the sky deepened to navy and the stars became brighter and more numerous. He started undressing and laughed. "Finally."

His skin rippled and shimmered with dark grey light as he started changing. He doubled over and curled up on the ground, twitching and laughing as he grew fur, claws, and fangs. The laugh turned into a howl and he stood before them on four massive paws, grinning.

A yowl came from behind them, and Dawn turned her head to see Jewel and Crown slink over to meet their wolf master. Geoff snarled and bristled his fur until they bowed to him, lowering themselves to the ground. He nodded and stalked over to Dawn. She forced herself to stay still as he sniffed her. Once he was satisfied, he licked his chops and circled her.

"You're a werewolf," she whispered.

Geoff flicked his ears and bared his fangs at her in another wolfy grin. He shifted his eyes to Dusk, then stopped pacing and readied himself to lunge.

"If you try that you'll change back," Dusk warned. "I'm still controlling the light."

Geoff snarled and snapped at him, then turned and ran off into the foliage. Jewel and Crown purred and rubbed against Dawn before chasing after him.

"Now what?" Dawn asked.

"Now we wait," Dusk answered. "And hope he burns enough energy that he'll be less dangerous when he returns." He looked at the black sky above them and frowned before cutting off the magic channel. "The wizards stopped. They must not be able to keep going now that I've interfered."

"Could we sneak out?" Dawn asked quietly. "While he's busy somewhere else."

Dusk shook his head. "He wants us to run or hide so he can hunt us. Since we can't force him to turn back to human, we're stuck until someone else comes."

"What happened to Diya?" Dawn asked.

Dusk furrowed his brow. "I sent him to get Robert for us, but he should have made it back by now."

"I'm sure he's fine," Dawn said. "Since we're with Geoff, there shouldn't be any trouble elsewhere."

Before he could answer, Dawn jumped as they heard a long, low howl. They turned towards the sound and saw three pairs of yellow eyes shining in the darkness as Geoff returned with the cougars.

Dusk grasped her thumb. "You can do this, just like in the Ruins."

Dawn took a deep breath and nodded. Dusk fluttered up out of her hand and she held it out for Geoff.

"I'm here," she whispered, taking one slow step. "It's all right, good boy."

Geoff put his ears back and bared his fangs, but stayed still as she crept closer. When she reached him, he sniffed her hand and relaxed, allowing her to pet him. She smiled and gently ran her hand along his head.

"There, that's better," she said.

Dusk relaxed and fluttered up to the cougars to calm them. As soon as he was away from Dawn, Geoff jumped at her, knocking her over. She gasped and dropped the lantern, then Geoff was on top of her, pinning her down. Dusk tried to reach her but Jewel swatted at him and sent him flying back. Geoff grinned at Dawn and licked her face and neck. She shuddered, and he rumbled like he was laughing.

"Get off of her," Dusk said and tried to dive around the cougars.

Crown snarled at him and he shot at her, slamming against her face and gripping her skin. She shrieked and recoiled, shaking her head to try to throw him off but he held on. After a moment she slowed and lay down, falling into an uneasy sleep as he forced magic into her. Jewel put her ears back and hissed at him, flicking her tail nervously. He stared her down, and she jerkily stepped back and lowered herself.

Geoff turned his head and barked at Dusk, then slammed his paw into Dawn's chest and glared at him. Dusk smirked.

"Try it," he said. "It won't kill her. You'll just activate my failsafe and prevent yourself from ever having her."

Dawn winced as Geoff howled and put more weight on her.

"Please," she said. "Don't do this. Let me help you instead."

She gasped as he pulled back, then screamed as he lunged at her shoulder and grabbed her with his jaws. He bit down, breaking her flesh and smashing against bone with his teeth, then dragged her as he turned to look at Dusk, who crumpled on the ground in pain. Geoff nodded at Jewel, and she leapt over, pouncing on the helpless fairy.

"Stop!" Dawn cried, and the cat froze with Dusk in her paws, mouth open to bite. "Leave him alone. I'll do it, I'll marry you, give you an heir, anything. Just don't hurt him."

Geoff crunched her shoulder, making her flinch, then turned to the lantern. Jewel gingerly grabbed Dusk by the neck and brought him over. He squirmed around, trying to free himself, but couldn't focus enough to use his magic. Geoff pawed at the lantern and shook his head, rattling Dawn.

"No," she said. "No. You can't make me, I won't open it."

She struggled against him, hurting herself more as she tried to pull out of his hold on her. Geoff rumble laughed and held her down with his paw while he pulled up on her shoulder.

"Geoff," Dusk rasped. He was still struggling to get out of the cat's mouth and spoke through layers of agony. "I can give you control of your curse, so you can transform at will and not be ruled by the light anymore. You can be stronger always, not just at night."

Geoff stopped pulling on Dawn and looked hard at Dusk for a moment, then growled around the shoulder in his mouth and looked behind Jewel. Dawn followed his gaze and watched as Crown approached and took over for Geoff in holding her down. Once he was satisfied Dawn couldn't get away, Geoff released her shoulder and stepped over to Dusk, sniffing him apprehensively.

"You have to let me go," Dusk said. "And I can't work if you're hurting her."

Geoff nodded and Jewel relaxed her jaws, dropping Dusk to the mossy ground. He landed with a thud and sat up.

"Are you all right, Dawn?" he asked.

"I'll be fine," she answered. Crown was heavy but had positioned herself well so Dawn could breathe easily. Her shoulder throbbed and made moving difficult and unappealing, so she relaxed as much as she could to relieve it. "Just worry about yourself."

Dusk took a deep breath and held his hand out to Geoff, who snarled at him.

"I have to read the curse," he said, and Geoff snorted and moved closer. Dusk placed his hand on Geoff's nose. Together, they were still for a few minutes. "All right, now I need something to enchant."

Geoff woofed at him and Jewel growled threateningly.

"I can't touch the curse directly. She designed it so you'll die if anyone tries to tamper with it," Dusk said calmly. "I'll have to enchant something else to work around it so you can use what she gave you whenever and however you want."

Geoff nodded and wandered over to his clothing pile. He rummaged for a moment, then returned with a heavy golden chain, which he dropped in front of Dusk.

"Good. Now just give me some time," Dusk said and set to work.

Geoff woofed again and went over to Dawn. Crown shifted out of the way and Geoff licked her bloody shoulder before laying down across her. He grumbled in her ear and relaxed, resting happily with his head against her cheek.

Dawn focused on her breathing, trying to keep it steady while she ignored her aching body. The less she hurt, the better for Dusk. Geoff was warm against her, and she listened to his heart beating the same it always did. Strong and steady, but not matching her. He was happy like this, had chosen this curse over her help, a fact that didn't make her feel any less guilty for choosing Dusk over him.

After what felt like an eternity, Dusk flitted over with the chain.

"It's done," he said, and Geoff lifted his head so it could be placed around his neck.

Once the chain was secure Geoff sat up and tested it. He shimmered again, faintly this time as the dark grey light matched his coarse fur. The fur pulled back into his skin, his snout flattened to just a nose, and the claws retracted into hands until he was human again.

"Nice job, fairy," he said and laughed. "Elegant little solution you've given me. Now allow me to return the favor." He grabbed the lantern and opened the door. "If you'll just get in, then I won't have to incapacitate you again. Although that was fun, and there's nothing better than freshly spilled blood." He looked down at Dawn and licked his lips.

"You're not getting any more of hers," Dusk said and flitted to her shoulder.

"Get away from her," Geoff growled. "She's not yours anymore; *she's mine*. You heard her, she gave herself to me to keep you safe. Which you'll be in the lantern, right where I want you."

Dusk ignored him and began healing her shoulder. "Do you want to get out here? Leave right now?"

Dawn sighed as the pain faded. "I do, but are we able to?"

Geoff grabbed her and pulled her into him, interrupting Dusk.

"You aren't leaving," he growled in her ear. "Your little boyfriend gave me my power, so now I can keep you here no matter how much you struggle. Your little tricks won't stop me."

"They don't have to stop you," Dusk replied and flitted up to his eye level. "If you look at your chain, you'll find that I gave myself an out. There's a spell in there, ready to attach to the curse and trigger its defenses if you hurt Dawn or me. If you try to harm her and she stops you again, it'll kill you."

"Then I'll just have to find a way around you," Geoff said, and his skin shimmered. "Won't be able to touch me if the girls do all the work."

He growled as he became a wolf again, and the cougars reacted. Jewel was ready by Dusk almost instantly, and Crown poised herself to rip into Dawn. Geoff grinned and pawed at the lantern, nodding at Dusk.

"And then what?" Dusk asked. "You still won't get to have her. I'll tell her to run, to escape without me. If you try to stop her, two things could happen. She could possibly still manage to kill you, even with her magic compromised, or you could activate her protection, and she'll get away regardless. As for me, Diya will see to it that I'm freed, however long it takes."

Geoff growled and snapped at Dusk, then straightened suddenly and turned his head, ears perked as he listened. The cougars put their ears back and twitched their tails with agitation. Geoff rumbled at them and sprinted off. Once he was out of sight, the cougars relaxed and settled around Dawn.

Dusk sighed and finished healing her shoulder, leaving only light scars where the teeth had punctured her skin.

"Shall we find out what's taken our host's attention?" he asked impishly.

Dawn closed the lantern and stood with it. "Think our backup finally made it?"

"Only one way to find out," Dusk replied as he followed her.

Jewel watched them go, then yawned and walked away into the undergrowth with Crown slinking along beside her.

38

"Diya!"

Diya froze in the hallway and looked around as he heard his name whispered at him. He spotted Paul peeking out from an alcove. The boy was a welcome face.

"You again. I know where I'm going this time if you were waiting to guide me," he said.

Paul shook his head and crept fully into the hallway. "Dusk is in danger."

"Yeah, I'm aware," Diya replied. "But he can handle Geoff on his own, and I'm bringing some help anyway. At the very least he can give me time to return."

"No, from Edmond," Paul said. "He wants to kill Geoff, and he'll hurt the princess if she's in the way. If he gets a chance, he'll also capture Dusk. We have to make sure he can't."

"So what are we going to do? I'd like it if he killed the wolf, but no one's allowed to do anything to Dusk," Diya said.

"We help the wolf," Paul replied. "Stall Edmond and ensure the wizards stop making the sun, then they can get away while the wolf is distracted."

"And let Geoff and Edmond worry about each other," Diya said. "One of them will get the other, and it'll be one less Kirkjufell for us either way. Right, you deal with the wizards, make sure Dusk can do something besides make it dark, and I'll take the uncle."

"He'll be angry, be careful," Paul warned.

"Nothing I can't handle," Diya said with a grin and sped away.

The lux fairy found Rob and Sarah sitting in the hallway in front of Dawn's room. They stood up as he approached.

"They ready for us?" Rob asked, hand hovering over his sword hilt.

"Got another little job first," Diya said. "Come on, we gotta go see the damn wizard again."

The humans followed him quickly to the next level and to Edmond's room. Sarah knocked on the door and Edmond answered almost instantly. He stared at them for a moment, taken aback by the unexpected visitors.

"Excuse me." He coughed and tried to compose himself, blinking quickly a few times. "Good evening, Sarah, Diya. And Robert, I don't believe we've met."

"Sarah?" Cedric said from inside. He shuffled over and frowned at them from over Edmond's shoulder. "What are you doing here? And at such a late hour."

"I could ask you the same thing," Sarah replied, and Cedric scowled.

"You don't need to, we know what they're doing," Diya said as he floated into the room. "Huh, you forgot to put away your things this time. What'd Berniece have to say?" He flicked over to the mirror on the desk and looked over the message Edmond had just received.

"Get away from there!" Edmond shouted and hurried over.

"Nothing about me, how boring," Diya said and moved away from the desk. "Thought she'd at least say hello or something—it's been a long time. Though I can't say I'm too thrilled that she's interested in Dusk."

Edmond threw his hand on the mirror and activated the spell to clear it. "What are you doing here?"

"Someone has to make sure you're occupied," Diya answered. "You kids go ahead and sit down. We'll be wizard-sitting for a while." Sarah skipped in, grabbing her father's arm on the way and pulling him to the armchairs. Rob stayed in the doorway and squared his feet. "Right, now let's all get comfy and enjoy the show. You might want to light a candle or something. I'm not bright enough for you to see by."

"What are you talking about?" Edmond asked, then frowned and went to his window. "What's happening to my sun?"

"Oh, that'll be Dusk," Diya said and shrugged. "Your nephew wants to show off for Dawn, so he's making it happen."

Edmond's face darkened. "Cedric, we have to move, now."

"I wouldn't do that if I were you," Diya said and flicked next to Rob as Edmond raced to the door. "Don't think the boy'll like it if you get in the way right now. He's been wanting to do this for a while, and he might be a little frisky."

"Get out of my way," Edmond ordered Rob, who pulled his sword out in response and held it ready to strike.

"Edmond," Cedric said wearily, drooping into his chair. "Listen to him: we've been foiled. It would be best to let Geoff be, at least for the time being. Perhaps you could acquire the original target while there's an opportunity for it."

Diya laughed. "You can look if you want, but I think you'll find the lantern isn't where it's supposed to be."

"It's with them?" Edmond shrieked. "You fools! You've given Geoff the very thing I need to overthrow him! I have to stop this. *Let me through!*"

"Am I allowed to kill this one?" Rob asked Diya hopefully.

Diya shook his head. "As much as I'd like that, we need him still. But that doesn't mean you can't rough him up a bit first."

Rob nodded and shifted to swing at Edmond's chest with his hilt. Edmond stepped back and held up his hands.

"If you try anything, I'll hit you first. My magic isn't sharp, but it can do worse things than cut you," he said.

Rob snorted. "Whatever it is, I've already gone through the worst thing possible. You won't get past me."

"Bert," Sarah said as she raced over, putting herself between them. "Don't. You won't prove anything by letting him torture you."

"Sarah!" Cedric cried. "Edmond, remember you agreed not to harm her."

"And you said she wasn't to be involved more, yet here she is," Edmond said and lunged at her. He grabbed her arm and she yelped as he twisted it behind her and wrapped his other arm around her. "Now, everyone get out of my way."

Sarah struggled against him uselessly, hoping her magic would spring to action, but it didn't. "They'll get out of your way when we decide it's time," she said. "We won't let you hurt Dawn."

"Dawn?" Edmond frowned. "But it isn't me that will hurt her. If you let me go I'll stop Geoff from doing any harm, which he's more than capable of, with or without my sun to keep him human."

"Well, he isn't human now," Diya said as the light shrunk away and only his weak glow remained. "And you know it could be worse for everyone if you got there now. I think you're aware how were-wolves are when they first change, especially if they haven't been able to for a while. But hey, you want to get your face eaten off, that's your business."

Rob paled and stared at Diya. "Are you sure Dawn's all right? It doesn't sound like she's all right."

Diya sighed heavily and looked up at the ceiling. "Oh, fine, just go, but don't say I didn't warn you."

Edmond released Sarah and looked pleadingly at Rob.

"There's still time to help her if you follow me, now," he said.

Rob stepped over to let the wizard pass, then ran after him as he sprinted along the hallway.

"Sarah," Cedric said softly before she could chase after them. He got up from the chair and crossed the room to her, his face wrinkled with sorrow. "Please, don't put yourself in more danger. Come with me, and we can start a new life somewhere else. I'll teach you about magic and help you find more beyond what I know. Just come, please."

Sarah gaped at him, wanting to say yes. Finally, he was on her side, offering her what she'd always wanted. Learning with him, discovering new things, finding happiness with each other like a real family. It was perfect, except for one thing.

"Dawn needs me," she said and turned to Diya. "Let's go."

Diya nodded and led her down the hall after Edmond and Rob. Cedric watched his daughter disappear and hung his head.

Edmond raced through the dark palace as only someone familiar with it could, Rob close on his heels. They reached the lift and he jumped on a platform.

"Get on," he said, and Rob nodded and took the next one.

Once Rob was in place, Edmond muttered a few words and the lift sped up, propelling them upwards at breakneck speeds. He jumped off on the eleventh level and reached over to grab Rob as he came up after. Somehow, Rob kept his balance, and they ran on. They reached a door, and Edmond tried the knob. It was locked.

"Of course it is," he muttered and beckoned Rob over. "Think you can break it?"

"Easily," Rob said and rammed his shoulder into the door, bursting it open.

They entered a dark sitting room quite like Edmond's, but larger and with fancier furnishings. Edmond quickly crossed to Geoff's bedroom and looked in, then turned to Rob.

"Where are they?" he demanded.

"That's exactly what I'd like to know," Henry said, sharp features highlighted in the light from the lamp he carried. He stepped into the sitting room, carefully avoiding the broken door, then glared at his brother. "But I'm also curious why the hell your wizards aren't doing their damn job."

Edmond gaped at him. "But they haven't stopped. It's the fairy—he's doing this."

"Like hell it's the fairy!" The lamp cut through the air as Henry gestured angrily, throwing shadows around. "I've just been to see your wizards and they've quit; they aren't doing anything! Why are you here, of all places, when my son is somewhere with the girl!"

"Didn't he tell you?" Diya said from the doorway as he and Sarah arrived. "He wants to kill your boy, and take over your kingdom."

"You!" Edmond shrieked at Diya. "You know where they are. Tell me!"

Diya grinned. "You already know where they'd be; you know your nephew."

Edmond stared at him, then sprinted out of the room. Rob jumped and ran after him again.

"Are they with the cats?" Henry asked icily.

"Kind of obvious, really, and I don't even know him that well," Diya said.

Henry sighed and fell into a chair. "Then it's already too late. How am I going to explain this to Leopold?"

"It can't be too late," Sarah exclaimed. "Dawn has to be fine. She has to be."

"Girl, you don't know anything of what could be," Henry said, laughing. "My son was already difficult to manage before the witch gave him this curse. Now he's controlled by base desires, and it's all I can do to keep him as close to human as possible. She won't make it if he wants to kill her."

"He *doesn't* want to kill her," Diya said. "Bet he'd like to kill your brother, maybe even you, but he likes Dawn, wants to keep her. No, what he wants with her is to get her away from Dusk. But he can't do that, it's impossible."

"But he'd be more than happy to break her if he thought it would do something to the fairy," Henry countered. "And once he starts, once he tastes blood, he can't be stopped."

"Yeah, that's why we sent the wizard to him," Diya said, and then added to Sarah, "It'll be okay. Dusk can handle things."

"You want Geoff to kill Edmond?" Henry asked. The shock seemed to be wearing off.

"Or the other way around," Diya answered, shrugging. "They're both bad."

Henry stood up and stomped out to the hallway, grabbing Sarah's wrist as he passed her.

"You people are going to fix this mess," he said, dragging her along while Diya flitted after them. "Everything would have been fine if you hadn't meddled. I'm not going to lose my son—or my brother if I can help it—and you little fairies are going to help me make sure they both live."

Diya snorted. "Even though Edmond is against you? And I don't think Geoff is really on your side, either, if I'm honest. He thinks everything is already his. Acts like you're just a placeholder until he's married, then he'll get rid of you."

"He is my son!" Henry yelled. "Of course he wants me gone. I've been grooming him to be king his whole life, teaching him to want power, to take it however he can. As soon as he marries that girl and gets an heir I'm giving him the kingdom. He knows he just has to ensure the line, and everything will be his. And Edmond... Do you think I was unaware he wants the throne? He does nothing without my knowledge."

Diya frowned. "Then how did Geoff end up like this?"

"The witch did it," Henry answered. "It wasn't Edmond's fault she had her own intentions with my son."

Diya shook his head. "But they're in on it together."

Henry stopped walking and Sarah almost slammed into him.

"Explain yourself," he growled at Diya.

"They're helping each other," Diya said. "Edmond wants your kingdom, and the witch wants something of mine. Something the Night Rise encouraged us to find and bring here. Now she wants your son dead because he's onto them."

"Is that why you're here, then?" Henry asked. "Why Leopold didn't mention you fairies were coming? Idiots, you knew what was going on and you did what they wanted anyway."

"We thought the witch was in Mantrisa," Diya argued. "We thought we were getting away from her. We didn't know she was here and had your brother helping her."

Henry glared at him for a moment, then yanked Sarah as he continued moving.

"Well, now you're going to help me stop this nonsense," he snarled.

"How?" Sarah asked as she tried to keep up.

Henry laughed. "If Geoff hasn't gotten Edmond or the girl yet, you're going to make sure he doesn't."

Sarah went pale. "You want to use me as bait? Let him get me instead?"

"What else are you good for?" Henry asked.

"This!" She focused on her wrist where he was grasping her.

Henry paused and glanced at her, then snorted. "What exactly are you hoping will happen?"

Sarah's vision blurred as her eyes filled with angry tears. "Why can't I do it? Why isn't it working?"

She closed her eyes and willed herself to make something happen,

NIGHT RISE ~ 385

anything. Her magic refused to act and she sobbed. Henry grinned at her and pulled her along again.

"That'll do nicely to get his attention," he said.

Diya flicked close and spoke quietly to her. "Don't worry, I won't let them do anything to you."

Sarah nodded shakily as they arrived at the terrace and Henry pulled her through the open doors.

39

"You go first," Edmond whispered to Rob when they reached the jungle terrace.

Rob nodded and readied his sword, then opened the right door slowly and peeked in. The entrance to the terrace was calm, only cricket chirps and a magic breeze gently stirring the tree leaves. There were no signs of humans—or animals.

"It's clear," he said and slipped inside.

Edmond sighed and followed him. "Be ready for anything. He's got cougars in here, and they'll do what he wants while he's a wolf."

They made their way carefully through the terrace, moving slowly and silently deeper into the plants. Edmond directed them towards the pool, and they were a few paces away when Rob stopped and tensed.

With a snarl, Geoff jumped out at him from the undergrowth and Rob stumbled back. Edmond gasped and dove to the side as Geoff pressured Rob towards him. The wolf grinned at them and pawed the ground excitedly as he crept closer.

"Where are your cats?" Edmond asked and glanced around as if he expected them to suddenly appear. He shifted away from Rob, concerned Geoff would jump at the knight again.

Geoff rumble-laughed and leapt at his uncle, easily pushing him to the ground. Without hesitation, he bit into his neck and Edmond screamed and flailed. Rob stepped over and shoved Geoff, knocking him off the wizard, then stood over him with his sword on his throat.

"You may talk big, but I know which one of us has real strength," he said. "You want to take life, but I'd give my own if it kept my friends safe."

He frowned as Geoff shimmered, then stared in shock at the human under him. Geoff smirked and got to his feet.

"Really. Trying to convince me to change, or just making excuses? We both know you couldn't kill if you had to," he said, then looked over at the wizard. "You dead yet, Uncle?"

Edmond wheezed and turned his head to see his nephew. "How are you human?"

"Turns out the fairy was useful for something," Geoff said. Rob snorted and he laughed. "You don't like him either. Shame I've already decided I want you dead. Since Ed didn't cooperate and die already, you can be my first kill as a wolf." He shimmered and jumped at Rob, changing back into a wolf as he slammed into him.

"No," Rob said, only stepping back while Geoff thudded to the ground. "You won't kill me. Where's Dawn?"

Geoff snarled and shifted back to human. "The girls are watching her for me. Why won't you attack? Are you afraid to hurt me? Afraid you might actually kill someone? You can't, can you? Too weak to take another life. You won't beat me like this."

"There's nothing weak about valuing life," Rob said and lunged at Geoff.

Geoff laughed and stepped to the side as Rob passed. He shoved him and Rob fell, unable to stop himself as the momentum carried him forward, and he hit the ground hard. Geoff shifted again and jumped on Rob's back, happily pinning him down.

"Geoff, don't!" Dawn shouted as she reached them and saw what was happening.

The wolf froze as he was about to bite Rob's neck and looked over at her. He growled and backed off of Rob, then changed to human again.

"Don't you even think about it," he said. "This fight has nothing to do with you. Where are the girls? You didn't do anything to them, did you?"

"They wandered off," Dusk said and flitted in front of Dawn protectively.

"Dawn!" Rob exclaimed with relief. He'd gotten himself off the ground and stood ready if Geoff tried anything else. "You're all right."

Dawn smiled and nodded. "I'm all right."

"Is that Edmond?" Dusk asked casually, glancing at the prone wizard.

"For now," Geoff said, laughing. "Won't be soon, though I might have to help him along."

"I'm not dying tonight," Edmond growled. He brought a hand to his throat and muttered a spell. There was a soft pink glow and he pulled his hand away and sat up. The deep gash Geoff had given him was messily sealed closed. It would scar, but it no longer threatened his life.

"Why must you ruin all my fun?" Geoff asked, pouting. "All I want is to kill someone, anyone, but no one will let me. Is it really so much to ask that you die when I break your throat? Since you insist on preventing me, I'll have to be more thorough this time." He shifted to wolf and raced towards Edmond.

The wizard was weakened, but ready for his nephew. He recited another spell and the air around him sparked with energy. Geoff noticed just before running into the field and skidded to a stop. He howled and stepped back.

Dusk glanced at Dawn and raised an eyebrow. She nodded, and they slowly made their way closer to the exit. Dawn caught Rob's eye and gestured for him to escape with them, but he shook his head and continued watching Geoff, waiting for his chance. Dusk noticed her worried expression and sighed quietly. She smiled as she felt a shimmer that seemed to say *if you must*.

Thank you, she thought back at him, and they stayed where they were.

Geoff became human again and glared at his uncle. "That's a new one. Did the witch teach it to you? Henry won't like it if you've been learning things and not sharing."

"Like I give a damn what Henry wants," Edmond said. "My whole life I've been giving him what he wants, and for what? So I can always be second and have less than him even when I'm more capable. It's past time for me to have what I deserve."

"But you're not more capable," Henry remarked as he reached the fight. He was still dragging Sarah and stopped a few feet from Geoff.

Diya fluttered up to Dusk while the Kirkjufells had each other's attention.

"She's coming," he whispered, and Dawn felt a cold tingle run through her. She glanced at Dusk, and he looked as worried as she felt.

"If you were, you'd have managed to take over the kingdom by now, but you haven't," Henry continued. "And I see you're failing to kill my son, though it appears he's gotten an edge on you that you weren't expecting." He looked at his human son with a touch of surprise and admiration.

"Nice of you to notice," Geoff snarled. "Took you long enough to get here. If you don't want me to kill you or your brother, you'd better get out of here before I change back. In fact, you can just leave the palace for good, since I'll be having my kingdom now."

"You'll have your throne when you have an heir," Henry replied.

"Until then I expect you to behave yourself. You want something to kill? Have her." He threw Sarah forward at Geoff, and she fell on her hands at his feet.

Geoff smirked at her and laughed. "No better than any other maid now, are you? Still think you're special? Or have you learned your place?"

She looked up at him fearfully. Her cheeks were stained from her earlier tears, and strands of hair were stuck to her face. With a yell, Rob lunged at Geoff and knocked him away from Sarah. They scuffled on the ground while she scooted back.

Dusk flicked up to Dawn's ear and spoke quietly to her. "I know you want to help your friends, but we need to leave now. Diya can watch them for us, please. We have to get you and the lantern out of here."

Dawn watched Geoff turn into a wolf and get the upper hand as Rob dropped his sword, then glanced at Sarah, who was getting shakily to her feet.

"I'm sorry," she whispered as she ran forward. "I can't leave them."

When she was a step away from Sarah, a hand grabbed her and yanked her back.

"You get out of here," Henry said and dragged her towards the doors.

"No!" Dawn exclaimed and struggled against him, but he continued moving forward, away from the fight.

"Dawn, you have to go," Dusk said, flitting along beside her. "Please. We aren't ready for Berniece, and I can't risk losing you."

Dawn looked back and watched Rob grapple with Geoff and end up on top of the wolf as he got a hold of his knife. Diya hovered near the fight and waved at her reassuringly. She closed her eyes and took a deep breath. They would manage without her; she had to trust them.

"All right," she said and ran with Henry back to the palace.

"Bert!" Sarah shouted once she was on her feet and had calmed herself with a deep breath. "You idiot, get off of him!"

Rob was about to stab Geoff in the chest when he heard Sarah and hesitated. The wolf rumbled and rolled over, throwing Rob off of him. Once he was on his paws again, he jumped at Sarah.

"Sarah!" Rob yelled as she screamed and tried to run, but was unable to get away from the wolf.

Geoff grinned and nipped at her, rumbling as she jerked away from him and kept attempting, but failing, to increase the distance between them.

Rob turned to Edmond, who was getting up, energy field still zapping around him like a shield.

"Are you going to do anything?" Rob asked.

Edmond watched his nephew toy with Sarah. "Let him finish. It'll be easier to kill him if he's had some satisfaction first."

Rob's face contorted with rage, and he raced at the wolf. Geoff grinned at Sarah one more time and turned to face Rob, easily knocking him off balance as he charged. With a shimmer, Geoff was human and kneeling on Rob's neck.

"Who's life is more valuable now, knight?" Geoff mocked and pressed his knee down on Rob's throat. "What do you think, is mine worth more alive or dead? What about yours? Certainly worth more to me after I kill you. But maybe I should kill your girlfriend first, so you can watch." He looked up and sniffed.

"After I finish Ed, though," he snarled and turned, changing as he did, to jump on Edmond sneaking up behind him.

Sarah seized her chance and grabbed Rob, pulling him to his feet.

"Let's go," she whispered. Rob nodded and allowed her to help him sneak away.

Edmond screamed as Geoff pushed him down and reopened the neck wound, too surprised at being caught to maintain his

392 - FRANCES DE LA ROSA

spell. Geoff held on and bit down harder, waiting until the wizard stopped moving to let go. Once he was still, Geoff released him and shimmered, shifting to human.

"Goodbye, Uncle," he whispered in the dead man's ear. "Was nice killing you."

Diya waited until Geoff was busy with his uncle, then raced after Sarah and Rob as they stealthily moved through the trees back to the palace.

"Come on, we have to hurry," he said quietly, moving in front of them to help guide them through the dark jungle.

"Aren't we done?" Rob asked. "We did our part. Edmond and Geoff are worrying about each other, and Dawn got away."

"Berniece is coming," Diya answered without looking back. "That's a bigger issue than any of the Kirkjufells. We need to get out of the palace altogether if we can."

They reached the doors and stopped—the way out was blocked by the cougars. Before they could go back, the wolf stalked up from the foliage behind them. Geoff grinned and shimmered to human.

"Didn't think I'd forget about you, did you? Trying to leave when I'm busy, just when it was getting fun," he said.

"So you got the wizard," Diya said. "Sad he didn't get you, but I've no qualms with his death."

Geoff laughed. "No? Maybe I'll let you live for a little longer. You're not entirely boring."

"You're not getting any of us," Rob said. He stood ready with his sword, Sarah tucked behind him.

"Thought you already figured out that I can beat you," Geoff remarked. "Guess I'll have to show you again." He shifted and started across the space between them.

"Hey," Diya said, and Geoff slowed and looked at him. "Not now.

The witch is coming, and you don't want her getting to Dawn any more than we do."

Geoff growled and shifted back. "So, you need my help? Is that what you're saying?"

Diya sighed. "Yeah, we do. Dusk'll get Dawn away from Henry easily enough, but I don't know where they'll end up after that. We need you to find them, so we can get there before the witch does."

"Don't think your little friend can handle things?" Geoff jeered. "Fine, I'll take you to them. But this isn't over." He shifted to wolf and sniffed the air a few times. Once he was satisfied, he nodded at the cougars to step aside, then jogged into the hallway.

"So why do we need him?" Sarah whispered as they followed the wolf.

Geoff snorted and snarled at her. He snuffed around for a few moments, then froze. With a growl, he sprinted down the hallway. He stopped at a turn and looked back, waiting for them.

"That's why," Diya answered, then called to the wolf. "Wait a second, would you?"

Geoff growled, but stayed put, tail flicking impatiently. Diya closed his eyes to concentrate, and after a few moments, his glow flickered and brightened until everyone could see several meters around him.

"That's better," he said, smiling to himself. "'Kay, we're ready now."

Geoff woofed and raced off again. He sniffed as he ran, speeding up until he was well ahead of the others, almost out of view as he neared the edge of Diya's light.

"Hey, the humans can't go that fast," Diya said, and Geoff bristled but slowed.

"Thanks," Sarah said softly, and Diya shrugged.

"I can go that fast," Rob muttered, and Sarah shoved him. "All right, we'll go slower. But it's on you if anything happens to Dawn."

"You two shut it," Geoff hissed at them. He'd stopped and shifted to human, and they almost ran straight into him. "Nothing's going to happen to her if you let me take care of things. Only one allowed to hurt her is me." He turned back into a wolf and sniffed around again.

Sarah blinked at him, then looked at Rob, who was glowering at Geoff. She nudged him softly and smiled when he looked at her.

"Thank you, too," she whispered.

"For what?" Rob whispered back, brow furrowed with confusion. Geoff woofed and started running again, forcing them to move.

"I'll tell you later," Sarah said. Diya glanced back at them and gave Sarah a knowing look. She glared at him and he grinned, then turned forward to chase the wolf.

40

"Where are we going?" Dawn asked Henry as he dragged her through the palace.

They were hurrying through the eleventh level. The king's hand was clamped on one wrist while she held the lantern in her other hand. He was taking Dusk and her somewhere of his own desire, and her map told her they weren't aiming for any place she'd been to yet.

"I'm putting you in my rooms, then I'm taking your fairy to Edmond's," Henry answered.

"You won't be separating us," Dusk said. "Dawn, time to go on our own."

Dawn nodded and zapped Henry's hand, making him jerk away from her. He attempted to grab her again, but she dropped to the ground out of his reach, clutching the lantern against herself. Dusk flew between them and glared at Henry. He shimmered red, engulfed in flames.

"Let her go," he said calmly.

Henry glared back at the fireball and straightened himself. "And what are you planning to do? I still need her for Geoff. She isn't leaving this palace before we have what we want from her. Until then, I can keep her quite comfortable in my rooms where I can watch her."

"No. She's leaving this place with me," Dusk replied.

Dawn scooted away and stood up. "I'm not giving anything to Geoff, but we don't have time to worry about that right now. If we don't get out soon, you might not have a kingdom to give him either."

"What are you talking about?" Henry asked with amusement. "My kingdom isn't going anywhere."

"The mountain witch is coming," Dusk explained. "If we go, then she won't be able to take your kingdom. Well, she'll still try, but it won't be as easy for her."

Henry sighed. "Is it true Edmond's helping her?"

"There's proof in his sitting room," Dawn answered. "If you want to check you can, but I know it's true."

"Show me," Henry said and walked towards the nearest stairs.

Dawn looked at Dusk, and he dowsed his flames and nodded. They followed Henry down to Edmond's rooms.

Henry went straight in and froze.

"You!" he exclaimed at Cedric, who was watching over Edmond's mirror.

Cedric stared at Dawn and Dusk, then noticed the lantern in Dawn's hand and gasped. "Why have you come here? And where's Edmond?"

"Where do you think?" Henry snarled. "You've been helping him. You know he went to kill Geoff. They were both alive when we left, and I've done what I can to keep it that way."

"Dawn, you must go," Cedric pleaded. "Berniece is close. I've endeavored to stall her coming, but I fear she is aware I am attempting to mislead her. You don't have much time."

"You're helping us?" Dawn asked. "Why?"

Cedric sighed. "I realized I had no hope of receiving my reward, and thought it was better not to also lose my daughter. Now please, take the lantern away before she finds you."

Dusk flew over to him and held out his hand. Cedric stared at him for a moment, then smiled and gave him his finger to shake.

"Thank you," Dusk said, then flew back over to Dawn. "Whatever she promised you, if I can, I'll try to get it for you."

Cedric shook his head slowly. "I don't believe even you can manage it. Now go, please."

"No one is going anywhere," Henry exclaimed. "Not until I get some answers about what the hell is going on here. My brother wants your lantern? How does that have anything to do with cursing my son and taking my kingdom?"

"It's complicated," Dawn said as Dusk tugged on her sleeve to get her moving. "Cedric can explain." Together they raced away before Henry could react.

After a few turns, they slowed so Dawn could catch her breath.

"Now what?" she asked, and the path to the side entrance appeared in her mind.

"Now we get out of here," Dusk said.

Dawn nodded and followed him along hallways and down stairways until they reached the exit. She stopped for a moment to take a few deep breaths, then looked at Dusk before opening the door.

"Well, isn't this convenient," said the woman standing just on the other side, a smirk playing on her lips as she brushed a strand of dark, curly hair out of her face. "Fancy running into the very thing I came to collect before I even enter."

Even in shadows, her features were sharp and defined, like a woman in the prime of her life, but something in the way she carried herself told of many years beyond her appearance.

Instantly, Dusk was in front of Dawn and on fire again. "Berniece."

"Ahh, Dusk," Berniece replied, sighing as she crossed one arm over herself and held the other up as though she were holding a glass. "How interesting that you of all fairies would be the one to return this to me."

She reached past him to grab the lantern and frowned as Dawn yanked it back and cradled it away from her. "Come, girl, give me my lantern."

"It isn't yours," Dawn said and slowly stepped back. "It belongs to my family, and I've been entrusted with its care."

"Poor, ignorant child," Berniece said. She closed her eyes and shook her head sadly. "What a pity you've been taken so willingly by this one." She nodded at Dusk who flickered angrily.

"So simple-minded, he and the other fairies are. They've no understanding of how unfortunate their lives are. So much potential—and power—stuck in the bodies of such tiny things. It's sad to see them fly around, happily oblivious of what they could be, what they should be. What good are his roses or tricks with light while dragons can make or destroy anything they please? What purpose in an eternal life if you've no ability to grow and change, become more than what you were when you were created?"

"And what good is your life?" Dusk asked. "What purpose do you have? The little good you do for humans you do for personal gain, yet you live alone in the mountains, unknown by humanity."

"Oh, you think I want something else?" Berniece laughed. "It's easier to gain power if no one else is aware you are after it. I've been patient since Coma left, and I was rewarded with another wizard. Not as powerful, it's true, but still able enough to help me form a plan for a new life. And in spite of your effort to ruin it, here I am, about to have my lantern *and* you to give it even more power. Really, it hardly could have gone better."

She pulled a needle out of her pocket and casually flicked it at Dawn. Dusk dove in front of it, and it bounced off of him and clinked on the stone floor.

"Is that how you want to play," Berniece said, pouting. "I was hoping I wouldn't have to rely on my stronger toys, but you don't give me much choice."

"I'd reconsider, if I were you," Dusk replied and pointed at her skirts, which started smoking.

Berniece gasped and grabbed at her dress, swishing her skirts to extinguish the flame that was starting to creep up them.

"Tut-tut," she said, shaking a finger at Dusk. "Trying to ruin a lady's clothing. You were never much of a gentleman, but I see you've only gotten worse in the last century. Really, what would Nova think?"

Dawn felt a shimmer nudging her, and she slowly crept back as Dusk kept Berniece busy.

"At least I'm still a fairy like he made me," he said. "Coma didn't die how he was created, and I know Nova still suffers from the loss. You may not think much of me or my power, but Nova appreciates what I do, and it's his opinion that matters."

"That's the issue right there," Berniece said. "You really believe it's enough to please someone else, even though everything you do is less than what he can. Even if you were stronger, he could end your life, as he did with Eachann. How can you still think you have a chance at anything more than what he decides?"

"I don't think that," Dusk argued. "I know I can only accomplish so much, and it doesn't even begin to compare to what Nova could do. But he made me that I might live and experience the world. If my existence is enough to make him happy, then I serve my purpose by simply being."

"Girl, do you think I don't see you?" Berniece smirked as Dawn froze. She'd made it a handful of steps away, out of arms reach, but still close enough that the witch could grab her if she lunged. "You bring that back now if you don't want any harm to come to Dusk."

"Your needle didn't do anything. Maybe you have nothing that can touch him," Dawn said. She felt a shimmer telling her to stay put and not to do as Berniece said.

"Oh, I have something," Berniece replied and looked past Dawn, down the dark palace hallway. "And here it comes now."

"Geoff!" Henry exclaimed as the wolf entered Edmond's sitting room and snuffed around. "Did you finish with the girl already?"

Cedric gasped. "Not Sarah!"

"What not me?" Sarah asked as she and Rob appeared in the doorway with Diya. Cedric sighed with relief.

"Where's Edmond?" Henry asked his son.

Geoff shimmered to human and smirked at his father.

"Back with the girls," he said. "Now if you'll excuse us, we're ensuring my other girl doesn't have any trouble with a certain mountain witch." Back in wolf form, he continued sniffing out his trail.

"You killed my brother," Henry whispered, and Geoff flicked his ears at him in response. "Tell me you at least left his body."

Geoff looked at his father with his yellow wolf eyes, then changed.

"He's not worth the time," he said and returned to wolf.

"Then you should have let him live!" Henry kicked at his son, hitting him in the side and knocking him into a wall.

Geoff yelped in surprise and looked at Henry. He bristled his fur and stalked forward, growling and baring his teeth. The king backed away, his face hard but his hands in front of him.

"Geoff," Diya said tiredly. "Later. We have to get to Dawn, remember?"

Geoff snapped at his father and turned to run out of the room. Diya and Rob were after him almost instantly. Henry sighed and jogged out also, hurrying to the terrace to find his brother.

"Sarah," Cedric said as she started following after Geoff. She stopped and looked at her father. He walked up to her and looked over her, then sighed and embraced her. "I'm glad you're all right."

Sarah smiled and hugged her father back. "And I'm glad you didn't leave. Now I've got to catch up to them."

Cedric nodded and released her. "Then allow me to come with you also."

"Are you sure?" Sarah asked. "We might run into Berniece." She thought of something and stepped back from him, eyes wide with worry. "Unless that's what you want to happen."

"No!" Cedric said. "I understand if you don't believe me, but I have realized what truly matters, and that is you. The fairy kept you safe before, and now I wish to repay that debt by ensuring the princess's safety."

Sarah looked him over intently—and saw the honesty in his eyes.

"You can come with us," she said, smiling, and led the way down the hall. "I'm sure we could use your help."

Diya paused as they caught up to him and scowled. "What're you doing?"

"I am coming with my daughter to protect her friend," Cedric answered.

"Really," Diya said. He flew off, and they did their best to keep up with him. "Sure hope you mean that. But I'll be watching you, in case you don't."

Cedric struggled to maintain the pace, breathing heavily as they ran. "I see I've quite a way to go to prove myself."

Diya snorted and didn't reply. They caught up to Rob, who was waiting for them at the top of a stairway.

"Finally," he said and started going down. "Geoff's about ready to go without us."

The wolf was pacing at the bottom of the stairs, snarling up at them impatiently. He shifted to human as they reached the bottom and glared at them. "The hell is the wizard doing?"

"He's coming with us," Sarah answered and glared back at Geoff.

"Like hell he is," Geoff growled. "You get out of here, now. I don't have time for this goatshit. Mountain witch isn't going to just give up if Dawn leaves the palace, and I won't have you getting in my way." He returned to wolf and sprinted away again, going so fast that even Rob struggled to keep up.

Diya shook his head and looked at Sarah and Cedric. "Come on, we'd better not let him get there alone."

"You are allowing me to continue?" Cedric asked, still having difficulty with all the running. "I had thought you might agree with the prince that I should do something else with myself."

"Said I'd keep an eye on you, didn't I?" Diya explained. "You want to prove yourself, might as well let you have a chance. Just don't make me regret it."

"Thank you," Cedric said, and Diya nodded his head.

"Hurry up," Rob called. He was waving at them from their next turn. "He got too far ahead; I can't see him anymore."

Diya scowled and sped ahead of them, going up and down several possible turns before buzzing back. "He left us."

"So now what?" Sarah asked.

"We keep going," Diya said. "Split up and try as many directions as possible until we find something." He buzzed away down the longest hallway until he looked back to see no one had moved.

"Oh," he said and drifted back to them. "Can't see much without me, can you? Guess we'll just have to stay together."

"We'll find them," Rob said. Diya nodded at him gratefully, and they made their way forward, going more by intuition than anything else.

After what felt like ages of searching, and more dead ends than any of them wanted to believe, Rob stiffened and held up a hand for them to stop.

"Did you hear that?" he asked under his breath. They all looked at him as he strained to listen, then relaxed. In moments they all heard the footsteps running toward them. Diya grinned and flew ahead of the group towards the sound.

"Paul!" he exclaimed as the boy appeared from around a corner.

"Diya!" Paul said and stopped. "Good thing I found you. The wolf is loose."

"We know," Diya said as the rest of his group caught up. "He's supposed to be taking us to Dusk, but he ran ahead. We need to find where he went, hopefully before the witch gets here."

"The witch will come here?" Paul asked, color draining from his face. "We can't allow them to face her alone." He turned and ran, waving for them to follow. "Hurry, the wolf came this way."

He expertly ran through the dark palace, keeping a pace that was easy enough even for Cedric while still being faster than a slow jog. Soon they made it to the ground level. They reached the final turn, and Paul halted them. He peered around the corner for a moment, then faced them with wide eyes.

"The wolf," he whispered.

Diya nodded. "And?"

Paul gulped. "And the witch."

41

Dawn slowly turned her head and saw wolf eyes glowing several meters down the dark hallway.

"Geoff," she whispered, and Berniece smirked.

"Seems you managed to best your uncle," the witch called to him. "Pity I've lost him, but at least you can serve my purpose once more before I destroy you."

Geoff snarled and charged at them. Berniece sighed as she reached into her pocket, then pulled out a little wooden whistle and blew it. There was no sound that Dawn could hear, but Geoff howled and came to a stop next to her. He collapsed on the ground, the howl turning into a scream as he shimmered and shifted in an effort to escape the sound. Dawn knelt by him and put her hand on his shoulder while he shuddered.

"Oh," Berniece remarked and clasped the whistle in her hand. "I see how you've managed to get Edmond, though I wonder how you got this ability." She cocked an eyebrow at Dusk, and he shrugged.

"I gave it to him," he said. "You did a sloppy job on the curse, leaving it so open to being altered. Wasn't any effort to help him."

"It was sufficient for what I needed," Berniece replied. "And you know I wasn't expecting anyone to try. The only person who cares about him is Henry, and he was easily convinced to let Edmond take care of things."

"I care about him," Dawn said as she stood. He was an awful person, with an appalling attitude, but still. She hadn't spent her entire life wanting to be there for him, only to stop when he needed it the most. "I may not want to marry him, but he's my friend. What you've done to him is unacceptable, and we won't let you take anything else of his."

"You're a strange girl, you know," Geoff said as he got to his feet, watching her curiously. "As if I haven't done just as terrible of things, and tried to do worse to you and your little boyfriend. But if you want to be nice and help me, I won't stop you. Once she's gone, though, we'll see how happy you are to say we're friends."

Berniece shook her head slowly and laughed. "When I'm gone, you say. But it isn't me that will be leaving this palace now that I've come to claim it. Edmond would have made a nice king, but I'm more than able to rule on my own. Now grab me my lantern, boy, and maybe I'll keep you for later."

She brought the whistle to her lips and smirked. Geoff glared at her and put his arm around Dawn's waist, pulling her up against him.

"Try it," he growled.

Berniece shrugged and blew the whistle again. Geoff winced and tightened his arm around Dawn, just barely enduring the sound.

"Hmm." Berniece lowered the whistle and frowned. "That won't do. Even with that girl to help you, I ought to be able to keep you on the ground. What else have you done, Dusk, that he can withstand the sound so well?"

"Nothing," Dusk said, shaking his head. "Whatever the cause, it must come from him. Unfortunate that Coma didn't share his knowledge of how to read alignments, or you might have an idea what it is."

"Such an impish little thing you are," she said, scowling. Her eyes flicked between Dawn and Geoff a few times, and the scowl became a smirk. "But perhaps there's another solution to this problem."

She pulled out a new needle and pricked her finger, making the tiniest drop of blood appear. Geoff sniffed and tensed. Dawn felt him rumble against her as his desire began to take over. Berniece laughed and flicked her finger at them, sending the droplet towards Dawn.

"Catch that," she said as it passed Dusk.

Dusk watched with horror as the blood landed on Dawn's necklace and shimmered with black light. "You've tainted yourself."

Berniece laughed again. "Why do you think I choose a wolf form for my minions?"

Geoff grabbed the necklace and brought it to his nose, then licked the blood off it and shuddered.

"More," he whispered and yanked the necklace hard. Dawn fell against him, barely keeping her grip on the lantern. He tugged again and the leather cord snapped and came away from Dawn's neck. "Blood."

He put his nose on Dawn's neck and breathed deeply, then tossed the necklace away as he gripped her waist. The pendant cracked as it hit the ground and bounced away, stopping under Dusk.

"I need blood," Geoff murmured in Dawn's ear before he bit down on her shoulder, reopening her scars from before.

Dawn screamed, and Berniece laughed as Dusk shuddered and dropped to the floor, landing almost on top of the pendant.

"Dusk!" Dawn cried as Geoff chewed on her. If he killed her without the necklace, they'd lose everything. But should she kill him first? Could she? "Is it time?"

"Not yet," Dusk said. He forced himself up through the pain, grabbing the pendant on the way. "Do you trust me?"

"Always," Dawn replied, then screamed again as Geoff shifted to wolf and they fell to the floor together. The lantern clattered on the stone floor and rolled away.

"Then hold on. It'll be all right," Dusk said as his wings buzzed.

Berniece watched Dusk float up into the air with amusement.

"And what are you hoping to do with that?" she asked and swiped at him. He barely dodged her hand and she frowned. "What does it do?" She tried again to snatch the necklace and hit him, sending him into the wall.

"You'll see in a moment," Dusk rasped and shot to Dawn, more falling than flying. He skidded over Geoff and pushed himself forward to Dawn's collarbone. "Now, Geoff." The wolf paused as he gnawed on Dawn's arm and looked at the fairy skeptically. Dusk stared back resolutely. "Kill her."

Geoff grinned and howled, then bit Dawn's neck. Dusk winced and held onto her and the pendant, struggling to stay with her as she flailed, then with a flash she was gone, leaving her clothes, the pendant, and Dusk.

"What have you done?" Berniece asked as Dawn vanished. "Where did she go?"

Dusk looked at the pendant glowing softly.

"I did it," he breathed and collapsed around it.

Geoff shimmered to human and looked at the unconscious fairy, then grabbed the lantern and stood.

"So you want this," he said as he fiddled with it. He glanced between it and Dusk, then turned to the witch. "But it belongs to Dawn, and she belongs to me, so I don't think I'll be giving it to you."

"But what's happened to her?" Berniece repeated. "How has she vanished?"

"She hasn't vanished," Diya said as he flicked around a corner, followed closely by Rob, Sarah, and Cedric. He flew to Dusk and landed next to him, smiling brightly.

"Knew you could do it," he whispered to his friend, then turned to look at Berniece. "Been a long time, witch. Not long enough, but will it ever be?"

"Diya," Berniece said, spitting his name out like a bite of rotten fruit. "After everything you've done, you still have the gall to appear now. You've never been anything but a thorn in Coma's side. Eternity wouldn't be long enough in the lantern to pay for it."

Diya flinched and scowled at her. "Coma was the obnoxious one, but he got what he deserved in the end. You want to know where she's gone? You can figure it out. May have been a long time since you tried to make one, but you remember it, don't pretend you've forgotten."

Berniece stared hard at Diya, then glanced at Dusk and the pendant, and brought her hand to her mouth in surprise.

"He's made an ethereal convertor," she whispered.

Diya grinned. "You always wanted to see one work, and now you get to. Well, this half, anyway. You ready, Rob?"

As he turned his attention away from Berniece she shot forward, fingers clawing towards Dusk and the pendant. The knight jumped in front of them, barely managing to block her, and she slammed into him instead.

"Why, you terrible thing," she grumbled as she stepped back less than gracefully. "I've waited an entire century for this chance, only to find myself stopped by a complete nobody. How utterly miserable."

"Is it?" Rob said, shrugging, and pulled his sword out casually. "At least I'm doing what I know is right. Maybe now would be a good time for you to surrender."

Geoff laughed, drawing everyone's attention. He continued fiddling with the lantern and made a gripping motion with his hand. "You really think that'll work? She's got something that stops me. I don't doubt she can handle you."

He winked at Rob, who furrowed his brow, then looked at the witch again and realized what was going on. He lunged at her, and she stepped to the side to avoid him. His sword grazed her right wrist as he went past and she dropped the whistle. Geoff was already jumping towards her, dropping the lantern as he did, and grabbed the whistle before she recovered. Sarah saw her chance and collected the lantern while the boys and the witch were busy.

"That's better," Geoff said as he crushed the whistle in his hand. "Not bad, knight. Quicker on the uptake than I thought you were."

Berniece cradled her wrist close to her hand and murmured a few words. The scrape Rob had given her glowed a soft blue, and she released the wound.

"So you got my whistle. But I used something else on you already, and it worked rather well, don't you think?" she said, reaching into her pocket for another needle.

"Go ahead," Geoff said, smirking. "There's not a single person here I wouldn't mind killing, except maybe the fairy, since his being here means Dawn is alive. Otherwise, I'd enjoy taking all of their lives. And while you're busy making sure I don't get you too, one of them will do something. You're outnumbered, and we've got you surrounded now. No escaping."

"Hmm, you really want the girl," Berniece said. "You've no idea what's happened to her, have you? You'll need me if you want to keep her, really, after all this is over."

"You think I want your help?" Geoff laughed. "Whatever's happened, I'll sort it later, after you're dead."

Berniece sighed heavily. "So stubborn you are. Then I'll just have to find a way around you, you immovable thing."

She looked over at Cedric and smiled. "You tried to delay me getting here, cheeky boy. But somehow it's worked out all right, in some ways. I might have gone right on to Edmond and missed them as they slipped out with the lantern. You still want your reward—

I'll give it to you. You just have to convince that girl of yours to help you."

Cedric pursed his lips and shook his head slowly. "Even if you are telling the truth, my wife wouldn't have me if I sacrificed Sarah for her. I won't betray my daughter."

"You promised him my mother?" Sarah cried, almost dropping the lantern as she brought a hand to her mouth.

Geoff crept around to Rob while they spoke and inclined his head. Rob nodded and got ready to jump.

"Simple enough to arrange," Berniece said. "If you cooperate on your own, you can have her instead."

"Don't listen to her!" Diya pleaded. "She can't give her back, at least not how you think."

"I can so," Berniece said and reached around her neck to pull a chain out from her dress. On the chain was a silver pendant shaped like a lily. "This is her magic. All I need to do is put it in a host, and viola, your mother."

Diya flicked up to Sarah's face, terror written all over his. "No, that's not how it works. She wouldn't be your mother anymore, just a body controlled by magic that happened to be hers. It wouldn't have her personality or memories."

"You lied to me!" Cedric exclaimed. "You told me I would get her back in whole! Not just her magic in someone else's body."

"Can I help it if you chose to believe what you wanted?" Berniece asked. "I never said it would be her body. Only that it would be her, which it is, in a sense. You can still convince yourself it's truly her: pick someone with similar features, close in age, and you'd never know the difference."

"I would know," Sarah said and backed farther away from Berniece. She held the lantern tightly, enveloping it in her arms. "Whatever you say, whatever you do with her magic, it won't change the fact that she's dead. I'll never help you."

Geoff signaled and Rob jumped at the witch, sword poised to kill.

"No?" Berniece said and turned to Rob, knocking the blade away with her arm and catching him in the stomach with her knee. He gasped and slammed to the ground, struggling to breathe.

"Bert!" Sarah shouted, kneeling next to him in an instant.

Berniece had another needle in her fingers and stood over them, ready to strike.

"All right girl, last chance," she said. "My lantern or this takes the boy's magic."

Sarah glared up at her. "Never."

"Very well," Berniece said, sighing, and let the needle drop. It twisted in the air until the point was aimed at Rob's head, then fell fast and straight.

Just as it made contact with his skin, Sarah placed her hand on him and gasped. Maroon magic surged through her and the needle reflected off of Rob and bounced back towards Berniece.

The witch jumped in shock and narrowly avoided the needle. Geoff grinned and shimmered into a wolf as he leapt at her, catching her before she realized what was going on. He knocked her to the floor and held her down while she struggled under his weight.

"Go on, kill me," she said, piercing black eyes glaring into the wolf's yellow ones. "Take a bite, see what happens. Or do you know you can't? The curse won't let you."

Geoff growled and pressed his paw down on her throat, trying to suffocate her. Her eyes widened in fear, and he rumbled.

"Diya," she whispered, shifting her eyes to look at him. "Listen. He isn't dead."

Diya snorted and glared at her. "Lies. Don't even try with me. Dusk might be dumb enough to fall for something like that but I'm smarter than him."

Berniece laughed, then coughed as she struggled for air.

"I got a message from a mirror," she rasped. "The signature was Nova's scale."

Diya froze and plummeted down, hitting the floor with a thud. His body spasmed for a few moments and he cried out in pain. "No. No!"

Geoff flicked his ears and pulled back slightly. Berniece laughed again and smirked.

"Good boy. Go get the fairy while you can," she said.

"Don't," Diya rasped. He was still curled on the floor and his breathing was shaky. "Kill her now, while you can."

Geoff grinned and pressed down again, then sniffed and turned his head. Everyone followed his gaze to Dusk, who was stirring.

"Let me see it," Berniece pleaded with the wolf. "Before you kill me, let me have this." Geoff flicked his ears and repositioned himself so she could turn her head and see, but kept his paw ready to crush her neck.

Dusk blinked a few times as he sat up, then looked down at the pendant that glowed brightly and began vibrating.

"She's coming," he said and smiled.

The glass of the pendant shattered and turned back into sand, falling away from the radiant flower. The rose glowed brighter and brighter until it was blindingly brilliant, then the light collapsed in on itself and pulsed deep in the flower's heart.

Dusk carefully picked up the bloom and held it as the light spread out and formed a human shape. The rose petals shifted and wrapped around the light like a dress, and Dusk adjusted his arms around it all, putting one around her shoulders and the other on her waist. Four points of light poked out from her exposed back and grew into wings. With a final blinding flash the light pulled back and settled into the soft glow of a lux fairy.

42

Dawn awoke at what she somehow knew was the middle of the night. She was aware that it was dark but could see well through a veil of light that was apparently coming from her. Under her, she felt the world slowly turning, and she could sense several living things around her, though she only recognized one: the one holding her. She looked up at him and thought she must be dreaming.

"Dusk?" she whispered.

"Dawn," he breathed back and kissed her deeply. She shivered and put her hands on his neck to pull herself into him, certain this was fantasy but determined to enjoy it while she could. He smirked and tasted her lips with his tongue, then sighed as she opened them slightly and allowed him inside.

"Dusk!" Diya shouted and jumped on them, jarring them both to reality. "You did it! And just in time."

He pointed at Geoff holding Berniece down nearby and watching them cautiously. Dusk looked around the hallway at all the watching faces and groaned.

"What did we miss?" he asked.

"Just the witch trying to talk her way out of us killing her, but Geoff's got it under control," Diya said.

Dawn looked between Dusk and Diya, struck by how odd they

seemed. They were the same size as her now, and was Diya brighter? She looked down at herself, wearing what seemed to be a dress made of rose petals, then glanced around and saw Sarah and Rob staring at her in shock. They were giant, and she realized what had happened.

"Dusk, am I a fairy?" she asked.

Dusk chuckled. "You're a fairy."

She smiled and looked behind her back. "I have wings."

"Yes, but don't try them yet," Dusk said, smirking. "We've got to finish this before we teach you to fly." He squeezed her and kissed the top of her head, then flicked his own wings and flew next to Berniece.

"Seems we've beaten you," he said, assessing her.

Berniece glared at him, eyes flickering with contempt. "You cheeky fairy, pulling off what Coma didn't, and acting like you don't want more. You could have been something. Become human and worked with me, and we'd have gotten somewhere. But you've chosen this path. Is she worth it? Is she everything you could ever want?"

"You were wrong before," he said, and she frowned in confusion. "When you said I couldn't grow, or become more powerful. It may be true for you, but I've realized what I was missing from my life, and it's her. You wanted Coma for power and ultimately got nothing. I want Dawn for love, and I have surpassed his ability now that I have her. Would you like to live?"

"Are you offering me a chance?" Berniece asked carefully.

"A deal of sorts," Dusk said, shrugging. "You share your knowledge—and help people—and in return, we won't end your life here. Of course, there won't be any more extensions to your life, but you can live out the rest of what you have in peace."

Berniece snorted. "And I suppose I'll have someone to watch me, and ensure I never try anything you don't like. Where would you put me? Since I doubt I'd be allowed to live in my own home."

"If Geoff would like to, I believe he would make a good care-taker. There is an opening for a mage, if I'm not mistaken," Dusk said. Geoff rumbled and nodded.

"So I'll be captive to my own creation," Berniece said testily. "Have you any other conditions for me, before I agree?"

"Anyone have anything?" Dusk asked, glancing around the cramped hallway.

"Her necklace goes to Sarah," Diya said.

Dusk shrugged and fluttered over to unclasp the chain, then carried it to Sarah. She looked at the pendant, and her eyes filled with tears as she accepted it.

"Thank you," she whispered.

Dawn looked closely at the pendant and gasped as she recognized the flower. Sarah giggled and looked at her friend.

"Guess you really are still you," she said quietly.

"I guess so," Dawn said.

Diya nudged her, grinning. "It suits you, being a fairy."

"Well, I think your glow suits you," she replied, her bright smile almost rivaling his reclaimed light.

Dusk flicked back to Berniece and spent a few moments cleaning out her pockets, tossing several more needles aside, then nodded to Geoff.

"She can't use her blood again, at least for now. You'll have to keep a close eye on her access to needles and such," he said.

Geoff grinned and shifted to human.

"Hear that witch? I get to own you now," he said and squeezed her throat with his fingers before releasing her finally.

Berniece gasped and sat up, rubbing her neck. "It's only a matter of time before I get my hands on what I need. You'll have to watch your back."

"Not after I finish his chain," Dusk remarked. "Now that I know what you have available, I can set him up to be immune to everything you can do."

Geoff laughed. "And you thought you couldn't handle her. Guess she's not as good as you believed, or you're really better than you pretend."

Dusk shook his head. "She doesn't have all of her things with her. I can think of several items she owns that could have stopped us, had she brought them."

"You're almost charming when you want to be," Berniece said, smirking.

Rob snorted and Dusk rolled his eyes.

"If everyone is quite satisfied, I believe we have some humans to get to bed, and a lantern to put away."

Geoff grinned and stood, then pulled Berniece up, wrapping his arm around her waist possessively. "Don't worry about us, I'll put her somewhere secure," he said. "We'll be discussing things later, though. Not going to take my girl and go on like it's nothing."

"I wouldn't expect anything less," Dusk said with a smirk. "Of course, I couldn't have done it without your help, even if you almost ruined everything when you broke the pendant."

"Had to try to stop you, didn't I?" Geoff said. "Wouldn't have been fair otherwise."

Berniece cackled. "As if you had any idea what it would do."

Geoff put his hand under her chin and pulled her face close to his.

"You be careful what you say to me," he whispered as his fingers moved down to her neck. "Don't want to make me angry."

"And you be careful not to hurt anyone else," Dawn said, remembering that she had what she needed to keep him contained. "Or I can activate Dusk's spell."

"Enough," Dusk said before Geoff could retort. "Robert, will you go with Geoff and Berniece to ensure they both get somewhere safe?

Sarah, if you could take the lantern back to Dawn's room please, and she needs a hand as well."

Rob stood up hastily and helped Sarah to her feet—still hugging the lantern—then stepped over to Geoff and the witch. Geoff scowled at him.

"I don't need an escort," he growled.

"Yes, you do," Dusk said. He flew over to land with Dawn and Diya, putting his arm over Dawn's shoulders. "Now go before I give you more."

With a grumble Geoff conceded and walked off, dragging Berniece, Rob following after.

"Ready?" Dusk asked as he dropped his arm from Dawn's shoulders to hold her hand. She flicked her wings curiously, and he shook his head. "You won't get very far with them. Better let Sarah carry you for now."

Dawn tested them once, flapping awkwardly, then let them fall and smiled at him. "All right."

"You'll figure them out," Sarah said, placing her hand next to Dawn for her to climb on. The lantern was tucked safely under her other arm. "Knowing you, I'll wake up to you rolling and flipping in the air."

Dawn stepped delicately onto her hand and sat. Dusk settled next to her and Sarah stood back up.

"I think I may need to get used to other things first," Dawn said as she pulled on the edge of her dress, trying to make it cover her knees. "You couldn't have made the skirt a little longer?"

Dusk laughed. "Not with a rose, but we can make you more clothes later."

"That would be nice," Dawn said, then looked up at Dusk anxiously. "Of course, that isn't to say I don't like it."

"I know," Dusk replied and chuckled at her. "I can feel how happy you are."

Diya fluttered next to them and winked at Dawn. "Just be glad it covers as much as it does," he said. Sarah made a face at him and he grinned. "Hey, I got you your necklace, remember?"

"Doesn't mean I owe you anything," she replied. They made their way back into the palace, seeing Cedric to his room, then continued to Dawn's.

When they arrived, Sarah caught herself as she almost knocked, then let herself in. She set her hand on the bed so Dawn and Dusk could get off, and Diya joined them. Once the lantern was tucked away in its chest, Sarah yawned and rubbed her eyes.

"Anything else I can do, or are you set?" she asked.

"Perfectly," Dusk said. He gave Dawn's hand a squeeze, then flicked to the door. "Dawn, would you keep an eye on Diya for me while I help Sarah to her room?"

"Of course," Dawn replied, grateful he would take care of Sarah for her. Dusk half-smiled and looked at Diya.

"I'll be fine," Diya said, and Dusk nodded and led Sarah away. The instant Dusk's light was no longer visible, Diya groaned and crumpled to the bed, bouncing slightly as he landed.

Dawn watched him closely, not sure if she should be worried or not. "Are you really fine?"

"Yeah," he said, turning his head to look at her. "Just need sleep."

"Oh," Dawn replied as she knelt by him. "I didn't realize you could."

"Yeah," he said again, closing his eyes and laying his head down. "I'm special like that."

His glow dimmed as he settled, then he cried like he was in pain and his body trembled. Dawn put a hand on his shoulder, but he jerked away.

"Diya?" she whispered, and he spasmed. His eyes opened, but they didn't focus, seeming to see things that weren't there.

She continued trying to gently touch him, and he moved away

from her each time. Was he hurt? Was it her fault somehow? Whatever was going on, she didn't think Dusk would be pleased when he returned. What a terrible way to repay him for what he did, to fail Diya within seconds of being alone with him.

"It's all right," Dusk said, and Dawn looked up to see him hovering over them.

"What happened?" she asked, eyes just blurring.

"It's nothing," Dusk said, landing with them. "He just needs help getting to sleep. It was quite the night for him." He carefully placed his hand on Diya's shoulder, holding tight as the lux fairy continued to squirm.

"Can I try?" Dawn asked. She may be new to fairy life, but sleep was something she knew plenty about.

Dusk looked at her and smiled. "If you want to."

He helped shift Diya's head into her lap, and she stroked his hair away from his face, humming softly. Eventually, Diya's eyes closed, and he settled back to shivering.

"Good job," Dusk whispered as he eased Diya into deep sleep with magic. "That will be nice and restful for him."

He lifted Diya's head so Dawn could get out from under him, then wrapped his friend in a corner of blanket. Once he was sure Diya would be comfortable, he helped Dawn to the far end of the bed so they could sit together.

"So now what do we do?" Dawn asked, looking up at Dusk's face. It was strange, seeing him the same size as herself, able to be touched and held. She loved it.

"Whatever we want," he replied, half-smiling as he put his hand behind her neck to pull her close. "And it just so happens I want to do this."

He kissed her, and she melted into him. Their hearts beat against each other, matching their rhythm so perfectly she would have believed they were one.

About the Author

Frances De La Rosa lives in Eastern Washington with her husband, two kids, two dogs, and one cat.

When she's not keeping after her family, she enjoys writing, singing, and sewing. Her first piece of fiction was a Choose-Your-Own-Adventure story in middle school. She sings almost daily, though her musical career is regulated to the kitchen while she's cooking. Her favorite thing to sew is frilly dresses for herself, and she hopes to teach her daughter to make her own dresses when she's older.

CPSIA information can be obtained
at www.ICGtesting.com
Printed in the USA
BVHW051009140522
636990BV00013BA/318

9 781087 944371